.25 CALIBER ETTIQUETTE

I stood in the middle of the shack. Wondering. Would it be rude to search the place? Yeah, I guess it would be rude. Emily Post had nothing to do with my decision. I just thought it would be dumb, given the squeak of the floorboards behind me. That and the voice.

"Get your hands up and turn around slowly."

The woman was silhouetted against the doorway. She was of medium height, and at another time and place I would have admired the lovely curve of her waistline and her long, bare legs. But I was distracted. A shaft of sunlight streaming through a crack in the wall reflected off the barrel of the .25 caliber Colt automatic in her hand.

The little black muzzle was aimed at a point in my abdomen where a second belly-button would have been superfluous and painful. Seemed a good time to break the ice. I smiled, friendly-like, and said good morning. She didn't return the greeting. Some people are grumpy early in the day.

Bantam Crime Line Books offers the finest in classic and modern American mysteries.
Ask your bookseller for the books you have missed.

COOL BLUE TOMB

PAUL KEMPRECOS

BANTAM BOOKS
NEW YORK ▪ TORONTO
LONDON ▪ SYDNEY
AUCKLAND

COOL BLUE TOMB

A BANTAM CRIME LINE BOOK / MAY 1991

CRIME LINE and the portrayal of a boxed "cl"
are trademarks of Bantam Books,
a division of Bantam Doubleday Dell Publishing Group, Inc.

ISBN 0-553-28881-4

Published simultaneously in the United States and Canada

PRINTED IN THE UNITED STATES OF AMERICA

RAD   0 9 8 7 6 5 4 3 2 1

FOR
Jan

ACKNOWLEDGMENT

I'd like to express my grateful appreciation to Arnold Carr who so generously shared his time and considerable expertise as a diver and shipwreck salvor; Sten Carlson for his technical advice; Bill Crockett, whose real-life encounter with a live artillery shell inspired the fictional account, and Joyce Johnson who gave me a tour of a Provincelands dune cottage. Any deviations from factual are mine alone. I owe special thanks to my agent, Meg Ruley, and editor, Kate Miciak, for their encouragement and guidance.

Evil deeds never prosper.

Homer, *THE ODYSSEY*

CHAPTER 1

The day had been a scorcher from first light. Hot and muggy, mercury in the nineties, sticky-shirt weather, when the skin prickles between the shoulder blades, underwear clings like a damp dishcloth to every body crease, and tempers go on hair trigger. The sun had awakened with a grudge against the world and no one was sorry to see it go. As the molten disk disappeared, finally, behind the western horizon, a collective sigh of relief arose, from the Cape Cod Canal to Provincetown, like a family watching the departure of a bad-tempered rich uncle.

Out at Race Point, the sunset watchers held their breath, half expecting the sun to sizzle as it plunged into the sea. But there was no steam, only a silent, gilt-edged explosion of red and orange, and a violet darkness. Then came a chorus of honking horns, applause rippled over the sand dunes like opening night at a Broadway spectacular, and the watchers headed out in the dusk, crossing the quiet desert hills of the Province Lands to the bright lights and noise of Commercial Street.

The narrow lane skirting Provincetown Harbor was mobbed. From the art association building to the Coast Guard station, a single line of cars crept bumper to bumper through the milling foot traffic. Tourists shuffled lethargically along in the lingering tropical heat, faces glistening with perspiration, searching for a cool breeze, but willing to settle for the diversions offered by the eclectic variety of bars, cafés, and shops. Long queues formed outside the soft-ice-cream stands. The hot-oven pizza joints were as lively as morgues. And the patrons in the sidewalk cafés didn't mind paying three-fifty for a dollar beer, as long as the glass was cold.

From his window seat in a smoky East End bistro the blond man stared at the passing street parade. His expression fluctuated. Boredom. Then annoyance. And boredom again. In between, he glanced impatiently at his wristwatch. A half-dozen empty bottles of Black Horse Ale stood on his table and he was working on another, chasing down each quick gulp with an angry puff on a Marlboro cigarette.

He checked his watch again. Then he frowned, mashed the cigarette into an ashtray overflowing with half-smoked butts, and got up, bumping into a young woman at the next table. She was drinking a Cape Codder—cranberry juice and vodka. The icy red mixture sloshed from her glass onto her lap and she yelped angrily. The blond man ignored her and staggered off.

He was in his midthirties and his well-tanned face had a boyishness that fooled people until they got close enough to see the hardness around the thin lips and green-flecked gray eyes. His hair was platinum, near white, and shoulder length like a 1960's flower child. He wore faded blue jeans, cut off at the thigh in a ragged fringe, and a purple T-shirt. The shirt was decorated in silver with swaying palms and the words *Life's a Beach*. His tattooed arms were thick and muscular. His narrow waist came up in a "V" to shoulders almost too broad for his medium height, like the physique Charles Atlas used to peddle to ninety-five-pound weaklings from the back cover of Superman comic books.

The dim room was jammed with sweaty college kids smelling of sunscreen, unshaven Portuguese fishermen wearing black shin-high boots, and gay couples and threesomes of both sexes. Foamy pitchers of beer swirled over the sea of heads like flotsam caught in a current. A couple of air conditioners with persistent death rattles spat drops of water and battled futilely against the BTU level produced by the press of bodies.

The jukebox pounded out a Rolling Stones number, "Sympathy for the Devil."

Mick Jagger's satanic guttural voice cutting through the din, and the Stones chanting like a chorus of deranged owls.

The blond man shoved a path through the crowd to the rest rooms marked "Buoys" and "Gulls." The men's room door was locked. He swore to himself, then pushed his way to the rear of the long bar. He stepped outside and descended a short stairway to the beach. Walking unsteadily in the soft sand, he picked his way around the rotting hulk of an old wooden fishing boat, stopped in the shadow of an abandoned pier, and relieved himself at the water's edge. He zipped up his fly and tarried, savoring the coolness of a light breath of air that whispered off the bay. Across the harbor fishing draggers sidled alongside the fish pier to disgorge the slimy contents of their holds.

The breeze died after a moment and the blond man turned to go. Before he had taken a step, the cement truck hit him. That's what it felt like. Something big and heavy smashing into his spine, hurling him forward like a missile thrown from a catapult.

He sprawled face down, hearing his rasping breath, someone moving behind him, the fishing-boat engines mumbling like old men, the jukebox blasting.

Planting his arms in the ankle-deep water, he struggled to push himself to a kneeling position.

A boot slammed into his right elbow. Hot pain shot through his arm and it crumpled like cellophane. He flopped back into the water. The boot crashed into the side of his head. Then again. The harbor lights blinked out.

And a voice from the jukebox shouted: *Oh yeah!*

Buffeted by green waves of nausea, the blond man groped for a handhold at the slippery edge of consciousness. After several unsuccessful tries, he held on, and the world slowly came into glassy focus. His head and arm throbbed with a dull ache. He lay belly-down, his face turned to the left on a flat hard surface that shivered with the low-end vibration of a powerful engine. There was a damp fishy smell in the air and the shush-shush of a bow cutting water.

He was on a boat, that was clear. How the hell? He remembered leaving the bar to take a leak. Then nothing. He tried to move, but his legs were bound securely. His left arm was pinioned to his thigh. His right hand curled uncomfortably up by his ear. A weight pressed down on his back. He shuddered as the faint light of comprehension glimmered in a corner of his mind.

Jesus! He was wearing diving gear!

The weight on his back was an air tank. He was looking

through the window of a face mask. The second skin clinging to his body was a dive suit.

Panic clawed at his innards.

Why in God's name was he fitted out for a dive?

He fought against the icy fear, taking deep and measured breaths to still the frantic jackhammering of his heart. Be cool, man. Don't struggle. Don't lose your head. You've been in tough spots before. Black water with minutes of air. Your regulator hose snagged on a jagged hull. Be cool. Think.

He rocked back and forth, gaining momentum with each motion, and finally managed to roll onto his right side. There was a hollow gong as the air tank banged into the deck. He tried to free an arm. It was impossible. He was wrapped as tightly as a mummy. He squirmed helplessly, like a beached eel, but the bindings holding him were incredibly strong. After a few minutes of desperate effort he lay on his side, panting and exhausted. Sweat stung his eyes. His nausea had returned.

The engine pitch changed from a rumble to a murmur. The boat lost headway and settled into the seas like a ballerina. Footsteps approached and stopped inches from his head. Rubber boots gleamed wetly in the faint yellow wash of deck lights. Hands reached down and grabbed him under the armpits. He was dragged a short distance and released. The slap of waves against the hull was louder. The hands reached down again and pulled his legs so the fins dangled over the side of the deck.

"No!" he shouted.

A boot thudded against his shoulder. He teetered for a long, terrifying instant. The boot battered him again. He rolled off into space and splashed headfirst into the chill sea. A hoarse scream escaped from his throat, but his words were lost in a gargled burst of bubbles.

He began to sink into blackness.

The immense weight of the sea closed in, welcoming him with an inexorable killing embrace that crushed his useless lungs. Daggers of pain stabbed his ear canals. He continued to sink, ever deeper. The contractions of his dying body had come to a fitful halt by the time he landed on the soft muddy bottom. The impact stirred up a cloud of silt and sent several crabs scuttling for safety. The body settled into the thick grassy carpet of vegetation. In time, the cloud subsided, the crabs returned, and the body rested quietly in its lightless cradle, becoming one with its surroundings. Then, brushed by a gentle current, the long pale strands of hair began to rise and fall, rise and fall, moving in rhythmic concert with the undulating fingers of seaweed.

CHAPTER 2

Be content with your lot, Aesop says; you can't be first in everything. Old Aesop was a fantastic teller of fables, no doubt about it, and generally his advice isn't half bad. Slow and steady wins the race or don't count your chickens before they're hatched still makes good sense after 2,500 years. But contentment was eluding me on this stormy day, the third in a row.

I lazed on a moldy green sofa and nursed my next-to-last can of Bud. The beer had gone flat, but I didn't care. Slurping another tepid mouthful, I reached over and picked up a comics-section page from last Sunday's *Globe*, read the Doonesbury strip, and didn't think it was funny, crumbled the page in a ball, then tossed it at a Boston Celtics wastebasket, imagining I was Larry Bird. Three seconds left in the game, tie score. Bird steals the ball. The crowd is on its feet. Johnny Most is yelping with excitement in the announcer's booth. Bird drives down the parquet floor. He shoots. The ball arcs prettily toward the basket. Ponk. It bounced off the metal edge and joined the pile of wrinkled newspaper littering the floor. Rimshot. Phooey.

Absentmindedly scratching the dark stubble that made an emery board of my chin, I read, for at least the hundredth time, the embroidered motto that mocked me from the opposite wall. HOME SWEET HOME. My gorge rose. If I weren't a civilized person, if I hadn't paid fifteen cents for the framed sampler at a yard sale, if it weren't covering a hole in the plaster, I would have ripped it from the wall and stomped the words to shreds. Instead, I dolefully surveyed my surroundings and sighed.

The boat house smelled as if it had floated ashore at high

tide. The incessant sound of raindrops splattering like machine-gun bullets against the windowpanes echoed in my skull. I looked fearfully toward the heavens every time the timbers shivered from the battering force of a southeast gust, half expecting the roof to fly off. The dank air was wet enough for a fish to swim in. A viscous slime coated the linoleum floors like some alien space blob out of a fifties horror movie. I glanced at the shaggy overweight black cat attached to my thigh. He was mildewing around the whiskers and tail, but he purred happily in his sleep. At least one of us had found contentment.

I was mind weary and bored. Even worse, I was broke. The dirty weather was more than just a nuisance. It meant no fishing and no paycheck.

I pried the cat from my leg without disturbing his noisy snooze, stood up, and walked over to the deck doors. On clear days there's a panoramic view of the bay, the low-lying dunes of the outer beach and the liquid immensity of the Atlantic Ocean stretching to world's end. Today, sheets of rain slanted down from slag gray skies and cut visibility to a few yards. I closed my eyes and concentrated, willing the rain and wind to stop and the sun to break through the clouds.

The phone rang. I guess that was something.

I opened my eyes and picked it up.

"How you doin', Soc?" A voice as crisp as dry leaves. Sam, my fishing partner.

"Lousy, Sam. How about you?"

"Yeah. Know what you mean. Still looks a little sloppy, don't it?"

Sam's lyrical description of the tempest raging outside was in character. His gift for Yankee understatement had surfaced the first winter we fished together. We were coming into harbor, loaded to the gills with cod, when his line trawler lost speed and sunk into a trough between two big waves. A following sea taller than the radio antennae slammed into Sam's boat like a locomotive. We could have pitchpoled end over end and landed in the breakers wearing a couple of thousand pounds of codfish for hats, but the Atlantic Ocean was merely reminding us it was boss, and we escaped that day with only a cold shower. Minutes later, soaked to the skin, we entered more placid waters. Sam was at the wheel. He looked up with a puckish expression of unconcern on his ruddy features. "Lost a little headway back there," he observed casually, ignoring the water that dripped off the tip of his nose.

Now he was quoting the National Oceanic and Atmospheric Administration weather report. It was good news for a change. Rain would end, wind would drop and come around to the southwest. We could fish tomorrow.

"That's great, Sam," I said. "I'll see you down at the pier, bright and early."

Sam answered with the fishermen's catchall word for everything good and wonderful. "Finestkind," he said.

Life had taken on new meaning. This called for a celebration. I hung up and liberated my last can of Bud from the refrigerator. I was in midswallow when the phone rang again. Probably Sam calling to tell me how his old crewman once lost his false teeth overboard and found them in a goosefish. I hadn't heard the story more than a dozen times.

It wasn't Sam. I put the beer down, quickly. "Hi, Ma," I said.

"Hello, Aristotle. Have you been away?"

"No, I've been home more than a week."

"Have you been sick?"

"No, Ma. Why did you ask?"

"You haven't called. You haven't come home to visit. So, you must be sick." The Socratic method at work. Asking a series of easily answered questions leading the answerer to a logical conclusion foreseen by the questioner.

Oh hell. "No, I've been fine. I'm sorry. I've been pretty busy lately. You know how it is."

"Yes, of *course,* Aristotle. I understand. Maybe sometime when you are not busy, your father and I will see you."

The years have scarcely touched my mother's voice. It has just enough trace of an accent to be charming and is nearly as rich and melodious as I remember as a kid. Yet it carries an unmistakable message of command. Not a Patton. More subtle. My childhood buddies worried about being spanked. I would have welcomed a swat on the behind as relatively painless. My misdeeds, however trivial, were considered stains on family honor. A raised eyebrow would cut me down to size. A pause after a sentence would have me squirming. It still did.

"You know," I said hastily, "it's an amazing coincidence

having you call. There's no fishing because of the weather, so I was just thinking of coming up to see you and Pop today."

"*Kalà*, Aristotle. Good. That will make Papa and me very happy. Drive safely," she added, and hung up.

I put the phone down and finished my beer, not really enjoying it, then went into the bathroom to shower my gamy body and scrape the weeds off my face. I exchanged my denim cutoffs for a wrinkled but clean pair of tan chinos, my T-shirt for a blue oxford cloth button-down, and my flip-flops for a pair of Top-Siders, worn over bare feet. It was still raining so I pulled on a slicker and a Boston Red Sox baseball cap. I walked outside and swung behind the wheel of a faded green GMC half-ton pickup truck in the advanced stages of body rot. The engine turned over a few times reluctantly and coughed to a sputtering start. I put the truck into gear and followed a half-mile-long dirt road to the macadam, splashing through puddles as big as Lake Superior.

Actually, I was glad of an excuse to overcome my personal inertia and get off Cape Cod. The boat house was as unfit for human habitation as a fever swamp. Acute claustrophobia had reached a near-terminal stage. And my sole foray into town to replenish my shrinking beer supply ended with a panicky and empty-handed retreat. Mobs of foul-tempered tourists who had fled their expensive cottages and motel rooms were driving aimlessly around with carloads of whiny kids in the back seat and murder in their hearts. The merchants love lousy weather because people don't go to the beach. The cash registers jingle merrily on rainy days, but the Cape is a traffic jungle.

The rain was tapering off forty-five minutes later as the truck passed under the parabolic steel framework of the Sagamore Bridge, one of three spans linking the Cape to the mainland. Far below, visible through the suicide fence, a rusty freighter sluggishly plowed a foamy furrow between the curving stone revetment of the Cape Cod Canal, fighting the stiff currents that rippled the wide waterway.

Two hours later I was about twenty-five miles northwest of Boston, looking at the far smaller Northern Canal, the three-decker houses and sprawling brick mill buildings of my hometown on the Merrimack River. The chamber-of-commerce boosters have taken to calling Lowell the Cinderella City. The old place had come a long way, but its story was hardly the stuff of glass slippers. It was more like the bank president who becomes a skid-row bum then claws his way back to respectability.

In its heyday before the turn of the century Lowell was the world model for the industrial town. Then came the Depression, the mills closed, and Lowell went into a funk that lasted more than fifty years. A local boy named Jack Kerouac made it big before drowning in a sea of booze and hopelessness, and the inevitability of his fate seemed like a metaphor for the city. In the 1970's, high tech and new political clout sparked a comeback. Today, instead of bone-tired immigrants toiling over clattering looms in the old mills, there were trendy boutiques, upscale ice-cream stores, and National Park Service rangers telling gaggles of school kids how it was. The old ethnic groups who really knew how it was had left the city to the newcomers, mostly Southeast Asians, all trying to carve their piece of the American dream, and not doing badly at it.

There were big changes in the Acre, the neighborhood where I'd loitered with my buddies and shredded the warm summer evenings with rock music from our car radios. The golden-domed Holy Trinity Hellenic Orthodox Church and the Hellenic Cultural Center were unchanged. But gone was the Greek grocery store on Market Street were you could buy dark wrinkled olives from strong-smelling tubs, and juicy roast lamb slivered with garlic and wrapped in heavy white butcher paper. In its place was a Southeast Asian import business. The corner gift shop that sells baklava and minia-ture Parthenons is flanked by a couple of Cambodian stores. The kids who play in the nearby housing project have black eyes and hair and round faces. Garbage litters the sidewalks and a couple of tough-looking bars that look like the last stop on the muscatel express have managed to hang on. The air vibrates with a nervous Asian energy, though, and big American cars line the curbs.

Near the edge of town I parked outside a converted three-story, brick mill building. I stepped through the front en-trance into a reception room and inhaled an overpowering fragrance of oregano, cheese, and tomato. Athena Kostas was seated behind a reception desk. Seeing her triggered pleasant memories. I'd had a crush on Athena when we were both kids struggling to learn old-country language and culture in the church Greek school. She was a few pounds heavier now and her black hair was touched by gray, but her dark almond-shaped eyes were still strikingly beautiful. I remembered my pang of teenage lust the time the back of her blouse lost a button.

She looked up and smiled. "Hi, Soc. How are things down on the Cape?"

I went behind the desk, impulsively pecked her cheek, just for old times, and said, "Busy, Thena. You look terrific. Is the family around?"

She blushed faintly. "Thanks, I needed that; it's been one of those days. They're out back. Be prepared. They're having an, uh, marketing session."

I squeezed her shoulder and stepped into an adjoining office dominated by an enormous color photograph of the Acropolis in all its magnificent ruin. Under the picture in the delft blue of the Greek national flag were the words "Parthenon Pizza. One out of every three frozen pizzas sold in New England is a Parthenon. Try a classic."

A door next to the poster flew open and an apparition in white burst in. White sneakers, white slacks, white T-shirt, and white arms. Face and mustache caked with enough flour to bake a week's supply of rolls at the Parker House. My younger brother looked as if he had fallen into a flour bin, which was probably what happened.

"Hi, George," I said.

"Soc," he gasped breathlessly, sending up a powdery cloud of flour. "You gotta come and settle an argument. I just read Pa's order for southeastern Mass. It's huge. He is cra-zee. Linguica pizza's a new product, for God sakes."

"I don't know, George. Lotsa people in New Bedford and Fall River can't get through their breakfast without frying up a few hunks of sausage with their eggs so they'll have an early start on the day's heartburn. Maybe Pa's right."

Speak of the devil. George was brushed aside by a stumpy white barrel. "You tell him, Aristotle," my father boomed in an accent as thick as yogurt. "George, you wanna make it big in the pizza business, you gotta thing big."

A gold tooth gleamed over Pa's shoulder and my mother, a slim lady who wore a black dress and her pepper and salt hair pinned back in a neat bun, edged in. My mother is related to half the people on Crete. Relatives are always dying and consequently she enjoys a perpetual state of mourning. Miraculously, she can spend a whole day in the bakery without getting a speck of flour on her dress.

"You listen to George," she yelled in Pop's ear. "Five thousand linguica is too much."

"Hello, Ma," I said.

"Hello, Aristotle," she replied, treating me with a sweet smile that lasted a second before she turned on my father and unleashed a torrent of Hellenic invective that would have impressed the avenging Furies.

George looked smug. "That's right, Soc old boy. Harvard didn't give you all the answers."

"Boston University, George. Harvard's on the other side of the Charles River."

"Charles, schmarles. It's all the same." He was scraping off the flour caked onto his pinky ring.

"You're right, George. Absolutely correct." As usual, I'd only been home three minutes and my voice was already rising. "I don't know a damn thing about pizzas except that they give me indigestion. You're probably right about the linguica too. But do we all have to yell about it?"

My parents stopped screaming. They looked at me, dumbfounded. Pa shrugged and stomped back into the bakery. He was shaking his bald head, wiping his hands on his apron and muttering, "You wanna thing small, we thing small." Beaming with vindication, George followed, slamming the door behind him, and I was left alone with my mother.

We stood in silence a minute, then I said, "I'm sorry, Ma. I didn't mean to lose my temper. George just drives me crazy sometimes."

"George is a good boy, Aristotle. He works hard, comes in every day and keeps the company going."

I don't think she meant to hurt me, but her words cut right to the quick. "Maybe that's why I get so angry. I don't contribute a thing to the family. Heck, I can't even sing the Parthenon Pizza jingle."

My mother is relatively tall for her generation, but the top of her head comes just to my chin. I've never known her to be intimidated by a difference in height—or anything, for that matter. She faced me square on, put her left hand on her hip, and waggled her right forefinger under my nose. Her gray eyes flashed.

"Aristotle," she scolded, "you make me *very* angry when you talk like that. The family is not the same as the business. George is like your father. An Athenian. To him, business is everything. *You* could never make pizza. You are too much like your great-grandfather Nikos." She shook her head. "Every time I look at you I see him. He was tall like you. Same hair. Same sleepy smile. And the eyes. Sometimes warm and innocent, like a little boy. Sometimes like dark pools with no bottom." She patted me lightly on the cheek. "Sit down, Aristotle."

Easing into a leather chair, I pondered how little I really knew about my ancestors. For the most part they were simply faded sepia photos of countless anonymous aunts, uncles, and cousins whose unsmiling faces seemed chiseled from the rocky terrain behind them. Their names were inevitably linked to disasters—drowning, falling, or wandering off—never-to-be-seen again tales that became object lessons to kids inclined toward disregarding the warnings of their parents.

My great-grandfather was different, however. He loomed larger than life in the family mythology. In the dog-eared photo albums he was a kindly looking old codger with an eagle nose and a walrus mustache. He wore baggy black pants tucked into shiny black leather boots and a black-fringed handkerchief on his head. I remember being fascinated by the antique pistols and the ivory-hilted dagger with its silver sheath stuck in his wide waistband, and the bandoliers across his chest, but never thought of them as more than photographer's props.

My mother seated herself on the office sofa and folded her hands in her lap. "When I was a little girl," she began, "I was my grandfather's favorite. He was old then, but still strong enough to lift heavy stones. I was like a tiny feather sitting on his knees. He told me stories of the old gods. He took me to the cave where Zeus was born and to Knossos where King Minos lived. *Everywhere* we went people recognized Papou and treated him with respect. I was so proud to be seen with him."

She paused thoughtfully. "After he died and I am old enough to understand, the family tells me more. How Nikos is a farmer when the Turks hold Crete. He is a peaceful man who minds his own business. Then one day a neighbor comes and says, 'Help me, the Turks take my son.' So Nikos goes to help. There is a fight and he kills two Turks. He escapes and becomes a hunted man living in the mountains. Then *he* becomes the hunter. He kills the Turks who come to catch him. They kill some of the family and the others must hide. Grandfather becomes a devil. He strikes and is gone. Turkish mothers tell their children Nikos will come if they are bad."

She stopped again, a distant look in her eyes. "When I heard these stories, I think about his hands. So big, yet so gentle. I remember how they hold me, braid my hair, pick me up when I fall. But Aristotle," she said, her expression growing more intense, her voice almost a whisper, "these were the same hands that *killed* men, cut off their ears and noses and did other terrible, terrible things. Even today, when I think of how those hands do both good and evil, it frightens me."

I took her hand and squeezed it. "Don't worry, Ma," I said. "I may look like Nikos, but that's as far as it goes. I never did anything like that, not even in Vietnam."

She touched my knee lightly.

"I know, Aristotle. You are gentle too. But you are also like your grandfather. A *pallikári*. A strong man. I could see when you were very young. That time the big boys pick on your brother and you put one of them in the hospital. *That's* why I push you into the university. Maybe if you study you will become a professor." She shook her head. "But blood always tells. First you become a soldier, then a policeman."

"And now I'm a fisherman and a private investigator with two cents to his name."

She took my other hand in hers and squeezed it. "Sometimes you help people, no?"

"Sometimes I do, Ma."

"Poof. Then you are what you are."

I chuckled. "Okay, Ma. You win. But I promise not to go near any Turks."

We stood and she hugged me. "You're a good boy, Aristotle. You keep doing what you do and leave the linguica pizzas to George."

As if on cue, the door to the bakery opened and George walked in. He had washed up and changed into a tan summer suit and pale blue sport shirt open at the collar. Around his neck he wore a thin gold chain that must have cost a bundle. When he's not covered with flour, George is a handsome man who turns female heads without trying. He has my dark brown hair and complexion. His nose is straighter, he's shorter by a couple of inches, and he wears his clothes with a Mediterranean jauntiness.

"Let's go out for a beer," he said with unexpected friendliness. "There's a terrific place opened up near here."

In the interest of family harmony I nodded, kissed my mother, promising on my life to call her soon, yelled goodbye at my father, who was busy in the bakery, and went outside. We got into George's car, a white Cadillac Allante convertible about two blocks long with a matching white top and a vanity license plate that read PIZZA. A few minutes later we parked near a bistro that had more ferns in the window than a Tarzan movie.

Inside, there were more ferns, a black, pink, and chrome art deco motif, and a long onyx bar crowded with successful-looking young urban professionals. The patrons, men and women, wore the kind of trendy overpriced clothes sold in stores named after French poodles. They were talking at each other with animated expressions of earnest avarice. George was no stranger here. He glad-handed the line of suits as if he were running for mayor before we sat in a booth with a mirror on the wall so we could see how terrifically good-looking we were. The waiter introduced himself to me by his first name, which I thought was forward. George ordered an imported beer that sounded like something a German says when a person sneezes. I asked our waiter for Bud in a bottle and thought he was going to faint with mortification. Which would have been all right with me.

George wasted no time getting to what was on his mind. As soon as our beers arrived he said, "Soc, I feel really funny talking to my older brother like this. But when the hell are you going to settle down and make something out of your life?"

I resisted the primal urge to reach out and rip the self-satisfied smile off his cocksure face. Instead I said, "By the way, George. How's Maria, and little Jimmy and Ariadne?"

"They're good, Soc. Real good. That's another thing you should be thinking of. A wife and kids. Hell, you're still a young guy." He waved expansively. "Look at me. I've got friends and business associates. I've got a five-bedroom house outside of town and a swimming pool shaped like a pizza. We've got three Caddies in the garage, all with car phones, and only two people to drive them. I got an exercise room and a media room loaded with state-of-the-art toys I don't know how to operate. I even vote Republican. Tell me, Soc. What have you got? Wait a second, I'll tell you. You got nothing."

My hand clenched the flaring pilsner glass. "George, I want you to stop right there before I forget you're my brother. You're way out of line."

George leaned back, a look of embarrassment on his flushed face, and put his palms out. He'd gone too far and he knew it. "Okay, okay, I'll shut up. I was just thinking about your welfare."

"Don't. I appreciate your concern, but what I do or do not do with my life is my business. Nobody else's. If I want to screw it up, that's my business. If I want to waste it, that's my business too."

We finished our beers in a tense silence that wasn't broken until a short while later when George drove me back to my truck. "Say good-bye to the folks for me," I said, getting out of the Cadillac. "And thanks for the beer." I slammed the car door, got into my truck, and nearly ripped the gearshift lever off the steering post. I shouldn't have let George get to me, but his pompous posturings contained splinters of truth that got under my skin. George could never understand me, not in a thousand years. Hell, I don't even understand myself. Even so, his well-meant counsel had started embers of resentment burning in my soul. I was still seething forty-five minutes later when I pulled into Harvard Square.

The prospect of a long uninterrupted ride home alone with my thoughts was too much to bear, so I decided to head into Cambridge and stop off at a Mexican restaurant for a frozen margarita or two and a couple of tacos. I like Mexican food, but it doesn't like me, and I looked forward to a little stomach distress to divert me from my brooding. There's a Mex cantina off the square I frequented when I was a Boston cop. It's a noisy place smelling of tequila and onions and usually jammed with Harvard kids whose innocent rowdiness used to be like a tonic to me when I was coming off some dreary case. I guess I was looking for a dose of the same medicine.

The tangle of narrow streets around the square is a parking nightmare any time of the day or night. I prowled for ten minutes before I saw a car leaving a space near the restaurant. I pulled ahead, started to back in, and slammed on my brakes. A blue Toyota Tercel was hugging my bumper. I leaned on the horn and, when the car didn't move, threw the truck into reverse and mashed the accelerator. The Toyota backed up so quickly it tapped the bumper of the car in line behind it. I parked, got out of the truck without a look back, and went directly to the bar inside the cantina. The bartender was a half-dozen drink orders behind and trying to catch up.

Minutes passed. I was becoming cranky. A tall, slim woman took the stool next to me. Her shoulder-length red hair glinted like copper in the light. It was obvious from the way she waved a five-dollar bill that she was thirsty too.

I finally caught the bartender's eye and testily yelled out that I wanted a margarita. The red-haired woman shouted her order at the same time. A glass of white zinfandel. Figured. I turned to give her an annoyed glance. She beat me to the punch, skewering me with a glare that didn't take away from the fact that she had remarkable blue eyes and was quite attractive. I shrugged and finally got my order in. When my margarita arrived in its salt-rimmed glass, I attempted to drink it in peace. The red-haired woman had other ideas.

She'd been stewing. "You know you almost hit me back there," she said pointedly. I gave her a blank look. "I was right behind you. You backed up so damned fast I bumped into the car behind me."

The blue Toyota.

I yawned. "You shouldn't have been so close to my tail."

"*You* shouldn't be behind the wheel of anything bigger than a tricycle."

"Look, little lady."

"I'm not little and I'm not a lady."

"I can see that," I said, and slammed the glass down without breaking it. No amount of refried beans was worth having to listen to a lecture from a woman who was probably a spoiled and overeducated grad student.

I slid off my stool, threw some bills on the bar, and stormed out of the restaurant, cursing softly when I got to my truck. There was the blue Toyota kissing my rear bumper.

I got into the pickup, threw the gearshift into first, and smashed into the car ahead of me. Then I put it into reverse and crunched the Toyota. After a few satisfying minutes I had pounded out several inches of elbow room. I banged the Toyota one more time, squeezed out another inch, and eased onto the street. I thought I heard a yell and looked in the rearview mirror. The red-haired woman was standing on the sidewalk waving at me. I waved back and drove off.

About two hours later I pulled up in front of the boat house. I had stopped on the way home for a wholesome Big Mac and fries. My mood had improved with the weather. The rain had stopped completely. The wind had died to a light breeze that sighed in the locust trees. The stars sparkled like fourteen-karat diamonds in the black sky. "Hello, Big Dipper," I said. "Thought I'd never see you again." The boat house still smelled like a penicillin factory but that would disappear with a few days of sunlight and open windows. I set the alarm for 4:00 A.M. and went directly to bed. Sam would be down on the shore first thing in the morning and I didn't want to keep him waiting.

CHAPTER 3

The fishing trip wasn't a complete failure, but it was close enough to qualify as one. Sam and I set hundreds of baited hooks in a honey hole about twenty miles offshore where the cod usually beg to be caught. Hook after hook came up empty. Even a fish learns to keep its mouth shut, I guess. By late afternoon our hold was still mostly air. I tried to put the best face on our depressingly slim pickings. Taking a break from the hauler—the mechanical gadget that pulls the lines in—I threw my arms wide apart, like a medicine man invoking the Great Spirit, and squinted up at the sky. It was cloudless, a brilliant blue.

"Okay, Sam," I said, taking a deep breath and letting it out. "So it's not a terrific fish day. So we're not high-liners. But some things are more important than money. Think of all those suckers in three-piece suits and briefcases toiling over a hot desk somewhere. They would positively kill to be out here."

My enthusiastic ravings were only part hucksterism. The weather was magnificent. A perfect ten. The rainstorm had scrubbed the air. Our faces baked like raisins in the warm light of the sun. The breeze was as light as a baby's breath. The ocean was calm and the trawler slid easily down the shallow slopes of lazy green seas. I would have wanted to be on the water whether I was catching fish or not.

You have to know where I'm coming from when I talk about the sea. I have a romantic affection for it that goes back a long way. Maybe it's in the genes. The Greeks didn't have much in the way of land. The country is mostly rocks and mountains, so their lives literally depended on the sea for thousands of years. They cultivated it and, most important, used it as a highway to the world. Then, too, there's my mother. She was born on an island and has always viewed the sea with a mysterious reverence. When I was a kid, she'd look at a runny knee scrape no amount of salve and epsom-salt baths would help and prescribe her treatment. *Thalàssa*. The sea. There followed the ritual bathing in the frigid ocean waters at a North Shore beach, and the wound would heal.

Later, a few weeks after I returned from soldiering in Vietnam, a noon whistle went off and I tried to dig a foxhole in the sidewalk with my fingers. I almost succeeded. Shaken and embarrassed, I drove to Crane's Beach in Ipswich and skipped flat stones in the surf. I got up to seven bounces before my hands stopped trembling. Later, when the wounds of war still festered in my mind, nightmares haunted my sleep, and life's overwhelming ironies became unbearable, I moved near the ocean, hoping it would soothe and heal as it once did. I found that the breeze going in one ear and out the other blew away some of the hurtful memories, the surf's roar drowned out the bad dreams, and that catching a fish was far more therapeutic than lying on a shrink's couch. Cheaper too.

As usual, Ma had been right. *Thalàssa*.

Sam, who stood a few feet away tending the wheel, rolled his eyes and said the day would be much more beautiful if we covered the cost of fuel and bait. He had a point. I reeled in more line. Nothing, nothing, and more nothing.

Then my luck changed. There was a flash of silver just below the surface. A whale-size haddock struggled on a hook. My heart flipped the way it does when a lovely woman casts an interested glance in my direction. This was even better. Haddock are as rare as smiles at an IRS audit and they fetch gold-coast prices.

Suddenly energized, I opened my mouth to let out a rebel yell. A long skinny shadow darted in toward the wriggling fish. The haddock vanished. The shadow disappeared. The yell died in my throat. A weird chickeny squawk came out instead. The haddock had been snatched by a blue shark around six feet long. The blue shark is a neon torpedo with an anvil head, hacksaw teeth, and big round eyes that have a dead look to them. The fish isn't in the same class with a great white shark. Nothing is. On the other hand you wouldn't mistake one for a rubber ducky. I swore, hauled in more line, and swore again.

Dangling from the next hook was a platter-shaped crea-ture called a skate. It's a worthless trash fish that steals your bait and raises your blood pressure. Normally I'd gaff it off the hook. Suddenly inspired, though, I dropped the skate back into the water and jiggled the line enticingly. The shark reappeared, circled a few times, and made its move. A second later he dropped the grisly morsel. Obviously a gourmet. He shot off in search of a more suitable table d'hôte. I grinned evilly. Sweet revenge.

Sam snorted like a Clydesdale. His weathered face was crumpled in laughter.

"Nice of you to feed that fella. Why don'tcha give that shark a gaff to pick his teeth with." He pronounced it "shahk."

"He ate my haddock," I grumbled, hauling in more trawl line. "The damned thing ate my haddock. Do you know what I could have done with that haddock? I could have sold it and bought a new truck. I could have taken a vacation in Maui. I could have bought the whole Hawaiian Islands. Listen, Sam." I tapped the side of my head with a forefinger. "I've got a better idea than feeding sharks. How about calling it a day?"

"Hopin' you'd say that," he said cheerily. "Fishin's a young man's game; every muscle in my body tells me that, but I hate to be the first to quit."

We gathered the last of the lines and brought in a few more cod. Sam set a course for home and gunned the throttle while I coiled the nylon line in round plastic tubs. Powered by a 360-horsepower Detroit diesel, the forty-eight-foot steel hull sheared the seas as easily as scissors cutting a bolt of silk. The light was waning and opaque clouds scudded across the sky as the trawler passed between the last pair of channel markers and eased up to the fish-pier unloading dock. Over-head a raucous mob of gulls dipped and wheeled in noisy search of leavings.

Sam and I pitchforked the meager catch into a rusty bucket that dumped the fish down a chute into wooden boxes which held about 120 pounds apiece. Packers shoveled crushed ice into the boxes and stacked them in the trailer truck that would take them to the Fulton Fish Market in New York. With the hold emptied, we tied up at a mooring in a small cove north of the pier, slipped over the side into a white wooden pram, and rowed toward shore. The pram's bottom scraped onto the sand near a beach where several other dinghies rested upside down.

"See you tomorrow, Sam?"

"Finestkind. You can sleep an hour later with the tide change."

"No complaints from me, Cap."

We emptied the pram of gear and oars and turned it over, then started up a small grassy rise. A man was waiting for us. It would have been hard to miss him. He was slightly smaller than a haystack. He had a red-haired mane tied in a pigtail and a bushy beard. He wore jeans tight over tree-trunk thighs and a black T-shirt with a grinning white skull and crossbones on it.

As we drew nearer, I saw that his eyes were brilliant but not cold the way blue eyes sometimes are. His skin was burnished from salt spray and sunlight reflected off the water. His left ear was pierced with a large gold ring. Put a cutlass in his hand, a black eye patch, and a drunken parrot on his shoulder and you'd have an N. C. Wyeth illustration for *Treasure Island*.

He greeted me. "How're you doing? I'm looking for a guy they call Soc. Might that be you?" His voice was deep and rich like a TV news anchorman.

"It is unless you're a bill collector in disguise," I said.

He chuckled, showing big white teeth. "My name is Mike Barrett, and I don't collect bills, unfortunately, I pay them." We shook hands. It was like putting my fingers in a padded bench vise.

At six foot one without my flip-flops, I'm rarely mistaken for a pygmy, but Barrett topped me by at least three inches and fifty pounds, none of it fat. I studied his face and tried to recall where I'd seen him before. I spend more time around gin mills than is good for me and sometimes have fascinating conversations with strangers who become bosom buddies for a couple of blurry rounds. Then we'll bump into each other sober and wonder where we've met. So I no longer get embarrassed at blanks in my memory. I would have remembered a man mountain like Barrett unless I was unconscious, which was entirely possible.

"I think I've seen your face somewhere," I ventured. "Should I know you?"

"Nope. We've never met before."

"Then to what do I owe the pleasure?"

"I've got a job I'd like you to take."

"Bad timing, Mr. Barrett. As you see, I have a position with Sam here hunting the wily codfish."

Barrett shook Sam's hand, then turned back to me. "I know you've got to go fishing when the fishing is good, but I'm in a real jam and could use your help. Could we just talk about it?"

"I'm afraid it might be a waste of time. Sam can't get along without me."

"Why don't you talk to the fella," Sam interjected. "Price of cod isn't so great. Be a good time for me to work a few days on that hauler that's been giving us trouble. Then if you're still busy, I can get the Nickerson kid to take your place."

"Sam's a great kidder," I said. "Actually I'm indispensable and he's making a substantial sacrifice. Okay, Mr. Barrett, let's go talk. But what makes you think I can be of help?"

"I know one good reason. His name is Joe Ford."

I raised an eyebrow. "How do you know Ford?"

Barrett grinned. "Joe and I go back a long way. We were kids together in Southie. Used to cruise around looking for fights just to show how tough we were. Then we became respectable, more or less. Coupla people around the shore here mentioned your name and the fact you used to be a detective with the Boston PD. I called Joe and asked him about you. He's a lieutenant now, by the way. Hard to believe. Anyhow, he said some people thought you were a wise-ass and a little rough around the edges considering you were a college boy. And a few soreheads around town still hate your guts. But Joe said you were honest as hell. And smart. Sounded like what I needed. He said if you gave me a hard time to tell you a sob story or say I have a pretty sister. You wouldn't be able to resist."

"And do you?"

"Sob story? Sure."

"Pretty sister as well, I suppose."

"Uh-huh. I've got that too."

"Joe talks too much." I led the way to my truck. "Okay, Mr. Barrett. Follow me to my office. You can tell me about your sister while I sob in the beer you're about to buy me."

I said good night to Sam and got in my pickup. Barrett followed me out of the parking lot in a black Chevy pickup truck. Five minutes later we pulled up outside a squat, green asphalt shingled building. Neon brewery signs glowed in the small windows. We went through the front door, found a corner booth, and ordered two beers. Slow-turning ceiling fans stirred yeasty eddies in an atmosphere heavy with stale cigarette smoke, Pine-Sol disinfectant, and ninety-proof dreams.

Back in the 1950's, when the place had been a bustling seafood restaurant named the Porthole, it had clean red-and-white-checked tablecloths, fish-and-chips seconds on the house, and was a must stop for families driving onto the Cape in their Hudson Hornets and Nash Ramblers. Business went belly-up after the state put in a new highway. The only ones who used the old road were people who were lost. The owners moved back to New Jersey and sold the restaurant to a defrocked Anglican minister with an aversion to food. He shrank the menu and expanded the liquor selection before transferring the restaurant to its current absentee owner, who probably kept it as a tax loss. The name had been shortened by popular usage to "The Hole." It fit it well.

The Hole was decorated in early jetsam. Wooden buoys with chipped paint hung from the mustard-colored walls. Lobster pots encrusted with fossilized barnacles shaded the fly-specked globe lights. The ashtrays were hand-size sea-clam shells. The tables had been butchered with the initials of every customer sober enough to open a Swiss army knife. Other shoreside joints had been transformed into pretentious cafés that sold walnut quiche and sandwiches with cute names and alfalfa sprouts on them. But not the Hole. It stood fast, an island of tackiness that resisted the currents of gentrification. This was no small thing, because it was more than just a place to drink. The Hole was a true haunt, a summer meat rack for the young preppy crowd, and in the winter, you could cash and drink your unemployment check in one stop. The way I looked at it, the Hole deserved preservation as a national historical monument.

Barrett drained his beer, then pulled a color snapshot from his wallet and handed it over. The photo showed a young, slender woman in a lime green almost-nothing bikini that provided nearly as much coverage as a couple of Band-Aids. Her hair was the same color as Barrett's, maybe a tad darker, and her near-luminous blue eyes were set against a complexion, unusual in redheads, that could turn sunlight into a tan. "Your sister?" I said.

"Yep, that's Eileen," he replied. "What do you think?"

"I think it's a damn small world."

"Huh?"

"Nothing. Lucky she doesn't have your physique." I handed the picture back. "Okay, Barrett, that's the pretty sister. Now tell me the sob story."

Barrett tucked the snapshot into his billfold and started talking. I sipped a Bud from a tall frosted mug, the plastic kind that always looks heavier than it is, and traced patterns with my forefinger in the beads of beer floating on the surface of the mutilated tabletop. I wondered if Fred loved Shirley as much as he did when he carved their names inside a heart a million drinks ago.

"Maybe you've read about us in the local press," Barrett was saying. "We're trying to salvage an old shipwreck off Provincetown."

I halted my damp doodling and looked up. "Aha. That cute little Jolly Roger on your shirt should have flagged me. You were the treasure hunter who was going to find a zillion bucks in gold and silver."

"We hype that media stuff as much as we can. The skull and crossbones is just to get their attention. The more ink, the better our chance of attracting investors. TV time is like gold to us."

"I don't mean to be disrespectful, but why would someone smart enough to make some money want to invest it in anything as risky as shipwreck salvage?"

"Good question." Barrett ordered two more beers. "A lot of investors figure pieces of eight are more fun than pork belly or soybean futures. The government has tightened up the law on tax shelters, but you'd be surprised at the number of people who don't mind throwing dollars in the water. Being part of a salvage project is pretty exciting to someone who normally deals in stocks and bonds. In this case, they are going to be entertained and make a few bucks to boot."

"Tell me more."

Barrett's eyes glowed with an almost boyish excitement. "The ship's name was the *Gabriella*. She was a British frigate that went down off Peaked Hill Bars in June of 1778."

The second round Barrett had ordered arrived. I took a cold sip and said, "What makes her so interesting to you?"

"The ship's manifests show she carried a couple of hundred thousand pounds sterling to pay the British garrison in Philadelphia. But the redcoats never got paid. The British army abandoned Philadelphia and retreated to New York. It was a mess. Most of the available shipping was held for the thousands of Tory civilians who were still loyal to the crown, for sick and wounded troops, and for heavy material. The Tories had flocked to Philadelphia during the British occupation. The *Gabriella* was supposed to go to New York, drop off money and goods, then head to Halifax, Nova Scotia, with the Tories. But she developed a leak, was separated from the convoy, and chased by some French ships. The captain decided to run straight to Halifax."

"How much is that payroll worth today?"

"Hard to say. One way to judge the value is by figuring out how much the coins would be worth if you melted them down and sold the metal at market value. You'd probably only do a meltdown if the coins were damaged. It would be better to sell any rare coins to collectors and investors, maybe at auction. Stick the others in a plastic case with a certificate of authenticity and you can get anywhere from a few hundred to several thousand dollars apiece, depending on condition. You have to be careful not to flood the market. The payroll is worth a big hunk of change, no doubt about it, but it's just the tip of the iceberg."

"How do you mean?"

"The manifest also lists a hundred gold ingots. That's ten thousand pounds of pure gold. Plus, more gold and jewels owned by British Tories who wanted to get themselves and their valuables out of town. It gets even better, Soc. When we did the initial research, we checked the passenger list. That's when we really got excited."

"Don't tell me. The *Gabriella* was carrying the Astors and the Vanderbilts."

"Better. Passengers included a half-dozen army and navy commissioners. Their valuables weren't recorded, and with good reason. The war made a lot of corrupt British officials incredibly rich. The commissioners were the biggest crooks of all. They charged the crown for bogus goods and supplies never received. The money lost to graft was mind-boggling, even by today's standards. That loot was on the ship, I'm certain of it."

"So that ups the ante."

"You bet it does. For a basis of comparison, there's an old pirate ship called the *Whydah* a few miles down the coast from my site. Divers have pulled up thousands of coins and other stuff off her. That baby's worth a bundle, millions maybe. The *Atocha* down in Florida is worth hundreds of millions, but I think the *Gabriella* will be up there in the big leagues." Barrett took a deep breath. "I estimate the total cargo is worth fifty million at the least. Maybe ten times that."

I whistled softly. "You're talking major bucks. What makes you sure someone didn't get to her first?"

"I had a few sleepless nights wondering the same thing. But the more I got into the historical research the less I worried. The locals undoubtedly picked the beach clean of everything that floated ashore, but I don't think they touched the mother lode. Salvage methods were pretty crude, to begin with. And the British were in hostile waters. The colonists just didn't have the resources. And by the time they did, the currents and the tides might have scattered or buried the treasure beyond reach. There are no records the treasure was ever salvaged."

This was getting interesting. "How did the *Gabriella* go down?"

"Combination of bad luck and bad judgment. She was running fairly close to shore. The ship was probably pretty safe, even with American privateers around. The frigates were smaller than the big ships of the line, but they still packed a wallop. She was 110 feet long and had twenty-six guns, and what she couldn't fend off, she'd outrun. She was trying to round the Cape—that was in the days before you could shortcut through the canal—when she was hit by one of those gales that sometimes come up real fast in the late spring. The captain was a guy named Morton Dinsmore. Dinsmore tried to work her around the tip of the Cape at Provincetown and into the shelter of the bay, but she hit the Peaked Hill Bars and went aground less than half a mile from shore. Dinsmore died in the wreck. Some people say it was all his fault. Court of inquiry pretty much upheld that view. Others say he wasn't alone to blame. That he was a convenient scapegoat because he wasn't around to defend himself."

"What's your opinion?"

"Dinsmore was the skipper, so final responsibility was his. But I'd like to think he was just in the wrong place at the right time."

"He wouldn't be the first one in that position."

"Damn right. That's what makes this whole business so fascinating. Not just the draw of treasure. It's the link with the past. Captains still make lousy decisions that lose them ships. Especially in these waters. There are hundreds of wrecks out there. That combination of shoals and easterly winds is a real keel catcher, even today. Just for a historical fact, most of the sailing ships wrecked in the last couple of hundred years sank in less than thirty feet of water, but that doesn't make it any easier to find them."

"But you have her."

"The *Gabriella*? Oh, sure. At least we *had* her."

"Past tense?"

"Past tense. That's why I need you."

"You need a nautical archaeologist, Barrett, not a part-time private cop."

He tugged at his red hair and shook his head. "I catch your drift, now see if you catch mine."

"I'm easy. Try bribing me with another Bud."

Barrett held two fingers high as a waitress walked by. She ignored him. I lifted my empty mug and winked on her next pass and she brought us another round. Being a notorious barfly has its small rewards. Barrett chugged down half a mug and continued his story.

"A couple of weeks ago my top diver, a guy named Kip Scannell, drowned off Provincetown. He was diving for lobsters."

"I'm sorry to hear about your crewman. I know from personal experience diving sometimes is dangerous."

"You're a diver? Joe Ford didn't tell me that."

"I haven't done any diving in a while. Got my certification in the service. Seemed like a nice hobby and a lot more hygienic than the Bangkok brothels. Going underwater was the ultimate R&R. Fish are a lot nicer than humans. They only devour each other when they're hungry. You still haven't told me why you need a private eye."

Barrett's reply was sidetracked by a commotion at the bar. A couple of husky young tourists who had succeeded in drinking themselves stupid were tossing a grubby white yachting cap back and forth like a Frisbee. The cap belonged to a regular customer named Geetch. The little guy dashed frantically between the two lunks, but all he got for his efforts were handfuls of air and a red face. Geetch would blow away in a stiff breeze; he didn't stand a chance against the pair of endomorphs tormenting him. I watched the fun for a minute. It was obvious the entertainment was just starting. I excused myself and ambled over to the bar. I rested my hand on the bigger man's shoulder. "Why don't you give the cap back?" I suggested amiably.

He turned and looked at me as if I had just stepped out of a flying saucer nude, then removed the cigarette dangling from his lips. "Butt off, asshole. This is none of your friggin' business."

I'm a patient sort of person. "I'm making it my business," I said with my winningest smile. "Game's over."

Friendly persuasion has its limitations when you're talking to a couple of hundred pounds of lager lout. He threw the cap on the bar. Then he reached out with a beefy arm and clamped onto the front of my shirt. He massaged my ribs with his knuckles so it hurt. Down by his side the right hand holding the cigarette bunched into a fist the size of a cantaloupe. He stuck his face in mine. "Oh, yeah?" he said. His breath smelled of old onions. Behind him, his buddy growled menacingly like a dog worrying a bone.

The situation was troubling. The kid was about my height, maybe twenty-five pounds heavier and fifteen years younger. Except for the barrel-size beer gut that hung over his belt, he was built like a fullback on the Boston Patriots. His eyes were small and mean. And he looked as if he ate nails for fun.

In my cop days I'd arrested guys who could have been his identical twin. They're almost a distinct species. *Homo halfwit.* They start out as drunken teenagers brawling with spectators they'd urinated on at hockey games, grow up thinking a marriage license is a permit to beat up on long-suffering wives, and father violent images of themselves. When they die of heart disease or their livers give out, the priest or minister has to bite his tongue to keep from cheering at their funeral. Their biggest mourners are the bar owners, and the attorneys who paid their kids' expenses through Boston College by telling judges who'd heard it all before that their clients are good family men who will pay for any broken bones or windows. It was definitely a mismatch, particularly with the guy's clone ready to back him up.

I considered a nifty boxing combination that's a real showstopper. Set up your man with a snappy left jab, follow through with a quick right cross, and send him to birdland with a left hook that starts at your knee. It doesn't work when you're standing nose to nose, so I had to come up with something else.

Improvising, I said, "You really should do something about your breath, me bucko. It's terrible."

Then I jerked my right fist in a short swinging uppercut, catching him in midsnarl. My arm sank to the elbow in his mushy midsection.

He went *"sooof!"*

His eyes bulged, but he simply looked like someone with a little gas pain. I could have swatted him with a copy of *People* magazine for all the damage I'd done. I hadn't even knocked the ash off his cigarette.

"Jesus," somebody whispered. Maybe it was me.

It's a humbling experience to see that you don't really have dynamite in your fists. Time to rethink my strategy. Since I didn't have access to a Louisville Slugger, maybe I could tell him his shoelace was untied then make a dash for the door. Luckily, I didn't have to resort to subterfuge. Or flight. After six months and a day he released my shirt. He sank in slow motion to the floor, where he held his stomach and stared up at a ceiling fan. The cigarette started to burn a hole in his T-shirt.

The bar had been as silent as a mortuary. Now there was a chorus of gasps, yells, and cheers. Geetch stood nearby, slack-jawed. It wasn't over yet. The guy's friend moved in on me like a tank, deliberated a second, and pronounced, "Hey! That's dirty fighting."

"You're right," I said. I bent and took the cigarette from his friend's limp fingers and squashed it out in a clamshell. "The Marquess of Queensbury would simply be appalled. Now get your buddy out of here while I'm still in a good mood. I'm not taking any prisoners today."

He took another step forward.

Geetch, who had snatched up his cap and now clutched it to his narrow chest, let out a squeak which didn't make me feel any better. I had lost the element of surprise. I needed firepower. I edged toward a wooden bar stool. There was the scuffle of feet and the crash of chairs overturning as customers scrambled out of the way. The guy advanced as I slowly retreated. A nasty grin crossed his broad face. I picked up the bar stool. As a cop I learned that a nightstick applied between the head and shoulders has a calming effect. Maybe it would work with a bar stool. On the other hand, it might only irritate him.

He took one more step. I cocked the stool like Ted Williams getting ready to smash a home run.

A wall of flesh loomed in the background.

"You fellas could use some air," said Joshua, the combination night bartender and bouncer. He clamped one hand on the drunk's neck, collared his still-motionless friend on the floor with the other, and hustled them to the exit as if he were playing a set of cymbals in a marching band.

I let my breath out, walked back to the table, and sat down. Barrett, who was nursing a fresh beer, said, "You and the bartender were a little rough on those guys."

"Not really. Joshua was pretty gentle. He's been tamed by marriage, fatherhood, and the discovery of religion. But if he were still in the Hell's Angels, he'd have bent a Stilson wrench over their heads. I had to resort to guerrilla warfare or they would have tossed me around instead of that hat. They might of hated themselves when they sobered up. Maybe they'd even bring me flowers in the intensive care unit after their bail hearing. So I did all of us a favor. This way no one really got hurt."

Barrett's eyes sparkled with laughter. "This is the first time I've hired a private investigator. I suppose I don't want someone who lets himself get pushed around in bars."

"Hold on, my friend. You don't exactly have yourself a PI yet."

Geetch shuffled over. He wore dirty white duck pants and a faded denim shirt. He plunked the cap back onto his greasy hair. "Thanks, Soc. Those guys—"

"No problem, Geetch, they were spoiling our conversation."

He glanced at Barrett then back at me. "I hate to ask. . . .

Got short on my bar bill . . . I know you got chopped out in Vegas . . . but I was wondering. . . ."

"Sure, Geetch," I said, pulling out my wallet. "Ten spot's best I can do. I'm a little light."

Geetch took the bill with infinitely gentle fingers, scrutinized the portrait of Alexander Hamilton as though looking at the features of a loved one, then folded it precisely in two and slipped it into his pocket. "Thanks, Soc. Coupla days. I promise." He backed away from the table in nervous little steps and joined the other regulars at the bar.

"So you were out in Vegas," Barrett said.

"Yep. But Lady Luck was in Atlantic City. You'd be surprised how quickly you can drop a bundle at the blackjack table. Now I know why you say 'hit me.' The dealers are very obliging when it comes to masochists."

Joshua came back in minus the two drunks and winked at me as he walked past. "Sorry, Soc. I was juggling beer kegs in the cellar when that ruckus started."

"You did just fine, Joshua. I owe you one."

Barrett was staring morosely into his empty mug. He looked up. "Look, Soc. I really need your help. Tell you what. My boat is in Provincetown. Show up tomorrow morning and I'll lay out my problem over breakfast. If you refuse after that, I'll never bother you again. What do you say?"

I would have considered taking the case even if I hadn't been sitting on an anorexic wallet. I liked Barrett and he seemed genuinely troubled. It took only a second to decide. I chugged down another swallow of beer, wiped the foam from my mustache with one hand, and proffered the other. "I would say, Mr. Barrett, that I drink my coffee strong, black, and hot. What time do you put the pot on?"

CHAPTER 4

A clatter in the kitchen woke me the next morning around six. I got up, pulled on my thrift-shop terry cloth bathrobe, and staggered from the bedroom. Sam had let himself in and was at the counter tinkering with my antique Silex coffee maker. "Hey, Soc," he said when he saw me, "why don't you get one of those new Mr. Coffee machines? Be a lot easier to use than this contraption."

"I don't like appliances you have to call mister," I sniffed, pulling a chrome and green plastic chair up to the chrome and green Formica table. "Would you believe it? Got that thing at a yard sale for twenty-five cents."

Sam gave me a look of despair. "I believe it."

Miracles never cease. The coffee didn't peel the enamel off our teeth. Sam joined me at the table where we dug into a package of fossilized powered sugar donuts and traded tidbits of gossip. Cape Cod has changed immensely since the days when you could shoot an arrow down Main Street after the Labor Day tourist exodus without danger of hitting anyone. Thousands of new people have moved over from the mainland. Parts of the Cape are now as impersonal and boring as suburbs. But there is still a nucleus of locals who have known each other for years, and they use the coffee-cup circuit like a wire service.

Sam passed along a bulletin on a burgeoning romance in the building inspector's department at the town hall, where his wife works as a clerk, then asked, "You going to be able to help that big fella we ran into yesterday down at the pier?"

"Dunno yet. I'm off to P'town in a little while to talk to him."

"Be nice if you could do more of that detective stuff.

Fishing business is up and down. Seems like there's less fish each season. Haddock have disappeared, now cod's going the same way. And the work gets tougher every year you get past thirty. Hell, Soc, you got too much on the ball to be breaking your back hookin' fish for a living."

"You sound like my brother," I said. "You haven't been talking to George lately, have you?"

Sam pulled a tan cap with a long black plastic duckbill visor onto his close-cropped snowy hair. "Don't have to talk to anybody. I got eyes and I know how to use them. Got to use them now to fix that hauler."

Like many veteran fishermen, Sam is a weather checker. He can't go five minutes without seeing what the weather is doing. It comes from years spent on the sea, where conditions can change rapidly, and reading the weather is a good way to ensure long life. He got up, walked over to the deck doors, peered outside, and grunted enigmatically. On the way back to the kitchen area he paused in the living room before three framed photographs standing side by side on the fireplace mantel. One picture showed a skinny kid wearing a smart-ass grin and a flak jacket. First division, U.S. Marines. Real world-beater. Going to make the universe safe for democracy. Just me, my fully automatic M-16 assault rifle and a sackful of claymore mines that could turn a man to chopped sirloin quicker than you can say kill zone.

The grin was gone and I looked a hundred years older in the group portrait of my police academy graduating class. But it was back on my face in the third photograph. I had my arm around a sable-haired woman in the kind of awkward embrace that comes from rushing to beat the self-timer on a camera.

Sam stuck his nose close to the last photo and said, "She sure was pretty." He looked at me, embarrassed. "I'm sorry, Soc. I didn't mean to—"

"That's okay, Sam. You're right. She sure was pretty. And she was just as nice as she looks." I glanced at a clock. "Time for me to head out."

Sam waited while I made a quick telephone call, then we left the boat house together. He got into his pickup and started the engine. "Be careful," he warned out the window. "Things have changed. Cape's not the same as it used to be."

I put my hand on his arm. "Nothing is, Sam. Not one blessed thing."

He puffed out his cheeks. "Guess you're right, Soc. But watch yourself anyways." He put the truck into gear and drove off, waving at me in the rearview mirror.

A frisky southwest breeze from Nantucket Sound tickled the whiskers of the codfish weathervane on the ridgepole. Sparkling like broken crystal on the bay was a dazzle of sunlight that hurt the eyes to look at it. Not a thread of a cloud marred the sky. I breathed in the heady beauty of the morning, then swung behind the steering wheel of my truck and bumped out to the paved road.

Forty-five minutes later I crested High Head in North Truro. A couple of miles distant, Provincetown hugged the curving bay shore where Cape Cod runs out of land and tucks into itself like the curlicue on a violin. The tall granite shaft of the Pilgrim Monument, towering high above the town, was bathed in a soft golden ocean light.

The highway descended gradually from the marine scarp of High Head, whose scraggy sloping bluffs were carved from the sea by Ice Age glaciers and sculpted by storm waves thousands of years before the invention of the fried clam. Below High Head were Salt Meadow and the placid, marsh-rimmed waters of Pilgrim Lake. Just beyond the lake, crowned by twisted vestiges of buried forest, the great tawny dunes of the Province Lands rolled to the Atlantic. On the left, along the bay shore, a row of white and aqua cottages stood like fence pickets. I cringe whenever I see them. The cabins are named for flowers, and back in my wild youth I had stayed in one and created a minor riot late one night after drinking the Provincetown bistros dry. Now was that Peony or Phlox? Whoops. Sorry. I haven't been back since.

Leaving Route 6, I drove onto a connector that crosses a couple of hundred feet of sand and beach grass onto Route 6A, the two-lane shore road. The truck rattled along past ancient wind-scoured houses bleached silver gray by the sun, cottage colonies and motels with names like Fore 'n Aft, Wind and Waves, Crow's Nest, Ocean Breeze, and Sea Gull. Beyond a group of sterile condominiums and time-sharing resorts the road broke into the open again and skirted the rippling mudflats that edge Provincetown harbor.

Commercial Street was practically deserted except for a half-dozen early-morning joggers and strollers. The guttural rumbling from the GMC's corroded exhaust system echoed off the quiet, closely spaced old houses. A mile later, where the residential neighborhood gives way to a hodgepodge of guest houses, restaurants, bars, galleries, and gift shops, I turned left at a massive anchor the tourists use as a backdrop for snapshots and drove onto MacMillan Wharf past the whalewatch boats gearing up for the morning run. The whalewatch fleet has made gawking at humpbacks off Stellwagen Bank a multimillion-dollar business. Eat your heart out, Ahab.

I parked close to where a clean-lined boat around forty-five feet long was tied up at the wharf. Lettered in white on the navy blue fiberglass hull was the name *Shamrock*. She had a cream-colored deckhouse and on the aft deck was a crane and winches. Two elbow-shaped aluminum stovepipes that looked like jet engines hung from a steel-pipe framework at the stern. I parked my truck and walked over to the boat. There was no one on deck.

"Ahoy aboard the *Shamrock*," I shouted.

Barrett poked his head out of a hatchway. "Ahoy yourself. Come aboard, you're just in time for breakfast."

I climbed a short dockside ladder onto the deck and stepped down a companionway into the galley. Barrett was slicing thick chunks of slab bacon and throwing them into a black cast-iron frying pan where they sizzled and sent out a smoky fragrance that made my stomach growl. "Pour yourself some coffee while I rustle up our grub," Barrett said. I filled a mug from the pot on the stove and sat down at a dinette table. Seconds later Barrett looked up. "Hi, Eileen. I'd like you to meet Mr. Socarides. Soc, this is my sister."

"Hi," I said, looking at a pair of widening blue eyes and a melting smile.

"Soc is going to help us, I hope," said Barrett, unaware the galley had suddenly become festooned with icicles.

"How do you do, Mr. Socarides." Eileen forced a smile back onto her lips but couldn't control the cold fury in her eyes. Giving her my most lopsided grin, I shook her hand. She held on just long enough to be polite.

"Sis, how about joining us for breakfast?"

"Not right now, Michael. I want to catch up on some paperwork. Nice to meet you, Mr. Socarides." Businesslike. "I *do* hope we can talk before you leave." It sounded like a command performance. She spun on her heel and climbed smartly back up the companionway to the deck. I watched her go. It was hard not to. She was wearing the green bikini, and from my angle at least, the snapshot hadn't done her justice.

I drank my coffee and surveyed my surroundings. For a workboat, the *Shamrock* was fairly plush. The airy interior was nicely trimmed in teak and mahogany, the brightwork varnished to a high sheen. The lockers appeared custom-built. The light let in by an abundance of ports reflected from the off-white bulkheads. Most important for Barrett, there was plenty of headroom so he only had to duck some of the time.

When breakfast was ready, Barrett joined me at the table and we dug into our meal. "Nice boat. Looks pretty comfortable," I said, dabbing a chunk of fresh Portuguese bread into a greasy egg yolk.

"Thanks. I like her. She used to be a Scottish seiner. I bought her primarily for the deck space and the lifting gear. Previous owner was a lawyer. Built her as an investment back in the seventies when the federal government was generous with its financial help. He didn't know zip about fishing, but he knew a lot about comfort, which is fine, because the *Shamrock* is more than just a boat to me right now. She's my home. And she's my past, my present, and with any luck, my future."

In between bites of crisp bacon, I said, "You know, you're a hell of a cook. You could make a fortune in the restaurant business if you ever decide to quit treasure hunting."

"Can't quit. It took me too much time and trouble to get into it. I used to sell condominiums."

"Down in Florida?"

Barrett shot me a quizzical and not entirely friendly glance. "How'd you know that?"

"You forget, I'm a master detective. It was elementary. Talked to Joe Ford this morning and asked him to run a check on you. He said he didn't have to and agreed you both broke more than a few heads in South Boston before you went straight. Joe knew you went off to Florida in search of the endless summer but he hadn't heard from you until you phoned two days ago."

Barrett chuckled. "Touché. You'd be pretty dumb if you didn't check me out the way I did you."

"That's funny, I said the same thing. Tell me, when did

you make the jump from pieces of property to pieces of eight?"

Barrett got up to refill our coffee mugs. "About three years ago I was at a sales convention in Miami, had some free time, and took a trip to Key West. I saw that museum down there, the one with gold from the Spanish galleon *Nuestra Señora de Atocha,* and I was hooked. I read everything about underwater archaeology I could get my hands on. Then I sold my business, learned to dive, and started volunteering for salvage operations. That's when I grew this beard."

"That took a lot of courage. Not the beard, but leaving the security of a good job."

"Naw, Soc. I was fed up with mortgages and bank closings. I could always go back to it if I wanted to. Besides, I made some bad investments. I would have taken a financial bath if I hadn't gotten out when I did. The sale of the business covered them. What took courage was selling my house and putting that money and my savings into this boat so I could make the gamble of my life."

"But you've hit the jackpot with the *Gabriella.*"

"Yes and no. Help me clean up this mess and I'll show you."

We scraped down the dishes and pans and moved up to the spacious pilothouse. Barrett pulled a NOAA National Ocean Service chart of the Cape from a cabinet and spread it out on a plotting table. It's not hard to see why Thoreau called Cape Cod "the bare and bended arm of Massachusetts." The seventy-mile-long peninsula curls off the mainland, bisected at the shoulder by the Cape Cod Canal, like someone showing off his biceps. Barrett pointed to a penciled "X" within a rectangle drawn in the Atlantic Ocean off the balled fist at Provincetown.

"That's about where the *Gabriella* went down." He stabbed the chart with his thick forefinger. "The state permit allows me to look for her within an area one-mile square." He unrolled another chart, this one drawn on a clear plastic overlay, and placed it on top of the first.

"This map was drawn a few weeks after the *Gabriella* sank in 1778. A government representative had been sent down from Boston to retrieve what he could. The Continental Army desperately needed hard currency for the war. Turned out to be a waste of time. The stuff that drifted ashore got scoffed up by the locals. They told him the British got away with the rest. In his report to the Massachusetts provincial government he wrote that the locals were all a bunch of thieves."

"Some of them still are," I said. "Try to get a motel room for under fifty bucks."

Indicating a Maltese cross on the overlay, Barrett said, "That's where the ship supposedly sank, according to eyewitnesses on shore. It must have been a sight to break your heart. The *Gabriella* was loaded with wounded British soldiers, loyalists, and their families and servants. You can just imagine them, men, women, and children, crowded into tiny cabins, exhausted, scared, wet, and miserable. The ship was probably top-heavy with all those people and baggage. The wind would have driven the frigate close into the shoals along the Cape. Like this." He swept his big hand across the chart. "The captain tried to claw off and work the *Gabriella* clear of the Cape and around into the safety of the bay. The wind kept pushing him back, though, so he threw out the anchor, hoping to keep her out of the breakers. But that didn't work. It seldom does off this coast. The ship ran aground, broached so she was thrown broadside to the incoming seas, and over she went. More than two hundred and fourteen people died."

He moved the overlay around until it coincided roughly with the map underneath.

"You see the problem," he said. "The Capes have somewhat different shapes. The map was drawn freehand from the ground, so it's not quite right proportionately. The coastline has eroded a lot in the past couple of hundred years. There's nothing special about this old map, by the way. I've seen it on restaurant placemats. Everyone has known approximately where the *Gabriella* went down, but not specifically. Another big problem, on top of the storms that might have moved her, is the sheer number of wrecks out there. One square mile doesn't sound like much. But looking for one ship in that jumble is like hanging from a helicopter over a junkyard at night trying to hook a 1977 Ford Fairlane. Man, talk about tough!"

"But you found her."

"Yep," Barrett said, "we found her." He took three coins

the size and color of U.S. silver dollars from his pocket and spread them on the maps. I picked one up. It weighed about an ounce. On one side was a cross. On the other, two pillars flanked a couple of globes surmounted by a crown. Between the columns was the figure eight, wavy lines, and the Latin moto *Plus Ultra*—"Farther Yet." The date on the coin was 1765.

"Got 'em on the first few dives," Barrett was saying. "These are pieces of eight. Some people call them 'pillar dollars.' Those are the Pillars of Hercules, gateway to the New World. The waves are the Atlantic. The earlier hand-struck eight reale pieces were mostly melted down for their silver once they got to Spain. These guys were machined. They were used as international currency, like the dollar is today, even in the British colonies."

I put the coin down. "Okay. I'm impressed," I said.

Barrett grunted, prodding the dully shining coins with a finger. "It wasn't easy. Took months to gear up, put together a corporation, and go through a mountain of paperwork for a state permit. But we finally got down to business and started doing serious survey work last summer and into fall. We weren't sure we located the *Gabriella* until this spring."

Barrett tapped a black metal box resting on a nearby shelf. "This is a proton magnetometer. The mag was a spin-off from the sub warfare research in World War II. Back in the 1970's treasure hunters began using them in Florida. This little beauty revolutionized the salvage business. You tow a probe behind the boat, the mag reads the bottom for ferrous materials like cannons and anchors."

He shoved the coins and maps aside and unrolled a wide strip of graph paper marked with squiggles and splotches. He indicated peaks made by a stylus. "These are called 'anomalies.' They indicate hunks of iron or steel. This one's an iron-hulled sailing ship that went down in the 1860's, for instance."

Barrett unrolled another length of graph paper. A pattern of horizontal and intersecting bars was set against groupings of wavy smudges. "This is from a subbottom profiler. We call it a 'pinger.' It's kind of a sonar that Harold Edgerton developed up at MIT. Those little dark lines that look like distant mountains are targets, objects the profiler picked up under the ocean floor. You use the pinger in conjunction with your mag to draw a chart that gives you a fair picture of what's under the muck."

He rolled up the paper. "As you're finding this stuff, it's critically important to know your position. We use Loran just like you probably do when you're fishing, so you know how it works."

Loran is an acronym for long-range navigation. Sam and I couldn't get by without the Loran system. In the old days mariners used a compass and the knowledge gained through a hard apprenticeship to compute their position. The new breed punches a button on a Loran-C set smaller than a shoebox. The receiver picks up electronic signals broadcast by shore stations and translates them into Loran bearings. Just check the readings against the figures on your navigation chart and you can pinpoint your location.

I nodded. "Loran should put you within fifty feet of your wreck."

"It's absolutely crucial. You also need shore landmarks, and various diagrams to verify your position. Eventually, we would have pinpointed the site with shore-based responders or marked it with a remotely triggered underwater electronic beacon. You can mark a wreck with a buoy, but risk being cleaned out by poachers."

Barrett organized the papers and replaced them in a cabinet. "There you have it. The basic tools of the modern treasure hunter. Combine that stuff with a boat, a depth sounder, some historical research, a little luck, an expensive lawyer, a state permit, and lots and lots of money, and maybe, just maybe, you've got yourself a treasure wreck."

"That's fascinating," I said. "So what's the problem?"

He stared out the pilothouse window a moment before answering. "The problem is that all the stuff I just showed you is for another ship. The instrument data, the mag readings and sonar charts and Loran and land bearings for the *Gabriella,* all that is missing."

I was finally beginning to see why Barrett needed me. I sipped my coffee and waited for him to get to the point.

"Kip Scannell was in charge of the site stuff. And I can't ask him where it is because he's dead."

"You're right," I said, "that is a problem."

The light had left Barrett's face and his boyish enthusiasm was gone. "Soc, I'd like you to find my site data. Without that information, particularly the Loran coordinates and the chart saying 'here it is,' my *Gabriella* project is finished. I don't have the time or money to start from scratch. I'd be eternally grateful if you took the case. Are you interested?"

I had already come to a decision. "Okay, Mike. I can't promise any miracles, and I have an obligation to Sam, so I'll have to fit you in around him, but you've just hired yourself a private investigator."

Barrett grinned. "Soc, you have no idea what this means to me."

I pulled the wallet from my pocket and handed him a business card. "That's my number if you have to get in touch with me. Rates are on the back. I'll need a little advance for expenses."

"You've got it." Barrett examined the card. "God, where did you get a monicker like Aristotle Socarides?"

Believe it or not, Barrett wasn't the first to ask me that question. "It is rather a mouthful," I said. "The last name was given to me by my father. The first name was given to me by my mother. She was the one who insisted I study Greek and Roman classics. 'Count no mortal happy until he has passed the final limit of his life secure from pain.' That's from *Oedipus the King*. Want to hear something from *Antigone*? How about the *Iliad* in the original Greek?"

Barrett shook his head. "Maybe later."

"Everybody says that. You mentioned the state permit. Wouldn't your application have the information you need?"

The question really set Barrett off. "Sure, only the permitting board *lost* my folder. Can you believe it? New secretary, they said. Plus they moved from one building to another. They said they were sorry and surely I must have duplicates."

"So much for that idea. Tell me, would anybody benefit if you couldn't relocate the wreck?"

Another raw nerve. Barrett scowled. "Yeah, someone would benefit. His name is Lucas. Claims he found the *Gabriella* before I did. Obviously we can't both excavate the same wreck, so he wants the state archaeological board to take away my salvage permit and give it to him. If I can't relocate the ship, Lucas could say I didn't have the *Gabriella* in the first place. He might use that to move in on me. In that case this whole expedition, this boat, and my life will go down the drain. I could lose a couple of hundred thousand dollars just on the boat alone. That doesn't count the time I've sunk into this project. I need that damn data."

"Where did Kip live?"

Barrett scooped up a piece of eight and glowered at it. "I don't really know. He'd bunk out on the boat occasionally, but he was on the move a lot. He used to make the rounds of the P'town bars, so if I needed him, I'd just leave a message around and it would get to him pretty quick."

"What about friends or relatives?"

"None that I know of. Look, I wish I could be more helpful. Kip just didn't talk much about himself."

I stood. "That's okay. Let me scratch around. If I learn anything, I'll get back to you."

We went onto the deck. Eileen leaned against a rail, scribbling in a notebook. She looked as if she had been waiting for us.

Barrett was suddenly acting as frisky as a kid on the last day of school, which was scary considering his size. He did a little hop-skip dance and slapped me on the back. Somehow my teeth managed to stay in my head. Then he went over and crushed his sister in an affectionate bear hug. She was almost lost in his embrace. "Great news, sis. Soc's going to help us."

Eileen pried herself out of his brawny, red-furred arms and put the notebook down. "I'll walk you to your truck, Mr. Socarides. I have to get something out of my car." I shook hands with Barrett and climbed up to the pier with Eileen on my heels.

"Mr. Socarides," she whispered harshly when we were out of earshot, "I want to talk to you."

"I got that impression."

Up close, she was even lovelier than I figured. Her eyes were slightly greener than her brother's, but they looked at the world with the same intensity. I wondered at the way nature had juxtaposed a strong, stubborn chin with a soft, yielding mouth.

"You are doing neither me nor my brother a favor by taking this case," she said.

I stopped and leaned against my truck fender. "Ms. Barrett, aren't you being a little petty just because I grabbed your parking space in Cambridge the other night?"

"That's not the only reason. Incidentally, for your information, the damage to my car from your Neanderthal driving is more than three hundred dollars. You *do* know what a Neanderthal is, don't you?"

"Yes, and I know they came in both sexes. Try trading that Japanese junk in for some Detroit iron. Look," I said, whacking my truck fender. Flakes of rust fell from the inside. "Good old American knowhow."

She put a hand on her hip and waved a finger at my nose. "Michael told me about that barroom brawl you started last night. I'm not a bit surprised. He may be desperate enough to hire you, but in my opinion you're no more than a no-good drunken bum."

"Ms. Barrett—"

"What?" she snapped.

"In my opinion, your opinion doesn't count. However, I sincerely hope we can cooperate, for your brother's sake." I got in the truck and leaned out the window. "As they say at the bank, 'have a nice day.' "

Hooking the truck in a U-turn, I missed by inches the blue Toyota Tercel parked on the pier. I drove off, chuckling at the look of horror on Eileen's face. Ho-ho. Pretty clever guy. Guess I showed her. Omigod. A sobering thought zinged in from the stratosphere. My glee evaporated. Something about the way Eileen had scolded me, with her finger dusting the tip of my nose and the other hand planted solidly on her hip, reminded me of another woman who frequently makes my life interesting. My mother.

CHAPTER 5

Kip Scannell's death had hardly made a ripple in the local press. I thumbed through back editions of the *Cape Cod Times* at the newspaper's Provincetown office. The four-paragraph story was buried on page nine under the headline DIVER DROWNED IN FREAK ACCIDENT.

The report said a fishing dragger hauled up the body of Kip Scannell, diver on the *Gabriella* expedition. The body was in scuba gear and tangled in a gill net. Kip's outboard skiff was discovered anchored in the bay. The police theory was that he became caught in a net while diving for lobsters. I checked the papers published the week Kip died for an obituary listing survivors and funeral arrangements. Nothing. No paid death notice either. Odd. I photocopied the story and a few minutes later was on Route 6 heading out of town.

I had two certainties to work with. First, Barrett's missing charts had been in Kip's possession. And second, Kip was dead. If I started with Scannell's death and worked backward, maybe one certainty would intersect the other.

Kip's body was brought into an Outer Cape village less than a half hour from Provincetown. The picturesque bayside town had a seafaring past and a busy harbor, but now the fishing boats were outnumbered by art galleries that sold large blobby canvases to New York psychiatrists. The police department was in a large, cupola-topped building. A bronze plaque bolted on the white clapboards said 1841. It could have been A.D. or B.C.

Inside, the police-station odor of old cigarette butts and musty paper gave me a feeling of déjà vu. A dispatcher with mahogany hair and a freckled face sat at a phone console reading a supermarket tabloid story about a teenager giving birth to twin UFO space tots. I asked to see the chief. She conducted a head-to-toe examination with her eyes, then treated me to a dreamy smile.

"Do you have an appointment?"

I smiled back. "No, I'm sorry, but I don't."

"I'll see if the chief is available," she said agreeably. Sometimes it helps to be irresistible. She punched a button on the phone, mumbled a few words, asked my name, and mumbled a few more. Then she nodded at me. "It's okay, Mr. Socarides. He's pretty busy but he'll see you for a minute."

The chief's office was marked by a door with a frosted glass panel that could have used a spot of cleaning. Printed on the glass were the words "Chief Francis X. Farrell." The "X" was smudged. The office was what an enterprising real-estate salesman would describe as a cozy nook. The space was made even smaller by the bulk of the man sitting behind the gray metal desk. The desktop was remarkably uncluttered. Blotter, pen set, telephone, calendar. A framed photograph of the flag raising at Iwo Jima stood where some men might have a picture of the wife and kids. That was it.

Chief Farrell looked like a football linebacker gone to flab. He was built for barroom brawls, and judging from the ruins of his face, he had seen a few. He wore a white shirt open at the collar and had the flushed look that goes with a pale complexion and a booze habit. His hair was light brown gone to gray, cut to the scalp, and if he was busy doing anything, it was nursing a hangover. He did not look overjoyed to see me.

"Mr. Socarides," he rumbled. "What can I do for you?"

I sat in an office chair without an invitation. "I need some help."

His red-rimmed eyes regarded me skeptically. "What kind of help?"

"I'm a private investigator. I'm looking into the death of a diver named Kip Scannell. I understand your department investigated the case and I was wondering what you could tell me about it."

I sat back and awaited the eruption; no cop likes an outsider trespassing on his turf. The reaction was immediate and violent. The chief slammed a huge hand down on the desk, hard. The shock waves toppled the Iwo Jima photo. So much for police/private citizen cooperation.

"What's this friggin' crap? I looked into that case and the friggin' book is closed." His bloodshot eyes bulged. I realized he was staring at the gold ring in my left earlobe. The ring wasn't half the size of the one Barrett wore, but it seemed to infuriate the chief anyhow. "I don't need some hippie private cop messing around my town. Now get the hell out of my office!"

"Does that mean I can't see the report on the case?"

He responded with an anguished bark. But before he could start dismemberment proceedings, the telephone rang. Thank God for Alexander Graham Bell. Farrell grabbed the phone and stuck it in his ear. He listened a few minutes and his mouth sagged. "I did?" he said. "I didn't. I did. Oh, jeez. You're sure? Damn. When? Okay. Good-bye." He hung up. His skin had developed an unhealthy pallor.

"That was the chairman of selectmen," he said to nobody in particular. "Says I got blitzed last night at the Bell Buoy Lounge and dumped some tourist from New Jersey onto the ice in the raw bar. Told the other customers the guy reminded me of a clam because he had a little neck. The selectmen have scheduled a hearing. I'll be damned." Farrell seemed to remember me for the first time. "Whatcha say your name was?"

"Socarides. They call me Soc."

The look he shot me held a glint of recognition. "You were a cop in Boston, right?"

"That's right."

"You got resigned as a detective for roughing up a customer."

I shook my head. "That's wrong. Story's a little more complicated. It goes like this. I ran into a fracas in Roxbury on an off-duty night. A city councillor's kid had taken a shortcut onto a sidewalk and hit a black woman and her baby. Her neighbors trashed the old man's Lincoln Continental and were starting on the driver. I got him away with only a few bumps then arrested him for driving under the influence. The case never went to court. The councillor held the key vote on a waterfront development package that would get the mayor's relatives and friends off his back and onto the municipal payroll. Hizzoner appoints the police commissioner who told me I was being unreasonable. The woman and her baby weren't badly hurt and she was being offered a city job. The kid's lawyer was squawking about police brutality. It wasn't the first time I ran up against city hall, but I had finally reached my fill of sleaze, so I left the department. End of story. What about you?"

Farrell grunted amiably. "I was a state cop working out of the Framingham barracks. Made it to sergeant with no hope of advancement at my age and a crummy pension years away. I read about this job in the *Boston Globe*. Nobody wanted it because of the screwy local politics. My wife had already left me, and my kids had moved out of state. I didn't feel like directing traffic around potholes on the Mass Pike until retirement, so I became a big blue frog in a small pond. Now I answer complaints about barking mutts in the winter and I scrape tourists off Route 6 in the summer. It's a living, though, and the scenery, what I see of it, is sure pretty this time of year. But once in a while it gets to me and I have to cut loose."

"Like last night in the bar." I reached over and carefully righted the picture of Iwo Jima. "You were in the corps."

The chief eyed me suspiciously. "Yeah. So what?"

"Served in the Pacific theater?"

"That's right. Last year of the war."

"You must have been pretty young."

"Hell, I was just a kid." He picked up the photo and gazed at it fondly. "Best time of my life."

"I went to the same school, different graduating class. Did most of my classwork in the Mekong Delta. I was just a kid too." It was definitely not the best time of my life, but I decided not to tell him that.

"You're kidding. You were a marine?"

"Vietnam."

"What the hell," he said, extending his big paw across the desk. "Semper fi."

Farrell's handshake only hurt a little. Maybe the hangover weakened him. "What the hell," I said. "Semper fi."

Farrell jerked open a desk drawer and pulled out a manila folder. He leaned back and leafed through the papers inside. The phone rang twice, but he ignored it. Somebody else got it. Probably the young woman at the reception desk.

"Your boy Scannell was last seen in a P'town joint. The

cops down there figure he went diving the next day, got caught in a net, and drowned off Long Point, where the water's eighty to ninety feet or more deep. Anyhow, he drowns off Provincetown, which is his business, but the body's found by a fishing boat from this town, so they bring it in here, which makes it my business. If'd been me, I would've shoved him back in so he'd be some other cop's headache. Hold on a minute." Farrell got up and went in the next room. When he came back he had another folder. "Here. I xeroxed the file for you. Looks open and shut to me, but maybe you'll see something I missed."

"Thanks, Chief," I said, rising. "If I find anything I'll pass it on so you can get the glory."

Farrell blew a raspberry. "Glory?" Farrell blew a raspberry, "You're a jarhead all right. All brass and no brains. Now get the hell out of here. I've got to call my lawyer and see if he can help me hold on to this crummy job."

Saluting with a forefinger, I backed out of the office and walked by the receptionist. Her nose was buried in a paperback romance entitled *Flaming Ecstasy*. She didn't look up.

Back in my truck I rummaged through a shoebox full of cassettes, found the one I wanted, and slid it into my tape deck. The sound of the Marine Band came clashing out of the speakers midway between the halls of Montezuma and the shores of Tripoli. I started the truck, pulled out onto the road, and listened to the tape a few minutes as I drove along. Then I popped it out. Then I threw it back in the box. Then I listened to nothing.

A half hour later I was looking at a mermaid. She had green skin, curly tresses of sea lettuce, and bosoms as big as bowling balls. Definitely not built for speed through the water. This may have explained why she sat on a giant clam at the bottom of the ocean being leered at lasciviously by two infatuated divers. The sign she graced said LARRY'S DIVE SHOP. It hung outside a converted fish shanty overlooking a busy little harbor crowded with pleasure boats.

Inside, the shop's walls were hung with diving masks, fins, snorkels, color posters of scuba divers nosing around barnacle-encrusted timbers, and neatly printed schedules for diving lessons and wreck dives. A half-dozen air tanks stood in a corner. The shop smelled of rubber from the regulator hoses and the racks of neoprene dive suits. "California Girls" blared from a set of shelf speakers.

Behind the counter stood a stocky man in his thirties who had ginger hair and a thin mustache to match. He wore a T-shirt with a scaled-down version of the mermaid and her admirers. He was tinkering with an air-tank regulator and bobbing to the music. He grinned and reached over to the stero dial when I walked in. The Beach Boys faded to a decibel level slightly under earsplitting. "Socko, my man. What's happenin'?"

I jerked my thumb toward the front door. "Hey Larry, how did that pornographic sign get past the blue noses on the zoning board?"

"Some people know art when they see it. Besides, the board's only interested in square footage."

"There's certainly plenty of that."

"Drawn from life at the bottom of the sea. So what's shakin'? You going to get serious and get diving again?"

"Maybe," I said, collapsing into a purple Naugahyde beanbag chair. Picking a dive magazine off a rack, I riffled the pages. "I may change my mind, though, after hearing about Kip Scannell."

"God, poor Kip," Larry said. "But you know, there's a chance in a million of something like that happening, especially if you buddy up like you're supposed to."

"No argument there. I don't think I knew Kip. What kind of a guy was he?"

Larry put the regulator down and wrinkled his brow. "Kip was an okay dude, I guess. Always good for a laugh. I got loaded with him a few times down in P'town, where he did most of his socializing. He liked to party. Liked his booze, and women too. Especially the women. If you listened to him, he was the king of studs. Maybe he was. He came in the shop once or twice to buy gear."

"I heard he was a pretty good diver."

"You heard right. He used to do industrial dives like bridges and oil rigs before he came to the Cape. Dangerous as hell, but a couple jobs a year will pay the rent. He was probably one of the best, in fact. That's why it's so funny, him screwing up regally on an easy dive. Hard to figure why he'd pull some dumb-ass trick like getting drowned. Wasn't his style, if you know what I mean."

"How long had he been treasure hunting?"

"Anyone who dives is a treasure hunter whether he admits it or not. You know that, Soc. We're all hoping to stumble on a big chest of gold. Kip told me he did wreck diving off and on down south, but he didn't go into detail. He didn't talk much about himself. Mostly about chicks, parties he'd been to. Played it real close to the vest. He was one of those guys you don't even know where he lives. Sometimes he's around and sometimes he isn't. He'd drop out of circulation for a while and reappear, just like that, as if he'd never been away."

"I don't ever recall bumping into him. Who'd he hang out with?"

"Everybody and nobody. He had a lot of bar buddies like me but no real friends as far as I can recall. There was one weird story. Don't go away, I'll be back in a second." Two customers had come into the shop. Larry went off to wait on them while I read dive magazines. He was shaking his head when he returned ten minutes later. "Incredible," he said. "Those people just ordered two grand worth of gear."

"People'll pay anything for a thrill," I said.

"Guess you're right. Where was I? Oh yeah, Kip. Anyhow, about a year ago this buddy of mine sees him in a Key West bar. Kip is sitting at a table with some very rough dudes and from the way they're talking, they seemed like old friends. My buddy goes over to say hello and Kip makes like he doesn't even know him. Later Kip comes by and apologizes. Says he was talking about buying a boat from these suckers who wanted to unload it in a hurry and that's why he wasn't friendly. Even buys my buddy a drink."

"Interesting." Rising with some difficulty from the sticky clutches of the beanbag, I said, "Let me know your dive schedule. I might want to tag along."

"Yeh, you bet. Hey, Soc, you really think that sign's pornographic?"

I stepped outside, looked at the mermaid, and stuck my head back in. "It deserves to be hung over a brothel."

Larry beamed. "Gee, Soc. Thanks. That reminds me." I stepped back in. "I'd seen Kip a coupla times squiring around a dark-haired girl. Real pretty with the kind of body you see in a *Playboy* centerfold. Dunno her name. Kip never introduced her to me or anyone so far as I know."

"I wouldn't blame Kip for not wanting his girlfriend to meet you and the rest of the hungry sharks in these waters. Catch you later."

Driving back to the boat house, I assembled what I had learned about Kip Scannell. I had the uncomfortable feeling something wasn't right. Detective work is mostly plodding around collecting and analyzing facts. In time, the persistent voice of intuition may whisper in your ear. If you're any good, you will listen to what it says.

CHAPTER 6

Not everyone is lucky enough to die peacefully in his sleep. But Kip's death had been a hard one any way you looked at it. He would have spent the last seconds of his life gagging for breath, struggling as helplessly as a fly caught in a spiderweb. I sat at the kitchen table shuffling through the file Farrell had given me. In the dispassionate language of officialese, the police and medical examiner reports summed up the life, and death, story of one Arthur "Kip" Scannell. Diver. Age thirty-five. The folder contained no surprises, but I hadn't expected any revelations to jump out at me.

The facts seemed straightforward. Scannell was last seen in a Provincetown bar. He'd been drinking heavily. The police assumed he went diving for lobsters early the next morning and got snagged in a drifting gill net. No one had seen him leave the Provincetown marina, where he kept his outboard tied up. The cops guessed Scannell succumbed to a lethal combination of bad judgment and bad luck. Gill nets hang vertically in the water. Fish swim into the mesh, are caught by their gills, and can't back out. The thin nylon monofilament is nearly invisible underwater and as strong as steel. Sometimes a gill net breaks free and drifts off. Fishermen call these free-floaters "ghost" nets. A ghost net will continue to catch fish. This one caught a diver. Scannell wouldn't have had a prayer.

The police were up to their badges in a sea of noisy parties and triple parkers and saw nothing fancy in the cause of death. The man was in the water. He was caught in a fishnet. He was not a fish. He was not breathing. Therefore he drowned. This was confirmed by the autopsy. Kip had traces of alcohol in his body, the medical examiner said when I called him. God, it had been a hellish week, the medical examiner complained. There was a fatal car crash on Route 6, a boy buried under a collapsed sand cliff, and a suspected suicide. If that weren't enough, his golden retriever had puppies. Real cute. He'd be glad to give me a deal on one if I were interested. The autopsy report routinely went to the district attorney's office, and a note was sent to the police. *Slam*. Case closed. Next!

I tapped a pencil against my lower teeth. It made a tok-tok sound. Something was askew here. A guy like Kip doesn't leave a bar just when the fun is starting so he can dive for lobsters the next day. It made even less sense for an experienced diver to dive alone, especially after a night of boozing. No one likes lobsters that much. Thinking of lobsters made me thirsty. But then everything makes me thirsty. I went to the refrigerator, liberated another can of Bud, snapped the top open and reflected on the genius of the person who invented payment in advance of services. I walked back to the table and picked up the file, ready to go through it again. A car door slammed and I glanced out a window.

A Mercedes the color of butternut squash was in my front drive, parked next to my truck, where it seemed to bridle like someone who's discovered a shopping bag lady in his box at the opera. A well-built young man who looked as if he spent a lot of time pumping iron stood beside the Mercedes. His black cap tagged him as the chauffeur, but his fawn designer slacks and a dark blue polo shirt did not come off the rack at Acme Uniform.

He opened the back door of the Mercedes. Something in the way he moved caught my attention, but I was soon distracted. A slim woman in her early thirties emerged from the car in a graceful liquid motion and brushed her long blond hair away from a Katharine Hepburn forehead.

She wore a thin white cotton dress and not much more over a tan that had taken some hard work; her shoulders were bare and lovely. She was a type I had seen on the rare occasions somebody mistakenly invited me to a cocktail party. She had a figure sculpted by hours on the tennis court and months of self-deprivation, and she exuded wealth and deep boredom in every step. In ten years her skin would look like burned leather from exposure to year-round sun and her arms and legs would develop a stringy and unattractive muscularity. But now she had a body that could make a man wish his wife would step in front of a truck.

She walked directly to the house and knocked. I opened the front door so quickly I startled her. "Excuse me," I apologized. "I just oiled the hinges."

The woman slowly removed a pair of rose-tinted sunglasses. Raising a professionally plucked brow that arched over a bold green eye, she said, "Mr. Socarides, I presume. Am I pronouncing it correctly?"

"I am and you are. Please come in."

She turned and nodded to the chauffeur, who was lounging against the Mercedes. He scowled at me. Obviously not a friendly fellow. Then she stepped inside. "My name is Laura Nichols," she said, offering her hand. I held her fingers a few seconds longer than considered proper. The engagement diamond she wore must have weighed four carats. It nicely matched the diamond on her wedding band.

"I'm very happy to meet you, Mrs. Nichols. Why don't we go out on the deck."

We passed through the boat house and out the kitchen door onto the wide deck. Laura Nichols appraised the view with its magnificent sweep of salt marsh, bay, and distant ocean and said, "I had no idea." She had a low, throaty voice you could get used to hearing.

"Pretty, isn't it? This was the boat house for an old estate. The main house is off in the woods there. I worked overtime and bought this place a few years ago when you didn't have to have a numbered Swiss bank account to own a home on the water."

Pulling a faded blue director's chair from under a plastic patio table, I said, "Have a seat," and settled into its mate. "You know my name, so obviously you aren't lost." The breeze came from behind her and I learned that Laura Nichols favored expensive jasmine perfume.

"You're a private detective," she said. "Someone mentioned your name at the yacht club."

The only people I knew at the yacht club were the ones who mowed the lawn, but I played along. "Of course, the yacht club. Good chaps. I take a case for them now and then. Stolen burgees and all that."

Laura Nichols said, "I would like you to take mine."

Clients were suddenly popping out of the woodwork.

"You'll have to tell me about your problem before I can make a decision, Mrs. Nichols. You may not even need my services."

She opened a white alligator-skin purse, pulled out a silver cigarette holder with a matching Cartier lighter, lit a Virgina Slim, and inhaled. "My husband Charles is in real estate and construction, Mr. Socarides. He is extremely good at what he does. He has made a great deal of money. Charles comes from a humble background. When he started out, he did business, shall we say, unconventionally. He borrowed where he could get money and rendered services in return that some people would call questionable."

"Some people are prudes about anything."

Laura Nichols smiled tightly. "I'm not defending Charles, Mr. Socarides. But he did leave that part of his life behind him years ago. Recently, however, the government began a crackdown on organized crime. My husband is likely to be called as a witness. I believe his life is in danger because he knows too much."

"You may be jumping to conclusions, Mrs. Nichols. Have there been any threats?"

"No," she answered. "Nothing like that. But my husband has been followed for at least two weeks and perhaps more that we are not aware of. We think someone wants to determine his habits and that an attempt eventually will be made on his life."

"Does he know you've come to me?"

"Of course."

"Have you gone to the police?"

She laughed. "Mr. Socarides, would you go to the police if you had a history like that of my husband?"

"I see your point, but what can I do?"

"Charles and I would like to know for certain if anyone is following him. And if it appears he is in danger, see him to a place of safety. At least until he is subpeonaed. As a private detective you must know about following people." The emerald eyes watched me carefully over the cigarette.

"Most of the time I follow them to motels and bars."

"But you would know, if necessary, how to prevent someone from being followed."

"Sure, Mrs. Nichols. You could follow the follower and

hit him over the head with a baseball bat. That would cramp his style."

She looked around for an ashtray, didn't find one, then dropped the cigarette and ground it out under the heel of her Gucci shoe. "There must be some other way."

Across the marsh, a lone sea gull balancing delicately on an updraft burst into a manic laugh. Maybe he knew something I didn't. Maybe he was telling me this was a bum case. Maybe . . . A whisper of air, heavy with the fragrance of salt-spray rose, tousled Laura Nichols's hair, and blended nicely with the jasmine.

"I've just agreed to take another case, Mrs. Nichols. I don't know how much time I could devote to this. And I wouldn't help a potential government witness evade a subpeona. Some folks might consider that slightly illegal."

"I'm not asking you to break the law, Mr. Socarides. My husband is prepared to come forward and testify when the time comes. Nor would you have to guard Charles twenty-four hours a day."

"It's a little more complicated than that. First I'd have to find out if your husband is being tailed, and try to detect a pattern. If he is being followed by professionals, and I get in the way, they might get pushy."

"But you have a gun, don't you?"

"Yes, I have a gun, but I prefer not to use it. If you're looking for a Dodge City marshal, I suggest you go to central casting."

"I understand. I didn't mean . . ." She sighed. It was a pretty sound. "Mr. Socarides, it doesn't take a detective to see I'm a spoiled rich woman. I have a bad habit of treating everyone like a servant. It hasn't made me any friends and has lost many old ones. I apologize for trying to tell you how to handle your business. It's just that I am terribly nervous about Charles."

The sea gull cackled again. I ignored it. "How about this for a suggestion, Mrs. Nichols? Let me poke around a little just so we'll know what we're dealing with. Then we can take it from there. You and your husband may have nothing to worry about."

Laura Nichols leaned forward unexpectedly and wrapped her arms around my shoulders, her breath soft and warm in my ear. "I don't know how to thank you, Mr. Socarides."

My nose was against her neck, her firm breasts hard against my chest. The scent of her perfume and the warmth of her body sent a tingle flying down to the tips of my flip-flops. With some reluctance I pushed her gently away, but not too fast. Then I reached into my wallet and pulled out a business card. At this rate I might need new cards printed.

"My fee schedule is on the back," I said. "I usually ask my clients for a small advance."

Without glancing at the card, she put it in her purse, drew several hundred-dollar bills out, and handed them over.

"That's a very generous advance," I said. "Would you like a receipt?"

She snapped the purse shut. "It won't be necessary. You have a trustworthy face."

My face has been called a lot of things, never trustworthy, but I accepted the compliment because it was the first I'd received that week. "You may have change coming," I said.

"It's little enough for the peace of mind you have already given me, Mr. Socarides. I'll call you in the morning with my husband's plans. We thought it best that he have no direct contact with you."

Suddenly Mrs. Nichols was all business, she stood and extended her hand. "I can find my way out." She turned and walked quickly through the house and out the front door. The breeze lifted the skirt of her white dress. I went around the side of the boat house just in time to see the butternut-colored Mercedes disappear down the driveway in an explosion of dust.

I walked over to my truck and tenderly patted a fender heavily patched with fiberglass. It was a good truck but I had neglected it in favor of bar tabs.

Holding the bills in front of the headlights, I said, "Look at this, old girl. If business keeps up this way, I'm going to take you to the body shop and give you the best face-lift money can buy." I'm just a sentimental fool. I slipped the money into my pocket and went back into the house. Settling into a chair, I reopened the police folder on Kip Scannell.

CHAPTER 7

In my dream I was being run over by a bulldozer. It crawled slowly upward from my knees, digging its treads painfully into my skin, coming to a crushing halt on my chest. The ragged engine roar grew to a near thunder. I lay on my back, unable to breathe, every muscle paralyzed, struggling to open my eyes. The left eyelid fluttered. Then the right. Success. Uh-oh. Two yellow circles of pure evil stared at me. I blinked the blurriness away.

"Kojak! For Chrissakes!"

Fourteen pounds of ratty feline fur the color of anthracite coal hurtled off my chest onto the floor and skidded around a corner. I sat up and looked blearily at the clock on the side table. Seven A.M. I groaned and lay back again, pulling the blankets over my head. The phone rang. I groped for the receiver and in a fairly impressive imitation of intelligible speech, grunted a hello.

"Mr. Socarides? This is Laura Nichols. I'm sorry to call you so early. I tried several times last night but no one was home. Your answering machine doesn't seem to be working."

Her voice was coming from far away. I reversed the phone and spoke in the correct end. "I don't have an answering machine. Don't like them. Something inhuman about talking to a box." I cleared my throat. "I was out last night working on a case,"

More like two cases. Of beer. In my bill it would be called "preliminary research." That meant making the rounds of the haunts frequented by divers, surfers, fishermen, and other waterfront types. I asked a lot of people about Kip Scannell, greasing the conversations with hogsheads of beer. Now my tongue tasted like flannel underwear. Being a private eye is no picnic.

Considering the extent of the beerover I was suffering, about an 11.5 on the Richter scale, and the number of brain cells destroyed, I had accomplished very little beyond making the breweries put on a night shift. The picture of Kip was the same one drawn by Larry. Scannell was a hot-stuff dude, womanizer, damn good diver, boon drinking companion. Then there was that great-looking chick with the dark hair. Nope, never did catch her name. Maybe Kip was a little strange, but it went with the territory. Oh yeah, a voice had cut through the boozy fog at one bar. That thing with Kip and Lady Brett at the Dunes Club in P'town. Talk about *weird*.

I croaked out another sentence. "What can I do for you, Mrs. Nichols?"

"I have my husband's schedule for you. Mr. Socarides, are you all right? You sound a bit . . . fuzzy."

"I'm fine. Just the hay fever acting up." I pulled a notebook to the phone, found a ballpoint pen that didn't work, found one that did, jotted down times and places, and hung up. I looked at the clock again. Maybe I could catch a few more winks. Kojak poked his head around a corner. He said, "*Mrrp.*" Translation: Feed me.

I eased out of bed and made my way unsteadily to the kitchen. My temples pounded like timpana with each step. *Boom, boom, boombidy boom.* While water boiled for instant coffee I spooned out a mountain of 9-Lives tuna and liver into Kojak's dish with the smiling kitty face on it. I hated this part of the day, but Kojak bites the fur off his tail at any disruption of his schedule, and people mistake him for a deformed possum.

I stayed in the shower until the hot-water tank went cold. After four mugs of strong black coffee, I concluded that I wasn't going to die. I pulled on my one pair of chinos and a clean blue oxford button-down shirt and slipped my bare feet into Top-Siders. It's the basic uniform for a Cape Cod yachtsman or condominium developer, often one and the same. Substitute cranberry slacks and you're a golf nut. Throw on a navy blazer and you're a real-estate broker. Add a silk tie and socks and you become a second-mortgage man. I grabbed my softball-team T-shirt and Boston Red Sox cap just in case I got into redneck country. I like to think of myself as a master of disguise.

By eight o'clock, after a stop at a local hang-out called Elsie's to wolf down bacon and eggs and home fries, I was tooling along the Mid-Cape Highway toward the Cape Cod Canal. The day was gloriously clear. The tape deck played a Jimmy Buffet cassette. Buffet was still wasting away in Margaritaville. Nice work if you can get it.

On the other side of the canal I picked up Route 28. Near Buzzards Bay I left the highway and followed a back road to a large construction site. A couple of earthmovers piled dirt in preparation for a new shopping-mall foundation. A sign identified a trailer as the site office of Nichols Construction, Inc. Funny. A late-model gray Mercury Monterey was parked a couple of hundred feet from the construction site. Just sitting there off by itself. No reason for it to be there. Then again, no reason for it not to be. I pulled in next to a Cumberland Farms convenience store across from the project. Ten minutes later a black low-slung Porche 911 coupe that looked like a spaceship pulled up next to my truck. Laura Nichols was at the wheel. I got out, opened the sports-car door, and slid in on the passenger side, wondering if I should remove my shoes first.

"Good morning." I glanced around at the luxurious interior. "Nice wheels. Mercedes having a tune-up?"

Laura smiled. "Good morning. It's Edward's day off and I don't like driving the Mercedes."

She had on aquamarine shorts and matching tank top. A ribbon of the same color tied her honey-hued hair in a long braided pigtail. Her sunglasses were aquamarine too. She looked intently through the windshield toward the construction site. I looked at her. My first impressions weren't exaggerated. Porsche should use Laura in an ad. They'd sell a lot of cars.

She pointed to the site. "There. That man in the white shirt and tie. That's Charles, my husband. He's planning to leave in about half an hour for his office. He knows you'll be following him. He'll stop a few times so you can see if anyone else is behind him."

"Fine. Would you like me to call you later?"

"I think it's best if I call you."

"I'm in and out."

Laura heaved a stage sigh. "Mr. Socarides, it would make a great deal of sense to get an answering machine."

"Have I told you how I loathe talking to boxes?"

"I do remember hearing something to that effect."

I got out and walked around to the driver's side, where I leaned in the window. Laura's fingers brushed my arm. "Please be careful, Mr. Socarides. I don't want anything to happen to Charles. Or to you." Then she started the car, backed it out, and sped off, shifting smoothly through the gears like Mario Andretti.

I watched until she was out of sight, then went into the store to buy three large black coffees and two bologna and cheese sandwiches. It might be a long day.

Thirty minutes later, right on schedule, Nichols emerged from the trailer and got into a white Lincoln Continental. He was a tall man in his midfifties, with silvery hair and a mustache, who moved easily, like someone who worked hard to keep himself fit. I waited until the Lincoln drove off. The game was afoot. I swung out onto the road to follow Nichols.

The gray Mercury beat me to it, pulling out behind the Continental. I took third place in line. Nichols drove directly to Buzzards Bay and stopped at a breakfast restaurant. The Mercury parked where the driver could watch the front door. I found a spot where I could watch the Mercury. Nichols emerged from the restaurant after twenty minutes, got into his car, and drove over the Bourne Bridge, back along the other side of the canal and onto the Mid-Cape Highway. The gray Mercury followed and I tagged along.

About a mile onto the Mid-Cape, something unexpected happened.

The Mercury turned off at a rest area. A dark maroon Buick passed me and took its place. The Mercury shot back onto the highway behind me. I was between a double tail. Interesting. And exceedingly professional. I sipped the last dregs of coffee, crunched the Styrofoam cup, and threw it on the floor. The plot was thickening nicely.

Fifteen minutes later the Continental turned off at the Hyannis exit and parked at the Cape Cod Mall. Nichols went into a drugstore and emerged with some newspapers under his arm. He drove to the neat village of Osterville on the other side of Hyannis. His office was in a building someone imagined to be of Colonial design. I parked in a nearby municipal lot. My fellow followers took up stations on opposite sides of the street, poised for quick movement in either direction. I couldn't see the drivers' faces.

I ate my sandwiches, leaving the truck only to buy a couple of magazines and for bathroom breaks in a public rest room. No one got out of either vehicle. They must have had bladders of iron. About 2:00 P.M. Nichols emerged and drove off. The entourage followed, with me straggling way behind. Nichols turned onto a private road and waved to the fat guard at the gatehouse. He was home for the day. His two companions pulled over to the side of the road. I made a U-turn and went off in the other direction.

I stopped off at the Hole and downed two Buds. Then went home and sat on the deck with a can of beer. I tried to sort out my impressions. The Nicholses were not imagining things. But what did it mean? I got up and went into the kitchen. I was hungry. I had my head in the refrigerator, rummaging through clumps of green mold that looked like lab cultures, when the phone rang. It was Barrett. "How are you doing, Soc? Got anything yet?"

"Nothing solid. Just bits and pieces. I'm still scratching around."

"Can you come up to Boston tomorrow?"

"This have something to do with the case?"

"Yeah. Remember Lucas, the guy I told you is trying to grab my wreck? His lawyer has been pushing the state archaeological board. They've called an unscheduled meeting to discuss my permit. This will give you a chance to see all the players in one room."

I took down directions and hung up. Then I kicked off my Top-Siders and stretched my legs onto a camel saddle hassock purchased in a moment of wild abandon from a silver-tongued flea-market salesman. Home sweet home. Where a man is king, and nobody tells him what to do. I closed my eyes for a snooze. Kojak jumped onto the back of the chair. He milked my head softly with his paws and shoved his wet nose into my ear.

"*Mrrrp*," he said.

CHAPTER 8

Late next morning I drove to Boston. I headed off the South-east Expressway at the Causeway Street exit. Leaving the truck in the Haymarket parking lot under the expressway, I entered a warren of narrow streets. Boston's North End is a small slice of Europe where provolone cheese balls and dead rabbits hang in grocery-store windows, a luscious smell of baking bread flows from a dozen doorways, and you're never more than a few paces from a restaurant or expresso house.

Near the white-steepled Old North Church, where the rebels hung the signal lanterns for Paul Revere, I turned down an alley and pushed open a pale green door lettered in faded gilt with the words PASTA—WHOLESALE AND RETAIL. Inside was a brightly lit room that smelled of dough being prepared by a half-dozen young men dressed in white uniforms. A guy with movie-star good looks glanced up from a pasta machine. He had more waves in his dark hair than the beach on a good surfing day.

"Hey, Soc," he yelled. "You come in for some fettuccine?"

"Naw. Looking for Sal. He around?"

"I'll check." The young man clapped the flour dust off his hands and picked up a phone. After a brief conversation, he gestured at a portal.

I walked through a space piled high with bags of flour and was buzzed through a steel door to a small air-conditioned office with no windows. A diminutive, wrinkled man of about sixty-five with huge bright eyes in a simian face that vaguely resembled Picasso's sat at an oak desk that was covered with order forms. He was wearing a wide-collared white shirt and a wide paisley tie. Behind him a

Red Sox game blasted from a radio. The old home team was losing.

"Soc!" The old midget had a voice like gravel sliding down a metal chute. "How ya doon?" The crooked stub of a cheroot crushed between his teeth didn't exactly help his diction.

"Good, Sal, how about you?"

"Can't complain." He turned down the volume. "Haven't followed the Sox since Ted Williams but we hadda keep the radio loud when the feds bugged us." He laughed. "Guess it didn' work too good. Most of the big shots around here doon time. Old habits, though, know what I mean?" He reached across the desk and pumped my hand warmly. Grinning, he said, "Hey, you're not wired, are you?"

"Got me, Sal. Microphone's in my jockstrap."

Sal guffawed. He turned to his right and rattled off a stream of Italian to a mass of flesh sitting next to him in a sharkskin suit. A horizontal slit near the top of the mound parted wetly and closed. I assumed it was a smile.

"Don't mind Angie," Sal said. "He don't speak a worda English. But he's a cousin, y' know, on my wife's side, so I give him a job, although I dunno what it is yet. Now whaddya need? You don't come all the way from the Cape to buy some linguini."

"If that's what I wanted, this would be the place." I settled onto a wooden chair. "I got a funny case I could use some help on. Client supposedly did some work for the Organization years ago and now the feds are going to make him tell all. His wife is worried. She thinks someone wants to shut him up. His name is Nichols, Charles Nichols. Ever hear of him?"

"Naw, but it don't sound kosher, Soc. You scare a guy, use some muscle maybe, but you don't wanna mess with a civilian unless you have to. Easier for your lawyer to chop the guy up on the witness stand if it ever gets that far. Without wire taps and bugs with the stuff from your own mouth, or you forget to pay taxes, they got nothin'."

I nodded.

Sal took the well-chewed cigar from his mouth. "Look, Soc, I never forget what you did with that kidda mine."

"How's Freddie doing?"

"Good. Graduated law school at Northeastern. Says he

can keep busy the resta his life just defendin' my friends. But if you'd booked him way back, he'd never have gotten the chance to be a lawyer. Imagine, my kid, swipin' a car. Then gettin' caught."

"Hard to believe. I knew you'd give him a tougher time than any judge."

"I did, right across his ass with an oven paddle."

"About my client . . ."

"Yeah, I don't think he's got nothin' to worry about. Look, I been outta the action for some time, but I still keep in touch. Tell you what, I'll give the Providence associates a call, ask around, you know? Maybe something goin' down I dunno about. If there is, it's better you don't get involved. Sounds fishy, though."

I got up to leave. "I know it does, but it's a crazy world."

"You're tellin' me." He waved his hand expansively. Light glinted off the diamond on his pinkie. "I grew up in this neighborhood. Now we got the Yuppies movin' in. They send the rents sky-high, so the old people gotta move out. The guys joggin' around here in purple suits, they're CPAs and business types. Steal the eyeteeth out of your head, all legal. Believe me, I know. Then one day I wake up. Got all this real estate, so I rent apartments to these people. They got money to burn, Soc. Gimme anything I ask. Hole ina wall for a grand a month, no problem. My gross is ten times what it was in the old days. The only headache I got now is leaks in the bathroom or the heat don't work. Big deal."

Sal chuckled. "Another thing. They tell their friends the landlord is in the cement overshoe business. *You* know I stayed out of the strong-arm stuff, Soc, but they don't. Makes a good conversation piece." He leaned forward. "I still charge the old people the same cheap rents and these new guys pay for it. Like Robin Hood. Hey, maybe next year I'm gonna run for city council, or maybe mayor."

"I'd vote for you, Sal. Got to go now. I'd appreciate anything you could turn up for me on this case. Give my regards to Freddie. 'Bye Angie."

The slit opened and closed.

Sal laughed. "Hey, Soc, when you go outside smile in case the feds take your picture."

I left the bakery and at the entrance to the alley glanced up and down the street, half expecting to see a surveillance van with smoked windows. Four elderly men stood outside a café, discussing the state of the world like pugilists. Volvos and Saabs lined the curb. But no van. Cape Cod wasn't the only place that has changed.

Following Barrett's directions, I walked under the Southeast Expressway, past Quincy Market and Fanueil Hall to an office building behind the State House on Beacon Hill. I took an elevator to the tenth floor. Just follow the sound of shouting, Barrett had advised. I poked my head through one doorway. About thirty people sat in a hearing room that was as hot as a health-club sauna. No one was shouting, but the tension in the humid air was thick enough to slice with a butter knife. Barrett, who was the tallest object in the room, sat near the front. He turned and winked at me. Eileen, who sat beside him, shot a brief, haughty glance in my direction. Hardly anyone else paid any attention as I slipped inside and took a seat.

Two areas of sartorial style were represented. The Suits, clearly lawyers and minor government types. And the Jeans, who looked as if they did their wardrobe shopping at marine salvage. Up front behind a long table were the nine men and women who constituted the board representing the interests of the Commonwealth of Massachusetts as guardian of the ancient wrecks in the state's waters. The chairman was a distinguished gray-haired man wearing a suit but no tie. He rustled a pile of papers on the table before him and peered over his horn-rim glasses.

"We have," he said pleasantly, "something of a dispute involving the reconnaissance permit issued Mr. Barrett for the sunken ship *Gabriella*. An objection has been filed by counsel for Mr. Lucas, which says in essence that this board acted contrary to the state's regulations. Mr. Mather." He nodded to a man seated near the front. "As attorney for Mr. Lucas, would you *briefly* outline your case."

A tall handsome blond man whose hair was cut Prussian close stood with a yellow legal pad in hand. He wore a pink polka-dot bow tie and a blue seersucker summer suit probably worth more than his secretary made a month. His clothes didn't have a wrinkle and neither did his presentation.

He referred to his notes. "Mr. Director, my client, Mr. Lucas, contends that he notified the board of his interest in a reconnaissance permit for the *Gabriella* two days prior to

Mr. Barrett's notification, but that his application was not acted on by the board. Under state law Mr. Lucas sought the permit to explore in a one-square-mile rectangle, as delineated in the map I distributed to the board before the meeting."

The director picked up a sheet of paper, glanced at it, and put it down. There was a soft rustle as everyone else at the long table followed his lead.

"Furthermore," the lawyer continued, "Mr. Lucas contends there is no evidence supporting Mr. Barrett's claim to have actually found the *Gabriella*. And he questions Mr. Barrett's financial ability to undertake the *Gabriella* project as well. Therefore, I would respectfully suggest, on behalf of my client, that the permit issued to Mr. Barrett be nullified and a new permit for the same area granted to Mr. Lucas instead."

The director wiped the sweat from his forehead with a handkerchief. "It would be nice if someone could fix the air-conditioning in this room. Mr. Mather, as I informed you by mail, Mr. Lucas possibly may have found the *Gabriella* before Mr. Barrett, but his letter was informal. Under the statute an appropriate form must be filled out, which Mr. Barrett did. Thus, by law, he is entitled to first crack at this shipwreck."

A swarthy, thickset man with curly black hair was seated next to Mather. He had the face of a bandit and looked as if he were wearing football shoulder pads under his blue workshirt. He stood up suddenly and pointed a finger accusingly at the director.

"That's *my* ship out there. I found her first and I claimed her first. She's being stolen from me just because I didn't write out your asinine form!"

"Mr. Lucas," the director interjected patiently, "may I remind you that the *Gabriella* is not *your* ship. It belongs to the commonwealth of Massachusetts, which eventually is entitled to twenty-five percent of the value of any find. Any permit holder is considered a temporary custodian only. That's the law."

"The law also says first come, first served. And I was first!" Lucas's face was purple. "Hell, I saw where his boat's been working. He's not anywhere near the *Gabriella* site."

Barrett, who had been sitting back in his chair, arms folded, turned and glowered at Lucas.

The lawyer put his hand on Lucas's shoulder. "My client—"

"Your client," growled a professorial-looking board member, "is jeopardizing his own case. We're a little sick and tired of his claims and the way he has criticized this board and competing salvage groups in the media. He didn't do his homework in the law and now he's trying to foist the blame for his own mistake on this board."

The director rapped the table with his knuckles several times. "Some of you may have noticed that it is getting warm in this room in more ways than one," he said serenely, eliciting a few soggy chuckles. He looked expectantly at Lucas, who hurled a furious glance at his attorney and sat own.

"As most of you know," the director said, "these proceedings are relatively new for this board. We move cautiously, staying within the letter of the law, so the Commonwealth will not be open to lawsuits—several of which, I may add, are currently being threatened."

Looking down at the papers before him, he went on, "Now my suggestion is this: that we give these competing salvage groups a week to present their case. I am predisposed, I must admit, to permit Mr. Barrett to retain his permit as it was the first formally applied for. But this is a new area of law for all of us, and I am willing, at the same time, to review Mr. Lucas's argument. What is the pleasure of the board?"

This time it was Barrett who leaped to his feet. "You can't do that! You've already awarded me that permit. You're the ones who lost my file because of your incompetence. My crew is ready to work. Any delay will cost me a fortune, shorten my season, and make this project needlessly dangerous." Eileen reached up and put her hand on his arm in a futile gesture of restraint. He pulled away from her, his blue eyes blazing.

I looked over at Lucas. He was either smiling or curling his lip. Either way, he had a face only a mother could love.

The director flipped the manila folder in front of him shut.

"Mr. Barrett, I'm sure a week won't make a great deal of difference in a project that could take years. Yours is not the only project under our consideration. I'm terribly sorry about the mix-up with your file, but if the board is willing to come into Boston on a hot summer's day, you should be willing as well. Let me point out that it would be to your advantage to get this cleared up now, before we go to the next stage. If there is a flaw in our procedures and this is successfully challenged in court, you could lose your permit anyhow. It is quite possible, you must admit, that neither you nor Mr. Lucas has actually located the *Gabriella*."

Turning to the other board members, the director said, "I move that the board vote to request Mr. Barrett and Mr. Lucas to appear here one week hence with all the evidence, including artifacts, historical research, and precise site data bearing on the *Gabriella*, along with financial statements, copies of all applications and letters to the board. At that time the board will make a final determination in this matter. In the meantime Mr. Barrett's excavation permit, which allows him to remove large artifacts from the site, will be suspended, although he may continue reconnaissance."

The motion was quickly seconded and approved, and discussion shifted to the next agenda item. Lucas leaned over to talk to his lawyer. When I checked to see Barrett's reaction, his chair was empty.

I stepped out to the hall. Barrett was lighting a cigarette. His big hands shook. "That little bastard," he said.

"Lucas or the director?" I said.

"Both of them. They've really screwed me up. I didn't bargain for a time squeeze. Look, Soc, you've got to find that missing data or we're sunk."

A young man holding one of those slim pocket-size notebooks reporters carry approached us. He said his name was Cooper and that he was from the *Boston Herald*. Could he ask a few questions? Barrett gave the reporter a black look.

"Some people say you don't really have the *Gabriella*," the reporter said. "That this is really just a scam to attract money from investors. Do you have any comment?"

"Sour grapes," Barrett said. "The people spreading those lies about our project are either archaeologists who think they're the only ones with a right to bring up an old ship . . ." He looked over at the hearing room door. "Or other salvage groups trying to cut in on our territory. There's no doubt in my mind we have the *Gabriella*."

"What makes you so sure?"

"For one thing, the coins we found."

"What about suggestions the wreck could have been salted with coins from some other location?"

"Absolutely not. I picked those coins off the sea bottom myself."

"Any other proof?"

"If the board cooperates, I'll give you all the proof you need. The *Gabriella* itself."

The hearing had wrapped up and people were emptying into the hall. Lucas and his lawyer were coming our way. As they drew abreast, Lucas, who was a full head shorter than Barrett, grinned up at him and said, "Can't win them all, big shot."

These guys were like fire and gasoline. Barrett moved menacingly toward Lucas, making a noise low in his throat. Lucas braced himself, spreading his feet wide, and brought both fists up by his belt. Despite the size difference, Lucas looked as if he could take care of himself, especially in the close confines of the hallway. He had enough compact power to give Barrett a tough time.

The newspaper reporter prudently edged a dozen feet away. Mather and I stepped between the two men. I was certain they would go right through us to get to each other. Eileen came out of the hearing room, saw the impending donnybrook, and joined the human fence.

"No, Michael," she said softly. I took advantage of the distraction and grabbed Barrett's arm. Like a tugboat nudging the *QEII* into harbor, I steered him to the elevators, careful not to get into the same one as Lucas and Mather. Eileen took up the rear.

A few minutes later we were out on the street. Eileen looked at her watch and said, "Michael, I have to get to a class. Will you be all right?"

Barrett nodded glumly.

"It'll be okay," I said. "C'mon, Mike. What we need is a nice cold drink."

Eileen seemed relieved. I was probably imagining it, but the frown of disapproval my presence automatically triggered was gone. She kissed her brother on the cheek and walked quickly toward the nearest subway station.

Barrett and I found a dark pub and ordered a couple of cool ones. Barrett was calmer, the way a volcano is calmer, but his eyes were still dangerous.

"Now you've met Lucas. What do you think? Is he the kind of guy who'd do anything to get at my ship? He gets the site data somehow, waits me out, takes over my permit area, and moves in. I've done all the work for him."

"I think I'd have to know a lot more about Mr. Lucas. At this point I couldn't even accuse him of double parking."

Barrett clenched his right hand, which had been resting on the table, into a giant fist. He stared for a few seconds at his whitening knuckles as if he were concentrating all the tension in his huge body into that balled hand, then slowly uncurled his fingers. The move was an odd one, but it seemed to relax him. He said, "You're right, I guess. But do you have any other leads?"

"No big ones. I will have in time, though. With the board putting the pressure on, I'll just have to work a little faster. I was hoping to talk to your crew. They might have something and not even know it."

Barrett nodded. "You'll get the chance tomorrow. We're going out on a recon survey. Maybe we can pick up the *Gabriella*. I know it's a long shot," he said bitterly, "but I can't just sit on my ass. You know, with Kip gone, I could use some dive help."

"You got it," I said.

We talked a little more about the hearing, finished our drinks, and went our separate ways. When I got home two hours later I dug my dive gear out of a closet and checked the regulator and hoses. My wet suit was a little snug around the middle, but fishing is a great way to work off a beer gut. I only felt a little like a giant sausage when I zipped up the jacket. I was standing in front of the mirror sucking my belly in when the phone rang. It was Sal.

"Got some news for you, Soc," he said. "I call Providence and talk to some of the boys. They all got business degrees now and wear three-piece suits from Brooks Brothers, so they get a little bent outta shape when I ask about what you said. They tell me General Motors wouldn't go around whackin' some guy who bad-mouthed a Chevy, that's what they got lawyers for. Besides, they said, they wouldn't waste time tailin' a guy. They'd just bonk him."

"Guess they got a point, Sal. Thanks for your trouble."

"No problem. But maybe you should tell your client not to knock the Organization." He chuckled. "One of those fancy lawyers might sue your guy for defamation of character."

"Good advice. Your buddies got enough trouble with the feds bugging their water beds. You know something, Sal. You're right. It certainly isn't like the old days."

"You said a mouthful."

CHAPTER 9

—

"Good morning, Mr. Socarides. You can stow your gear on the deck for now. My brother is in the wheelhouse. He's expecting you."

Eileen was wearing denim shorts and a blue hooded sweatshirt. Her copper hair was tucked under a tan baseball cap. She wasn't smiling, but I surmised our relationship was definitely on the upswing. Fifteen seconds on the *Shamrock* and she hadn't once called me a no-good drunken bum.

It was around 6:00 A.M. and still dark. Sodium lights cast an eerie glow over the quiet wharf and sleeping harbor. The *Shamrock*'s engine idled at a low rumble. I set the big duffel bag holding my diving equipment near a rack of air tanks. Barrett was bending over a chart when I stepped into the wheelhouse. The storm clouds produced by yesterday's hearing had moved off his brow. He looked up and said, "Hi, Soc. We're almost ready to leave. Just checking our course."

A guy in his forties with curly black hair came into the wheelhouse. Barrett introduced him as Joe Santos, a Provincetown fisherman who helped run the boat from time to time. Santos shook hands vigorously and frowned in mock disapproval. "You another one of these crazy treasure hunters?"

"Worse than that, Joe. I'm a crazy fisherman."

Santos laughed and said if anybody needed him, he'd be below.

Barrett made a few more navigational computations and set his pencil down. "Okay," he said. "Let's go."

We cast off from the pier and steamed past the breakwater. The *Shamrock* passed Long Point and the friendly beacon of Wood End light, following a spiral course northwest and easterly around the knuckle of the Cape at Race Point, then southeasterly into the Atlantic. The stars faded as the sky lightened to a predawn gray and a fiery eyebrow of sun peeked over the edge of the ocean. Eileen appeared with three hot mugs of coffee and lingered in the cabin. Barrett was at the wheel, Eileen stood next to him. I sat in a tall swivel chair sleepily watching the foamy wash as the bow pushed through metallic blue-gray seas.

"The weatherman was right," Barrett said over the noise of the engine. "Going to be a fair day. We should be on site shortly. The area I've marked for reconnaissance isn't too far from here. I want a closer look at some interesting magnetometer readings I picked up on a preliminary recon. Without the exact coordinates, it's pretty much a crapshoot as far as the *Gabriella* is concerned, but it's worth a try."

"Long John Silver had it less complicated," I said. "Yo-ho-ho, and a bottle of rum."

"That's for sure. But some things never change. Even with all the electronic gadgets, you still gotta have a diver. Treasure diving used to be real simple. Just hold on to a big rock, fill your lungs with air, and jump over the side. Lucayan Indians in the Bahamas supposedly dove to a hundred feet and stayed under fifteen minutes. Maybe that's why they all got killed pearl diving for those greedy Spanish bastards. The Spaniards brought in African slaves to replace the Indians. The Africans became the best divers in the world. English used them later on to salvage Spanish wrecks. How's that for irony? They salvaged hundreds of millions off the Spanish fleet. Divers for William Phips, an English salvor, brought up thirty-four tons of precious metals in 1687. That was in six to eight fathoms using primitive salvage methods."

"You could use a couple of those guys yourself. Want me to spread the word that you're looking for a diver?"

"Don't go out of your way. I know you're busy. We'll do okay for now with this team until we relocate the wreck. Santos handles the helm while I dive. Eileen is our nautical archaeologist. Whoops, we're almost there."

I stepped over to Eileen and said, "You're an archaeologist? I'm impressed." I wasn't trying for brownie points. I meant it. Only one of us was impressed. She turned her back on me and I found myself looking at a tuft of red hair poking through the opening in the back of her baseball cap.

"Don't be," she said over her shoulder. "I'm only here

because the state wants someone with an archaeological background on board. I come cheap and I happened to be handy. When we start serious excavations, we'll bring in a professional archaeologist. My specialty is anthropology. But many nautical archaeologists are self-taught. The field is relatively new."

"Is the historical stuff much help in pinpointing a wreck?"

Eileen faced me again. She didn't reply immediately. Her lovely mouth was set in a contemplative pucker. Probably wondering if my interest was phony or not. The parole board in her mind took a vote and I was put on probation.

"Yes, Mr. Socarides," she said after a moment. "Historical records or anecdotal stories are often the touchstone for determining the worth of a salvage project. Eyewitness accounts of a shipwreck can be invaluable. Unfortunately the first people on the scene were probably looters and they would tend to be closemouthed. Sometimes even with good eyewitnesses, details are added later or left out. Reference points change too. A house used as a landmark may be gone or perhaps the owner had another house you don't know about."

She pointed to the tan bluffs and dunes around a half mile off our starboard side. "Natural landmarks can be tricky too. That beach erodes about two-to-three hundred feet a century. You have to figure in the effects of tides, currents, and storms. You end up with a shaky case of circumstantial evidence. Then you mix in the electronic remote sensing data and cross your fingers."

I had been studying Eileen's face as she ran through her textbook narrative. It may have been the competition with the sun-sparkled sea, but her eyes had lost the laser blue intensity of our first encounters.

"Amazing," I said.

Eileen looked surprised, then laughed self-consciously. "I suppose it is amazing when you find what you're looking for," she said in a detached way. Suddenly all business, she picked a clipboard off a hook and started toward the door. "You'll excuse me. I have a few things to do."

I went back to my seat. The sun had risen above the sea and the pearly sky was changing to azure. A fresh southwest breeze wrinkled the water with catspaw puffs. Santos came up to take the wheel. "What course, Cap?" he said.

"Keep 'er on a southeast heading," Barrett said. He pored over his navigational charts and checked the boat's position. None of us spoke for a while. Barrett finally straightened, tugging at his beard. "Okay. We'll start our mag runs from here."

Santos reduced speed just enough to maintain headway. There was a good view aft from the wheelhouse. I watched Barrett as he went onto the deck and threw a buoy over the side to mark our starting position. He came back and said, "We'll run a series of parallel tracks along the shore for a quarter of a mile. Eileen will ride herd on the magnetometer. When she gets a high reading, she'll yell 'hit.' You keep an eye on the Loran and jot our positions down on this pad. I'll run the boat. Joe, get ready to toss the fish overboard."

Santos went on deck and picked up a white plastic torpedo around three feet long. Fins protruded from one end. At a signal from Barrett, he threw the torpedo off the stern and played out the cable attached to it.

"That's the magnetometer probe," Eileen told me, her eyes on the ocean where the torpedo had splashed into the water. "It'll run along the surface about two hundred feet behind us and read any concentrations of iron-type metal on the sea bottom."

Barrett gunned the engine and the boat picked up speed, following an imaginary straight line on the water, turning after several hundred yards to start along another track. Eileen carefully watched the magnetometer's digital readout. From time to time she yelled "hit!" I noted each Loran coordinate.

The work fell into an easy rhythm with Eileen shouting, me scribbling. It wasn't tough to take. The pale sun shed brilliant flakes of light that sparkled whitely on the sea. A seaweedy breeze tumbled in through the open wheelhouse windows. Black-capped terns darted out of the sky to skim the low wave tops in fitful bursts of speed. The crystalline air was so clear you could pick out, in the traffic lanes several miles distant, freighters and oil tankers moving imperceptibly along the wide curve of the horizon. Passing closer to us was an occasional sailboat and a steady procession of Provincetown fishing boats commuting to and from the cod grounds.

After two hours, Barrett cut the *Shamrock*'s engine to an idle. The boat rocked gently in the one-foot swells. Barrett went out on the deck to help Santos reel in the magnetometer probe. I took my notepad over to Eileen. During the last several minutes, I had become aware she was watching me. Probably trying to decide if I was animal, vegetable, or mineral.

I smiled. "Nice day."

"Yes, it's gorgeous."

Silence. Maybe she was thinking what a sweet, sensitive fellow I was.

"Mr. Socarides," she said after a minute. "Exactly what *is* your game?"

Can't be right all the time. "I'm afraid I don't understand, Ms. Barrett."

"I think you understand me very well. You're much more intelligent than you appear under that uncouth guise you wear. All right, let me put it bluntly. What do you hope to gain from working on this project? You're not here simply for altruistic motives."

Suspicious little bitch. "You're right, Ms. Barrett. I hope to abscond with every ounce of gold and silver Mike finds. Maybe I'll steal this boat. Better hold on to your purse. I might snatch that too."

Her face flushed. "Sarcasm is a clever way to deflect my question."

"C'mon, Ms. Barrett. Get off my back. Do you really think I'm that kind of guy?"

She paused as if she were thinking it over. Then, quite firmly, she said, "Yes."

"You certainly are a shrewd judge of character."

"And you are a boor."

A boor. I was crushed. Luckily, I didn't have to blink back the tears. Barrett came into the wheelhouse. Gathering up our data, he penciled a series of small circles on a chart.

"These are major mag readings," he said. His voice had turned boyish again. "Normally we'd crank this information in with the sonar stuff and put it on an overlay. If we really wanted to get fancy, we'd feed the whole mess into a computer. But we're doing this quick and dirty today. Some of these hits are bogus. This one that nearly blew off the top of the mag is an old iron hull I checked before. But this is the baby we're interested in." His pencil indicated a dense cluster of circles. "Let's go back there and put a buoy on that spot."

Barrett moved the boat into position and asked me to take the helm while he went on deck and tossed a buoy over. Then he and Santos threw two anchors off the bow and two off the stern so the boat was at the midpoint of an "X" formed by the anchor lines. Returning to the pilothouse, Barrett said, "We can adjust the anchor lines so we can move around in a general area. Now we'll try blasting a few holes with the mailboxes."

"The mailboxes are those big stovepipes in the stern," I said.

"That's right. The anchors will hold us while we goose the engine. The mailboxes divert the force of the propeller wash downward. You want to blast the sand off the site so you can see what's buried underneath."

"Wouldn't explosives be quicker?"

Barrett smirked. "Come take a look." We went out onto the deck, where Barrett opened a light blue fiberglass watertight compartment just behind the pilothouse. Inside was a wooden box with the word EXPLOSIVES stenciled on it. "I've used dynamite off Florida to dislodge wrecks that lay in coral," he said. "The state archaeological people would never tolerate it here, and anyhow, the hole would fill in almost immediately in these waters."

"So why do you keep the stuff around?"

"For emergencies. I might be tempted to clear out something that got in my way, but the prop wash is the only way to go in a sandy bottom. Dig a crater ten feet deep with hardly more than an idle. Deeper if you rev it higher. You have to be careful. Prop wash can pick up an artifact, even something as heavy as a cannonball or ballast stone, and fling it out of sight. Later you can clean the site a little at a time with an airlift, which works like a vacuum cleaner."

Recalling yesterday's hearing, I said, "I thought your permit only allowed you to look and poke, not blast."

Barrett's lips pursed. "Look, Soc, I don't like to go against the state board. But you won't get into any trouble, I promise. The most they can do if they find out I've been excavating is yank my permit. The way things are going, I could lose it anyhow, so I'm willing to take the chance." He broke into a grin that made him look about ten years old. "Besides, desperate times call for desperate measures."

Barrett's argument didn't convince me, but I was feeling

guilty because I hadn't found his missing site papers, so I went along. "Okay. You've got a partner in crime. Let's go to work."

The diverters, which were about three feet across, were attached so they could swivel. Using a winch, we lowered the elbow-shaped pipes over the stern and fastened them down. One end of each mailbox pointed straight into the water, the other toward a propeller. The concept was simple but effective. The pipes would aim the tremendous force from the turning propellers at the sea bottom. The high-velocity water columns would blast away the sand.

With the diverters locked in place, Barrett stood in the stern while Santos took over the helm. When all was ready, Barrett gave a thumbs-up signal. Santos gradually increased power to 1,200 rpm. Engine roaring, the *Shamrock* surged forward, straining against the aft anchor lines until they were stretched taut as violin strings. Santos gave the engine more throttle. The stern bobbed spastically. More power. The *Shamrock* shuddered with vibrations as it pulled against its unyielding restraints.

Sand whirled to the surface, creating great brown billows that churned in our wake as the prop wash cut through the first layers of sea bottom. Santos ran the engine at high speed for about three minutes before Barrett signaled again. Santos killed the engine. The boat settled quietly back to its rhythmical rocking.

I went out to the deck where Eileen was helping her brother climb into a Day-Glo orange dry suit.

"That blast should have gouged out a humongous hole," Barrett said when he saw me. "I'll make an exploratory dive. Meantime, you get suited up. We've got plenty of spare air tanks. I'll send up a marker buoy if I find anything interesting. Follow the line down and I'll be waiting on the bottom unless I'm busy wrestling an octopus."

"Aside from the giant kraken, what other deadly dangers of the deep can I expect?"

"None that I know of. Water's only about thirty feet deep here, so you won't have far to travel. Current's a half knot and the temperature runs fifty to sixty degrees. We've been using dry suits because it gets chilly after a while, even now during the summer, but you'll be okay in your wet suit if you don't stay down too long. Weight your belt slightly on the heavy side so you can hover above the bottom in case we have to do some hand digging. The biggest problem is mung weed. It's like a brown blizzard sometimes, but the current is taking it offshore, so the visibility should be five to ten feet."

Barrett's regulator was attached to a long hose that ran through a harness on his back to an air compressor on deck. "I've gone over from air tanks to a surface air supply," he said. "The hookah rig lets me stay down longer. With only one diver we need all the time we can get on the bottom. Eileen's going to get her dive certification, but I can't wait." His voice was grim. Hundreds of thousands, maybe millions of dollars were at stake and the clock was ticking away on his one week grace period.

Santos started the compressor. Its noisy popping drowned out all other sound. Now fully fitted, Barrett bit down on the regulator mouthpiece and pulled the mask over his face. He lowered himself onto a metal platform hanging off the side of the boat. With a quick wave, he stepped into the water and disappeared in a swirl of bubbles. The plastic hose slithered behind him like a giant anaconda.

I stripped to my bathing suit and squirmed into my wet-suit pants, then pulled on my boots and strapped a five-inch knife to the inside of my calf where I could reach it easily. I slipped on my hood and jacket, followed by my fins and weight belt. Santos helped me into the buoyancy compensator, basically an inflatable vest with a harness to hold your air tank.

It was hot standing in the sun wrapped tightly in rubber, so I was glad when the basketball-sized spherical buoy popped up near the boat. I rubbed spit on the inside of my face-mask lens and rinsed it in the ocean to prevent fogging, and tested the seal by breathing in. Finally I clamped the plastic regulator mouthpiece between my teeth and, holding on to the mask so the impact wouldn't knock it off, stepped off the platform. There was a shocking chill as the ocean seeped under my suit, but in a moment the water trapped against my skin rose to a comfortable temperature.

I was excited. There's a sense of exhilarating freedom underwater. Just before the dive you waddle awkwardly about like a strange alien creature, encumbered by weight, tripping over your fins. The mask limits your peripheral view. The hoses for your pressure gauge and regulator dangle off your body like spider legs. But once in the water, you glide weightlessly through a blue-green haze like an astronaut in free-fall, exhaling gentle explosions of bubbles with each breath.

I felt as free as a porpoise. I pinched my nose to equalize pressure, then kicked my legs in an easy scissors rhythm and followed the nylon buoy line toward the bottom. The brown blizzard of mung weed reduced visibility to six feet. A splash of orange loomed against the murk. Barrett was at the edge of a crater about twenty feet across and two yards deep. He motioned for me to follow him around the rim. A few seconds later he swam into the conical hole. I followed a few feet behind. He stopped and fanned sand away from something that stuck out of the sloping side. I moved in closer and touched a hard, rough surface.

Barrett scribbled the words "Small cannon?" on a white plastic slate strapped to his wrist. I borrowed his pencil and wrote "?" He jerked his thumb upward, indicating an ascent.

We surfaced about twenty feet from the *Shamrock*. Barrett yanked the regulator from his mouth and shouted breathlessly to Eileen on the deck.

"I think I've got something! Maybe a signal gun. Move the boat ten feet closer to shore and give her a real hard blast for three minutes like before. Soc, you climb aboard and lend them a hand. I'll keep an eye on things below." He stuck the regulator back in his mouth, rolled forward in a cannonball-tuck surface dive, and with a flip of his fins, he was gone.

I inflated my vest and breast-stroked to the boarding platform. Hanging on with one hand, I slipped my belt and tank assembly up to Eileen. Then I pulled myself onto the deck and removed my fins and mask, unzipped my jacket.

"That may have been the shortest dive in history," I said. "Is it safe for him down there while you're blasting holes?"

A look of concern flickered across Eileen's face, but she smiled and nodded. "It's usually a good idea to stay out of the water while the propeller's going, especially with a surface rig, but Mike's an experienced diver and he's worked near prop wash before." Still, she kept her eyes fixed on the air hose.

When Barrett was about thirty feet away, Santos and I readjusted the boat's position by letting out the stern anchor lines and hauling in on the bow anchors. Santos took the helm again, checked to make sure the air hose was clear, and engaged the engine. As before, the *Shamrock* shuddered and strained against the stern anchor lines. He notched up the power.

I was aft, watching the brown roiling water, when the boat lurched violently. Thrown off balance, I smashed my right knee against a gunwale. Pain rocketed up my thigh but I kept my footing. I looked forward. Eileen had fallen to the deck. She was up in an instant, rubbing her elbow gingerly. I started toward her, but she shook her head, indicating she wasn't seriously hurt, and pointed toward one of the stern anchor lines that had been keeping the boat in place.

The line hung slackly in the water like a piece of overcooked spaghetti. I pulled at the end attached to the boat. It should have resisted me, but it came up easily and its frayed end told me why. The anchor line had snapped.

No longer held in place by the anchor, the *Shamrock* was swinging relentlessly toward Barrett's air hose. I sprinted toward the wheelhouse. Santos still had the boat at full power. I reached past him and killed the engine. Too late. The boat mashed Barrett's air hose like a rolling pin. The plastic umbilical wrapped under the *Shamrock*'s hull. The engine sputtered, then died. Above the clatter of the now useless air compressor, Eileen screamed.

I ran back to the stern and pulled at the hose, but it was hopelessly snarled in the propeller shaft, cutting off Barrett's air supply.

No time to waste. Precious seconds ticked by while I yanked on my fins and mask and zipped up my jacket. Eileen had recovered from her initial shock. An impressive lady. With quiet determination, she held my weight belt so I could just back in and snap it on. Santos had come out of the wheelhouse and was ready with my tank harness. The whole operation took about half a minute, but we seemed to be moving in slow motion. Buckling the straps as I went, I clambered onto the dive platform and jumped into the ocean, breast-stroked around behind the boat, did a quick tuck dive, and express-trained to the bottom, holding on to Barrett's air hose as a guide.

The water was still thick with sand and mung stirred up by the prop wash. But after a few seconds I could see a dull orange blur against the gloom. The blur became a blob that sprouted arms and legs and a head. Barrett dangled from the useless air hose, floating limply a few feet above the bottom.

I darted in closer. Barrett's face mask was twisted, its seal broken. Water had flooded in, but bubbles streamed from his mouth. Maybe there was still a chance.

Grabbing Barrett by his shoulders, I took a deep breath and pushed my regulator into his open mouth. There was no reaction. I wasn't even sure if he was still alive. I put my face inches from his and looked for a sign of life. His eyelids twitched and he moved his head slightly. He coughed and gulped air hungrily. I pulled his mask down onto his face. He tilted his head back and exhaled through his nose, clearing the water from his mask, and opened his eyes. I pointed to my mouth to signal a buddy breath. For a moment I was sure I'd lost him, then there was a light of comprehension in his dazed expression. Barrett curled his finger and thumb in an okay sign. I took the regulator back, filled my lungs deeply three times, and gave it back to him.

While Barrett took his ration of air, I slid my knife from its sheath and sliced the hose behind his head. Replacing the knife, I pointed up. Barrett nodded and clutched my vest. I hit the inflate button on my buoyancy compensator. Air hissed from my tank into the vest. Continuing to share my regulator, we began to rise, slowly at first, then faster.

It seemed like years, but less than a minute later our heads popped up at the surface. I inflated my vest fully to keep us afloat. Still clinging to each other, we swam to the boat, helped slightly by the current.

Eileen stood on the dive platform, her face pale and strained. She and Santos pulled Barrett aboard while I pushed from behind. It wasn't easy, but we got him on deck, where he collapsed into a sitting position. Santos helped me aboard. We removed Barrett's mask and hood and stripped off his harness, easing him onto his back. Eileen tucked her sweatshirt under his head for a pillow. Barrett's broad chest heaved as he swallowed great gulps of air.

Eileen knelt by her brother's side. "Michael! Can you hear me?" There was no immediate response. She looked devastated.

I squatted next to her and watched Barrett's face for signs of serious injury. I was most worried about an air embolism from the sudden pressure change of being yanked off the bottom. For a diver, an embolism is about as bad as it gets.

The lungs rupture, air bubbles are forced into the blood-stream. Within a few minutes, you die. Barrett must have had his rabbit's foot with him that day. Color returned to his cheeks. His breathing was becoming more subdued and regular. He blinked his eyes open and croaked, "What the hell happened?"

"Stern anchor line broke," Santos said. "The boat swung over and picked up your hose in the prop. I'm sorry, Mike."

"It's okay, Joe," Barrett said. He coughed a couple of times. "Figured I was in the clear. Never expected the fool boat to move sideways. Shoulda covered that damn prop with wire mesh a long time ago." He looked disgusted with himself.

"Soc killed the engine and brought you up. You're lucky you weren't—" Eileen's mouth clamped shut.

Barrett sat up and rubbed his jaw. "Stunned me for a second when I was jerked around, and first thing I knew I was breathing water. Guess I owe you one, Soc. Give me a few minutes to rest and we'll go down and fetch that cannon."

"You are *not* going to dive again today." His sister was furious.

I said, "Mike, I agree with Eileen. You're in no shape to dive."

Barrett struggled to his feet and stood on the deck unsteadily, his red hair and beard matted down, bellowing like a bull. "I'm not going to let that cannon sit on the bottom after almost getting killed for it."

Eileen exploded. She grabbed her brother's arm, her face flushed with anger. "Michael, be reasonable!"

He brushed her aside and staggered over to the air tanks. With one hand, he plucked a heavy tank from the rack as easily as someone picking a daisy. The exertion may have made him dizzy, because he shook his head a couple of times as if he were trying to clear the fog from his brain and slipped the tank back into the rack.

This was quickly getting out of hand. I went over and clamped him on the shoulder. "Look, Mike, I don't mind making the dive. I'm curious about that thing too."

Barrett turned to his sister. Fire burned in her eyes. He backed down. "I do feel a bit woozy. Okay, Soc, all you have to do is go down and get the nylon straps under that hunk. Can you do it alone?"

"Piece of cake," I said.

The operation went smoothly. While Santos slipped into the water and hacked away with a sharp knife to clear the hose tangled in the propeller, I suited up again and went over the side. I swam to where Barrett and I had surfaced, then dove. I found the crater within five minutes and slowly made my way along the rim. The mailboxes had done their job well and the object lay in the clear.

A few fin kicks propelled me in for a closer look. The thing was roughly cylindrical, about three and a half feet long and at least eight inches across. I took out my knife and poked at the blackish green incrustation. It was as hard as concrete.

I let a marker buoy fly to the surface. The *Shamrock* started its engine. The low throb grew louder and stopped directly overhead. Minutes later, two wide nylon straps attached to a hauling line were lowered from the surface. Using my hands as shovels, I scooped sand away from around the cylinder then tucked the straps under each end. All was ready. I jerked the line as a signal to lift.

The winch on board the *Shamrock* yanked the cylinder from the sand. With me hanging on to the line just above it, the load rose slowly to the surface. About halfway to the top the winching came to a halt. I could hear the sound of a second engine. The muffled rumrum grew louder. I looked up.

The dark underside of another boat was silhouetted against the shimmering surface. The *Shamrock* had company.

CHAPTER 10

I had a bad feeling about our visitors.

I swam up to take a look, surfacing between the *Shamrock* and a black-hulled vessel. It was stubbier, beamier, and about ten feet smaller than Barrett's boat, but, like the *Shamrock*, had twin prop-wash diverters mounted aft. The name on the stern was *El Toro*. Lucas stood on the deck being his usual charming self. He was shaking his fist. His features were twisted with rage.

"Barrett," he yelled hotly. "Whatever the hell you've got down there is mine. You're poaching on my claim!"

Barrett grasped the rail as if he were going to tear it off and glared across the thirty-five feet of water separating the two boats.

"Go to hell, Lucas! This is my turf until the law tells me different."

Lucas bounced around on the balls of his feet, fighting mad. "The law says you got no right digging. Where's your permit to pull something off the bottom?"

In answer, Barrett stepped into the deckhouse and emerged with a hunting rifle in his hands. He lifted the rifle to his shoulder and aimed it at Lucas.

"*Here's* my permit. Now move your ass out of here." Eileen, her face pale, appeared beside her brother.

A crewman on Lucas's boat called out, "Hey, Cap," and tossed a shotgun down from the upper deck. Lucas caught the gun neatly. Sunlight glittered on its barrel.

"Now what, big guy?" He sneered. He raised the shotgun to his shoulder and aimed it at Barrett. "You wanna have a shoot-out, we'll have a shoot-out."

Mexican standoff.

The two men faced each other like a couple of buccaneers in an old Errol Flynn pirate movie. Neither one was willing to give an inch. Nobody spoke. One twitch and someone could be dead. A shotgun blast could hit Eileen as well as Barrett. On the other hand, in the event Barrett was quick enough to get off the first shot, I might have a client charged with murder.

I waved my arm and shouted, "Hey, you guys. Cool it. I don't want to swim home."

In the excitement, nobody had noticed me bobbing like a champagne cork between the two boats. Lucas looked over and did a double take that was pure Three Stooges. Taking advantage of the diversion, I swam to the platform on the *Shamrock*. Barrett stepped back and handed his rifle to Santos, who'd been out of sight from my vantage point. Then he climbed down onto the platform and grabbed my hand. He hauled me out of the water, dive equipment and all, as if I were a bag of goose down. "Sorry, Soc," he said. "Forgot all about you."

I massaged my shoulder, amazed that the arm was still attached to it. "Thought you'd never ask," I said. I pulled my mask off and looked across at the *El Toro*. Lucas had handed his shotgun to a crewman, but he was scowling darkly in our direction.

"Okay, Barrett. Today was your lucky day. But I'm making a formal complaint about this to the state board."

He charged into his wheelhouse and gunned the engine. The *El Toro* swung away in a big half circle, spitting out a purple cloud of exhaust fumes. Seas churned up by the angry wake slapped the side of the *Shamrock*, so the boat rolled.

Barrett put his arm around Eileen. "Sorry, sis. You too, Joe. And Soc. I could have gotten us all killed. I just lost my temper."

"Don't worry about it," I said, although I was worrying about it. "Let's get your cannon up and go home."

Santos started the winch again. Within minutes the cylinder was hauled into the light of day and lowered onto the deck. Like a baby with a new toy, Barrett grabbed two chisels and wooden mallets, handing a set to me. "You chip that end, I'll chip this. Be real careful, don't damage anything delicate."

The incrustation was several inches thick, but the brittle

crust peeled off easily in big hunks. Eileen and Santos sat nearby on the deck and watched our progress. We tapped diligently for several minutes. Coaxed by a particularly hard rap from my mallet, a fist-sized piece clunked onto the deck and revealed coppery metal underneath. I brushed away a few crumbs of concretion and looked closer at the gleaming surface. With a sharp intake of breath I said softly, "Barrett, stop hammering."

Barrett's mallet halted in midair. He looked up. "Dammit, Soc. What the hell's the problem?"

"The problem," I said as calmly as the situation permitted, "is that this appears to be a live artillery shell, courtesy of the U.S. Navy."

CHAPTER 11

The shell encased within the black lump was an old-timer, probably left over from World War II target practice, but it had enough punch to sink the *Shamrock* and blow us into oblivion. I stared at it, remembering a couple of guys back in Vietnam who dove into a foxhole during a mortar attack. The VC had the range and dropped a round right on top of them. A tough twenty-four-year-old sergeant in my outfit looked at the charred and smoking shreds of cloth and the hunks of red meat that had been a couple of human beings only seconds before and whispered in a Georgia drawl, "Keerist. Looks like somethin' for the friggin' barbecue." I haven't touched shish kebab since.

Sweat trickled down my armpits. I was too proud to faint in front of other people, but I began to hyperventilate when I thought of how I had happily whacked away at the chisel like a kid pounding a hammer-and-peg toy. The shell had been soaking in the sea for decades. I had no idea how it would behave. Like others, though, I had heard the stories of fishermen who spent the last, horrified moments of their lives looking at an old World War II mine or U-boat torpedo snagged in their nets.

I stood up slowly. "Look," I said, "there's no telling how sensitive this thing is. It didn't go off when we were hammering away, and it may even be a dud. But we've got to treat it as if it just came off the production line."

"JesusMaryJoseph," Santos murmured.

"All right," Eileen said. "What do we do with it?" The girl had spunk.

I would have suggested carefully winching the shell over the side. Barrett, who was still squatting next to the shell, had other ideas. Before I could answer Eileen's question, he growled, "We get the damned thing off my boat. That's what we do."

He placed a hand at each end, curled his huge arms, and hugged the shell to his bare chest, like a weight lifter pumping iron, then stood and walked over to the dive platform. The muscles in his arms and back rippled. With its heavy incrustation, the shell weighed about 150 pounds, I guessed, but Barrett handled it as lightly as if it were made of balsa wood. He knelt near the edge of the platform, lowered the shell into the ocean, and released it with hardly a splash.

We watched the bull's-eye ripples where the shell went in. Minutes passed. Nothing happened. A rash of nervous grins broke out among the crew, me included. Santos clapped his hands and grabbed Eileen in a hug. "This Sunday I'm going to church and make a big donation," he said.

The color was creeping back into Eileen's cheeks. "You may have company," she said softly.

"Should have let Lucas have it," Barrett mumbled. Santos laughed sourly.

I leaned against a bulkhead and reflected on my day. I was troubled. The obsessive nature of treasure fever was starting to dawn on me. None of it made any sense. Within the space of a few hours, Barrett nearly drowned and almost got himself and his sister shot up in a gunfight. All over a phony "cannon" that could have exploded and ended his dreams and ours as well.

Barrett and Santos got the boat ready and we headed back to Provincetown. Eileen had wandered off to the other side of the deck. She stared stonily at the horizon. Hoping to console her, I walked over and said, "Look, Eileen. I'm going to do my best to find Mike's missing data."

She turned to me with a bleak smile. "Mr. Socarides," she said quietly, "as far as I'm concerned, you can save your energy. I don't give a *damn* if those papers ever see the light of day again."

CHAPTER 12

The lobster was at least six feet tall counting the eye stalks. It stood on Commercial Street outside a Provincetown bistro, forlornly waving a pillow-size pink claw at the passing tourists. For $14.95 the folks from Ohio could get the real thing. A lobster special. Plastic bib, a nutcracker to open the shell, and a couple of ounces of soggy meat. Maybe the come-on works, but today nobody was biting. Normally, I don't talk to strange crustaceans that are as big as I am. But as I drew nearer, I recognized the ruddy face peering from an oval hole cut in the faded cloth covering the lobster's upper abdomen.

I stopped and looked closer. "Is that you in there, Sebastian?"

"Good evening, Soc," the lobster replied. "You don't happen to have a cooler, do you?"

The voice that used to reach the balcony seats at the Old Vic was still deep and strong, even if it had a jagged edge to it. Two decades ago, Sebastian had been a promising Shakespearean actor. Now the only bright lights he saw exploded behind his eyes when his brain cells short-circuited on cheap whiskey.

"Wish I could help, Sebastian. You must be warm with that thing on."

"Hotter than Hades," he grunted lugubriously. "The sacrifices I make for my art."

"The Bard would be proud of you." I patted him where I thought his shoulder might be, and continued along Commercial Street.

The *Shamrock* had arrived back in Provincetown an hour earlier. At my suggestion, we stopped off for a sudsy libation to the sea gods who had enlivened our day. It wasn't such a terrific idea. The mood at our table was glum. Barrett and his sister stared out the windows fronting on the harbor and brooded. I stared at their untouched glasses of warm beer and licked my lips. Santos went off to chat with a couple of buddies. I wanted to break the uncomfortable silence, but couldn't think of an appropriate bon mot. Finally, Barrett spoke.

"I guess this day wasn't a total loss," he mused. "Now you see how vital that missing data is to the *Gabriella* project."

"Mike, I'm sorry I don't have them for you. But don't give up hope. It's not over till the fat lady sings."

"Don't get me wrong, Soc. I have every confidence in you. I know this is a tough case."

"Which is why I should be chasing down a possible lead," I said, pushing my chair back.

Eileen said, "Good-bye, Mr. Socarides. Thanks for getting Michael out of trouble today." I sensed she was glad to see me go. I left the bar and plunged into the near-gridlock foot traffic, thinking about the offhand comment I heard the first night I went pub-hopping for information on Kip.

That thing with Kip and Lady Brett at the Dunes Club in P'town. Talk about weird.

Not much of a lead, really, but better than nothing.

The crowd milling along Commercial Street was a chowder of young families trailing whiny wakes of sticky kids, and overdressed older couples, gay twosomes, threesomes, and quartets making the most of the chance to let their hair down.

The chittering, chattering, chuckling human stream flowed in and out of the bars and restaurants, the leather and T-shirt shops. Tributaries ran into the sidewalk-artist stalls and the souvenir stores that sold rubber chickens, model fishing boats made in Taiwan, and wall plates with John F. Kennedy's portrait on them. Hungry eddies circulated around the foot-long hot-dog stands and the fried flipper-dough counter at the Portuguese bakery, where business was brisk.

The nightlife was cranking into gear. A chunky man in a flowered dress, ill-fitting henna wig, and high heels that looked as if they were killing him stood on the sidewalk outside one bar hustling tickets for the early drag show. At another watering hole a fat bald character with a barbed tongue tickled the piano keys and insulted customers who couldn't get enough of it. Old men and women, the locals, gossiped on the benches near the antique town hall and skeptically eyed the procession like judges in a beauty contest. Behind them, town kids jaded by overexposure to the annual invasion of oddballs, eccentrics, and just plain folks sat on the shadowed lawn around the statue of the World War I soldier and admired each other's sneakers.

You could say a lot of bad things about Provincetown. You could cluck about how the place had gone steadily downhill since Eugene O'Neill and the artsy Greenwich Village expatriates staged *Bound East for Cardiff* in a fog-kissed fish shanty, and wonder why anyone bothers to deal with the crowds and the traffic and honky-tonk. But on a hot summer night you can still stroll out on MacMillan Wharf and look back at the old town, at the floodlit crenellations of the Pilgrim Monument tower and the tiara of lights glittering in the harbor. The breeze smells of old wood and old fish. The music drifting across the water from the clubs and bars on Commercial Street teases your memory like the gentle fingers of a pretty girl, and somehow it all makes sense.

I dodged an oncoming baby stroller aimed at my kneecap and stepped into a narrow alley between two sagging wooden buildings that fronted the harbor. A graveled walkway inadequately illuminated by imitation gas lanterns led to a blue door with the words DUNES CLUB scrawled on it in dripping white letters. Beyond the door was a cozy vestibule where a diminutive woman sat at a table collecting cover charges.

She eyed me lazily. "You won't like it here," she said in a sleepy sort of way. "Take a look." She indicated the portal to her right. It was a challenge. Nicely said, but still a challenge.

I poked my head into a large dim room lit for the most part by candle flames that flickered at a couple of dozen tray-sized tables like a convention of fireflies. The room was occupied entirely by women. They were dancing, drinking, or simply listening to the low throb of the Woodstock-size sound system. I stepped back and grinned.

"No problem," I said. "I like women."

She wasn't impressed. "They might not like you. Nothing personal. I can't keep you out by law if you want to push it, but some of the customers could make things uncomfortable."

"That's discrimination."

She shrugged. "That's life."

"That's okay. I'm not into the club scene anyway. But I would like to see Lady Brett. Is she around?"

The young woman shot me a quizzical look. "What's your name?" she asked. I could swear she was smiling. I handed her my card and she carried it up a flight of stairs near her table. She returned a few minutes later. "Go on up," she said, lifting her voice in a musical lilt.

The second-floor landing opened into a room that looked like a psychological torture chamber. A plump sofa and chairs of shocking pink squatted on a rug the color of a rabbit's-ear lining. The throw pillows were black and white zebra stripes. The wallpaper was cerise. There was a pale green marble table supported by a stylized pedestal of three frowning catfish. A sheer red scarf with yellow butterflies hung over a lamp that cast a diffused rose-tinted light.

No thumbscrews. No electric shocks. Leave your prisoner in a space like this for twenty-four hours and he'll get down on his knees and beg to tell you the secret-invasion plans.

A honey-sweet voice called: "Ah'll be right out, dearie." The voice had just a tinge of a southern accent and came from behind a set of padded pink doors flanked by gilt Corinthian columns topped with black funerary urns. I walked to a window and looked out between beet-dyed drapes at the harbor, trying to phrase my questions.

"Now, dearie, what can I do for you?"

I turned. "I was just admiring your . . ."

The sentence lodged in my throat like a chicken bone. A sequined apparition in canary yellow with a beehive of golden hair that soared several inches above my head on the way to the moon stood there coquettishly fluttering eyelashes the size of pocket combs.

"Admiring my what, dearie?"

". . . view," I said.

"I'm disappointed."

The creature pouted, pirouetting so the flouncy skirt of the evening dress swirled at ankle height in a frothy blur. The maneuver produced a breeze as heavy with French perfume as the Place Pigalle on a Saturday night. The voice dropped several octaves. "What's wrong, Sunny Jim? Haven't you ever seen a female impersonator before?"

Talk about weird.

"It's not quite what I expected," I said. "Not at all."

"No?" Lady Brett reverted to the sultry southern accent. She sounded more like Rhett Butler than Scarlett O'Hara. "Well, ah surely didn't mean to disappoint you-all." The voice dropped again. "Go ahead, throw one at me."

"Throw what?"

"A *name,* silly. Female vocalist. Somebody vintage. Not one of your upstart rock tarts. I'll only go as far as Streisand or Midler."

"How about Judy Garland?"

"Pish-posh. Everyone in town does Judy," Lady Brett scolded. "But I'll do it anyhow." He took a deep breath, puckered his lips, and belted out a couple of verses from "Over the Rainbow." It was a tolerably good impression of how Dorothy might have sounded if she and the Wizard had closed down the Emerald City Bar.

"I've never heard it sung quite like that before," I said. "How about Pearl Bailey?"

"Hmmph. Doncha have nothin' harder'n that, honey?" Louis Armstrong with a bad cold.

"I'm impressed, I'm really impressed." I was telling the truth.

"You should catch my act downstairs. Well, maybe not." He looked me over. "I've never met a private eye before. I thought all you shamuses wore trench coats and slouch hats. What can I do for you? Are you on what they call a caper?"

"You could say that. Actually I'm trying to learn what I can about Kip Scannell, and I understand you knew him."

Lady Brett lit up a cigarette in a black plastic holder decorated with grape-size rhinestones, took a deep and decidedly unfeminine drag, and exhaled dramatically. "Kip was a dear boy. A very sweet boy. Why are you interested in him?"

"Nothing complicated. Kip had some property that belongs to my client. I'm trying to track it down."

"I'm not sure I can be of help."

"I'm not sure either, but I heard that you and Kip were acquainted. I thought it might be worth talking to you. Were you good friends?"

"In a manner of speaking. We had mutual interests, let us say. Kip was attracted to men. You knew that, of course."

I raised an eyebrow. "Quite the contrary. I was told he

was very much a ladies' man. I believe the term used is 'stud.' "

Lady Brett laughed sardonically, waving the cigarette holder. The motion set the plumes in his coiffure bobbing. "Oh, he was that too. But Kip liked men as well. I wasn't one of them. I don't go for the overmuscled beachboy type myself, but sometimes I host private cocktail parties for the lads and lassies. It gives them a chance to meet someone without doing the dreary bar scene."

"Do you know anything about a friend of his, a pretty, dark-haired girl?"

"He never brought her around here." Lady Brett looked at a pink plastic wristwatch. Diamonds flashed on his fingers. "Pardon me, I don't mean to end this fascinating conversation, but I have to do a show in a couple of minutes."

"That's no problem, I appreciate your help. Maybe we can talk again in a day or two. In the meantime, you have my card, so please feel free to get in touch if anything occurs to you."

"You can come up and see me *anytime*," Lady Brett said in a breathless imitation of Mae West.

"I'll do that," I said. I left the apartment and descended to the vestibule. The ticket taker smiled innocently at me. "Okay," I said. "The joke's on me. But in my copy of Hemingway, Lady Brett *was* a lady."

"I guess Hemingway never spent any time in Provincetown," she said.

"He didn't know what he was missing," I answered, and walked out the door into the night.

Commercial Street was still crowded, but Sebastian had shed his lobster shell and sat at a sidewalk café nursing a boilermaker. He waved at me and I sat down and ordered a Bud.

Sebastian raised his beer glass. "I'm celebrating the end of my short-lived but illustrious career as a giant lobster. The town fathers, and mothers, I presume, have banished me from my stage. Nothing personal. Seems the costume doesn't fit in with the upscale image they are trying to promote. I can see dark clouds gathering, my good man. Next they will banish drag queens." He drained the glass, chased it down with a shot of whiskey and wiped his mouth with the back of his hand.

"Speaking of drag queens," I said, "what do you know about Lady Brett?"

Sebastian swept his white mane back over his ears as he must have before he stepped onto the stage in the old days. "Ah, the good lady. You've met her, er, him."

"Whatever. I just had the pleasure. What's his pitch?"

"Rather mediocre female impersonator. Does all the obvious ones. Did he do Mae West for you?"

"Yeah. Wasn't half-bad, but I prefer the original article. Do you know anything about his business connections?"

"He owns the Dunes Club and has a few other interests in real estate here and there, I've heard."

"Is he in business with anyone else?"

"Well . . . There are rumors." Sebastian studied his empty glass pensively. "Sometimes it's not good to spread gossip, you know."

I ordered him another boilermaker. It's great being a private cop. For a $950 license and $50 bond you get the opportunity to loosen an alcoholic's tongue by pouring drinks down his gullet. I let him swallow a few gulps.

"What sort of rumors?"

Sebastian took another slug and wiped his mouth again. "I've heard he has an interest in a couple of gay bars up around Boston."

"Did you know Kip Scannell?"

"Ah, young Kip. Sad. Very sad. Yes, I knew him. Anyone who frequents the public houses on a regular basis was bound to run into Kip. He bought me drinks several times."

"What was his connection with Lady Brett?"

"Some say they were business associates. Ask around. I'm sure others know better than I."

Booze or no booze, it was obvious my source had dried up. I stood. "Thanks, Sebastian. And good luck."

He grinned up at me. " 'If we do meet again, why we shall smile; if not, why then, this parting was well made.' " He hiccuped. "Shakespeare. *Julius Caesar*."

" 'From his tongue flowed speech sweeter than honey.' Homer, from the *Iliad*," I said.

He smiled blearily.

"Can you get home okay?" I asked.

Sebastian waved an arm carelessly toward the street. "I live just a few steps, or should I say, a few staggers from here. I have traced the path so well my feet know it without me. Besides, the muscular lads at this establishment are most kind about seeing me home. It wouldn't do to have one of their best customers fall into the harbor."

"It was good to see you, Sebastian."

"And you." He focused an eye on me as well as he could. His voice slurred, he said, " 'In thy face I see the map of honor, truth, and loyalty.' *Hic*. Pardon me. That was from *Henry VI*."

I bent close to his ear. " 'There is a time for many words, and there is also a time for sleep.' That's more from Homer."

He dug into his memory to forehand another quote. The effort was too much. He slumped over, his chin on his chest. I motioned to a waiter, who smiled and nodded. He and another husky young man lifted Sebastian gently from his chair. I paid his bar bill, gave them a generous tip, and stuck a twenty in his shirt pocket. He would use the money to drink himself into another stupor, but I couldn't blame him. It's not every day you lose your job as a lobster.

CHAPTER 13

As fond as I am of low life and high adventure, it was great to be home. I collapsed into the smoky ripeness of a gardenia-print overstuffed chair liberated at great personal risk from a flock of surly sea gulls who'd used it for a dump roost. My hand, as usual, was wrapped around a frosty can of beer. Kojak leaped kittenishly onto my lap and purred with contentment. A cold beer and a warm cat. What more could any man want? The telephone ended my R&R. Laura Nichols was calling and she sounded nervous.

"Mr. Socarides? I must see you."

"What's the problem?"

"I'm . . . afraid."

"Afraid of what, Mrs. Nichols?"

"I can't talk now. Can you meet me at my boat? It's the *Laura N* at South Harbor."

"I'll be there in forty-five minutes. Is that okay?"

"Yes, but please don't be any longer than that."

I wrote down the directions, hung up, and took a shower. I wasn't really concerned about Laura's safety. It's not the first time a panicky client has called me. Often, their indefinable fears are little more than tree shadows on the window. Besides, no sense looking for trouble with a gritty body.

After lathering away the sea salt and grime, I pulled on a pair of faded denims that had reached that exquisite state of softness between respectable and threadbare, and a natty T-shirt with a picture of Tecate beer I had paid far too much for at Hussong's Cantina in Ensenada, Mexico. I took a souvenir from my police days out of a dresser drawer. It was a .38 Smith & Wesson police special, an ugly thing whose sole function was to punch holes in people.

I wasn't lying when I told Laura Nichols I didn't like guns. I knew firsthand there was nothing romantic about the way a bullet tears flesh and splinters bone. But if she were in danger, I rationalized, it wouldn't hurt to have insurance. Irritated at compromising my own principles with only a token internal struggle, I clipped the holster onto my belt. Then I piled, squeaky clean, into my truck.

About thirty minutes later I parked on a bluff overlooking a pretty harbor enclosed by the mainland on one side and a hilly island, really a peninsula, on the other. Swinging gently at anchor within this basin were about two dozen sailboats and cabin cruisers, nothing less than thirty feet long. Lights twinkled on the yachts and the laughter and clink of cocktail glasses and the scent of tobacco wafted on the breeze. It would have been a pleasant exercise in voyeurism just to row among the boats catching scraps of conversation, or a good tip on the stock market. Maybe someone would say, "Hey there, young fellow, climb aboard and have a couple of pops."

I took the gun off my belt and stuck it under the seat. It seemed to weigh a hundred pounds. I cursed at my weakness in bringing it. I locked the truck and descended the wooden stairway that spilled down the bluff, picking my way past some fish shanties. I pushed a six-foot fiberglass pram into the water, stepped inside, set the oars in their locks, and started pulling.

Nearly every boat in the harbor was registered in Delaware. It was a nice little tax dodge for the well-to-do. Register your boat as a Delaware corporation and avoid Massachusetts taxes. No one asked me aboard for a drink; maybe they thought I was a revenue cutter.

The *Laura N* was off by itself near a point of land. The forty-foot-plus motor sailer had lots of teak and brass. It was top-heavy and boxy, built more for carrying hors d'oeuvres and martini shakers than cutting through the seas.

Laura Nichols saw me rowing toward her. She set her drink on the deck as I tied the pram alongside the boarding ladder and reached down to help me. I almost fell into the water. She wore white shorts and a minimal halter that were practically luminous against her dark, slim body. She looked nuder than if she'd been wearing no clothes at all.

I stepped on board. Laura smiled and said, "You must need a drink after rowing way out here."

"Yeah, it was tough trying to get through all those floating cocktail parties without succumbing to terminal thirst. Delaware must have a bigger fleet than the U.S. Navy. I think I deserve a scotch on the rocks, Mrs. Nichols."

"I think you do too, but please call me Laura. Mrs. Nichols makes me think I should be wearing a granny shawl."

"I wouldn't want to be guilty of making a lady age prematurely, Laura."

"Fine, then. Do I call you Aristotle?"

"My friends call me Soc."

"Then Soc it is." She disappeared below and emerged into the soft glow of the deck lights with the bottle of Dewar's and a large tumbler that tinkled enticingly. She poured herself another drink. We sat a few steps down from the wheelhouse in a nicely appointed living space that had a couple of deck chairs, side tables, and a supply of ice. Neither of us spoke.

The summer night had a drowsy sensuousness to it. The harbor was like one of those East Indian ports Joseph Conrad used to write about where jolly good Englishmen sipped quinine while painted bodies rustled along the shore and spears clicked in the black liquid darkness. I drained the last gulp of scotch, felt the warmth in my stomach, and handed the empty glass over to Laura for a refill. She was ready for another drink.

"Well, how can I help you?" I said.

Laura said, "I wondered how you were coming with my case."

"I could have told you that over the phone."

"I know. That's why I was a little more dramatic than I had to be when I called you."

"It wasn't necessary to try for an Oscar nomination. I would have come even without the theatrics."

"I thought you would, but I wasn't sure. And I *am* afraid, really."

"For your husband? Don't worry. We'll get him out of this in one piece."

"No, it's not that. I fully trust you. It's just that . . ." She laughed nervously. "This sounds so silly, and perhaps I've become paranoid, but I think perhaps I'm being followed too."

"What makes you say that?"

"Oh, woman's intuition mostly. Glimpses here and there. People looking at me."

"I'm not surprised at that."

We went back to our drinking. A few minutes later, I drained my glass again and handed it over for a refill. The tips of my fingers were getting numb. So was my judgment, but it had been a tough day and I find it hard to resist a good scotch, especially when it's free.

Laura filled our glasses and leaned against the rail, crossing one long leg over the other. We drank some more. "I'm curious," she said finally. "What do you think of me?"

With my eye I measured the gleaming length of her leg between the knee and the ankle, appraised the slim waist, the sculpted breasts, the curve of her bare shoulders, the elegant profile, and the honeyed hair. I sipped my scotch and said, "I think you're very attractive, but I'd be surprised if I were the only one who thought so. I think you collect pretty things like jewels, expensive cars, and boats and maybe you collect men the same way." I belched, not too loudly I hoped. "I think you make a hell of a drink."

She laughed casually. A lovely sound. "You certainly don't mince words."

"Forgive me. It's the scotch talking. Speaking of which." I extended my empty glass. The bottle of Dewar's was looking sick. She filled the tumbler and sat on the deck next to me. Her hair smelled of jasmine.

"You're only partly right about me," she said. "I do like pretty trinkets that cost money, and the shinier and more expensive they are the better. But there are things you don't know."

She lit a cigarette, took a deep drag, and stared out over the harbor. Someone in a nearby boat had put on a Billie Holiday tape. Lady Day's soulful voice floated like smoke on the night air. We listened until a cabin door closed and the music stopped. After a minute Laura said, "I suppose you've been to Vermont. Everybody has."

"I used to ski down Bromley mountain when they still used barrel staves," I said.

"That's what most outsiders see. The après ski, the pretty

autumn foliage, and the oh-so-quaint covered bridges. But the poverty in the backwoods is as bad as anything in Appalachia. A girl might be pregnant at fourteen and an old woman at thirty." She took a gulp of scotch. "Where I grew up, there are men who think having sex with their daughter or sister is just part of the natural order of things. When my mother died, my stepfather decided I should take her place. And not just with the cooking and washing. That's when I ran off."

I looked around at the yachts in the harbor. "You've come a long way from the backwoods."

"I was sixteen when I arrived in Bennington and got a job in a coffee shop. I took secretarial courses and went to work at the college. That's where I learned how to act like a rich girl long before I became one. So you are right. I enjoy being wealthy and I'm determined never to be poor again. Never, no matter what it takes. May I fill your glass?"

She emptied the rest of the bottle evenly into our glasses. I raised mine in a toast and said, "*Yasou.* That's Greek for 'to your health.' Or in this case, to your wealth. As Aristophanes would say, 'Quickly, bring me a beaker of wine so that I may wet my mind and say something clever.' " Not that my mind was dry.

"You're quite a surprising man." There was a slight sadness in her eyes that didn't fit the mood of the night. It was only there for a second. She grabbed the empty bottle and said, "I'll get another one of these." She went below. I was glad to see she had trouble navigating the stairs. A few minutes later she called out, "Could you come down here for a minute?"

Laura was sitting on the edge of the double bed in the master stateroom. It's considered highly unprofessional for a private investigator to find himself in a darkened bedroom with an attractive client, especially if she is married. But I've never claimed to be the Pinkerton Agency. I went over to her. Laura stood and tilted her chin up. I kissed her lightly. Her mouth tasted of scotch and cigarette smoke. She shivered, although the night was steamy. I slipped an arm around her slim waist and pulled her to me. She put her arms around me and gave me a kiss that nearly melted the rubber soles of my Top-Siders.

We sat on the edge of the bed and she trembled and

whispered hoarsely in my ear, "Hold me, hold me close," the way Grace Kelly might have done it in a clinch scene.

We lay on the bed and I brushed her long hair and her graceful neck with my lips, kissed her mouth softly, then harder, tasted the sweetness of her, inhaled her, explored the curves of her body with my hand, felt the warmth of her, heard her breath quicken, felt my temperature rise, felt her stiffen.

She sat up suddenly. "What's that? I thought I heard a noise on deck."

I ran my hand down her thigh. "It's probably just some boat sound."

"No," she insisted. She sounded alarmed. "It was something else."

I sighed. "Okay," I said, easing off the bed. "I'll check it out."

I crept up the companionway into the living-room area and looked around. One small lamp was on. Nothing was awry. No intruders. No pirates swarming aboard with knives clenched in their teeth. I climbed the short set of stairs into the pilothouse. Again nothing. I stepped out onto the deck and looked around. More nothing. I was coming to the unhappy conclusion my amorous adventure had been interrupted by the normal squeaks and burbles of a boat tugging at its mooring when a shadow detached itself from a pile of sail bags off to my right.

Something whisked by my ear. Something black and as hard as a miser's heart. It didn't quite remove the top of my skull but my brain bounced around inside my cranium the way a suitcase tumbles down an airport luggage chute. The deck jumped into my face and a burgundy curtain slammed down and left the stage in darkness.

It could have been worse. I could have been sober. I could have resisted and been really hurt. But with incredible prescience I had drunk myself into a relaxed mindlessness and the tap of the sap that launched me into the center of the spiral nebula only finished a lift-off started with my first slug of Dewar's.

A planetarium ceiling whirled above me.

"Velcome to Astronomy 101," the professor was saying in a Teutonic vaudeville accent. Orion was riding Pegasus and the Big Bear was dancing with the Little Bear and the Dish running away with the Spoon.

My eyes creaked slowly open. The professor vanished. The stars remained, fuzzy and out of focus. My head hurt, so I knew that I wasn't in heaven. But an angel bent over me.

I groaned.

"Thank God," the angel said appropriately.

The groan felt good, so I groaned again.

"Just lie there for a minute," said the angel, who had Laura's face. "What happened?"

"I think someone slugged me," I said. Brilliant deduction. I had trouble wrapping my tongue around the sibilants, but Laura got the message. She looked around, fear in her eyes.

"Are you sure you didn't slip and fall? I came up as soon as I heard the thump. There was no one aboard, I'm sure of it."

"Maybe he went for a swim. Check the pram and the motorboat."

She was back a few minutes later. "The launch is still here but the pram is gone."

I sat up by degrees and asked her to wrap some ice in a napkin and bring it to me. I held the ice pack gingerly on the egg growing out of the side of my head. Then I asked for some more ice, this time in a glass with a splash of scotch. I sipped from the glass without retching. The fiery liquor trickled down my throat.

"I don't think you should stay here," I said.

"Yes, you're right. I'll go back with you."

We climbed into the launch and motored to shore. I saw Laura safely behind the wheel of her Mercedes, checking the backseat first to make sure there were no uninvited passengers, and said I would follow her home.

I got into the truck and sat on shards of glass, pieces of the smashed window on the passenger side. I groped under the seat where I had left my gun. It was gone. I eased out carefully, swept the glass away with a rag, got back in and started the truck and put it into gear.

Whump-whump.

The GMC lurched forward and stalled. I got out and circled the truck, swearing mightily and at great length in the tongue of my forefathers, then walked over to the Mercedes.

"What's wrong?" Laura said.

I slammed my hand against a fender so hard my palm stung. With little lip movement I said, "You don't suppose you could give me a lift to a gas station? Some joker with a sharp knife has been practicing surgery on my tires."

A gray mist was creeping in off the ocean as I turned into the crushed clamshell parking lot at the Hole. The foggy sky above the building glowed with a grainy orange-and-blue neon halo. I got out of the truck and kicked one of my new tires. Laura had driven me to an all-night garage and insisted on paying for the treads with her platinum American Express card.

The teenage kid who followed us back to change the tires muttered several times as he worked, "Jeez, mister, somebody sure don't like you." I needed a new head too, but the garage didn't have my size in stock. Using the garage phone, I called the police station to report my stolen pistol. Just in case someone intended to use it to pull a bank job. I told the dispatcher, whom I knew, that I'd come by in the morning to take care of the paperwork.

The Hole was as quiet as a church on Monday. The tourist crowd had left to rest up for another grueling beach day. A couple of regular customers were having one more for the road. The late shift would arrive around midnight and stay until last call before scattering onto the highways in search of accidents to happen. It was the time of evening every bartender waits for, when the boss has gone home to complain that the help is robbing him blind and the top ten in the drunk parade have slipped into their nightly coma.

I bellied up to the bar, still woozy. Hoppity frogs danced in my stomach. Joshua had the night off. The alternate night bartender came over to wipe down the bar top with a rag. He looked at me and gaped noticeably.

"Hey, Soc. You okay? You look a little green around the gills."

"Yeah, I'm just fine. I'll be even better after you open a Bud. Make that two."

He set two bottles down on cardboard coasters. I stuck one bottle in my face and pressed the other against my neck. The cold, wet glass felt marvelous against my skin. Then I chugged down that bottle. The jukebox was miraculously quiet. I prayed no one would play "Rock and Roll Is Here to Stay." I was working on my third beer when I heard a nasty chuckle.

"So you're Barrett's hired gun. You don't look so tough to me."

Somewhat stiffly, because of the agony associated with moving, I swiveled on my bar stool. Lucas stood there. He was grinning. His teeth were yellow, like a rat's. He swayed slightly as if he were on a moving deck. He either wore a rum after-shave or he'd had more to drink than I had.

"Hired guns went out with Billy the Kid," I said. "Can I buy you a beer?"

Lucas ignored the offer. "I know all about you. Cop from Boston, got kicked off the department for knocking around some boneheads."

"Wrong again. If you don't want that beer, I'll have it myself." I signaled the bartender.

Lucas climbed onto the stool beside me. "I heard around the shore that you're an okay dude. So how come you're working for a creep like Barrett?"

"I'll work for almost any creep who helps me pay my bar bills. I might have worked for you if you'd asked."

His face sagged as the insult sank in. For a moment I thought he might take a swing at me. Lucas wasn't a tall man. Maybe five foot seven. He had a brawler's physique, though. Thick muscular arms and a powerful chest. A neckless head that rested on his broad shoulders. A look in his eye that said he wouldn't think twice about breaking a bottle and shoving it down your throat. Just your ordinary scary fellow. I was feeling too beat up to care. He grinned again. "Yeah, they said you were a wise guy too. What kind of job you doing for Barrett?"

I grinned back. "Would you be surprised if I said it was none of your business?"

"Naw. Is the beer offer still on?"

I held two fingers up and the bottles arrived almost instantly.

"Let me ask you a question," I said. "That little argument you and Barrett had out there on the water today. Somebody could have been killed. What was that all about?"

"You were there. You saw Barrett pull that rifle on me. I was just acting in self-defense."

"Guess I can't argue there. But how come you and Barrett hate each other so much?"

"We go back a long way, ol' Mikey and me. I knew him down in Florida."

"Salvage stuff?"

"Yeah. He jumped my claim and got away with it. There was an old silver wreck off the Florida Keys. One of my crew gets drunk and talks too much. Next thing you know, someone thinks my boat needs some sweetening. Pours a bag of sugar in the gas tank. The engine bearings don't work so great after that."

"What makes you so sure it was Barrett?"

"When I finally fixed my engine and got back out to the wreck, Barrett was diving on her. Somebody must have cleaned out the wreck years ago, cause Barrett got nothing, but that son of a bitch screwed me royally. I'm not the type that forgets."

"It's not just sour grapes because he got to the *Gabriella* before you did?"

Lucas let out a whooping laugh that made heads turn. "I'm out to even the score, but that's not the only reason I'm busting Barrett's ass. I found the *Gabriella* first. She's my wreck and what's on her is mine. Hell, from where you guys were diving today, he doesn't even know where she is."

"What about those coins Barrett found? Doesn't that prove something?"

"What about them? They don't prove shit. You can pick that stuff up by the thousands in Florida. Just walk into a coin store. If you ask me, those coins had a nice flight on the Miami shuttle." Lucas slid off the stool and stuck out his hand. "Thanks for the beer. Look, no hard feelings about needling you?"

"Naw," I said, gripping the heavily callused palm. "I knew you were just trying to get a rise."

"Yeah. Doesn't matter anyway. Barrett's going to be history. I don't care what kind of paperwork he brings into the state board. When I get through telling them he dug when he wasn't supposed to and tried to use me for target practice, he'll be lucky he doesn't end up in jail. Let me know if you need a job. I'm looking for divers."

"I'll think about it."

"Good luck," Lucas said over his shoulder, weaving off to rejoin his table. "You'll need it working for Barrett."

I stared into my beer, trying to read the foam like tea leaves. Events were moving much too fast, sweeping me along like a riptide, when the water piling up on shore squeezes through a sandbar and takes you with it. You can purposely ride a rip current out for a deep-water dive. You can fight it to exhaustion, and drown. Or you can conquer your instincts, swim parallel to the beach, then safely back to shore.

I threw some money down on the bar and headed for home, an ice pack, and a good night's rest. It was time to get clear of the current before I found myself too far from land to swim back.

CHAPTER 14

The sea gull swooped in low, swung up in a graceful arc, danced on sun-gilded wings as lightly as a milkweed seed, and released the oyster in its beak. The oyster shot down and smashed against the massive boulders of a jetty like a bomb on target.

Splat!

I flinched and lowered my binoculars. The gull dove onto the rocks and picked its snack from the shattered shell. I rubbed my scalp tenderly. Poor oyster. I knew how its head must feel. The gull's success was depressing. I had to wrestle with an oyster for ten minutes before I pried it open. And I was attacking my cases the same klutzy way. The lump on my head was painful proof of my ineptness.

I sat at the driftwood coffee table on my deck, squinting against the sparkle on the bay, puffing without enjoyment on a stale unfiltered Camel left over from my smoking days. Kojak was curled up on the table purring in his sleep, probably dreaming of a 9-Lives Mount Everest. I toasted the gull with a cup of Mexican coffee and mashed the cigarette into the pile of butts in the clamshell ashtray. Then I went inside the house and returned with a cordless phone. I set the phone down in front of me and stared at it. I had been dumb. If I stared long enough, maybe the phone would ring and someone would call and make me smart.

Nothing happened. After a few minutes, I picked up a red ballpoint pen and made some marks on the yellow legal pad on my lap.

The person who had played a xylophone solo on my skull the night before did me a favor by calling attention to my unprofessional behavior. Strike one was getting drunk with

Laura Nichols. Stupid. Strike two was trying to seduce the aforementioned client. Asinine. Strike three was carrying a gun I didn't intend to use. And strike four was losing it. Foolish and imbecilic. Definitely bush league. Time to act like a detective instead of a defective.

First the Scannell puzzle. I reread the photocopied news story reporting Kip's death. I had worked backward from that starting point with little success, trying to learn what happened before Kip died. How about working forward, instead? Try to learn what happened afterward. Okay, start again. Scannell was dead. Most people don't keep dead bodies around the house. They must be disposed of, usually by an undertaker. I congratulated myself on my searing insight and pawed through the Yellow Pages, stopping at the listing for funeral homes.

A few calls later I had established that Kip's mortal coil reposed at the undertaker's only long enough to be collected by a hearse sent from a Searsport, Maine, funeral home. A call to Searsport told me funeral arrangements were made by the next of kin, one Kate Scannell, address unknown. I thanked the undertaker and hung up, wondering what relation Kate Scannell was to Kip. Okay, try something else. Kip spent a lot of time in Key West. I looked up the long-distance information number for Florida.

"Directory assistance, what city please?" The operator spoke with a friendly drawl.

"Key West. Do you have a listing for an Arthur Scannell?"

She checked the computer. "Sorry. There is no A or Arthur Scannell in Key West."

"Look, miss," I said in my most avuncular tone. "I hate to put you to any trouble. But this is Sergeant Dudley, Massachusetts State Police. We're trying to track down Mr. Scannell. Unfortunate car accident involving a family member, if you know what I mean. It would be a great help if you could read off all the Scannell names with their numbers."

"Guess ah can be of help, Officer."

She relayed four names from her computer screen. I jotted them down, thanked her, and hung up. One number was listed simply under K. T. Scannell. Could Kip have used his nickname? I called the number and let it ring a long time. While I waited, I poked Kojak with my bare toe to see if he were alive or just in suspended animation. Still asleep, he rolled onto his back with his paws sticking up in the air. Ridiculous feline. Finally, a groggy male voice came on the phone.

"Good morning," I said nasally, with a decidedly imperious inflection. "I'm trying to get in touch with a Mr. Kip Scannell. Do I have the correct number?"

"Kip doesn't live here. This is his cousin's house."

"My name is Hanscomb Calder at Mr. Scannell's insurance agency. Our office has a refund check for Mr. Scannell. Unless we hear from him"—I lowered my voice in a thinly veiled threat—"I'll be forced to refer the matter to our unclaimed funds department."

That got his attention. "Kip's up in Massachusetts doing some diving or something."

"Are you his cousin?"

"Naw. She's not here."

"Would his cousin know how to get in touch with him?"

"Probably."

"May I speak to her?"

The man yawned loudly and said, " 'Scuse me. I work nights. Kate's on Cape Cod for the summer. I'm just house sitting."

Bingo.

"Do you know where I might reach her?"

"Just a second."

The telephone clunked down and there was a rustle of paper. The man came back; he reeled off an address in a bayside town about ten miles away from me. "Listen, if you talk to Katie, tell her to give Bob a ring. She hasn't called for a while and I had to take her mutt to the vet for some worm pills. She owes me twenty bucks."

"I'd be happy to. Are you a relative?"

"Naw. Just a friend. Who'd you say you were?"

"Mr. Calder. Our company cares for all your needs, from womb to tomb."

"Yeah, that's cool, man. Look, I have to go back to bed, okay? Catch you later." He hung up.

Kojak the miracle cat returned from the land of the living dead. He looked frantically around and jumped onto the safety of my lap. He may have had a bad dream about a mouse. Kojak fears mice second to not being fed; I think he watched Tom and Jerry movies as a kitten.

I absentmindedly scratched his ears and tried to figure Laura Nichols. She had been as subtle as a Fourth of July fireworks display. She didn't come across as one who gave away favors easily. On second thought, what had she given away except half a bottle of scotch? And why would someone clobber me and run? I certainly hadn't posed a serious obstacle to anybody who wanted to hurt Laura. And who would bother to steal my gun and make rubber garters out of my tires? Questions and more questions. I picked up the phone and dialed Laura's number.

She answered on the second ring. "I'm so glad you called," she said. She sounded glad. "Are you all right?"

"I'm fine. A little sore, but I have a thick skull, I guess. I'd like to track your husband again. Is he going out later?"

"Yes. After dinner he plans to go to the Harbour Club. He has some friends there he plays cards with once a week. He usually leaves the house around seven."

"Good. I'll tag along to see if he stirs up any action."

"Soc, please be careful. I'd feel terrible if anything happened to you."

"You're not the only one. My creditors would cry a river. I'll give you a report later. 'Bye."

I drained my coffee mug and said good-bye to Kojak. Before I left the boat house, I cut a piece of plywood the size of my broken truck window and jammed it into the door. It wasn't pretty, but it would keep the rain out. Then I drove to the police station to fill out a theft report for my stolen gun. Everyone in the department thought it was a big joke. Street-wise city cop loses his gat. Ho-ho. Humiliating.

About twenty minutes later I turned down a narrow back street and parked. The Bide-A-Wee Arms was a two-story, elongated building manufactured by joining together two more or less similar houses. Curls of white paint peeled off the gray underlayer, giving the outside a shaggy sheepdog look.

In the city it would have been a flophouse or condemned. But on Cape Code the rooming house fulfilled a need for summer lodging. The college kids who lived there couldn't have cared less how the house looked. Most put in barbarically long hours sweating over fryolators, slinging fish and chips, or chasing down customers who get amnesia when it's time to tip. Hours off were spent at the beach or partying. Sleep was optional.

I walked up the stairs onto a wide veranda that extended the length of the house. The front door was open. I stuck my head in and yelled, "Anybody home?" No answer. Silly me. The sun was shining. People would be working on their tans. I went back to my truck and minutes later parked on a quiet, maple-shaded lane in front of the Outer Cape Historical Society. The society was in a yellow dollhouse of a cottage heavily decorated with white gingerbread trim. Just inside, an ample gray-haired woman sat behind a wooden desk. She squinted at me through wire-rim glasses, then smiled. If she were the gingerbread witch, Hansel and Gretel would have nothing to worry about.

The historical society occupied the former cottage living room. The walls were lined with bookshelves and glass cabinets holding lacy fans intricately carved from whalebone, ornately decorated scrimshaw whale teeth, and snuffboxes, the kind of thing sailors labored over during voyages that lasted years. Hanging on the primrose wallpaper were framed newspaper clips, primitive oils of sailing ships painted by China Trade artists, and portraits of steely-eyed captains and their thin-lipped wives. The room smelled like an attic.

"Neat place," I said, looking around. There were just the two of us in the building.

"Built in 1850," my hostess said, happy to have somebody to chat with. "Campground Gothic architecture. Moved here in 1867 from Millennium Grove in Eastham where the Methodists used to have their big revival meetings. What can I do for you?" She talked as if she were reciting from a catalog card.

"I'm interested in a ship named the *Gabriella*."

"Ah." Her eyes lit up and the magnetic tape in her head went on fast forward. "British frigate. Sank off Provincetown June 21, 1778, in a squall. Supposedly carried thousands of pounds in silver and gold to pay British troops."

"Yep, that sounds like her, all right."

"You a writer or a historian?"

"Little bit of both, I guess you could say."

"Lotsa people been writing about her. Been in all the papers. My name's Mrs. Eldredge. That's Eldredge with an 'e.' The Eldridges with an 'i' were the horse thieves." She grinned. "*We* Eldredges, on the other hand, would steal *anything*. I'm the curator. Have a seat."

She indicated a chair next to a massive oak table with claw-ball feet and disappeared into a back room. A filing cabinet opened and shut, and a moment later Mrs. Eldredge returned and plunked two fat manila folders on the table. "I'll be in the workroom catching up if you have any questions."

I sat down and opened the first folder. It contained a hodgepodge of material in reverse chronological order. I glanced through yellowed newspaper clips going back to the turn of the century.

In the years following its sinking, the *Gabriella* acquired a mythic patina. No longer a mere sea tragedy, the frigate had become a legend, joining witches, giant Indian braves, and Viking dragon ships as part of the local folklore. The treasure became more fabulous with each new telling of the story. The circumstances of the wreck grew more bizarre and confusing to a point where it was hard to separate fact from fantasy.

Arguments raged over the treasure. Had the local inhabitants hidden it away? Who was the mysterious stranger who was seen digging out on the lonely moors? Was he a survivor who buried loot so he could retrieve it years later? Occasionally a beachcomber would come across an eighteenth-century coin, fueling even more speculation. The treasure began to achieve the status of a king's ransom. Chests of emeralds and diamonds, rubies and sapphires lay tantalizingly close to shore.

Ghosts entered the picture. Mostly the shades of British soldiers, presumably still waiting for their paycheck. But there were also imaginative tales of spectral figures who roamed the cliffs and moorlands in eternal wait for husbands and sweethearts who had perished in the wreck.

On April 4, 1902, the *Provincetown Advocate* carried the report of a phantom sailing ship. A fisherman swore he saw a vessel, with a British union jack at its masthead, glide in and out of a fog bank. Skeptics suggested the story was in the same spurious league as the six-eyed sea serpent Professor George Washington Ready saw off Provincetown in 1886.

A cutting from the September 8, 1928, *New Bedford Standard-Times* recounted the testimony of an unidentified Coast Guard surfman who swore he witnessed an unearthly crew unloading chests of gold on the beach near where the

Gabriella was said to have sunk. His report was suspect, coming as it did during Prohibition, when smugglers commonly landed treasure of a different sort and the back way to Provincetown used to be called Rum Boulevard or Whiskey Road.

A few intrepid souls dragged for the ship with grappling hooks. Occasionally they brought up a hunk of rotten wood that sparked a new round of controversy over the *Gabriella* and her buried millions. But as Barrett had pointed out, the technology of the time wasn't sophisticated enough to find and salvage the wreck. The *Gabriella* had remained a myth on the Outer Cape for more than two hundred years.

Once I had an idea of the perimeter of the subject, I dove into contemporary accounts. There were photocopies of early records that included the report of Isaiah Dawes, major in the Continental Army. Dawes must have been the government representative Barrett mentioned. Accompanied by two aides, Major Dawes sailed to Provincetown from Boston a couple of days after the wreck to see what he could salvage. I followed the graceful flowing quill-pen script, closing my mind to the present, putting myself in Dawes's boots as he stood at the crest of a high bluff watching hundreds of Cape people greedily scour every stick of wreckage off the beach.

The *Gabriella* had gone down off Peaked Hill in Provincetown, one of the most dangerous stretches of water on the East Coast. The Peak Hill Bars consist of two lines of shoal water that run parallel to the coastline for a distance of about six miles. Like many vessels before and since, the *Gabriella* was driven over the outer bar only to be lethally battered by the surf near Dead Man's Hollow.

Cape Codders had a well-earned reputation as wreckers who could pick a doomed ship clean while the crew was still buckling on its life jackets. Wrecking was a heritage that went back to their ancestors on the English coast where some enterprising souls were involved in the activity known as moon cursing, or "moon cussin'." The moon cussers waved lanterns from the beach on moonless nights to lure a ship aground where it could be looted, and cursed the moonlight that made their dirty work impossible. Surviving mariners were greeted with a brick in a stocking. And according to one story, a shipwrecked sailor dove back into the sea after learning he had landed on the Cape. It may have been a bum rap for Cape Codders, who often risked their lives to pull shipwrecked people out of the surf and later provided the backbone of the Lifesaving Service. But it was also true that a few locals vigorously opposed the building of a lighthouse near some dangerous shoals. Bad for business.

Dawes tried to retrieve the *Gabriella*'s cargo from the local inhabitants. They told him the British had salvaged the wreck and carried it off in another ship. Dawes threatened people with arrest. When threats didn't work, he appealed to their patriotism. General Washington needed money to fight the British, he told them. That didn't work either. All Dawes received for his trouble were a few worthless pieces of ship's hardware and the headache associated with disposing of the remains some 200 of loyal British subjects. It was Dawes who drew the rough map Barrett had shown me.

The second folder contained sketchy accounts of an admiralty court investigation into the sinking, some broadsides and newspaper stories and excerpts from a diary kept by a Thomas Powers, one of only a dozen survivors of the wreck.

Powers was born in Bristol, England, in 1752. He joined the Royal Navy as a ten-year-old cabin boy. He was a lieutenant when he shipped out on the *Gabriella,* and lived to the ripe old age of eighty-one, spending his last days as a country squire. In his diary he painted his own actions in colors that were positively iridescent. At the other extreme he portrayed Dinsmore, the captain, as a blundering, stubborn fool who was totally responsible for the loss of his ship, its cargo, and more than two hundred lives.

Lieutenant Powers had a flair for drama. As I read a typewritten transcript of his diary, I could almost hear the panicky commands, the howl of the storm, and feel the desperation of the crew as the ship capsized in the savage waters. Many on board couldn't swim. Others died of exposure. Powers was lucky. He made it to shore and crawled to a house, where he was given shelter. The transcript stopped there.

I got up, took a seventh-inning stretch, and rubbed my eyes. Then I carried the files out front. "Mrs. Eldredge, I was wondering if you could help me."

She scuttled over, holding a scrapbook she'd been working on.

"The Powers diary here is incomplete. I was wondering where I might find the rest of it."

"Hmmph," she said, sorting through the papers. "That certainly is peculiar. You don't suppose anyone took it? I wouldn't put it past some of the people we get in here, and as you can see, I can't keep an eye on everyone." She clucked. "Of course, I wouldn't worry about a nice young man like you. Come to think of it, though, I'm not sure there were more diary pages in here. Oh dear, it's been so long since I've read this myself. Maybe I was thinking of another file." She slapped the folder shut. "Sorry I can't be of more assistance."

"You've been extremely helpful. I appreciate it." I took some bills from my wallet and stuck them into a donation box. Near the front door I paused by a white ceramic object on a shelf.

"Oriental prayer vase, eighteenth century," I said, "probably brought over by some deep-water skipper in the China trade."

Mrs. Eldredge beamed. "Dear me, no. Nineteenth-century chamber pot, manufactured in upstate New York."

From the Outer Cape Historical Society I drove to the telephone booth outside a Route 6 gas station and used my charge card to dial a Boston number.

A woman answered. "Beacon Research Corporation. Norma speaking."

"Hi, Norma, how's it going?"

"Soc! Is that really you? How's my favorite Hellenic hunk? Are you in town?"

"I'm calling from the Cape, Norma."

"That's okay. Drive up to Boston. Max is away. We can have an orgy."

"You can't have an orgy with just a couple."

"Why not? Since my diet I've lost the equivalent of one person and I've got two people left. You're one. That's three. So we'll have a ménage."

"That's the best offer I've had all day, Norma, but I'll have to take a raincheck. I'm up to my eyeballs in work for a change, which is why I called. I need your help."

"Oh, all right. Be a party pooper. I'll just have to take a freezing shower instead. So, my Athenian Adonis, what can I do for you?"

"Remember those corruption cases we worked on, how you and Max always said, 'follow the money trail.' "

"Sure. You follow the money, look at where it can go astray, and then poke around."

"I'd like you to poke around for me. There's only one problem. The money trail could be a little cold."

"How cold?"

"A couple of centuries cold."

"Yikes, Soc. Our data base doesn't go back *that* far."

"Look, Norma, this could be important. I'd like you to see if there's any record of what happened to the money that was on a British ship called the *Gabriella*. She sank off Cape Cod in 1778. She had a guy named Thomas Powers in her crew. He was a lieutenant. I'm particularly interested in anything you can turn up on him. There may be a diary with some missing pages somewhere. Think you can help? I'll send you flowers."

She gave a heavy sigh. "You've given me *so* much to go on. But we'll check around. Sure you don't want to come up?"

"Sorry, Norma, I'd love to, but I'm really busy."

"Okay, but don't forget."

"Don't forget what?"

"Those flowers. I like roses. Red ones with very long stems."

When I got back to the Bide-A-Wee Arms, a pretty, well-scrubbed blonde sat at the top of the front-porch stairs. She wore a cranberry-colored uniform with a white lacy apron and a cap that looked like an upside-down coffee filter.

"Hi," I said. "I'm looking for Katie Scannell. She around?"

The girl smiled and put away her nail file. "Hi, my name is Judy. Katie hasn't been here since last week." The smile vanished. "You heard about her cousin, didn't you?"

"Yes, I know about Kip. Pretty rough deal. Did you know if Kate left a forwarding address?"

Judy tilted her head. "No, she didn't. I mean it was really weird."

"What do you mean?"

"The way she left. Katie didn't tell anyone where she was going."

"Maybe she's still in Maine," I suggested.

"No, she came back after the funeral. I guess she was pretty much the whole family. Her cousin's father ran away when he was a kid and his mother's got Alzheimer's, so Kate had to make all the arrangements. She was gone a few days, then she showed up at the Arms and took some of her stuff and left. She was only here a few minutes. She left some of her clothes, that's why we figured she'd be back. Are you a friend of Kate's?"

"Kip's, really. From the old days. I was away, but when I heard about the accident, I came back to see if there was anything I could do. Didn't Kate even give a hint of her plans?"

"Nope. She just loaded her stuff in the beach buggy and off she went."

"Beach buggy?"

"You must have seen it. The one Kip drove. An old green Scout."

"Oh sure, the old Scout."

She looked beyond me. "Sort of all rotted out, like your truck. Say . . ." Judy checked her watch. "I have to go to work. Could you give me a ride?"

"I'd be glad to. Let me guess. You wait on tables at the Captain Elijah House, right?"

"Right. How did you know? Oh, I get it. This uniform. Isn't it just too quaint? Hold on and I'll be right with you." She disappeared into the rooming house and emerged carrying a canvas bag. "Change of clothes. Someone is bound to have a party after work." She got in the truck and looked around. "Yep, corroded, just like Kip's Scout. Do you drive out in the dunes too?"

"No," I said. "This is only two-wheel drive. Got rotted out from the salt they used to put on the roads." I caught the "too" at the end of her sentence, held on to it, and took the thought a step further. "Sounds like Kip hadn't changed since I saw him. Usta get out on the dunes whenever he had the chance."

"He still did. Guess he loved that shack."

This was starting to get interesting. "God. That old thing is still standing. Did Kip ever take you there?"

"Oh, no. Kate says he liked having a place where he wouldn't be hassled. Even Kate only got invited out once or twice. Said it was quiet as the moon. Oops, here's work."

I stopped in front of a large Victorian house. Two clean-cut car valets gave the truck a puzzled look, then smiled when they saw my passenger.

"Thanks for the info," I said.

"Thanks for the ride," she said. "Come by again."

I watched her go up the walk and shook my head. Young enough to be my daughter. Dammit.

Manny's Service Station was a gray-shingled building that had catered to the beach-buggy crowd since the days when you slapped a set of oversized tires on your Model-A Ford, loaded it with fishing gear and sandwiches, and whipped along just out of reach of the surf on the hard-packed sand that ran like a highway on the lower beach.

The Model-As had given way to converted bread trucks fitted out with camp stoves and port-a-potties. Now the garage was surrounded by nimble jeeps and massive camper trucks that could carry a full living-room set, including the color television and stereo. I found a space in the parking lot next to a camper that rocked with kids engaged in pitched battle over a bag of Cape Cod potato chips and strolled to the station.

The office smelled of tire rubber and oil changes the way old garages do. Dressed in stained and patched overalls, his thin face grease-smudged like a commando about to go on a night raid, Manny sat behind a huge and messy oak desk. He was tucked in a corner, flanked by shelves crammed with mufflers, fan belts, suntan lotion, and cans of dry-roasted peanuts. He was talking rapidly into a phone. He waved when he saw me and rolled his eyes toward the ceiling. A few minutes later he banged the receiver down.

"Jeez, these parts distributors are something. I haven't got enough to worry about with all these beach buggies driving me buggy. How are you, Soc? Long time no see."

A chubby boy banged the door open. "Can I have the bathroom key? And my dad says there's something wrong with the air hose."

Manny handed the boy a key attached to a six-inch-long piece of wood. "Tell your dad to make sure the hose rest is up or the pump won't work. See what I mean?" he said to me. "Every year I say I'm going to give up this crazy business, sell out for a princely sum, and just hang around bars all summer and go to Florida in the winter."

"You hang around bars and go to Florida now."

"Yeah, that's right," he reflected. "Maybe I'm having a good time and just don't know it. What can I do for you, old pal?"

"I'm helping out a friend of Kip Scannell's. You know, the diver who drowned off Provincetown. Heard he had a dune shack in the Province Lands. Do you know where it is?"

"Kip's place? Sure. He was pretty closemouthed about it, but I'd seen his Scout around. Pretty hard to keep a secret out on the dunes. It's like a little village. Everybody knows everybody's business. Took a waitress out there once for a private party. My wife had worked out a property settlement with her lawyer by the time I got home. Incredible. I still can't figure how she knew I was fooling around. They didn't even have CB radios back then."

He ripped off a piece of lined notebook paper and drew a rough map. "It's sort of hidden between a couple of dunes so you wouldn't see it from the track. Nice place I heard, but I never got inside it."

The chubby boy came back with the bathroom key. "My dad says your air hose is still busted. And your toilet just overflowed when I flushed it."

Manny rolled his eyes again and told the boy he'd check the air pump in a minute.

"I'd like to go out and take a look," I said, picking up the map. The ragged paper was covered with Manny's oily fingerprints. "Could I rent a four-wheel drive?"

"Hell, Soc, you can take the Bronco gratis. I'll give you the keys so you can get past the gates the national park put up. That's interesting what you said about helping a friend of Kip's."

"What do you mean, Manny?"

"I know you should have respect for the dead," Manny said. "But to be perfectly honest about it, I didn't think Kip had any friends."

CHAPTER 15

Ten minutes later, I turned the Bronco off Route 6 onto a
fire road and partially deflated the oversized tires to improve
their traction. I shifted into four-wheel drive and headed into
the Province Lands, following the sandy track that runs
between the mirror-flat waters of Pilgrim Lake and a big
dune called Mount Ararat on the old maps. The windblown
sandhill is constantly on the move. It's swallowed all but a
few hundred feet of stubborn scrub forest and would cross
the highway and start burying houses if it weren't chopped
back regularly by state road crews.

The Province Lands are part of the Cape Cod National
Seashore. The National Park Service has placed this part of
the dunes off limits to vehicles except for their own, the dune
taxis that carry sight-seeing tourists, and the beach buggies
people use to reach the shacks. The way was blocked by a
cable hanging between two rusty posts. I got out and used
Manny's key to unlock the gate, then pushed on. The track
ascended to the crest of a hill, where I paused to sweep
my eyes across the narrow land wrist separating ocean from
bay.

Gripping the steering wheel loosely, I let the fat, low-
pressure tires more or less follow the ruts on their own. The
nude desert landscape gave way to scraggly stands of pine
and oak so stunted you could almost jump over them, so
tough fire can't kill them. Dark-leafed bayberry, beach plum
bushes, and ground-hugging bearberry formed shadowy thickets bordered by snowy clusters of dusty miller. The air smelled
of sea and growing things and hot sand.

I stopped to unlock another gate, then drove past an
abandoned Coast Guard station. The crumbling concrete

foundation could have passed for the ruins of an ancient Sumerian temple.

The dunes rolled to either side like great green seas the way the ocean looks when there's a storm working offshore. Sparks of sunlight glinted off razor-edged blades of compass grass whose sharp points drew circles and semicircles in the sand with each breath of wind. The valleys between the dunes were cool puddles of blackness. I began to catch glimpses here and there of dune shacks. They were so much a part of the landscape that you couldn't be sure if you were looking at the corner of a roof or a tangle of gnarled branches, a weathered chimney or an old stump.

Before long I was lost. Manny's quickly scrawled and grease-smeared map was totally confusing. I could have made better use of the diagram by blowing my nose in it. The countryside resembled a scene from *Beau Geste*. Any minute, I expected to see a band of Bedouins leading a camel caravan. Maybe I could ask directions. I turned the Bronco around and backtracked, pointing the four-wheel drive up a slope between two towering dunes that had looked interesting on the first pass. I regretted the decision almost immediately.

Pinched in by steep dunes on either side, the track narrowed until it was barely wide enough for the Bronco. I had hoped it would widen out and give me some breathing room. Nice move, Soc. Looks like a dead end. You're gonna have fun backing out. My side mirrors were practically digging into the encroaching dunes. After a few hundred feet the path broadened and became more level. A galvanized steel stovepipe poked like a submarine periscope from behind a grassy knoll. Hmmm. My unerring detective instincts. Knew I was on the right track all the time.

The plywood and tarpaper shack was nestled just around a corner in a bowl-shaped depression that hid it well. A small outhouse with a crescent moon cut in the door stood on a rise behind the shack. Sandwiched between the two buildings was a green Scout.

As I got out of the Bronco, there was a crashing in the bushes. I tensed, then relaxed. Nerves. Just a cottontail dashing for cover. His frightened hops through the shiny patches of poison ivy triggered miniature avalanches that flowed down the dunes with a *shhhh*. The only other sound was the breeze rustling faintly in the scrub. Not exactly like the surface of the moon. Quieter, maybe.

I went to the front door, knocked, and yelled, "Hallo." No answer. I tried the door. It was unlocked. I opened it and poked my head in. "Anybody home?" All was quiet. I stepped inside.

The one-room shack was about sixteen by twenty feet and it smelled of wood smoke and bacon grease. A potbelly stove with a profile like a Boston traffic cop I used to drink with at J. J. Foley's took up one corner. Over the sink was a black cast-iron hand pump. Gas stove and gas fridge. New cabinets, a couple of bunks. Stained-glass windows threw trapezoids of red and yellow light on the hardwood floor. A bad oil painting of the shack hung on the wall. The artist had used too much cobalt in the sky.

I stood in the middle of the shack. Wondering. Would it be rude to search the place? Yeah, I guess it would be rude. Emily Post had nothing to do with my decision. I just thought it would be dumb, given the squeak of floorboards behind me. That and the voice.

"Get your hands up and turn slowly around."

When you're a gumshoe, you can make those astounding deductive leaps that baffle ordinary mortals. With dazzling speed my keen analytical computer of a mind had assembled the circumstantial evidence. Fact one. Behind me stood a young woman. Fact two. From the tone of her voice she was deadly serious and more than a little jittery. Fact three. I would bet my stash of Silly Putty eggs that she had a gun pointed at my spine and a nervous finger curled around the trigger. Conclusion: Do what she says.

I had developed a sudden itch at the small of my back. It was just above the elastic of my undershorts, probably the remnants of the label tickling my skin. I resisted the urge to scratch. Instead, I reached for the nearest stratus cloud and turned very, very slowly.

The woman was silhouetted against the doorway. She was of medium height, and at another time and place I would have admired the lovely curve of her waistline and her long, bare legs. But I was distracted. A shaft of sunlight streaming through a crack in the wall reflected off the short barrel of the .25-caliber Colt automatic in her hand.

The little black muzzle was aimed at a point in my abdomen where a second belly button would have been superfluous and painful. Seemed a good time to break the ice. I smiled, friendlylike, and said good morning. She didn't return the greeting. Some people are grumpy early in the day.

"Who are you?" She didn't beat around the bush.

Neither did I. "My name is Socarides," I said. "I'm a private investigator. And I'm hoping you're Kate Scannell."

"What are you doing here?" The edge in her voice was sharper. Maybe I broke the ice too quickly. It's disconcerting when someone you've never seen before says your name. The last thing I wanted to do was disconcert her.

"As I said, I'm a detective. I made a few phone calls and asked around. This shack is no secret. There was a chance you were here. I came out to take a look. Kip's Scout is parked outside. Your friends at the Bide-A-Wee Arms miss you, by the way. And your roommate in Key West said to tell you your dog has worms but the vet's given him pills."

She remained as motionless as a statue. "What proof do you have that you're a detective?"

"You can look in my wallet. I'll remove it real slowly from my back pocket and put it on the table, okay?"

She didn't answer. I waited a few seconds. When she didn't shoot me, I eased the billfold out of my pocket with the tips of my fingers, put it down, and backed a respectable distance away.

Kate stepped from the shadows and walked slowly over to the table. She picked up the wallet and studied my investigator and driver's licenses, the business and credit cards. I studied her. She was about twenty-five, with glossy black hair that just brushed her shoulders. She could have passed for a young Liz Taylor. Too old for *National Velvet*. Rebecca in *Ivanhoe*, maybe. She was dressed in denim cutoffs and a flowered halter, Daisy Mae style, and disgraced neither article of clothing. She was barefoot and looked as if she spent a lot of time that way.

She put the wallet back on the table. She didn't lower the gun.

"All right. What do you want from me?"

"I was hired by Mike Barrett, Kip's boss. He wants me to find some missing papers Kip had. They're quite important to him."

"Go on."

"The papers haven't showed. I was hoping you could help me."

She seemed to wilt and her hand wavered slightly, then she caught herself and brought the gun up again. I wasn't so sure I liked the glint in her gray eyes.

"Sit down," she said. "Don't try anything because I still don't trust you."

I nodded. I've always been a sucker for a cute little snub-nose automatic. "By the way, where were you when I drove up?"

"Hiding in the outhouse. I watched you through the hole in the door."

Smart move.

I sat in a chair and leaned one elbow on the table. "Here's the story," I said. "Kip was in charge of the charts and other site data that pinpointed the location of the *Gabriella*. That stuff has disappeared, and without it, Barrett's whole salvage project goes down the drain. So he hired me to try to locate his papers. I've gotten nowhere. When I heard Kip had a relative on the Cape, I decided to look you up. Maybe you can help me, maybe not, but I thought it was worth a try."

"What do you want to know?"

"Basically, anything you can tell me about Kip's movements in the weeks before his death. Where he went. Who he was with."

Kate Scannell nodded and seated herself in a chair next to the potbelly stove. She placed the revolver in her lap with the muzzle still aimed so she could squeeze off a shot if I twitched.

"First, you have to understand that Kip and I were family to each other, all either one of us had. When he moved to Key West, I followed him. Then Kip got the dive job here. He called last spring and told me the restaurant money on the Cape was good, and he wanted me around because he was onto something really big."

"Was he talking about the *Gabriella*?"

She shrugged a tanned shoulder. "What else? Anyhow, I came up in May and got a job. I didn't see a great deal of Kip because we both worked long hours. But sometimes he would show up out of the blue, flirt with the waitresses living at the Arms, and take me out for a drink."

"What about his big score? Did he ever make it happen?"

Her brow furrowed. "I don't know. I never heard anything about it again. But I was starting to worry."

"What about?"

"I saw less and less of Kip. When I did see him, he seemed happy and nervous at the same time. He told me that after July thirteenth, I was through waiting on jerky tourists. He said he'd buy me a restaurant. But he always talked like that. I didn't pay much attention."

"What do you mean about his being nervous?"

Kate shook her head. "It's hard to describe. Sort of always looking over his shoulder. It got worse about a week before he died."

"In what way?"

"One night Kip took me out for a great steak dinner, but hardly touched his food. He said if anything happened to him I should just disappear."

"Did he say what was worrying him?"

"No. He gave me some money to live on. And this gun. Two days later he was dead. . . ." Kate paused, gnawing at her lip. She cleared her throat softly, and went on. "I took care of the funeral, then came back to the Cape. I didn't want to go back to Key West. It was like I couldn't believe Kip was dead and that I'd be admitting it by leaving. So I got some things and came out here."

I chewed on her story. Kip had been afraid for his life. But afraid of what? Of whom?

"What are you going to do now?" I asked.

"I don't know."

"I might offer some advice. I won't pretend to know what's going on, but Kip obviously thought you'd be in danger if anything happened to him. That's why he wanted you to disappear. If I can find you, anybody could. I'd suggest you get out of here. Get off Cape Cod. Maybe even avoid Key West for a while. Do you have someplace to go?"

Kate said, "Yes, I have friends around the country. I could stay with one of them, I suppose."

"Good. Do it today, and don't leave a trail anyone can follow."

"I still don't know if I should trust you."

"That's a healthy attitude. Hold on to it. Why should you trust me? We met for the first time ten minutes ago." I retrieved my wallet, extracted a business card, and put it on the table. "Give me a call once you've settled someplace. You don't have to tell me where you are, it's probably safer that way. I'd just feel better knowing you made it out of here. I'll see what I can dig up in the meantime. If I find those missing charts, they may tell me something. Is it okay to go?"

She stood up and stuck the pistol in the waist of her cutoffs. "Not yet," she said. She went over to a large wall cupboard and opened the door. There was a large blue duffel bag inside. "This is all Kip's stuff. Maybe there's something here that will help."

I went over, opened the bag, and examined the scuba gear it contained. The regulator and hoses seemed in good condition. Kip owned two sheath knives, which told me he was a cautious diver. I pulled the dry suit out of the bag. A dry suit is stiffer than a wet suit, which fits snugly and allows in water that warms on contact with the body. In a dry suit, the insulating material and the air trapped against your skin keep you comfortable.

Kip's suit was an orange and black Viking Pro with detachable gloves and hood. The fabric seemed fine. No holes or apparent leaks. I found the gloves, but the hood was missing. Strange. The hood is indispensable. It's not just a question of comfort. The head has very little fat, so it loses heat faster than other parts of the body. A cold diver burns up air almost twice as fast as a diver who is comfortably warm. I rummaged through the bag, but still no hood. I asked Kate if this were all the equipment Kip was wearing the day he died.

She nodded.

Okay, so the hood was missing. Maybe the cops or the undertaker took it off Kip's body and threw it in a drawer. I pulled out the weight belt. I had to put my back into it. The belt is basically a nylon band that has a quick-release buckle you can open with one hand. The rectangular lead weights slide onto the nylon. I hefted it in two hands, tried to imagine a diver swimming with it. Couldn't.

"How much did Kip weigh?" I asked Kate.

"About 150 pounds, I guess. He wasn't tall but he had muscles from working out a lot."

This was crazy. The belt was weighted with about fifty pounds of lead.

I placed the belt down and pulled a shoebox from the bag.

"By the way, Kip was supposed to be lobstering. Did he have a license?"

"Not that I know of." Kate smiled tentatively. "But Kip wasn't big on stuff like licenses and permits."

I opened the shoebox. Inside were a well-worn man's wallet with a Scorpio design on the leather, a diver's waterproof wristwatch, credit cards, driver's license, a half-used pack of book matches from the Dunes Club. I put everything back in the bag and shoved it into the closet.

Kate was watching me expectantly. Anticipating her question, I said, "I didn't really expect to find anything. Sometimes all you have is scraps of information that seem unrelated. Eventually all that stuff comes together."

Kate walked me to the Bronco. "I guess you're right about leaving," she said as I got behind the wheel. "There's nothing I can do here." I offered to keep her company while she got ready to go. She thanked me and said she'd be fine, so I headed out toward the main track. I looked once in my rearview mirror, but Kate had vanished. There was only the dune shack sitting in the sun, looking old as the ages.

CHAPTER 16

My telephone started jangling the minute I stepped into the boat house. Brother George was calling. He didn't say hello. He never says hello. "Soc. Ma's coming down the Cape. She wants you to meet her in three hours at the Poseidon Restaurant in Hyannis."

"Is everything all right?"

"Yeah, yeah. Don't worry. Family's all okay. Don't be late. You know how she is." He hung up. George doesn't say good-bye, either.

I shook my head. This was unbelievable. George *never* calls me. And the last time my mother came to Cape Cod was to see the boat house. She liked the view, but when she finished her drill-sergeant inspection, she said grimly, "Aristotle, you need a wife."

After a couple of hours spent sketching out notes for the written reports private detectives are supposed to make to their clients, I got in the truck and drove to Hyannis.

The Poseidon Restaurant was in a white stucco building on a side street in the west end. It was marked by a blue sign with a black trident pointing to the door. Parked in front was the white Caddy with the unmistakable PIZZA license plate. George lounged against the car smoking a cigarette. He was dressed in white-duck cruising slacks with a string waistband and a pale green print sport shirt. He looked like a Parisian gigolo on a break. He parodied a salute when he saw me.

"We've only been here a couple of minutes. Ma's inside." I stepped toward the front door. George flipped his cigarette in the gutter and caught me by the arm. "Hey, Soc. About all that stuff I said the other day at the bakery. I'm sorry. And Ma didn't tell me to apologize either," he added quickly.

I put my arm around his shoulders. "C'mon, George. Hell, I know you didn't mean it."

He looked relieved, but something was still bothering him. "That's just it, I *did* mean it. Look, Soc, nothing against you, but like that crazy argument over the linguica order the other day. I gotta put up with that kinda stuff all the time. So when you walk in, free as a bird, and get treated like the Prodigal Son, maybe I get outta line. They think you're God. You're the educated one, the guy who went to college. Some-one mentions Homer to me, I think they're talking about something the Red Sox hit out of Fenway Park. So I gotta show how much better I am by bragging and telling you how to run your life."

"Look, George," I said. "The folks depend on you. They know they're not getting any younger but it's tough for them to let go, so they have to make a federal case every time a question comes up. Sure they treat me like a big deal, but I'm an embarrassment to them. I'm the older son, but I left the family, I left the church, I left the business. Hell, George, you know the Greeks. They think a hundred hours is a minimum work week. They invented the work ethic three thousand years before those blue-nosed Puritans claimed credit for it. I cause the folks a great deal of pain, and believe me, George, it doesn't make me feel very good. Another thing. You've got a lot to brag about. Maria's a terrific lady and you've got two great kids."

George frowned skeptically. He knew his kids were two incredibly spoiled brats who should have been named Calig-ula and Agrippina, but he appreciated my fib. "Hell, Soc, you know you could settle down if you really want to. Maria's got some friends who are looking for a husband and—never mind," he said, catching my glare. I'd met some of Maria's friends. "Better go inside. Ma's waiting."

The restaurant was a single room with stools and a counter along one side, booths on the other, and plastic-topped ta-bles in the middle. The predominant color was Aegean blue. A mural ran the length of the wall over the booths. It showed the sea god Poseidon poised ready to hurl his trident at Odysseus and his black ship. It wasn't a bad painting. The colors were electric, but it was far more interesting than the idyllically boring fish shanties, dories, and red sails in the sunset found in most Cape restaurant murals.

Odysseus was in a tough jam. On the starboard side were the Sirens. Odysseus was tied to the mast so he could listen to their fatally beguiling song without jumping overboard to his certain death. Scylla and Charybdis were on the port side. A hungry one-eyed Cyclops hovered on shore, hoping to snatch a nice juicy crewman for dinner. I looked at Poseidon's face again. Incredible! Except for his shovel beard, Poseidon bore an uncanny resemblance to my uncle Theo, the bookie in Cleveland nobody in the family talks about. Except Theo was maybe a hundred pounds heavier and smoked Havana cigars.

There were only three people in the restaurant. A portly man in his midfifties with thinning hair and a face that was mostly nose sat at the counter, his chin cradled in his hands. Behind him was a woman with lovely deep-set eyes. And next to her in a black dress, with her back to me, was my mother.

She was standing in a way I had often seen when she was working out a problem: right hand on right hip, left foot slightly forward, head down slightly, the fingers of her left hand resting lightly against her cheek. She turned at the sound of the door, flashed a fourteen-karat smile, and came over and hugged me.

Taking my arm, she led me to the counter. "This is Mr. and Mrs. Pappas." Her tone said: Aristotle, be on your best behavior. The woman smiled. Her husband gave me a sullen glance without lifting his chin. "Our families have known each other a long, long time, Aristotle, going many years back to Crete."

The man stirred. "Crete." His accent was thick. "That's where I belong. Not here. America. Hah." He shook his head ruefully. That's when I noticed the angry bruise on his cheek.

"How long have you been in America?" I asked.

He cast a baleful glance in my direction. "Twenty-five years."

"Mr. and Mrs. Pappas have a problem," Mother interjected. "I told them our family would do everything to help."

Oh, hell. "What sort of problem?" I was wary. She'd done this to me before and it always meant trouble.

The smile evaporated from Mrs. Pappas' face and she rubbed her beautiful eyes vigorously with the corner of her apron. "Two nights ago a robber came into the restaurant.

He had a gun. He hit Pericles. He says he will shoot him. We had to give him all our money. He ties us up. Look," she said, presenting her arms. Ugly rope burns circled her wrists.

Pericles shrugged. "Robbers. Guns. America." He had a point.

Mother said firmly, "I told Mr. and Mrs. Pappas that you were a detective and would help get their money back."

"It's really a job for the police. Aren't they working on it?"

"Police. Hah," Pericles contributed.

"America," I said.

He looked at me for the first time. A kindred soul.

His wife said, "The police, they say they have someone, but they cannot prove he did it."

Excusing myself, I took my mother aside and we sat in a booth. "Ma, this is awful timing. I've got more work now than I can handle."

Mrs. Pappas brought us two demitasse cups of thick, syrupy Turkish coffee and a plate of baklava that oozed honey like a beehive. Mother took a sip of coffee and a dainty bite of the diamond-shaped pastry. "*Kalà*, good," she said approvingly. Mrs. Pappas beamed and returned to comfort her husband.

"It's very sad about this," Mother began. "For years, the Pappases have saved their money, always working for others, so they could open this restaurant." She glanced up at the sea-god mural. It was very rare anything caught my mother by surprise, but this time her mouth dropped open. She raised an eyebrow. "Ah. That looks like your uncle Theo in Cleveland, the one who's always in trouble."

Wisely, I said nothing.

"But Theo's not so skinny." Mother likes precision. The diversion was momentary. She wasn't through with me. "I was telling you about the Pappas family. They have no money and may have to shut down. We cannot allow this to happen."

The emphasis on the word *we* was unmistakable. I tried a bite of baklava that was so sweet I almost went into insulin shock. "I'd love to. But I'm very, very busy."

"Yes, I *know* that. And you must do what you must do. But first listen to me, Aristotle, then decide. Many years ago back in Crete my father and a cousin of Mr. Pappas were neighbors. Our families were always fighting. Over pigs or cows that get loose and climb fences to get into the Pappas yard. Then one day they stopped fighting each other." She paused dramatically. "Instead," she said, "they fight the Germans."

She had me hooked. Just when I thought I had heard every family story, she pulled another one out of her memory. "The invasion in World War II," I said. "That was in 1941, I think. Very bloody, from what I've read."

She nodded. "It was a terrible thing, Aristotle. Terrible. The fighting was very fierce. The people of Crete do not give up their soil. Many, many people were killed. My father was at the Pappas farm that day. He was looking for a lamb. It was in with the Pappas flock. Mr. Pappas said the sheep must have wandered through the fence. My father said the sheep did not move the stones by itself." She shrugged. "Maybe they would have killed each other over the lamb, but the Germans came out of the sky with their big white umbrellas. One soldier landed near the two men. He is young and frightened. He tries to shoot my father. Mr. Pappas had his pitchfork." She gestured at the mural. "He throws it like Uncle Theo up on the wall. No more German. They hide the body so there would be no revenge from the German soldiers. Later Mr. Pappas joins the fighting and is killed."

I thought I could see where she was going. "But why not just give them money to replace what was stolen?"

"You are a smart boy, Aristotle. Our family and the Pappases have been bound together since that day. This is a blood debt. They are much too proud to take money. But you are a detective. You can get their money back. Then our debt will be paid. It has been much, much too long." She paused, sipped some coffee, and looked me straight in the eye. "Of course, if you are too busy . . ."

I looked up at Odysseus tied to his mast. I knew exactly how he felt. Then I looked back at my mother. She waited patiently for an answer. I reached across the table and took her hand. "I'll do my best, Ma. That's all I can promise," I said.

She smiled confidently and patted my cheek. She said, "I know you will, Aristotle."

CHAPTER 17

Hyannis used to be a bucolic backwater that bustled nonstop for thirteen weeks as a summer resort, closed up tighter than a clam after Labor Day, and didn't come out of hibernation until the Fourth of July. Today it's like a mini-city that bustles twelve months of the year.

The police station in Hyannis is an institutional brick building a few minutes from the Poseidon. I asked the dispatcher if I could see Lieutenant Souza and was buzzed into a maze of offices. Typewriters clacked in the background against a murmur of conversation and the ring of telephones.

The lieutenant was in his office cubicle reading a copy of the *Cape Cod Times*. Souza is a short man, plump as a smoked ham. He favors white shirts, mortician dark suits and ties regardless of the season or occasion. He uses a macassar to keep his dark brown hair shiny and in place and a hurricane couldn't dislodge his coif. He has a sallow complexion and sad eyes. If he weren't a cop, Souza would have been counseling married couples. People open up to his unthreatening, sympathetic face. A few of them have talked themselves into a reserved suite at the Barnstable County House of Correction.

He smiled wearily when he spotted me. "Hi, Soc," he said. "Just going through the local rag, thinking how when I was a rookie you could close the police station at five and the biggest thing was someone stealing a basket of quahogs from a pickup truck."

He brushed aside a pile of papers and a couple of empty styrofoam coffee cups and spread the paper out on his desk. Tapping the pages with a forefinger, he said, "Look at this—assault and battery with a dangerous weapon; ninja stuff that'll turn your stomach. Here's a heist. And a woman over in Sandwich murdered." He puffed out his fat cheeks. "I liked it better when it was quahogs."

"Speaking of heists." I pulled out a chair and sat down. "What can you tell me about the robbery at the Poseidon?"

He leaned back in his creaky swivel chair and locked his fingers behind a thick neck. "You interested in that? Oh yeah, the place is run by a couple of your countrymen. Had breakfast there a few times. Home fries were crispy the way I like them." He shook his head. "The owners got that old-country mentality, though. They don't trust banks, so they keep their money in a hidey-hole, their own private safe. Kid who works in the kitchen sees where they put it. He lives next door to one of the local punks. Tells his buddy, who pulls a stocking over his face, walks in around closing time with a gun, roughs up the owners, and rips off five grand. Open-and-shut case."

"So why don't you open and shut it?"

"Christ, Soc. You sound like the chief." He shifted his weight forward. The chair protested. "Listen, before you became a private cop you used to be a flatfoot at some place north of here that's famous for its baked beans, so you probably vaguely remember something called an alibi. Then there's due process. And evidence. It's always nice to have a little of that. I know who did the job. He knows it. And so does half the world. But I can't prove the jerk jaywalked across Main Street."

Souza pulled a folder out of a precarious mound of papers and handed it over. Inside was a rap sheet. Two photos, front and profile, were attached. The mug shots showed a dark man in his midtwenties with street-wise eyes, a pigtail, and a feminine mouth that would have been pretty if it weren't permanently twisted in an expression of contempt. His eyes had that vacant expression that seems to stare out at you from every picture in the rogues' gallery.

"Let me guess," I said. "John Dillinger when he was still a punk."

"Naw. Dillinger had class. The suspected perpetrator is a kid named Perry. I've known him since he was tall enough to steal hubcaps off a tricycle. His sheet's got mostly minor stuff like housebreaks and traffic violations, but the lad is young yet and has a long distinguished career ahead of him, particularly now that he's sampled the delights of armed robbery. He has three buddies, equally fine upstanding citizens, who'll swear on a stack of Bibles he was playing cards with them all night. Probably bridge. Didn't even go to the bathroom."

Souza took the folder back. "Didn't leave anything at the scene. No way to ID him with the stocking over his head. Can't crack his story. The victims were so scared they can't remember what day it happened. No one saw a getaway car. Oh yeah, the kid in the kitchen is gone. His mother says he's in Alaska or Texas, she can't remember. I'd track him down but our bloodhound is having a nose job. You know how it is."

"Are you sure this guy Perry did it?"

"Positive. Affirmative. No doubt about it."

"I'd like to talk to him."

Souza spread his hands and hunched his shoulders like a pawnbroker making his final offer.

"Hey, it's a free country. No one can stop you from talking to the guy. But a little advice. He lives in a tough section of town. Definitely not Hyannisport where the Kennedys play touch football. Close as you'll get to Hell's Kitchen around here. The neighborhood produces punks like other parts of the Cape grow cranberries. Whenever there's a felony we automatically send a couple of heavily armed cruisers over there to round up the usual suspects, like in the Bogart movie they keep showing on TV. Say, was that Bergman or Bacall? I always forget."

"Bergman."

Souza sighed and his tired eyes lit up briefly. "Yeah. God, she was some beautiful woman. Bacall was the skinny one. She was nice too. Look, Soc, if you talk to this kid, be careful. He ain't the brightest little jerk in the world and his elevator doesn't go up to the top floor, if you know what I mean. You can never count on a guy like that to do the smart thing."

He scribbled a name and address on a piece of paper, put it on the corner of the desk where I could see it, and smiled his sad smile.

"As an officer sworn to uphold the law I can't condone any sort of vigilante action on the part of private citizens. But if your independent investigation leads you to this, er, gentleman, and if in the course of a calm, reasoned conversation you should elicit information that might help the authorities with their inquiries, please feel free to pass it on. Then maybe we can toss the little bastard in the slammer, where he'll be so busy watching his pretty little ass in the shower that he won't think about beating up on folks for a long, long time. Oh yeah, don't forget to read him his Miranda rights."

I got up and memorized the address without touching the paper. Souza crumpled it into a ball and tossed it toward the wastebasket. It missed, but he didn't pick it up. "Larry Bird's got nothing to worry about," I said.

The address was on the other side of town. I drove down a sunbaked dead-end street into an older subdivision of small and tired-looking one-story houses that had the unkempt mien of orphans. The house I was looking for stood alone in a cul-de-sac. The shingles on the sides and roof had turned rusty brown and were starting to curl like toenails. The white paint on the trim was a faded memory. The weed-choked front yard looked like the Matto Grosso. A waist-high chain-link fence enclosed the whole property. A crooked BEWARE DOG sign hung on the front gate. Someone who thought he had a sense of humor had pasted a vapid smiley face sticker over the "A."

I sat in the truck a few minutes to get a feel for the place and the neighborhood and didn't like either one. I got out and walked over to the fence. There was no car in the yard, only a rectangular area of faded yellow grass splotched with oil stains. I opened the gate and shut it. No dog either. I went in and stepped up to the door and rang the bell. Then I knocked. Nobody came to the door. I thought for a minute how I seem to spend half my life knocking on doors where there's nobody home. I walked around the house and looked into the windows, but the shades were down. I went back to my truck and waited to see if there was any interest in my visit. There was about as much activity as a wax museum after closing. I drove off.

It was dinner time and I was getting hungry. I stopped off at a wharf restaurant, washed some fried clams down with a couple of beers, and watched the boats glide in and out of Hyannis harbor. When I got bored with that, I fetched a battery-operated razor from my glove compartment, went into the men's room, shaved off the day's accumulation of chin fuzz, and washed my face. Then I went back out to the truck, pawed through my disguise bag, and changed into a pale blue polo shirt, tan chinos, and a lightweight navy blazer. It was early evening when I parked just off the road about a hundred feet from the gatehouse Nichols had passed the first day I tailed him. I was not alone. Nichols's other shadow, the maroon Buick, was parked down a side street.

Thirty minutes later the white Continental emerged from the drive and nosed its way toward my truck. I ducked down behind the steering wheel and stayed there until the Buick took up the chase, then started the truck and latched onto the train like a caboose.

The parade followed a winding shore road for several miles. The Continental pulled off at a long drive marked with a sign that said HARBOUR CLUB. The Buick followed it in; I kept going and found a package store. I bought a couple of king-size cans of Bud and a bag of Doritos, and drove to a beach parking lot, where I watched the sun fall into the phosphorescent blue bay waters. Then I drove back to the Harbour Club. Time to get a closer look at my client, Mr. Charles Nichols.

A wheezing green GMC pickup might be conspicuous next to all those Mercedes and BMWs with their burnished skins, so I avoided the car valets and parked in the deep shadows of a massive catalpa tree. I carry an old aluminum ladder, some pipes, and a couple of boards in the back of the truck. People tend to assume it belongs to a workman. Nobody who drives a Mercedes pays attention to a workman.

I strolled over to the club, a rambling gray clapboard building with a roof like a coolie hat. It was perched on the brow of a hill overlooking a pretty tidal inlet that glittered from the reflected light cast by dozens of pastel Japanese lanterns. People dressed for a Gatsby party sat at the tables on a circular patio and sipped tall candy-colored drinks that matched their clothes. A piano inside the club played Cole Porter songs and the music floating through the French doors was as cool as lime sherbert.

I climbed a broad brick stairway to the patio and went into the club. The room was dominated by an oval bar as big as the Wonderland racetrack in Revere. The bar was jammed with people who liked to drink and knew how. I elbowed out a space just wide enough for my arm and signaled the bartender. It wasn't likely a place like this would carry a beer made in the U.S. and I didn't want to attract attention by ordering one, so I asked for Harp even though I don't like it.

The beer came in a glass slightly bigger than a whiskey shot and the bartender took the best part of a five-dollar bill, so I let him keep the change. Then I walked around the bar and past the open door of a small room. Nichols was playing a game of stud poker at a green baize table with four other men under a gray umbrella of cigar smoke. I went back to the bar and tried guessing which patron drove the Buick. It was a lost cause.

The crowd was middle-aged, affluent, and preppy in an old-school sort of way. There were so many whales on belts, ties, skirts, and slacks that I could have been at a reunion of cetologists. I wandered around, nursing my Harp until it went lukewarm and flat.

Around nine o'clock the card game broke up. Nichols came out with a cat-eats-canary grin on his face. Luck must have been good to him. He sat at the bar and ordered a Stolichnaya martini on the rocks. There was an open stool next to him, so I sat down. He was chatting pleasantly with the young bartender, asking about school. Nichols had tanned skin that was comparatively unlined. His silver hair was thick, and professionally styled so it wouldn't look cut. He was a handsome man until you looked close. Then you noticed the way his friendly smile didn't match the calculating look in his green eyes.

I ordered another Harp. When the bartender set the glass thimble in front of me, I said, "Say, do you know if Frank Melville has been in tonight?"

"Melville? I'm afraid I don't know him, sir."

"Yeah, I guess not. He's a big-time developer, but he's new around here."

Nichols's head turned a few compass points in my direction like a radar antenna homing in on a blip.

I began to lay it on like putty. "Ah, Christ, I was supposed to meet him to talk about some land I've got down in Chatham," I said, slurring my words slightly. "Say, you wouldn't want to buy ten acres all zoned for condos, would you?"

Nichols's head was nearly lined up with his shoulders.

"I'm afraid not, sir," the bartender answered politely. He was a good kid. Probably working his way through Yale. "It's a bit beyond my means."

I laughed with what I hoped was the proper amount of sloppy irony. "Don't feel bad, it's a bit beyond my means too."

Taking the bait like a trout snapping at a fly, Nichols leaned toward me. He wore an expensive cologne and a used-car salesman's smile.

"Excuse me, I couldn't help overhearing you. I'm in the development business myself, but I'm not sure I know this Melville chap. He's new, you say?"

"Maybe around the Cape. He's been doing a lot of major stuff along the Maine coast. He was coming to the Cape for a few days and I was supposed to show him these lots I've got over in Chatham, so I came down from Boston." I glanced at my watch. "Dammit, we were supposed to meet here, but maybe he got caught in traffic."

"Yes, that's probably it," Nichols said. He gave me a lizard smile. "My name is Charles Nichols."

"My name is Tom Johnson," I said. "Pleased to meet you." We shook hands; his skin was smooth and cold.

"May I buy you a drink?" Nichols waved to the bartender, who brought us another round. "You've got some land in Chatham. That's pretty valuable property. I'm surprised you want to get rid of it."

"It's not a question of wanting. I'm a builder, one of those little guys with a pickup truck, a hammer holster on my belt, and an office in my back pocket. Kinda new around here. You know how the market's been. Things were so good I thought I'd go big-time. Mistake. Shoulda stayed small. Got in over my head. The bank's getting nervous. Now I've got to dump some of the stuff I bought before I go down the tube, even if I have to take a loss." I looked around. "Melville could be missing a fantastic deal."

I drained the last of my beer. The piano player had switched from Cole Porter to Irving Berlin. Nichols ordered us two more drinks.

"A lot of people got caught by the slump, you're not alone." He was sympathetic. "But bear in mind, Johnson, you're sitting on a very valuable property. Condos, you say. I've built a few of those in my time."

"No kidding," I said. I fidgeted with my glass as if I were wrestling with a tough decision. "Look, Mr. Nichols, I don't usually do business with people I meet in a bar, but Melville's only got himself to blame if he can't keep an appointment. If you're interested, maybe you and I could talk."

"I wouldn't want to cut in on another developer." He sounded as sincere as Red Riding Hood's wolf. I was surprised he didn't lick his chops. "Of course, it certainly wouldn't hurt just to chat. And if we did work something out, I'd be prepared to move quite quickly. You'd have a check in your hands as fast as it took to write it."

"Migod," I said, awestruck. "That's wild. But look, I owe this guy Melville. Let me take one more crack at reaching him, and if I can't, it's his tough luck. I'll be right back." I slid off the stool and headed for a phone booth. I dialed my number and talked to no one while the phone rang at my house. Never could teach Kojak to pick up the phone. I went back to the bar. Nichols flashed his con-man smile. I sat down and shook my head.

"I got his secretary and she said she was just about to call me. Melville had a flat tire on Route 3 near Plymouth. He'll be down in a little while but I'm going to meet him somewhere else. She says he's pretty hot on buying my land. I'm afraid I'll have to see him, but if it doesn't pan out and you're still interested, I'd like to talk to you."

Nichols's smile didn't waver. He pulled a card from his billfold and handed it to me. "I understand your commitment to Mr. Melville. But if the deal doesn't go through, I'd be very pleased to discuss business with you. Frankly, I like the cut of your jib, Johnson. Just give me a call and we can have lunch."

I took the card and looked at my watch. "God. I've got to get moving. It was nice talking to you, Mr. Nichols. Thanks for the drinks. I've got a feeling we'll be in touch again." We shook hands and I headed out the door. Not far from my truck I saw the red Buick parked in the shadows at the edge of the parking lot.

It's hard to believe, but sometimes I do something that isn't very smart. I was enjoying a slight buzz from the high-priced beers, but it didn't mask my general frustration over the slow pace of my cases and the added headache of fulfilling a family obligation. Or maybe it was just the Harbour

Club. Expensive joints that pretentiously spell their names in the English manner and serve miniature beers give me a pain. In fact, lately just about everything was giving me a pain.

Whatever the reason, the sight of the Buick just sitting there stirred something mischievous in my guts. I remembered my poor little truck and its plywood window and four flat tires. Maybe, just maybe I've got the guy who did it. Having played judge and jury, I pulled a buck knife out of my pocket, kneeled down, and jabbed a tire. The air swished out satisfactorily. I jabbed another. The Buick sagged with a lovely *fump*. I went around to the other side, so pleased with myself that I almost giggled, and stabbed another tire. The noise of escaping air covered the footfall behind me.

"Hey, what the hell."

I half stood, leaving the knife stuck in the tire, spun right, and instinctively swung my left fist in a short hook that ended in a soft midsection. The man went *"ooof."* He doubled over. I followed through with a quick right chop to the jaw. He crumpled and hit the ground like a side of beef. He didn't get up. I quickly checked the parking lot. The car valets were on the other side, and the Buick had screened our scuffle.

I rummaged through the man's pockets, found his wallet, and moved into the light cast by the nearest lamp. His billfold held about a hundred dollars, some credit cards, a driver's license, and registration in the name of Harold Williams. There was something else. An identification card.

I looked closer. Oh hell. I had just coldcocked a state cop. Williams groaned.

"Ho boy," I said, and quickly inserted the wallet back in his pocket. Formal introductions would have to wait. I yanked my knife out of the sidewall, tucked it into my pocket, jogged over to the truck, started the engine, and pulled out of the parking lot with my lights off, turning them on when I got to the main road.

I nailed the accelerator. "Ho boy," I said softly.

Sam called shortly after I got home. He said his hauler was fixed, the Nickerson kid decided there was better money sea scalloping out of New Bedford, the price of cod had gone up, and if I could spare a day on the bounding main, he'd be mighty pleased. I said I'd have to think about it and let him know.

I felt guilty about taking time away from Barrett's case. On the other hand, I rationalized, maybe a day at sea would do me good. I wasn't accomplishing much on land. The state board meeting on Barrett's permit was four days away. I still hadn't found his missing papers. Maybe I never would. The search had been overshadowed by my uneasiness over Kip's death. The Nichols case was starting to smell like a week-old haddock. Oh yeah, there was my assault on a state cop too.

The telephone rang and the call made up my mind for me. It was my mother. She said Mrs. Pappas would have some baklava for me when I brought the money back. It was her way of saying she was giving the Poseidon case top priority and expected big things of me. Sort of like the Spartan mothers telling their warbound sons to come back with their shield, or on it. Nice to be appreciated. It would be even nicer to be out of reach of more motherly telephone calls. Although you could never tell with Ma. She'd find me a hundred miles at sea, but it was worth a try.

I picked up the phone and called a number.

"Sam," I said. "About that fishing trip tomorrow. Finest-kind."

CHAPTER 18

___

It was Euripides who said that those whom the gods would destroy, they first drive insane. That explained it. What a relief! I was on the Zeus hit list. He had zapped my sanity with a thunderbolt and I had flipped out. Why else would I be sitting in my truck, tired and dirty, when I could be inside the boat house taking a hot shower, popping a cold beer?

Dumb. I got out and stood in my front yard. Listening. Only the insect chorus broke the hush of the moonless summer night. Nothing was amiss. Still. I waited and watched the darkened boat house. Something wasn't right.

I had just come home from fishing. The ocean winds had not blown the cobwebs from my brain as I hoped. On the good side, Sam and I lucked into a new honey hole. We unloaded fifteen boxes of cod and it was with sincere regret that I told Sam to round up another warm body to take my place for a few days while I devoted my efforts to detective work. Barrett's deadline was fast approaching and I had just been spinning my wheels on his case.

My paranoia attack began at the fish pier. Seconds after I started my truck, headlights blazed in my rearview mirror. No big deal. Just a funny coincidence. Even more so when the headlights followed me out onto the road. I took the long way home to see what would happen. The road wound through some woodsy sections and past lonely cranberry bogs. The headlights stuck with me, tagging a few hundred yards behind, slowing when I slowed, speeding up when I did.

I turned off onto my drive and stopped. A dusty black Dodge van with tinted windows sped by. Its taillights disappeared around a curve. I waited five minutes to see if the van came back. It didn't. Probably a lost tourist. I put the truck into gear and bumped down the road.

Now I was leaning against the truck's front fender, reluctant to go into my house. Remembering. Thinking back to recon patrols that were supposed to be as safe as a walk in the park. The alarm screaming in my head. My arm snapping up reflexively. The column screeching to an abrupt halt. Down on one knee, each man facing out in the opposite direction from the guy in front of him. Pulses pounding on an adrenaline high, mouths so dry we couldn't have licked a postage stamp. Sometimes the moment passed, and we'd trudge on. Sometimes the jungle jitters kept us alive.

But this was ridiculous. This was quiet old Cape Cod. In one of the quaint little villages here and there that Patti Page used to sing about. I couldn't spend the whole night in my front yard. I walked toward the house, then veered off, avoiding the front door, soft-shoeing around to the back, where I climbed onto the deck and listened. There was only the rhythmic slurp of the incoming tide. I relaxed. Probably just the product of an overactive imagination and a weary mind.

A match flared orange in the darkness, outlining chiseled features and a shaggy beard. The light breeze carried the scent of cigarette smoke my way.

"Nice little place you got here."

"Thanks, Mike," I said. "I like it. Want a beer?"

The cigarette glowed. Barrett had settled his huge body into a thronelike wicker chair I'd bought for five dollars during a wild spending spree at a yard sale. "Don't mind if I do," he said.

I went in the house and came out with two cold cans of Bud. We popped the tops and sipped our beers in silence. The night was warm and humid, with just enough moving air to keep the flying insects away. I sat on the edge of the deck, my legs dangling over, with my back to Barrett. After a while he spoke again.

"I asked around, got directions here. Parked in that little hollow just off your driveway. Not trying to be a wise guy, but I didn't know when you'd be back and I didn't feel like explaining myself in the event one of your friends dropped by."

"Funny," I said. "I sort of knew somebody was here. Maybe I smelled your cigarette."

"Maybe," Barrett said. He sounded as if his thoughts were a million miles away. "I was sitting here enjoying the night. You can see the lights from the fishing boats out there. They look like stars. Planets, maybe. Hard to see where the sky ends and the ocean begins." He paused. "Tell me, Soc, did you ever wonder why I'm so intent on salvaging the *Gabriella*?"

"Not really, Mike. You didn't have to."

"Well, it's crazy, I guess, but I've got a dream. I want to bring to light something nobody has touched or even seen for centuries."

"Every man has his dreams. Yours is no crazier than most. Hell, my dream is to break the bank at a Monte Carlo blackjack table."

Barrett chuckled softly. Then he said, "I've never told you about the day I found the *Gabriella*."

"Not the details, Mike. I'd like to hear them."

"Good. It will help you understand. I'd been looking for weeks, months. Covered the same ground again and again. All I picked up was a lot of junk. Every sorehead who ever thought of finding the ship but didn't have the guts to try got on my back. Telling the newspapers, TV, anyone who would listen, that I was chasing a phantom wreck. That I was lying, or pulling some scam."

"I read that some people don't even think the *Gabriella* exists," I said.

"Right about that," he fumed. "Hell, I began to believe them myself. The stories that the treasure was gone, the ship scattered up and down the coast from Maine to Nantucket. I was pretty discouraged, and down to my last few dollars. I knew that if I didn't find the ship on my next trip out, I wouldn't be able to put together a project like it for years. Never, maybe. I'd be the laughingstock of the treasure-hunting business. They'd call it Barrett's Boondoggle or something like that. God, I wanted to show they were wrong. Not only prove the wreck existed, but that I found it. That's when I began to think about the voices."

Voices. This was a new one. I perked up my ears. "What voices are those, Mike?"

Barrett laughed. "Don't worry, Soc, I'm not going to pull a Joan of Arc and go marching off to war because I got orders out of the clouds. Sometimes, though, when I was lying in my bunk, half-asleep, letting my mind ramble, thoughts would come to me, almost like whispers in my ear. Eerie. I'm sure it was just all the project stuff rattling around in my subconscious."

"Probably," I said. I've heard a few voices myself; usually telling me I've had enough to drink. Unlike Barrett, though, I ignore them.

He went on. "I know this sounds nutty, but something or someone was down there, deep under the boat, calling me, saying don't give up. Keep trying. And I did. I went back to where the magnetometer had picked up some anomalies, and blew off the sand. I had a feeling we hadn't gone deep enough the first time, and I was right. This time when I dove I saw what looked like big cigars lying in the sand. I chipped the crud off one. The metal underneath had a broad arrow engraved in it."

"A broad arrow? What did that tell you?"

"It told me I was looking at property of the British crown. It was a simple, three-line design. The Royal Navy used it everywhere, on knives, forks, bottles, and on its cannon. I touched the iron barrel and a chill went up my spine. It was like shaking hands with ghosts."

"Rich ghosts," I said.

"It's not just the treasure, Soc, believe me. Sure, treasure is important if you want to keep your operation afloat, but there's more to it than that. The archaeologists think you're risking your neck for a buck, but that isn't it. They sit in their neat museum offices writing papers pooh-poohing everything you say. Then if you do hit it, they yell that you're raping history. They'd rather have a wreck rot on the bottom where only the fish can see it than have a treasure hunter like me bring up something for the world to look at. I'd love to see their faces when I find the *Gabriella* again." He paused. "I guess I got carried away, Soc. Sorry to be so boring."

"I'm the one who should apologize, Mike. I haven't found your papers yet, but I did chase down one lead." I told him about Kate Scannell and the dune shack.

He listened without interrupting, then said, "Are you sure she wasn't lying about the site data?"

"As sure as you can be about anyone. Yeah, I really don't think she's interested."

I started to tell Barrett of the questions Kip's death raised in my mind, but he spoke again and I decided to hold my tongue, at least until I had some hard evidence.

"Well, keep in touch, let me know if you learn anything," he said. "And don't forget, the clock's ticking on my permit."

I nodded and looked out across the water, thinking about my encounter with Charles Nichols. He didn't seem worried about being knocked off by the Mob. Nor was he hesitant when I waved my fictitious land deal in his face. Then there was the state cop I had oh-so-cleverly assaulted. Why was he following Nichols? I needed another beer. I asked Barrett if he wanted a fresh brew.

No reply. I turned and checked the chair. It was empty. For a big man, Barrett moved quietly. The wicker hadn't even squeaked. A minute later an engine started. I sat on the deck watching the twinkling fishing-boat lights until a hungry mosquito strafed my head and drove me inside. Kojak was lying on my pillow. I tumbled him indignantly onto the floor, crawled between the sheets, and with some effort, got to sleep.

The next few days would be long ones. If I'd known how long, I would have set the alarm for the following year.

CHAPTER 19

By morning a southeast breeze was nudging an ocean fog bank onto the outer beach. Silky tendrils of mist snaked over the narrow finger of sand and into the bay. A gray-white wall that chilled the bones and muffled sound encircled the boat house and isolated it from the outside world. The air smelled of kelp, schooling fish, and barnacled leviathans, like the breath of a giant sea monster. A distant foghorn grunted with a croupy urgency. Just offshore the muted buzz of outboard motors mingled with the shouts of skiff fishermen guiding each other with good-natured oaths of encouragement.

I was throwing clothes onto the bed from my closet and dresser. I wanted a tough-guy disguise. Really tough.

A black biker T-shirt with a skull and *Rebel from Hell* written on it caught my eye. Perfect. Worn jeans and work boots. I skipped the morning shave and shower. I wanted to *smell* mean too. I wrapped a camouflage bandanna around my head, Rambo style. Nice military touch. I picked up a black eye patch left over from Halloween. Too melodramatic. I tossed it back in the dresser drawer and put on a pair of southern-sheriff reflecting sunglasses that added a hint of menace and hid my eyes.

I stood in front of the mirror, stuck my thumbs in my ears, and wiggled my fingers. "Boo!" Not exactly Genghis Khan. But nobody would mistake me for Little Lord Fauntleroy, that was for damned sure.

The fog thinned out away from the shore and the emerging sun quickly burned off the overcast. It was mostly sunny by 7:00 A.M. when I stood in front of the Hyannis house with the overgrown front lawn. A shiny black TransAm was parked in the yard. Bright painted tongues of flame spread back from its hood. Leaving the truck, I walked over and leaned against the fence.

There was an explosion in the long grass. Something slammed into the fence like a battering ram and the chain links rattled from the shock. It scared the hell out of me, and I jumped back. It happened again. I peered cautiously over the steel mesh. Glittering up at me were two mean and ravenous eyes set in an ugly frog-flat head full of pointed teeth. The head lunged. I pulled back again, but I didn't really have to worry because the bow legs supporting the squat powerful canine body were not made for jumping.

The dog was a tawny brindle with a splash of white on its chest and murder in its heart. I had seen American pitbull terriers before. Despite all the noise about banning them from the countryside because they occasionally chewed up a child or, even worse from some people's view, dined on a poodle, I found them no more dangerous, just more game and aggressive, than your average mutt. But nasty people have nasty pets. This dog, who wanted to tear my face off and have it for breakfast, was telling me a lot about its owner.

I strolled along the outside of the fence softly whistling "How Much Is That Doggie in the Window?" The pit bull followed, growling wetly, daring me to try something foolish. I turned and retraced my steps. The terrier paced me like a sentry on guard duty. I turned once more, strode to the gate, and quickly opened it.

The move confused him. The beast looked at the gate. He looked at me. He couldn't believe his good luck. I could read his thoughts. Ohboy! This must be the stupidest human alive. The kill message flickered along his brain synapses. He dug in with his short legs and hurtled through the open gate. I vaulted over the fence and slammed the gate shut from the inside. He spun around, even more confused. I wasn't where I should be and he couldn't figure it out. He tried to knock the fence down again. When it didn't fall over, he just sat on his haunches with his tongue hanging out, giving me the bad eye.

I went up to the house and leaned on the bell. I figured the TransAm's owner was a nocturnal creature. He would not be at his best early in the day. There was a stirring inside and the door swung open. Standing there was a wiry man whose pigtailed profile I had seen on a police rap sheet. He was blinking at the sunlight like a mole. His face had sleep wrinkles in it. He was wearing pink bikini shorts and a tank top.

"Who the hell are you?" he croaked. Irritated.

I smiled. Friendly, even though I despise men who wear pink.

"Acme Collection Agency, Mr. Perry." Bluff and hearty. "You have an outstanding account with the Poseidon restaurant. About five thousand dollars, I believe."

That woke him like a pail of ice water. His eyes shot past me. "Where's Kilo?"

"Kilo got tired of munching on neighborhood kids. Little fella went to buy himself some dog yummies." I'm just too funny for words when I get going.

Perry didn't think so. He tried to slam the door, but I stuck my steel-toe boot in just like the vacuum salesmen used to do. I pushed him inside, shut the door behind me, and looked around. We were in the living room. On the floor was a worn-out rya rug the color of mustard. Pinups from a motorcycle porn magazine and heavy-metal rock groups were artfully pinned to the wallpaper. The best piece of furniture in the room was a stereo. Probably so hot you could fry eggs on it. Not exactly *House and Garden,* but to each his own.

Perry tried to bolt. I grabbed his greasy pigtail and skinny neck and guided him to the bedroom. There was a rumpled mattress on the floor with no one in it. I checked the bathroom and a junk room. We were alone in the house.

I pushed him back to the living room. He squirmed energetically, but I was stronger, about six inches taller, and had my mean clothes on. The little maggot tried to knee me in the groin. It was a bad move. I remembered the bruise on Mr. Pappas' cheek and the fear in his wife's gentle eyes. And I was feeling peckish for having been dragooned into the case by a little Greek woman in a black dress who knew how to punch the ticket on a guilt trip. I deflected his bony knee with my own, grabbed him by the front of his tank top, and slammed him against the wall with both hands.

"You have the right to remain silent," I said.

He opened his rosebud mouth to say something saucy.
SLAM!

"Anything you say can and will be held against you in a court of law."

SLAM!

"You have the right to an attorney."

SLAM!

"You have the right to come up with that five grand before I push you through the wall."

His eyes rolled back in his head. I stopped playing handball with him. He didn't bounce well anyhow. Perry hadn't been hurt as much as he thought, but being picked up and thrown at a wall by someone bigger than you is a humbling experience. I know, because it's happened to me a couple of times. I dragged Perry to the sofa and pushed him onto the cushions. Then I pulled over a wooden chair, turned it around in front of him, and sat down.

His head lolled. He wiped his mouth with the back of his hand and glanced up sullenly, trying to read the expression behind my mirrored shades.

"You a cop?"

"Naw. I'm the tooth fairy. I bounce punks like you around while I say their Miranda rights just to exercise my wings. Listen, dirtball, if I were a cop, I couldn't even come through the front door without a warrant. You know that. And I couldn't smash your kneecaps or cut up that lovely face of yours so even your mother wouldn't recognize it." Sometimes I get shamelessly swept away. Blame it on a misspent youth watching Jimmy Cagney movies.

Perry glared. "I don't have the money." I started to come off the chair. "Okay, okay!" he yelled. "Don't matter anyhow. Friggin' load didn't come in."

I sat down again. "What the hell are you talking about?"

"The load, man. Dope supposed to come in July thirteenth. I was gonna buy a cut with the dough and turn it around on the street."

It took a second for the information to sink in. When it did, I came up so fast that I knocked the chair over. I stuck my knee on his chest and grabbed his windpipe. "Run that by me again, dirtball," I whispered, my face inches from his. "Especially the date on the drop-off."

His skin went blue. I released my grip on his Adam's apple.

Fear flickered in his eyes. "Jesus. You're crazy."

"That's right," I said. "Like in the movie. *Psycho*. So give."

Catching his breath, he whimpered, "I told you man, July thirteenth. Look, let me go. I'll get your money."

"Not yet. Tell me more about the dope. How was it supposed to come?"

"Christ, I don't know. How does the shit ever get here? Somebody brings it up from Colombia. Me, I just deal with a middleman."

"What kind of dope was it?"

"Hard stuff, man. The hardest you can get."

I hoisted him out of the sofa. "Get me the money."

Rubbing his neck tenderly, he hobbled toward the kitchen with me stepping on his heels. He took a quick look over his shoulder, wisely decided I'd probably get a lot of pleasure out of slamming him against the wall again, and grabbed a canister off the shelf. It had a duck's face on it surrounded by roses.

I took the canister out of his hand and dumped the contents onto the counter. A plastic bag plunked out in a cloud of flour. I picked the bag up. It was tight with bills. I shook them out onto the counter and counted the money. There was ten dollars missing. I glanced at Perry.

"I bought gas for the car, okay," he whined, reaching to protect his neck. I ushered him back to the living room and threw him onto the sofa just so he wouldn't get cocky again.

"Where's the gun you used?"

He shook his head as if he were talking to a slow child. "I got rid of it, man. Sold it to some guy from Somerville. That's the first thing the cops would look for."

"I want you to know who I'm working for, smart-ass. Just in case you're thinking about getting another gun. That restaurant you hit is a front for some people with connections who like to clean dirty money. You dig?"

His eyes widened. "You talking about the *Mafia*, man?"

The Pappases would not be thrilled to have their lifelong dream described as a laundering outlet for the Mob, but it would be good insurance against further mischief.

"I'm talking about some heavy hitters who'd step on you like an ant if you ever go near the Poseidon again," I said. "Consider yourself lucky. My employers are here on vacation. They don't want to worry about punks floating ashore with lobsters hanging on their noses while the kids are building sand castles on the beach. *Kapeesh?*"

He nodded his head vigorously. Pretty Perry wasn't as dumb as he looked.

I stuffed the money in my pocket. "And *that*," I told him, "goes for your little dog too."

The pit bull was curled up outside the gate taking a snooze in the early-morning sun. His ears perked up when he heard me coming. He opened one eye sleepily. When he saw me, the humiliation he suffered in our earlier encounter welled through him. He launched his body at the gate. I swung it open obligingly and scaled the fence. The mutt skidded into the yard with an I've-got-you-now-you-bastard yelp. I clanged the gate shut behind him and leaned over. He stood there, a look of defeat on his Froggy the Gremlin face.

"I know exactly how you feel, puppy. I've had days that started just like yours. But look at it this way. If I were the dogcatcher you'd be doing time at the pound. Ta-ta."

A few minutes later I stopped at a pay phone and called my mother. "I got the money back for Mr. and Mrs. Pappas," I said. "All except ten dollars."

"Aristotle," she replied, "I *knew* you would do it. But so soon ... You are a good detective. I am very proud of you. Now take the money to the restaurant so Mr. and Mrs. Pappas won't worry. And, Aristotle ..."

"Yes, Ma?"

"Put ten dollars from your wallet in with the money. I'll pay you back next time you come home."

I called Lieutenant Souza to let him know he could sit on the case. The money, I told him, had been returned anonymously.

"What about Perry?"

"I don't think he'll go near the Pappases again. But he's an up-and-coming lad, so I'd reserve space for him at the Cedar Junction home for careless felons if I were you."

Cedar Junction was the pastoral name some state genius had given the state prison at Walpole a few years ago. It was a euphemism largely lost on the inmates. A thought struck me. The day I had seen Laura Nichols's chauffeur at my house he had moved with a peculiar wariness, an unhurried saunter and a lazy swing of the shoulders. It was a movement you pick up when you don't have any place to go and you're always watching your back.

"You know a guy named Charles Nichols?" I asked Souza.

"Yeah," he said. "Big developer. Deals cooking all over the place. He's always up before the planning board with one project or other. What about him?"

"He's got a chauffeur named Edward. Wondering if he ever did any time. Can you find out?"

"Yeah, I think so. I owe you one on this restaurant thing." He sighed. "I still miss the old quahog days, though."

I headed to the Poseidon. The restaurant was half-full of breakfast customers. A Nana Mouskouri tape was playing from a couple of shelf speakers. Mrs. Pappas was working the grill while her husband sat hunched on the same stool as before. He looked up at me with his basset-hound expression. I smiled and reached into my pocket, dropping the money on the counter in front of him. He stared at the wad for several seconds, unbelieving, before he picked it up, counted the bills, and let out a yelp of joy. Some of the breakfast customers curiously glanced our way. His wife bustled over.

"The money," he said, bubbling. "We have the money back." He burst into tears. She burst into tears. They hugged each other. Mr. Pappas pumped my hand. Mrs. Pappas hugged me. I almost got misty-eyed myself. Most of my clients react with a what'sitgonna cost me? Mr. Pappas rushed into the kitchen. I was hoping he was going to put the money in a safe place, like a bank vault. Instead he emerged a minute later with a slim girl in tow.

I guessed she was his daughter. She had huge brown eyes, a full mouth, and auburn hair cut short like a boy's. She was wiping her hands on the apron worn over her jeans. She was not happy to be thus exposed to the public, but stood there patiently as if she had been through this routine before. She had the same lovely smile as Mrs. Pappas, though her eyes sparkled with a wary defiance her docile mother could never have mustered. Her father spoke to her in Greek. She replied in English. He growled, took her arm, and pulled her over for an introduction. Her name was Helen. Then he hustled his wife behind the counter and disappeared into the kitchen, peeking momentarily from one of the diamond-shaped windows. Helen and I awkwardly faced each other.

"I think we're supposed to start hearing violins," I said.

She regarded me grimly, then cocked her head and smiled. "Would you like a cup of coffee?"

I nodded. She filled two cups with American coffee. We went and sat in a booth. Mr. Pappas' appraising eyes appeared fleetingly in the kitchen doorway, then disappeared.

Helen folded a napkin marked with a trident into a fan, then smoothed it out. "Pop's a good guy. He enjoys grumbling, but he means well. He's just convinced if he doesn't do something I'll be an old maid or, even worse, marry someone he doesn't approve of. So he drags me out whenever there's an eligible Greek male around. When you came in with the money just now, skyrockets must have gone off in his head. Thanks, by the way; you saved our lives."

"My pleasure," I said.

"Look," Helen said, "I already have a boyfriend, but Poppa doesn't approve of him."

"Tell me about your boyfriend. Is he Greek?"

She laughed. She had a nice laugh. "No. That's the problem. John is Scotch Protestant. A WASP, for God sakes. Can you imagine? But he's no bum. He's got a good landscaping business and he's really ambitious. Just the kind of guy Pop would like me to marry, but he's the wrong eth, as in ethnic. He doesn't have an 's' at the end of his name."

"Don't give up hope. Your father will come around. Meanwhile, we should dream up a story to tell him. We're hitting it off so well he's probably on the phone lining up a priest and a bouzouki band. How about this? Say that I am trying to get a business going independent of my family, but I can't even consider the possibility of marriage until it's successful. It could take years, and it would be unfair to put a claim on you. The business could fail, then I'd have to start all over again. It's just a delaying tactic, but it will give them time to get used to John."

She grinned. "Perfect."

"Great." I finished the coffee and stood up. "It was nice meeting you. Thanks for the coffee. And good luck."

I ambled over to the counter and hugged Mrs. Pappas again. She gave me a small white box tied with a red ribbon. Pericles had come out of the kitchen. I shook his hand and wished them both good luck in the restaurant. With a last glance at Uncle Theo up on the wall, I headed out, carrying my payment of baklava.

The Poseidon case had been enlightening as well as profitable. Perry said a dope drop was canceled. Nothing remarkable about that. What was odd, though, was the date. Kip Scannell had told his cousin Kate July thirteenth would change their lives. And then he died.

CHAPTER 20

My aunt Aphrodite from Astoria owned a homely mongrel named Hermes who was part sheepdog, part timber wolf, and slightly larger than a Volkswagen. Hermes was the sole object of my aunt's affection, having replaced three husbands who happily worked themselves to death in the restaurant business and left her a wealthy woman. In spite of a ferocious feral look, caused by an unfortunate underbite, Hermes was a good-natured slob who frequently sought release from his pampered life. On these occasions he'd joyfully wander about the countryside looking for something dead to roll in.

When I was a teenager, Hermes went AWOL during a visit from my aunt. My mother handed me the keys to the family car and assigned me to find the dog, quietly, before Aunt Aphrodite missed him and went into hysterics. He wasn't hard to locate. I followed a trail of terrified children and overturned garbage cans and found Hermes in a field contentedly chewing on an old ham bone.

Tracking Hermes may have been the genesis of my detective career. Collaring him was something else. After a half hour of playing catch-me, I gave up and decided to fetch my aunt. When I opened the car door to leave, Hermes jumped in and licked my face.

The incident taught me a good lesson. As Aesop pointed out in the Tortoise and the Hare, the race is not always to the swiftest. Or in Soc's Corollary, don't get in a sweat chasing something you can make come to you.

I was recalling fond memories of Hermes and my aunt, both now dead, as my truck crept along behind a Volvo station wagon with Connecticut plates. Two kids made faces at me out the back window. The snail's pace suited me fine. I had deliberately taken Route 6A home, cutting across to the north side of the Cape from Hyannis, because I knew traffic on the Old King's Highway moved slower than conversation on a blind date.

The two-lane road meanders prettily along the shore through a historic district and past graceful captains' houses built a century ago by deep-water skippers who seldom saw them, past velvety marshes, salt meadows, and glimpses of distant water. I paid little attention to the scenery. I was oblivious to calendar art in the raw no matter how charming. I wanted to think.

I was thinking about Aesop again. When you grasp at shadows, he says in the fable of the Dog and the Shadow, you may lose the substance. Kip Scannell was mostly shadow. Every time I tried to get a handle on him, he eluded me. Larry had given me one side of him, Kate Scannell another. Lady Brett had added still another dimension, but I didn't have much confidence in a female impersonator who did such a lousy impression of Judy Garland. I felt like a police artist drawing a composite of a suspect based on witnesses who describe a suspect by saying he had hair, two eyes, and a mouth.

Now I had something solid. The connection between Kip and the drug drop was tenuous, to be sure, but if I believed it was coincidental, I'd still be setting out cookies and milk for Santa on Christmas Eve. I made a face at the kids in the station wagon. They giggled the way kids do and ducked their heads, only to pop up a moment later.

What next? I could continue my brilliant detective work and hope another connection would serendipitously surface. I could go on chasing shadows. Or I could use the Hermes gambit, which had worked when nothing else did. I turned off Route 6A and waved good-bye to the station wagon; the kids waved back enthusiastically. I stopped by the boat house to get rid of my mean clothes. Ten minutes later, I swung by the fish pier, parking near the bulkhead where a pretty white-hulled Maine lobster boat was tied up.

The thirty-five-foot boat was named *Sprite*. She belonged to Geetch, who cared for her as lovingly as some men treat a mistress. Geetch was puttering about the pilothouse when I stepped aboard. He seemed glad to see me. He didn't get many chances to show her off.

"Hi, Geetch," I said. "Could you to do me a favor?"

He stopped polishing the metal fittings with a chamois cloth. "Anything, Soc. Just name—" He caught himself. "Except for dough . . ."

"Naw," I said, sitting on the engine housing. "Nothing like that. I'd like you to shoot your mouth off."

He gave me a blank look.

"Let me explain," I said. "You knew Kip Scannell, didn't you?"

"Yeah. Kinda. Seen him around . . ." Geetch avoided my eyes and started rubbing a compass housing vigorously. "That was his boss . . . at the Hole. . . . You clocked that fat kid. . . ."

"That's right. Here's the thing. I've picked up some scuttlebutt that says Kip was involved in dope. Big time."

He stopped his polishing. "Jeez, Soc. Dope. Wow." Geetch used oral shorthand when he got excited. "You really onto . . . ?"

I winked. "Fill you in as details develop. But here's the pitch. The way I heard it, Kip had something to do with a major load of stuff. Supposed to come in a couple of weeks ago on July thirteenth. I got the inside track and I'm going to bust this thing wide open."

Geetch shook his head. "How come, Soc?"

"I'm sick of fishing. Sam's a great guy, but I want to get into the detective business in a big way. If I can bust this case, I'll get my name and face in the papers. The publicity will be terrific advertising. Clients will be banging on my door. But I need your help. I'd like you to get it around that I'm going to break open a case that involved Scannell and a dope drop on July thirteenth. That's the important part, the date. Say that I'm going to spill the beans on the whole mess. Can you do it?"

He took off his beloved cap and wiped his thinning hair with it. "Yeah, Soc. Dope. Pretty heavy . . ."

I got up and patted his bony shoulder. "If you want to exaggerate a little," I said with a wink, "that's okay with me."

Geetch gave me a Machiavellian wink of his own. "No problem. Elsie's place first. . . . Then the Hole . . . The whole world will . . ."

In the old myths, Daedalus figured out how to pass a

thread through a spiral shell. He bored a hole in one end, tied a thread to an ant, put the little critter through the hole, and it navigated the twists and turns, coming out the other side. Maybe Geetch could do the same thing for me.

I gave him a thumbs-up sign and stepped off the boat. "I'm counting on it," I said.

Chief Francis Xavier Farrell was grinning like someone who'd won Mass. Megabucks.

He sat at his desk and grunted affably into the phone that was largely lost in his hand. He gestured toward a chair when he saw me in the doorway. I went into his office and sat down.

"Don't worry about a thing," he purred lionishly, drawing out the vowels. "No problem at all. You've got a job to do and you did it. Nobody can blame you for that. Ooh . . . kaay. Buh-bye." He slammed the phone down, glowered at it, and scornfully hissed through his teeth, "You insignificant little worm. Hah."

"Hah?"

"Yeah. Hah. What of it?"

"You don't know a guy named Pericles, by any chance, do you?"

Farrell said, "Yeah. Trooper out of the Framingham barracks. Polish guy. No, wait. His name was Pulaski. Any relation?"

"Never mind," I said.

Farrell leaned back. "That was the chairman of selectmen on the phone," he said. "Remember the little bar fracas with the tourist? The selectmen held a hearing the other day. They were after my scalp. Know what happened?" Farrell was triumphant.

"Either you're wearing a toupee or they weren't too successful."

"Hah. They almost got fired themselves. Tourist never showed up to lodge a complaint. But a big crowd of townspeople came out to back me up. Lot of the ex-hippies I left alone even though I know damn well they were growing a little pot for home consumption. And the old retired folks I'd been nice to when they drove up on the sidewalk or backed into town hall and knocked off a few shingles. They beat up on the selectmen. Threatened to kick them out of office come election if they touched a hair on my sweet little head." He smiled smugly and gripped an imaginary steering wheel. "Hell, I'm even getting a new cruiser out of the deal, so I can junk that antique I've been driving."

"Congratulations. And thanks for letting me take a peek at this," I handed Farrell the Kip Scannell file.

"Oh yeah," he said, suddenly interested. "Anything in there?"

"Not too much. Nothing conclusive. But I wouldn't be surprised if Scannell had a little help getting dead."

Farrell whistled softly. "JesusChristAlmighty." His nostrils flared like an old hound who'd heard the distant horn of a hunt. "What the hell have you got?"

"No smoking gun. The whole deal just smelled from the beginning. Scannell's death was completely out of character. Car crash on the way home from a bar. Or shot by an angry husband, maybe. But not snagged like a flounder. Scannell had spent more time underwater than most fish. Divers know their limitations. They tend to get more careful with age. I guess it was Kip's weight belt that really started me thinking."

"What about his belt?"

"Scannell was diving with enough lead on him to sink the *QEII*. The idea is to have just enough weight to make you neutrally buoyant. That means you don't go up, or down, unless you want to. A guy his size needs maybe thirty-five pounds, but Scannell was carrying around fifty. He would have swum like a rock with that extra fifteen pounds hanging on his belly."

Farrell tapped his cheek pensively. "Yeah, I was there. The EMT guys had a hell of a time lifting the body onto a stretcher."

"Uh-huh. There's more. Most divers carry one knife. Scannell carried two, one strapped to his leg, a smaller one on his arm. That tells me he was a guy who liked insurance. So picture this. Scannell gets caught in the net. He reaches instinctively for a knife to slash his way out. Maybe he was too tangled to use it. Maybe he drops it. But Kip's knives never left their sheaths. Too damn neat. You can help on this next thing. Was Scannell wearing a hood when his body was found?"

"Naw. I remember because the guy had blond hair, almost white. Long, like a girl's. Maybe the hood got ripped off in the water."

"Practically impossible. The hood tucks under the suit. It fits real tight, like a rubber glove. So if the hood didn't come off, maybe it was never on. Kip would not have left his boat without his hood. You dive with no head protection in these waters and you'll freeze your brain within minutes. Hood's almost as important as your air tank. Okay, you say. There are questions about Kip's gear. Doesn't prove zip. I agree. There's something else, though. The strong possibility Scannell was in a high-risk business. And I don't mean diving."

Farrell crinkled his brow. "Spit it out."

"Does July thirteenth mean anything to you?"

He scowled. "Nope. Should it?"

"There was supposed to be a major drug delivery on the Cape that day."

Farrell slapped the desktop with his palm. "Damn. So *that* was it. I started picking up street talk this spring. Rumors about something coming in. But I can't do much about it unless someone unloads a boat load of bales at the town pier. How's Scannell figure in this?"

"Scannell let it be known that he was expecting to make the score of his life on July thirteenth."

"Aha. So you figure he was knocked off in a drug deal."

"The thought had crossed my mind. That still doesn't explain why someone would kill him."

"All kind of things coulda happened." Farrell said. He ticked his theories off on his fingers. "Maybe Scannell wanted to cut in on the big boys. Maybe he didn't pay his bills. Coulda got careless, flashed a roll or shot off his mouth."

"Maybe, maybe and maybe."

"You got a theory?"

"Nope. But Scannell was real nervous about something. I'd guess he was playing it real close to the edge, and for high stakes. Kip was cautious, but you can't keep looking over your shoulder all the time. Even the best plans can get screwed up. Reminds me of my uncle Alex and the apple pie."

"Could be," Farrell said. He tapped the Scannel file. "This isn't exactly grand-jury stuff you've dug up. Scannell was in the drug business and got himself killed. Big deal. Happens all the time, maybe more than we know."

I got up to go. "You're absolutely right. I couldn't even get through the DA's door with what I got, which isn't much when you come right down to it. I'll scratch around. Shake a few trees and see if any fruit fall out."

"Hmmph," Farrell grunted. "Just be sure no fruit bonks you on the noggin, Socarides. If you get into any heavy-duty stuff, call in the troops."

"Don't worry chief. I'm not in the market for another Purple Heart." I gave him a thumbs-up. "Semper fi."

Farrell managed to laugh without breaking any windows. "Semper fi," he roared. "Hah. Waitaminute, what was that you said about apple pie?"

"Something my uncle Alex used to say. He ran a greasy spoon in Brockton. We had to eat there occasionally to keep the family peace. My mother carried a cloth to wipe the dishes clean when Alex wasn't looking. Anyway, Uncle Alex always gave me the same advice. He'd put his arm around me and say that if I was in a strange city and didn't know where to eat, to find a Greek-run restaurant, which was usually pretty easy, and order the apple pie. You can't go wrong, Aristotle, he'd say, you can't go wrong."

"What's that got to do with Scannell?"

"I don't like apple pie."

Farrell crinkled his brow. "So?"

"Simple," I said. "It just goes to prove that even when you *can't* go wrong, you *can* go wrong."

CHAPTER 21

It was around noon when I left Farrell's office and drove to Provincetown. My stomach must have overheard me talking about Uncle Alex's apple pie, because it was rumbling. I stopped at the Portuguese Bakery on Commercial Street, bought six of the meat pastries called Pasteis de Mesa Tenra, and had them zapped to a juicy sizzle in the microwave oven. Then I walked out onto the wharf and climbed aboard the *Shamrock*.

"Lunch time," I yelled. "Anybody home?" Eileen Barrett emerged from the wheelhouse. She was wearing the green bikini again. Eileen was among the one percent of the female population over the age of eighteen who can wear a bikini and make it look the way it was intended. She was blessed with a body that was boyish, with slim hips, and well-formed breasts on the smallish side. But not too boyish, not too slim, and not too small.

"Oh," she said. "It's you."

The greeting was underwhelming, but I persisted, waving the paper bag. "Peace offering. Portuguese meat pies. Get 'em while they're hot."

She didn't smile. There was a glimmer of amusement in her eye, though. I had caught her in a moment of weakness.

"I must have been sending hunger vibrations out all over town," she said. "Hold on." She went down to the galley and reappeared minutes later carrying paper plates, napkins, wineglasses, and two cans of Coca-Cola Classic. She had put on a workshirt to preserve her modesty. I could understand that, even if I didn't like it. We dragged a couple of deck chairs over.

The meat pies were shaped like half-moons. Eileen bit

gingerly into the hot brown crust. There was something erotic about the way she neatly wiped the grease off her mouth, but maybe it was in the eye of the beholder. "Mmmm," she said. "You know what I like best about these? I like finding that little green pimiento olive. It's almost like . . ."

"Like finding treasure?"

She grinned wryly. "Yes," she said. "A lot like finding treasure."

We munched in contentment for a few moments. "What brings you to Provincetown?" she said. "Business or pleasure? If you're looking for Michael, he went to Hyannis to meet a prospective investor. He won't be back till tonight."

"I was looking for Mike. I'm glad to bump into you, though."

"Oh?"

Not exactly loquacious, but hope springs eternal.

"I was hoping we could talk. Civilized. Not casting stones. Or aspersions."

"Mr. Socarides . . ."

"Soc."

She wiped her fingers clean with a napkin. "Mr. Socarides," she said firmly. "It's nothing personal. I'm eternally grateful to you for saving Michael the other day. He could have died. And you showed surprising presence of mind during that frightening affair with the bomb. Now you've seen how this whole treasure business can warp reality. This project has become an obsession with Michael. And I'm afraid it will break his heart."

"I don't get you, Ms. Barrett."

"I'll be blunt, then. I don't believe Michael has found the *Gabriella*."

I wasn't expecting this bombshell. My meat pie almost landed in my lap. "Hold on. What *did* he find?"

"I think he's found a wreck, but that it's not the ship he's been looking for."

"What about the coins, and the cannon?"

"I've seen the coins and pictures of cannon, but that doesn't prove a thing. In archaeology, artifacts alone don't tell the whole story. You have to know *how* they got there. Let me give you an example. A few years ago salvors off Florida found British cannon on a 1715 Spanish wreck. Does that mean the wreck was British? Of course not. It only means the cannon were. The sea off the Cape is littered with wrecks. Michael may be only a hundred feet from the *Gabriella*. He may be a thousand feet. Hold on, I want to show you something." She went over to a deck locker, came back with a clear plastic bag, and handed me the dull gray object inside.

It was a plate, on the heavy side, octagonal in shape, around nine inches across, with decorative beading along the edge. I looked up at Eileen. "Pewter?"

"That's right. Now look on the back."

I flipped the plate over. Stamped in the center was a circular cartouche about an inch high. The circle enclosed a prancing unicorn and the name Joseph Foster.

"Michael brought the plate up on one of his first dives," Eileen said. "Pewter's a great find because it's usually in a good state of preservation and relatively easy to date. That mark is called a touchplate. The design identifies the person who made the piece. Pewter manufacturing was strictly regulated for centuries by the London pewterers' guild. After you served an apprenticeship to a master pewterer for at least seven years, you could be elected to the Freedom or Yeomanry of the London Company of pewterers. Then you were allowed to go into business for yourself and strike your own touchplate. It had to go on every piece you made. Thousands of touchmark designs were recorded and documented. Each mark tells its own story."

"What did this mark tell you?"

She ran her forefinger over the unicorn. "The book of marks says Mr. Foster was elected to the Yeomanry on February 24, 1757, and that he opened a shop at 236 Leather Street in London."

"That fits," I said. "The *Gabriella* didn't go down until 1778."

"True," Eileen said. "But that's only half the story, the part I told Michael."

"Tell me the other half."

"All right. Even after an apprentice got his freedom he might go on working years for a master as a journeyman before he could strike his own mark. First he had to save enough money to go into business for himself. Then he appeared before a board with his master to vouch for him and did a test piece. Mr. Foster was apparently short of pounds and pence. His touchplate wasn't struck until 1783."

I rubbed the plate on my knee and examined the mark again. "I think you're telling me this plate was made at least five years after the *Gabriella* went down."

"Right. Even if Michael has found the ship, the site may be contaminated by another wreck. Not necessarily English. Most of the eating utensils you'd find on any ship back then would have been made in England. The English manufacturers had cornered the market. This could have come from a Spanish or French vessel. Personally, I think Michael has found a small English schooner of war wrecked in the same general area. It would have been carrying cannon."

"My God. Have you told Mike this?"

"No, I haven't. When I first began to have doubts, he was already heavily invested in the project. I didn't want him hating me for dashing his hopes. I couldn't stand that. There was always the chance I was wrong. So I did nothing. I hoped for a miracle. When he lost the site data, I breathed a sigh of relief, thinking that would end it. That he'd be forced to give up the search and I wouldn't be responsible. Then you showed up with the promise of finding the missing material. I overreacted."

"Paradoxical, don't you think? You're also aiding and abetting this project."

"True, I'm afraid. I was glad to help when Michael asked me to come on as ship archaeologist last year. I've been doing grad work at Harvard. That's why I was near the Square the night we met. Michael was on the bounce from a broken marriage and a failed business. I thought it would do him good to plunge into this project, that it would take his mind off his troubles."

"Obviously, you see things differently now."

"Yes, I do. I never guessed how utterly the project would possess him. He had a touch of treasure fever at the beginning, with all the crazy fantasizing and unreal expectations that go with it. But now he thinks of little else. I know I'm overprotective, which is silly when you look at the size of him, but I always have been, and I guess I always will be."

"It's not silly at all. You love him. There's no need to make excuses. I can see why Michael would be single-minded. There's a lot of money involved."

"It's not just the treasure now. I think Michael was after the money at first, but now that's just become a means to an end. He's so consumed with the desire to reconstruct the past that he's lost sight of the present. Sometimes I think the poor souls lost on that ship are more real to him than the living. It makes him tilt at windmills."

"Do you plan to tell him he may be on a wild-goose chase?"

She studied the horizon. I watched the way the sun gleamed in her red hair. "It may have gone too far," she said. "I'm not sure if it would dissuade him at this point. He's determined to go down in the books as the man who found the *Gabriella*."

"Well, from the way my investigation has been going, you may not have to worry about that possibility."

"Please don't get me wrong, Mr. Socarides. This is certainly a worthy project from many standpoints. It's been fascinating for me."

I handed back the plate and she put it in the bag. "Tell me a little about your historical research," I said. "I've just heard bits and pieces."

"It's been quite a labor. There weren't a lot of dependable historical data. The Royal Navy normally conducted an exhaustive investigation when a ship was lost. There was an inquiry, but it was more perfunctory than thorough."

"The British were losing a country," I said. "Maybe one ship didn't seem that important."

"Perhaps. There are a few good sources. The record of the inquiry and the cargo manifest. I even went to London to look in the navy archives."

"But that didn't tell you where the ship was."

"Correct. We narrowed the search area down as tightly as we could, then Michael began his magnetometer surveys. After a lot of hard work he found a concentration of cannon, anchors, and ballast rock. On the strength of that discovery he got a reconnaissance permit from the state, made some dives, and picked up coins and wood. Then he applied for the excavation permit so he could start digging, and began dredging up investors to finance the work. But soon after he got his permit to excavate, Kip drowned and the *Gabriella* papers disappeared. You know the rest."

"Let's put your doubts aside for now and assume for a

moment that he has found the *Gabriella*. Would the wreck be intact?"

Eileen went into the pilothouse. I watched her go. Yep. She definitely had the best figure I'd ever seen on an archaeologist. She returned with a clipboard. "Most people think of a shipwreck as a whole ship sitting on the bottom, masts and all. But it's not like that in these waters. Look at this."

The diagram in the clipboard showed the shoreline and arrows pointing away from a cross-marked wreck site. "The *Gabriella* would have broken to pieces on the sandbar here, and the currents and tides spread the wreckage for hundreds of yards. The wreck site would have been closer to the beach, which has eroded in the last two hundred years. The deck cabins and the mast and rigging would have gone over first. The cannon and ballast would spill into a concentrated area. They'd be on top of the hull. Before long everything would be covered with sand."

"Where would the treasure be?"

"It was stored in or near the captain's cabin where he could keep on eye on it. When the ship sank, its own weight probably drove the hull into the sand. The treasure would be in the vicinity of the hull." Eileen widened her eyes and put a Bela Lugosi quaver in her voice. "Today the treasure lies in the briny deep guarded by the skeletons of British redcoats pointing their bony fingers at intruders who would deprive them of their pay." She grinned. "The press loves quotes like that."

"Quite a story. Did you ever learn what became of Lieutenant Powers, the first mate?"

She cocked her head. "You've been doing your homework. So you probably know Powers survived and gave his version of the disaster at the admiralty inquest. Losing a ship was a hanging offense back then. The surviving officers could be made to pay with their lives. Ultimately, the ship was the captain's responsibility. But as senior surviving officer, Powers could have been in for a rough time. Even if he weren't hanged, his naval career could have been ruined. So he was smart enough to paint a picture of the captain acting against his advice. Apparently he was convincing. The captain was dead and couldn't defend himself. Powers stayed in the navy and eventually retired. I believe he died in his sleep."

"I read part of his diary, but it stops with the rescue."

"That's right. There are further entries much later, but nothing more about his naval career. Powers was recuperating from his ordeal in the months following the wreck, then he had to contend with the court-martial. He did start a diary after he retired, but it mentions nothing of the sea."

"Quite a saga," I said. "You don't sound like someone who's new to the game."

"Marine archaeology is relatively young and many of those in the field are serious amateurs like me. The first ship excavated under archaeologically controlled conditions was in the 1960's off Turkey. For years the land archaeologists said you couldn't excavate properly underwater. Today they say nobody *but* an archaeologist should get his hands on a wreck. They'd have a wreck sit on the bottom another hundred years rather than risk some gold-hungry treasure salvor plundering it."

"Maybe the archaeologists have a valid point."

"I agree. As an academic I believe a shipwreck is a unique piece of history that should be brought to light scientifically. As part of a treasure-hunting expedition I've seen what a heartbreaking and expensive occupation this is. Any professional archaeologist who works for a commercial salvor is shunned as a pariah by his colleagues. The archaeologists want it all their way, and I can't go along with that. I'd like to see salvors and scientists work together. Florida treasure salvors, after all, developed the use of the magnetometer and mailboxes."

Eileen tended to rattle off like an oral history text, but when she forgot herself, she talked with a passion that reminded me uncomfortably of her brother's. I had the feeling that if I ripped the cover off the book I'd find the contents were X-rated.

"Mike feels the same way?" I asked.

"He's even less compromising. Michael's taken a lot of criticism from professional archaeologists, and it hurts, because he is very much aware of the historical significance of his work. The barbs have hardened his feelings, and made him even more driven. He's become proprietary about the *Gabriella*. You'll notice he calls it 'his' wreck. Michael is unequivocal. He believes if you're willing to risk life and money to find a wreck, it should belong to you. That you should fight for your turf."

"Sounds like war."

"It is. Even after you find a treasure you have to battle for it. But it's always been that way. William Phips was probably the first commercial salvor. In 1687 he took treasure off the *Nuestra Señora de la Concepción* galleon in the Caribbean. He had to face rebellious divers, bargain with rival salvors, and outrun a French privateer. Then the Spanish tried to put a claim on the treasure. Mel Fisher, who found the *Atocha*, had to fight the state of Florida in the courts to keep his treasure. There have been other court cases in Texas and Massachusetts. Even Congress has gotten into the act."

I made a sharp detour in the conversation. "Tell me," I said. "What did you think of Kip?"

Eileen took the question in stride. "Kip was a good diver," she said. "His death was a great loss to the project."

"I understand that, but you still haven't answered my question. How did you feel about him?"

She smiled. "I forgot about your persistence. Well, if you must know, Kip and I didn't get along very well. He tried to add me to his string of conquests right at the start. I had to step on his toes. It was sort of a cold war after that."

"What was Mike's relationship with him?"

"Michael tried to be professional, but they clashed sometimes. Kip constantly questioned Michael's decisions. He seemed to forget it was Michael's project. But I don't think that would've changed things even if it had occurred to him. Kip was just very headstrong and liked to meddle." It was Eileen's turn to detour the discussion. "But enough of Kip. How about you? How did you come to this point?"

I made it short and sweet. "I was born in Lowell where my family has a thriving frozen pizza business. I studied the classics in college, did a stint in Vietnam, worked for the Boston Police Department, retired early, and now live in a boat house that might get blown away in a good wind. I keep body and soul together fishing on a friend's trawler. I own a twenty-two-foot fiberglass Privateer I use for scalloping or flounder fishing. And when I'm not fishing, I do a little detecting."

She frowned. "Your family is Greek, isn't it? I thought pizza was Italian."

"That's what the Italians say. We Greeks look at it this way. The Romans stole all kinds of Greek culture, so we've just taken some of it back, improved on it, and do a better job of marketing and distribution. You can find a Greek mom-and-pop pizza house in practically every city and town in New England. My parents started out that way before they went from retail to wholesale. We can further explore the historical perspectives of Greco-Roman cultural transpositions over dinner some time this week, if you're agreeable."

She regarded me with those incredible blue eyes, casually twisting strands of coppery hair between her fingers. I studied her, visually caressing her soft mouth, her flawless skin, the graceful curve of each brow. Our eyes locked. Then the instant passed. But it had been there, bursting with possibilities. No doubt about it.

She laughed. "You summed up your own history rather succinctly. Surely there must be more than that. For instance, were you ever married?"

"Almost," I said. "When I was a Boston cop. I was still dealing with Vietnam. Still waking up in a cold sweat and smelling death. I was carrying a lot of baggage. Lot of guys went through it. Then I met a woman who helped me rejoin the human race. The nightmares stopped. Life started to have meaning again. We got engaged. Might have been a good thing."

"What went wrong?"

"Fortune's wayward tyranny, Sophocles would have called it. She was driving home from tending a sick friend. She was killed when a bunch of drunken Charlestown kids in a stolen car slammed into her. I moved down here not long after that. I've steered away from serious involvements, though. Makes life less complicated. Whenever I feel myself weakening, I go fishing for a few days. Or I take a case and get wrapped up in somebody else's problems."

She looked down at her hands. "I'm so sorry," she said. "I've never had to deal with anything like that."

"Tell me about yourself."

"Compared to yours, my life has been pretty uneventful. My parents were poor working class like most everyone else in Southie. We grew up in the housing projects. Mom and Dad both died comparatively young, so Michael and I were on our own almost from the first. I attended Girls' Latin, got some scholarships, and went on to college. I've been working so hard to cut the ties to the old neighborhood that I haven't had much time for personal life. There have been a couple of men, but what starts out as a romance seems to end up as friendship. When the salvage project is over and after I finish my degree work, I'll have more time to think about other things."

I watched the sunlight play in Eileen's hair and wished I could do the same, thinking that she was one of those women who men fall in love with as naturally as breathing. They go through life never quite aware that behind them lies a trail of men, living in a purgatory of frustrated yearnings, who have become their friends only because they can't be their lovers. Maybe Eileen wasn't like that. Maybe she could brush her career or her brother or her own undefined ambitions away without even thinking about it. But if I weren't careful, I'd have a charter membership in the Eileen dream club, paying my dues with silent longings and unrequited wonderings. It took about three seconds to throw caution to the winds.

"About that dinner?" I said.

A wary look flashed in her eyes. Curses. Back to no-good drunken bum. Then she smiled. "The lunch you brought was my idea of food heaven. But I'd be delighted to accept your invitation. I'm going to Boston tomorrow, and I'll be back the next evening after the state board meeting. I'll call you and we can arrange a time."

We stood and faced each other, inches apart. We didn't speak, but there was communication, definitely, electrically, on a very primitive level. Sight, sound, and smell. All senses of distance. Maybe touch and taste would come later. I said good-bye and shook hands like a proper Victorian gentleman, climbed back onto the pier, and walked toward town. It had been a productive lunch. A history lesson, a dinner date, and more confusion about the *Gabriella*. Was she a phantom or not? I was beginning to wonder.

Footsteps padded behind me. "Excuse me, sir!" I looked over my shoulder. A guy in a plaid sports jacket loped along the pier in my direction. A canvas photo bag slapped against his hip. I waited until he caught up. Rivulets of sweat trickled down his face.

"Hi," he said, gasping for breath. "You probably don't remember me."

I looked him over. "Sure I do. You're Cooper, the *Herald* reporter from Boston. Barrett give you a good story the other day?"

He shook his head and wiped the perspiration off his face. "It would have been better if my editor let me write about that clash out in the hallway. God, I thought those two guys were going to start World War III. My editor said I was exaggerating for dramatic effect. I wasn't, was I?"

"Your editor was all wet."

He laughed. "Thanks. That makes me feel better."

"You in Provincetown to sample the waters?"

"I'm nosing around for a story on the *Gabriella*. Say, do you work for Barrett?"

"Sort of. You could call me a consultant."

He checked me out, from the earring to the leather sandals I was wearing.

"You don't look like a consultant."

"What's a consultant look like?"

"Yeah. See your point. Would you mind if I asked you a few questions?"

"You can try. I don't have to answer them."

"Fair enough. I've been hearing two versions about the *Gabriella*. First, that Barrett doesn't have diddly-squat. That he hasn't found the ship. And even if he has, the treasure's probably long gone. Second, that the treasure is much more fabulous than anyone thinks. What's the *real* story?"

"Take your pick. Whatever makes a better headline. I don't think anyone knows. There's only one way to get at the facts. Go down there and take a look."

"No thanks. They don't pay me enough to imitate a fish. Bad things can happen underwater. Besides, the whole thing may become academic."

"Talking about the permit?"

"That too. I've been asking around. Barrett's up to his eyeballs in debt to the banks and other places. Even if he holds on to the permit, I don't know how long he can keep his operation together. He needs a quick infusion of cash. You've got to give investors something for their money. They won't shell out on the basis of a few coins, especially with people going around saying he salted the wreck with mail-order pieces of eight."

"I've heard that story. Doesn't make sense. Suppose Barrett were operating a scam, he could only carry it so far. He'd need to come up with hard evidence eventually."

"True. But he could keep going for a good long time,

living well on investment money. This deal falls through, he finds another project, another boat load of suckers, and he's off again. Florida. Bahamas. Not a bad life."

"You may be being too hard on him. Treasure hunting's a tough racket. Give him a little time. If he doesn't back up his claims, then you can draw-and-quarter him."

"God, I don't want to pillory the guy. I'm just looking for a story."

"I know where you can get one. Barrett's out of town, but his sister is on board the *Shamrock*. She's beautiful and she's smart. Ask her about the bony fingers of British soldiers."

"Huh?"

I started down the pier.

"Hey, wait a minute, I didn't catch your name."

I stopped and said, "I didn't throw it. My name is Aristotle."

"Aristotle." He gave me a what-do-you-take-me-for look. "Right. And my name is Plato," he said. I smiled and continued along the pier. Plato? I think he may have been pulling my leg.

CHAPTER 22

Somebody with a rich contralto voice was trying to get my attention. "Yoo-hoo, shamus. Over *here*, you silly boy."

A large man in a short-sleeve, flamingo-hued safari suit waved frantically at me from an outdoor café on Commercial Street. I walked over to his table. In his hand he clutched a giant drink the same shade as his outfit. He wore a Panama hat with a peacock feather in the black band. The wide brim was rakishly rolled up on one side like a fancy French pastry. His sunglasses had oversized split bamboo frames and blue-bottle lenses. A Malacca walking stick leaned against his fat thigh. He wore pale green snakeskin cowboy boots with high heels and pointed toes. He smelled like a perfume factory.

"Haven't we met someplace before?" he crooned. "Tangiers, perhaps, or Paris?"

I sat down. "More likely Tijuana or Hoboken. I don't get around much these days. And one gin joint looks like the next after a while."

"True," he sighed. "Sad but true." He wiggled his fingers at a passing waiter. "Would you like a drink, Mr. Sleuth?" He held his glass to the light as if it contained a fifty-year-old Bordeaux. "I highly recommend the Lady Brett cocktail. They named it just for me."

I glanced at the concoction with a gimlet eye. "What's in it besides Pepto-Bismol?"

"Triple sec, vodka, grenadine for starters."

"No thanks. The last time I drank out of a fishbowl I got seasick and the little paper parasol got stuck up my nostril. I'll have a Bud," I told the waiter.

Lady Brett clucked like an indignant hen. "Well, if you must."

When the beer arrived I slurped the foam off the head and said, "You may have blown my cover. But I'll forgive you this time because I was on my way to see you."

Lady Brett blew a wet kiss to a handsome young Narcissus who walked by with springs in his Reeboks, and turned back to me. Despite his name and delicate ways, and a couple of pounds of eye shadow, Brett was definitely no lady. You can't say he didn't try, but he had big, strong-looking butcher's hands and the physique of a wrestler. He was probably six feet tall without his beehive wig on. He fluttered his fake eyelashes. "Well, this *is* my lucky day. Were you coming by to tell me you solved the Kip caper? Maybe we should call it the Cape Kipper." He giggled. "Kip did end up like a sardine, after all."

"Still working on it. I thought maybe you could help."

"I'll help any way I can," he said agreeably.

"I appreciate that. I've asked around. Some people in town say you and Kip were in business together. Something to do with a string of gay bars up in Boston."

Brett flicked his manicured fingers with an airy gesture of dismissal. "*Some* people in this town are dreadful gossips. You know how rumors start."

"No, I don't," I said ingenuously. "Tell me about it."

"Oh, you impetuous savage," Brett breathed. "There's nothing sinister about all this. Kip was a thrifty lad who made a tidy sum from his diving. But he didn't have a drop of business sense in that pretty blond head. As an acquaintance and successful business person, it was perfectly logical for me to suggest investments."

"What kind of investments?"

"Vice."

"That's not exactly a blue-chip stock."

"To the contrary. There's nothing sounder. Just about everybody profits from the sex dollar. The hooker gets a good price for her product. The churches and the politicians sermonize us about the evils of the flesh as they're passing the hat. The vice-squad boys get a week's pay and all the graft they can carry. I simply put Kip in touch with people in Boston whom I knew through my club. I'll bet even you private eyes do a bit of networking. Kip may have owned a few stools in a leather bar, but it wasn't my business."

I grinned. "What exactly *is* your business?"

Lady Brett leaned forward onto one elbow. His voice dropped a couple of octaves. "Long before I was big enough to try on my mother's dresses," he said, "she told me the story of the curious little boy who wanted to see what was in the cave and was devoured by a hungry lion."

"I must have missed that one. Did your mother ever tell you about the diver who was involved in drug smuggling before his rather inglorious and highly suspicious death?"

Lady Brett took out a lacy pink handkerchief and removed his hat. His head was shaved completely bald. He dabbed at his polished scalp and carefully replaced his chapeau. "If you mean Kip," he said, "I suppose *anything* is possible. But foul play? Oh my. What exactly do *you* think?"

I crossed my arms on the table and leaned so close I could see my distorted reflection in the Vick's Vaporub lenses.

"I think you want me to think you're an airhead who's got an identity problem and a hormonal imbalance, that's what I think. You *are* kind of a doll when you're wearing makeup, anyone can see that."

"I'm flattered."

"Don't be. Because I'd bet my Captain Midnight decoder ring that the black heart of a wheeler-dealer beats under that cuddly, bubble-bath exterior. So here's where it stands. I make a few calls to my friends on the Boston vice squad—you know, the guys taking all that graft. I'll bet they know all about you. Then I call the Bureau of Taxation and Corporations, the IRS, and the state alcoholic beverages commission."

"Why, I do believe you're trying to frighten me."

"You catch on quick. How about this for scary? The town fathers might be interested in knowing who your business associates are when your liquor license comes up for renewal. And I'll bet there are hundreds of bored bureaucrats sitting around in government enforcement agencies who'd get a kick out of costing you thousands of bucks in legal fees and hounding you into bankruptcy. You might even have to close your charge account at Bloomingdale's. Of course, you could be clean, but it's amazing how bad a manure pile smells when you turn over a few shovelfuls."

Lady Brett's mouth widened in a crimson clown smile. I would have been willing to bet the eyes hidden behind the sunglasses didn't have little laugh crinkles at the corners.

"You have the Greek gift for metaphor, Mr. Socarides. You're truly missing your calling as a writer of fables."

"I've always preferred fairy tales. Try this one on for size. Goldilocks has a partner who's a potential embarrassment. He's been getting into some foolishly high-risk ventures and might be caught. He knows a little too much about Goldilocks and her business with the three bears. Goldilocks arranges for an accident. People have been killed for a lot less."

Lady Brett tapped his fingers together in a prayerful attitude. "I assure you this Goldilocks had nothing whatsoever to do with Kip's death. Assuming it wasn't an accident. Surely you don't think I was involved."

"Me? Oh, of course not. But you know that some people have nasty minds. And if I thought throwing you to the big bad wolves would stir up some action, I'd have to do it. Nothing personal."

Lady Brett's eyes narrowed. "If I *did* tell you what you wanted to know," he said slyly, "might I expect a little quid pro quo?" He offered a coy translation. "I scratch your back, you scratch mine."

"If you're asking me to keep your name out of the papers, that would depend on the quality of your information about Kip."

"Fair enough." Brett ordered another drink that looked like an upset-stomach remedy. "First of all, any suggestion I was involved in poor Kip's death is absolutely preposterous. I've read enough trash detective novels to know private eyes like to bluff their suspects into a dramatic confession, so it won't work with me, darling. But no one likes his laundry washed in public, particularly in a small and politically charged community like this. So I'll be perfectly candid with you. Kip wasn't gay. As you suggested, his interests lay elsewhere. Tsk, tsk. Such a waste."

"So why the masquerade?"

"The story was a cover for his occasional business meetings with me. The natives do get upset over kinky goings-on around the bas-relief commemorating the signing of the Mayflower Compact, but sexually speaking, pretty much anything goes in P'town. As long as it's between consenting adults. Kip had no doubts about his manhood. The game amused him. He said it even helped him with seductions.

Wolf in sheep's clothing, you see. Every woman longs deep in her heart to convert a gay man."

"What about your joint business ventures?"

"Kip and I were partners in a few bars in Boston and the suburbs. Lately, he had a lot of money to invest. I didn't ask him where he got it. Our investments were all perfectly legal, I made sure of that. Some people may view that as laundering dirty money. I saw it simply as investment diversification. No different than dabbling in the stock market."

"People who play the stock market don't usually end up dead in a fishnet."

"If you're implying that Kip's drug connections, if he had them, got him into trouble, you may be right, darling. On the other hand, you may be wrong."

"On the other hand, I'm probably right. Did Kip have any other business partners?"

"He sometimes mentioned them in passing, but never by name. I wasn't the only one helping Kip dispose of his money, and I'm sure there were those who helped him make it in the first place."

"Did anyone hold a grudge against Kip?"

"It would be hard to find someone who didn't dislike Kip. Disgruntled husbands or boyfriends. Spurned females. When one indulges in bedroom Olympics, one runs more than just the risk of venereal disease. He made a few enemies with his business dealings too. Kip didn't care who got in the way of his ambitions. I was aware of this aggressiveness and could deal with it. Even use it."

"Did Kip ever talk about his salvage work?"

Brett waved his hand airily. "Only that he liked diving a great deal. But I had the impression it was a close third after money and women, in that order."

"Did he ever mention Barrett, his boss?"

"Sparingly. I got the idea the big boy was a fanatic about this shipwreck business and a bit of a bore."

"What do you know about July thirteenth?"

If I hoped to catch Lady Brett by surprise, it didn't work. "What about it? The week after the Fourth, I suppose."

I drained the last of my beer and got up. "Thanks for being so cooperative."

"No problem, darling," he gushed. He was either doing Tallulah Bankhead or Humphrey Bogart, I couldn't tell which.

"It was simply *grand* seeing you again. Maybe sometime you can catch my act."

"Maybe I just did," I said.

If the Pilgrims were alive today, they might wonder why their 1620 landfall in the New World was marked by a monument of Italian Renaissance design, but they'd probably appreciate the gesture. The Pilgrim Monument was copied from the tower of Torre del Mangia in Siena, Italy. The tower is more than 252 feet high. It was built on a hill that raises it another hundred feet over Provincetown. At the top is an observation platform where you can see Cape Cod's slender arm wrapped around the bay like a teenager cuddling his first drive-in movie date.

After leaving Lady Brett, I walked over to the monument and bought a ticket, thinking the gull's-eye elevation might give me some perspective. There's no elevator in the monument. There are 116 stairs and sixty ramps between you and the top. It was like climbing the Matterhorn. My body was paying for many nights of dissipation. My tongue hung out as I cleared the last ramp of the tallest all-granite structure in the United States and stepped out onto the observation platform. There were about a dozen sightseers ohing and ahing over the view. I limped to the chain-link fence and made a breathless and totally insincere vow to lead a cleaner life.

A muzzy haze lay over Cape Cod Bay, blurring the distant dunes and low-lying hills to a few impressionist brush strokes. Marked by its stubby white lighthouse, the narrow spur of Long Point hooked in from the right. Provincetown lay at my feet. Its confusing jumble of narrow lanes and closely built antique houses crowded the edge of the harbor. Two long wharves jutted from the beach. Farther into the harbor, a freestanding stone breakwater sliced across at a right angle to the wharves. Fishing boats maneuvered inside the horseshoe formed by the wharves and the shore, and the whalewatch vessels took on passengers for the afternoon trip to see the humpbacks.

Provincetown looked like a maze. It's easy to get lost in a maze. Pathways leading nowhere. Blind alleys. All meant to bewilder, like the Cretan labyrinth, whose twisting passages trapped those who entered. Theseus strung a ball of thread behind him so he could find his way out after killing the Minotaur, the half man, half bull creature that liked to dine on young Athenians. He simply anchored a ball of thread to the door and strung it out behind him and unwound it in the maze. I quartered the town, looking for a place to tie one end of my thread to, and my eyes came to rest on a black-hulled boat with two stovepipes at the stern. The *El Toro*. I wanted to know why Lucas would name his boat the Bull. But there were a lot of things I wanted to know.

It took only a few minutes to descend to street level. I ambled over to the harbor. The *El Toro* was moored about a hundred yards from the beach. A pram was tied alongside, so somebody was on board. Borrowing a dinghy, I rowed to about twenty feet from the boat and yelled Lucas's name. A few seconds later he leaned over the rail, a wolfish smile on his face. He waved me aboard. I tied up, climbed a ladder, and stepped onto the deck.

Lucas said, "So you took my advice and dumped that creep Barrett."

"Nope. I'm still working for Mike. This is just a social call. Sort of."

Lucas eyed me as if I had just offered to sell him the Cape Cod Canal.

"Whassat mean?"

"It means I want to know why you call this boat *El Toro*."

He chortled. "That's *all* you want to know?"

"Not really. It'll do for a start, though."

"Huh. I thought so. No big secret. The boat is named after me. That's my nickname on account of the way I do things. I stick my head down and charge full speed ahead. Anyone in my way gets knocked down. Bango."

"That's not the way it works in the bull ring," I said. "When El Toro goes El Bango, he ends up El Deado."

"Yeah? Well that's the way it works with me. So, has Barrett found the *Gabriella* yet? You don't have to answer. He doesn't have a rat's ass of an idea where it is."

"And you do?"

"Yeah, I do. I found it before Mr. B. Remember? And if it hadn't been for the state's stinking red tape, I'd be counting my treasure by now."

"You really think there's a big treasure out there? Some people say the moon cussers got to it before anyone."

"Yeah, I heard that. I also heard she was carrying a big redcoat payroll. Gold too. If the locals scoffed up the treasure, they'd never be able to keep it secret. Some of that stuff would have worked its way into circulation by now. I think it's still down there. Barrett's going to lose his permit and I'll start scooping treasure off the bottom into my bank account. Want in on the action? I'm still open."

"No, thanks. I'm still gainfully employed. Tell me," I said, "did you ever try to hire Kip Scannell away from Barrett? He was a top diver, I hear. It would have hurt Barrett's project if he came over."

"Might hurt mine too. Remember me telling you about my crewman, the guy who told Barrett about my silver wreck down in Florida. That was Kip. Maybe he was drunk, and maybe he wasn't. I probably would have fired him even if he hadn't screwed me. He was a good diver, but a boat can't have two captains. Kip likes to run things. He kept butting in and caused a hell of a mess. That's just the way he was, always trying to be one up on the other guy."

So Kip worked for Lucas. That was a new one. I pitched a spitball from the outside, slow and curving. "Scuttlebutt says Kip was in on some dope stuff. Ever hear anything like that?"

Lucas squinted, then chuckled. "Yeah, you weren't just interested in the *El Toro*. P'town's a pretty tight place. You hear things. Kip may have picked up some change moving stuff. But so what, a lotta guys do that."

He caught the unspoken question in my eyes. "Naw, not me. Made a run once in Florida and got lost in a fog bank looking for the mother ship. Coast Guard found me. I was lucky. Guys on shore were nailed with a couple of vans fulla grass. Got some tough questions from the grand jury, but the DEA wanted the big guys and didn't waste time on me. It was a good lesson. Looking to salvage treasure doesn't always give you a day's pay, but if the cops do come around, it's to make sure nobody steals your gold."

"What are your plans if you get Barrett's permit?"

"No ifs about it. Sure thing. Especially when the state board hears how he pulled a gun on me. I may even call you as a witness." He made a sweeping arm gesture. "Boat's set to go. I'll relocate the wreck, blow the sand off, and start diving."

"How do you think Barrett will react?"

Lucas smiled unpleasantly. "I hope the overgrown ape chokes on a banana skin."

I rowed back to shore and dropped by the East End bar where Kip Scannell was last seen in public. The après-beach crowd was straggling in for liquid dehydration treatment. I sat at a table near the front window, where I could watch the Commercial Street traffic, and ordered a Bud draft. When the waitress put the frosted mug in front of me, I asked her if she knew Kip Scannell. She had the dark hair and pale complexion you see on many women of Portuguese extraction in Provincetown. She was about forty and attractive; twenty years earlier and she would have been stunning. Her name was Rose, she had worked at the bar a long time, and she was talkative. "Sure, I knew Kip. You a friend of his?"

"Friend of a friend, but I feel like I've known him all my life. I do some diving. Lot of the guys have been talking about his accident. I guess he came in here a lot."

"Enough so I knew he liked Black Horse Ale. And boy, was he putting them down the last night he was here."

"Sounds like Kip, all right."

"It was and it wasn't. Kip's usually a fanny pincher when he has a few. But he was a real sourpuss that night. Just kept drinking and drinking. Sat right at this next table, in fact. Dumped a drink on another customer. She got bent all out of shape. That was the last anyone saw of him."

"Did he say he was diving the next day?"

"He wasn't prepping for a dive, if you ask me. He was getting ready for a giant hangover, that's all."

"Sounds like he was waiting for somebody."

"I think you're right. And I'll bet it was a woman. Whoever she was, she didn't show and he was getting ticked off. Kip wasn't the kind of guy who got stood up."

"Maybe he got lucky and found someone else to leave with."

"Could be. But I didn't see it. I was straight out. Hotter'n hell that night and everybody in the world was in here trying to cool off. Nice talking to you."

She whirled off to take an order. I sipped the foam off my beer and looked out the window. Commercial Street was at its narrowest here, just over one car wide. The front window of another bar was only yards away. I drank up, crossed the street to the other place, and ordered a beer, carrying it to a window seat. There was a clear view of the table where I'd just been sitting. I drank my beer slowly, and when it was gone, I left.

Near the end of MacMillan Wharf about a dozen fishing boats were clustered like a Hong Kong floating village. I asked a fisherman on one of them if Joe Santos were around. He directed me to the edge of the pack. I climbed across three draggers and stepped onto a rusty vessel that had seen some hard time at sea. Santos was unraveling a tangle of nets.

He looked up when he saw me. "Hey, the treasure diver," he said cheerfully. "Dig up any bombs lately?"

"Uh-uh. I'm too old to wet my pants. How about you?"

"Barrett gave me the day off. Gives me the chance to catch up on my own boat."

"You do much work for Barrett?"

"Off and on. You could never tell with those guys. He and Kip would go whenever they felt like it. Day or night."

"Night? Must be pretty hard to look for treasure at night."

"Guesso. I never went out on night trips. They didn't need me. Said they were doing electronic stuff. That was okay. My wife puts up with enough crummy work hours as it is."

I looked over his boat. It was smaller and wider than Barrett's. "It must be fun to run the *Shamrock* for a change," I said.

"Oh yeah. This is a real workhorse. Drives like a dump truck. The *Shamrock* is sweet, even in dirty weather. She'd get temperamental sometimes, though."

"What do you mean?"

"Hard to explain. Some days she'd have a mind of her own. You handle boats, so you know what I mean. Wheel just feels different."

I went over to a pile of pale green monofilament net and poked it with my toe. "How do you like gill netting?"

He made a face. "I don't. Stuff catches fish, but it's not real fishing, if you ask me. You throw the thing over, it hangs there, and the fish swim into it. Then you haul it up and pick the fish out. Most of the guys around here still use trawls. That's more like hunting. Find the fish, set your net, and scoop 'em in."

"Why do you keep doing it?"

"I ask myself that fifty times a day. The answer is simple. They catch more fish. More fish, more money. What kinda fishing you do?"

"Hook and lining. I'm a purist, I guess."

"You're lucky. Maybe when I pay off the mortgage on this rustbucket, I'll get back into trawling. Gill netting's too much like factory work. Boring. Sometimes I wish all my nets had been ripped off."

I gave him a sharp look. "What do you mean?"

"I had a net stole from the boat coupla weeks ago. It was an old one, so I didn't give a damn." He laughed. "Maybe someday they steal the whole boat and I get smart and open up a fish market."

I picked up a section of gill net and pulled hard against the mesh. The nylon dug deep into the fleshy part of my hand and left thin pink welts on my skin. A simple but effective killing machine any way you looked at it.

Leaving Santos to his work, I walked back to my truck in the town parking lot. I was preoccupied and didn't notice the black van with the tinted glass until I was halfway home. It followed me until I turned off to the boat house. I made a note of the license-plate number and watched it continue by, like last time. And just like last time, it didn't stop.

CHAPTER 23

The Federal Express man knocked on the boat house door about a half hour after I got home from Provincetown and handed me a parcel as thick as a Manhattan telephone directory. Norma had worked fast. I went into the kitchen, sat at the kitchen table, and opened the package. Inside was a packet of papers and a letter:

Dear Lover Boy:

That was some assignment. Reminded me of the corruption cases I've handled in the Commonwealth. As the French say, the more things change . . .

I assigned three of my best operatives to chase down the info you were looking for. There were the obvious sources like the state archives, Massachusetts Historical Society, and maritime museums. But if you really want to learn about your ship, you go to the British Public Record Office. That's where you find Royal Navy data like ships' logs and court-martial proceedings. Then there's the admiralty archives and Lloyd's of London, contemporary press, broadsides and pamphlets, and so on. I called in a few markers in London and had the info faxed across the Atlantic and it lies now in your hot little hands.

Here, in brief, is the skinny on your shipwreck.

The *Gabriella* manifest lists payroll worth a couple of hundred pounds sterling scheduled to go to the British troops in Philadelphia. But the Brits were evacuating Philly, so the payroll stayed on board with some five tons of crown-owned gold bullion, stored in chests and supposed to go to New York for safekeeping. Plus personal goods being spirited out of town by the Tories before the rebels got them. Taking an educated guess, though, I'd say a big hunk of cash wasn't on the manifest.

To explain: The Revolution made a lot of good British citizens rich. They defrauded the crown of huge amounts of money. There's one estimate corruption cost King George twenty million pounds sterling. More than a hundred million bucks back then. And that was before the IRS, so it probably would have been billions in today's dollars.

James Michael Curley (bless his dishonest heart) would have been green with envy. He didn't come close to that in all his years as mayor of Boston and at least the poor people got a hodful of coal out of him on Christmas.

The guys scoffing all that cash from the Crown were the quartermasters. They ran the commissaries that provided supplies to the army and navy. They'd steal horses and carts and livestock from the locals and charge the government inflated prices or put together sweetheart deals with their friendly contractor in return for a kickback. The Philadelphia Commissary of Prisoners appropriated two-thirds of the dough that was supposed to buy food for the prisoners. A lot of our guys starved to death so some official could line his pocket.

Some of those vultures were on the *Gabriella*. Crooks are not known to entrust other human beings with their money, so I would say there is prima facie evidence anyhow that the ship carried a pile of dirty money. How much is impossible to say.

The whole thing seemed cut and dry until I read the court-martial record a couple of times. Take a look and see if you see what I see.

I picked up several sheets of paper from the admiralty library headed "Minutes of the Proceedings of a Court-Martial Assembled and held on Board His Majesty's Ship *Intrepid* at London on the 12th day of November, 1778."

"His Majesty's late Frigate *Gabriella*, having on the 21st

day of June 1778, run aground at Cape Cod, where she was totally lost, when on her passage from Philadelphia to Halifax," the board was directed "to try Lieut. Thomas Powers and such of the surviving Officers and Ships Company of His Majesty's late frigate *Gabriella* for their conduct on that occasion accordingly."

The Royal Navy did not take the loss of a ship lightly. Lieutenant Powers was the highest ranking officer aboard the *Gabriella* to survive, and his neck or at the very least, his career, was plainly on the chopping block as the board, made up of eleven captains and presided over by a rear admiral, gathered in the *Intrepid*'s great cabin.

A letter from Powers was presented, giving his version of the disaster. Two surviving crewmen were brought in and asked if they thought the *Gabriella*'s loss "was occasioned by any misconduct on the part of Lieut. Powers." They answered no. Then the lieutenant took the stand and expanded on his written comments.

Powers politely blamed the late Captain Morton Dinsmore for the loss of the ship. He was mildly critical of Dinsmore's decision to continue on to Nova Scotia once they had lost the French ships pursuing them. He testified that he had advised Dinsmore against running with full sail at night before a high wind. He said he questioned the course laid out by the captain as taking the ship too close to land, but Dinsmore pooh-poohed his doubts. Powers implied that since this was the first time he served under Dinsmore, the captain may not have had full confidence in him. Also, Dinsmore was worried about the leaking ship.

In any event, the captain changed the course plotted by the master. Navigation was still somewhat of an inexact science. On top of that, Dinsmore had been going with no sleep for twenty-four hours and was exhausted when he calculated his position. His figures were off and he was actually further west than he had assumed. The combination of miscalculations and storm winds drove the *Gabriella* onto the sandbar, where the surf hammered her. Under the pummeling, the cannon broke their lashings and skidded across the decks, smashing into crew and passengers. Some people climbed into the rigging to escape the loose cannon and the seas sweeping over the deck, but that haven was short-lived. The mainmast was the first to go and the rest of the rigging followed.

After all hope for saving the ship was lost, the captain ordered his gig, which was a personal lifeboat, made ready to launch while he burned documents, dispatches, and the signal book in his great cabin. Powers and the gig's crew got the lifeboat ready, lowering it partway, and waited for Dinsmore.

Pounded by a succession of giant seas, the ship heeled sharply over and capsized. The gig was knocked into the sea. The gig's crew drowned. The captain went down with his ship. Powers made it to shore alive. The next morning he and the other survivors were rescued by the British sloop *Nautilus*.

The court-martial board next examined a man named Stark, master of the *Gabriella*. He was legally responsible for the navigation of the ship under the command of the captain. Under British navy regulations, the master was supposed to warn the captain of potential danger. Or if the captain was not available and the danger was imminent, he had to tell the lieutenant of the watch, who happened to be Powers.

Stark had laid out a course that would have given the *Gabriella* plenty of sea room even with the storm shoving them closer to land. When Stark came on deck to relieve Powers, he was alarmed to discover the captain had ordered a new course. He saw danger in the new heading. But because the exhausted captain had gone to bed, Stark testified, he told Lieutenant Powers it would be wise to shorten sail and change course immediately.

Stark was quizzed about the on-deck exchange.

Q: What was the reaction of Lieutenant Powers to your advice?

A: He said he was reluctant, because of his newness to the ship, to press the captain on this matter, but that he would do what he deemed best.

Q: Did Lieutenant Powers, to your knowledge, convey your warning to Captain Dinsmore?

A: I don't know for a fact, sir. But the course remained as it was.

Q: Did you attempt to press your opinions on the captain yourself?

A: I was only on the ship five days out of Philadelphia and assumed my conversation with Lieutenant Powers would be sufficient.

Stark concluded Powers would tell the captain of the master's forebodings. Yet there was no change in orders. The ship, now less than a mile off the Cape, kept its disastrous course. If Stark had any doubts Powers had relayed his message, he wasn't, as a new man, likely to go over the lieutenant's head. He didn't see Powers again until after the wreck.

The question was put to Stark directly.

Q: Do you have any reason to believe Lieutenant Powers did *not* carry your warning to the captain respecting the danger in running on this new course?

Stark was on sticky ground here. The court-martial might understand his reluctance to go directly to the sleeping captain, given his short tenure as master on the ship. But Lieutenant Powers could be in hot water if he had been too timid to exercise his duty and failed to tell the captain of the master's warning. Stark's answer could be the smoking gun. Tension was probably high in the great cabin as Stark pondered his response. He didn't indict Powers, but he got his doubts across in a subtle way.

A: If Lieutenant Powers said he spoke to the captain on this matter, I must presume it to be so, sir.

The next question went directly to the heart of the inquiry.

Q: Do you believe the loss of the frigate *Gabriella* was due to any misconduct on Lieutenant Powers's part?
A: I have no knowledge of that, sir.
Q: Did you see Lieutenant Powers in the captain's boat?
A: No, sir, I was too busy trying to save the ship and helping those trapped under fallen rigging.

Again, the criticism was implied. Powers was sitting in the captain's gig while all hell was breaking loose and his crew and passengers struggled for their lives. There were certainly grounds to question Lieutenant Powers's conduct as an officer, but curiously, the court-martial was short and perfunctory. No more witnesses were called after Stark. A letter from a Royal Navy official named Harcourt was read in Powers's behalf, attesting to his sterling character and superlative skills as an officer and urging not only that Powers be exonerated, but commended for his behavior.

The cabin was cleared, the board members deliberated, the audience readmitted, and the verdict read: *"That the Court is of the opinion that the loss of His Majesty's late Frigate the* Gabriella *was occasioned by the captain's haste, and by his failure to heed the warnings of his officers."* No blame was attached to Powers or others in the ship's company, who did everything possible to save the ship and *"they were acquitted accordingly."*

I went back to Norma's letter.

"Pretty interesting, eh? I hope you picked up the name of the guy in the letter saying what a terrific officer Powers was. Now look at document B."

I read the copy of a letter in which Powers applied for leave several months after the court-martial. He said he needed rest to regain his health, which had been impaired "in consequence of my late suffering." A navy document showed his promotion to commander a few years later. Shore duty at Bristol. A newspaper clip noted his marriage to one Sarah Harcourt, daughter of the late naval quartermaster of Philadelphia. Another showed he retired to the country, far from the ocean breezes, and died peacefully, leaving several children and many grandchildren.

Back to Norma:

> Okay, Mr. Detective. Why did the court-martial bend over backward to whitewash Powers when there was at least some circumstantial evidence indicating that he didn't have the guts to tell the captain the ship was in danger and he beat it the first chance he got? Why did the quartermaster send a letter on his behalf? And how come the cozy relationship with the quartermaster's daughter Sarah?
>
> The other papers are pretty interesting, but I think there may be some stuff not here that holds the key to the main question: What happened to the

dough? I've got a lead I'm chasing down. In the
meantime, if you're not doing anything, give me a
jingle. Max is home for a couple of days, but he's
scheduled to leave town. Hmmmm?

I smiled and prepared to plow through the documents.
But first I called the florist and ordered a bouquet of roses
for Norma. I made sure they were long-stemmed.

CHAPTER 24

The next morning I put on my bathing suit, smeared my body with enough tanning oil to fill a Liberian tanker, stretched out on a chaise longue, and cooked like a sirloin steak in an overhead broiler. Contrary to appearances, I was working. Feedback is essential in an investigation. You have to stop, catch your breath, and bounce ideas off a willing ear. I poured a glass of canned lemonade from a plastic thermos and looked over at Kojak. He was in a cat coma at the edge of the deck. His ratty fur was streaked with dust.

"Kojak," I said, "let me run this by you. See what you think. The view from all fours, so to speak."

He opened one eye a slit and twitched his tail.

"There's this dead diver, see. And maybe somebody did him in," I said. "Probably connected with dope stuff. Dope is sorta like catnip for humans, Kojak. Costs lots of money and makes 'em chase their tails. Anyhow, this guy was business partners with a lady in Provincetown who is really a man. And he worked for a big bearded fellow who says he's found an old ship that has lots of treasure on it. But maybe he hasn't found the ship. And maybe there's no treasure. I've got two days to figure it out, and I'm not doing so well. Any suggestions?"

Kojak twitched again.

"Okay, put that one on the back burner for now. Chew on this. A beautiful rich lady shows up at my door. Says the Mob is going to bop her husband. But the wise guys say they never heard of him. And he acts like the only thing he's worried about is the supply of Stolichnaya vodka running out. Oh yeah. How come the state cops are tailing him? And how come I got knocked on the head when I made a move on the rich lady, which serves me right for trying the monkey around with a client. And why was my gun stolen and my truck trashed?"

Kojak yawned, jumped off the table, and sauntered into the house.

"Thanks a lot, buddy," I said to the back of his head. "I'll remember this at munchy-munch time." I closed my eyes and lay back to enjoy the sunlight on my face.

The cordless phone rang on the table next to my chair. It was Souza.

"Hey, Soc, you know that chauffeur guy you asked me to check on?"

"You got something?"

"Yeah. You still got an eye for spotting bad boys."

I sat up in the chair. "Tell me about it."

"Name is Eddy Merkin," Souza said in his marriage-counselor tone. "Eddy the Wheelman, they call him. Didn't know we had such a distinguished citizen living in our town. Originally from Chelsea. Worked on boats around the Boston fish pier as a kid, so he can handle himself on the water. He's been up on assault and battery, assault with intent to murder, and that sort of thing. Suspected of driving a get-away car on a couple of robberies. But his specialty is auto theft. He could hot-wire your ignition and deliver your chariot to a chop shop while you were buying coffee to go at Dunkin' Donuts. Got sloppy one day and was invited for a vacation at Cedar Junction. The Commonwealth of Massachusetts in its great wisdom let him out early. Good behavior and the fact the jails are bursting at the seams."

"Looks like you'll have to keep an eye on that young man," I said.

"Already got his file in my cabinet. Don't know what he's doing working for a big shot like Nichols. Guy must be interested in rehabilitation."

"Either that or his wife is," I said.

I thanked Souza and hung up, then fetched my Rolodex from inside, looked up a number, and punched it into the phone.

"State police," a woman answered.

I asked for Mr. McCormack. Seconds later a sandpaper voice rasped, "As I live and breathe. Is it yourself? Mr. Socarides."

"That it 'tis. And I'll be needing some information from you."

"Well now. It won't come without a price."

"I'll buy you a beer at the Hole."

"Gag. No thanks. I'm allergic to trench mouth."

"Aw c'mon. It's not that bad. Well, it's almost not that bad. Okay, martinis at the Harbour Club."

"Now you're talking. Fire away."

I shaded the truth slightly. "Got a client who's been asked to do a business deal with a contractor named Charles Nichols. Good move or bad?"

McCormack whistled. "If I were your client I'd find something safer, like a deed to the Brooklyn Bridge. Nichols is hotter'n a ten-dollar pistol."

"He's not connected with the Mob, is he?"

"Hell, no." McCormack lowered his voice. "Nichols has got his own deal going. He disposes of unrespectable money through respectable channels like real estate and construction. He's a double-dipper too. Takes government contracts and swindles Uncle Sam by padding the payroll with nonexistent minority workers."

"Uncle knows this, of course."

"Of course. And he's a bit peevish. The U.S. attorney's been getting stuff together for a bust. Our office, the FBI, and the DEA have been keeping an eye on Nichols in case he decides to fly the coop. He may know what's coming down the pike. Funny you should mention the Harbour Club. One of our boys followed Nichols there the other night. Got roughed up in the parking lot by some goon and had his tires slashed. Guy blindsided him."

"He get a look at his assailant?"

"Naw. Probably some two-bit gorilla Nichols hired for protection."

"That must be it," I said. "Thanks for the info. I'll tell my client he'd best invest his dough in soybean futures."

"Good idea. He'll be reading about Nichols in the papers soon enough. Just forget where you got the stuff I told you."

"Okay. But I'll remember I owe you a beer at the Hole."

"I thought it was martinis at the Harbour Club."

"Jeez, Mac. I'd love to. I dunno after your guy getting beat up there. Sounds too dangerous."

"You're a card, Soc. 'Bye."

The doorbell was ringing. I hung up and went back through the house and opened the wooden screen door. Two things stood on my front doorstep. They were definitely not the Jehovah's Witnesses who sometimes stopped by on their missionary rounds. I wished they were.

One of them was around six feet tall and looked like he could use a square meal. His gaunt face was a moon surface of pockmarks. He had a purplish five o'clock shadow on his shaven scalp. He wore cheap sunglasses with upturned plastic frames, dirty jeans, and a green and puce Hawaiian shirt with a design like an old tattoo. He was all tics and jerky movement. He couldn't keep his hands still. He touched his nose, his chin, wiped his jeans, started over again. The guy definitely had a problem and it was making my skin crawl.

Behind him was a long-haired man about five foot ten. A single thick eyebrow slashed darkly across his swarthy forehead. He was dressed in black jeans and a black leather vest over a black T-shirt. The shirt had a picture of a coiled snake and the words *Cobras Motorcycle Club, Fall River*. Charming. He looked like one of those fungi you find growing in your yard after a lot of rain.

A dusty black van stood in my driveway. The door was open. A couple of foam cubes hung from the rearview mirror.

Fungus spoke. "We're looking for a guy named Socarides."

I guess he meant me. "You found him," I said.

"Our boss wants to have a word with you."

"Who's your boss?"

He smirked. "I'm not at liberty to say. But he surely would appreciate a few minutes of your time." He wasn't pretty, but at least he was polite.

Skinhead stepped forward. "We'll even give you a ride." He gestured at the van.

"No, thanks," I said. "My mother told me never to ride with strange men who hang fuzzy dice from their mirror. Have your boss give me a call."

I started to close the door.

Skinhead reached around to the small of his back. He must have been wearing a hip holster because he pulled out an ASP 9mm P. He laid the short black Teflon-finished barrel across my left cheek and leaned in closer.

"Did your mother ever tell you about this? Suck on a lollipop, scumbag."

The move caught Fungus off guard too. He was smarter than he looked, and was trying to sweet-talk me along. It might have worked.

"Am I supposed to be quaking in my boots?" I said.

My mouth sometimes works as if it were independent of my brain. A bluff may be smart when you're dealing with a rational person, but Skinhead definitely wasn't playing with a full deck. Probably stuffed firecrackers in a frog's mouth as a kid. My voice sounded as if it were coming from deep in a cave. My voice was cottony. I was thinking about that twitchy St. Vitus finger on the trigger.

Skinhead was even more surprised at my reaction than I was. He gaped, revealing bad breath and an orthodontist's dream. He played with his tongue, trying to think of a snappy comeback. I saved him the trouble.

I slammed the heavy wooden door and held on to the knob, digging my heels in. The hard edge scrunched his skinny arm against the jamb. I tensed, expecting an explosion to remove my ear and half my face. Skinhead shrieked with pain instead. Some tough guy.

The gun dropped from his hand and thumped onto the floor. I scooped it up and kicked the door open. Skinhead clutched his right arm and whimpered. His partner backed away.

I held the pistol under Skinhead's chin. In my best Dirty Harry imitation I said, "You're about to become the first man in history shot dead with a lollipop." I put my mouth close to his ear. "Bang," I whispered softly.

"Hey," his partner said. "Take it easy with that thing."

I said, "I don't usually shoot people who come to call, but in your case I may make an exception. This is my town. I know every cop on the police force by his first name. I also know the judge. Coached his kid in Little League. The team wasn't very good but I'd bet the old man wouldn't get any more excited if I offed you guys than if I got a speeding ticket. Tell your boss that if he wants to see me he makes an appointment. I'll count to three, and if you're not out of here I'm gonna start using you for target practice. One . . ."

Fungus grabbed his partner, who was examining his arm, and pulled him toward the van. Skinhead went along reluctantly, looking back at me with murderous glances. They got in the van, but didn't start the engine. Dammitall. I should have followed them out. The van could be filled with UZIs and hand grenades. Skinhead's pride had been hurt, and he looked crazy enough to try to blast his way back.

A black pickup truck pulled into the yard. Barrett stepped out. He looked at me standing in the doorway with a gun in my hand, then at the pair in the van. They looked at him, all six foot five, and apparently decided it would be dumb to go up against a guy built like an eighteen-wheeler, guns or not. The van took off down the drive in a cloud of dust. The potholes in my road can rattle the teeth in the back of your head. I hoped they broke an axle on the way out.

Barrett came over. "What the hell is going on?"

"Just a couple of Girl Scouts peddling cookies." I hefted the gun, hoping my shaking hand wasn't obvious. "It's amazing what they can do in the kitchen. Looks almost real? Come out on the deck. We'll have some lemonade and talk about it."

I put the gun in a hall-closet shelf where Kojak would be unlikely to find it. He's an awfully smart cat but I wouldn't want him licking the sweat off the trigger.

Barrett and I went onto the deck. I portioned out the rest of the lemonade.

"Eileen said you came by the boat yesterday looking for me," Barrett said. "Anything new on the case?"

"Wish I could say yes. I'm still trying."

Barrett slammed a fist into the palm of his hand. "Damn," he said.

"We still have a couple of days, Mike. Don't give up hope yet."

"It's not you, Soc. I just heard the NOAA weather report on my radio. There's a storm due in three days. Even if we find the charts by the board's deadline, the whole *Gabriella* site could be obliterated by the time I get out there."

"You could find it again."

"Sure, but any delay could kill me. I'm running low on money. I can barely afford to fill my gas tank. This project was short on capital to begin with. I had to borrow hundreds of thousands for the boat and equipment. There might be mechanical problems or more bad weather. Lucas could sock me with a lawsuit. My legal bills are already incredible. It could be weeks before I get on site again and any chance of investment money will go out the window."

"I'll do my best, Mike. That's all I can say."

Barrett sighed heavily and stood. "I know you're trying, Soc. Look, I want to apologize for the other night. Showing up here without warning then going off without even saying good-bye. I was in a weird mood, I guess."

"No need to apologize. We all have our moods. I'm glad you stopped by. I wanted to ask you a few questions about Kip. Did he always stay on the boat?"

"Only nights when we were working," Barrett said. "When he wasn't there, I just assumed he was staying with a girlfriend. Didn't know about the place on the dunes. Why do you ask?"

"The dune shack is a damned inconvenient place to live. It's a pain to get to. No electricity, running water, or telephone. If Kip did have another place to roost, he may have stashed your papers there. There's something else, Mike. I think Kip was murdered."

Barrett mouthed a silent *what?*

"I don't have any solid proof, but there's circumstantial evidence pointing in that direction."

"I knew it. Lucas."

"Hold on, Mike, it may be more complicated than that. Did Kip ever give you any reason to think he might be involved in the drug trade?"

"I knew Kip did drugs on a recreational basis, but he stayed clean when he was diving and that's all I cared about. Was he dealing? Can't say. Anything's possible, I guess. You think it ties in?"

"People have a tendency to play hardball when there's big money at stake."

"Did those two freaks who piled out of here in such a hurry have anything to do with this?"

"Maybe. I expect to know fairly soon."

"Murder. I can't believe it, I just can't believe it." A hard look crossed his face. "I'm sure you know what you're doing, Soc, but if you're right, things could get nasty. I'd like to help you even up the odds."

"I may take you up on that."

I told Barrett I would get in touch with him as soon as I knew anything. About forty-five minutes after he left, the phone rang. A friendly voice said, "Mr. Socarides? My name is Jones. I understand my boys were a little rude to you. I'm really sorry about that. I had asked them to invite you to chat and not to take no for an answer. They tend to follow my orders literally at times."

"You'll have to be careful about that," I said. "You might hit your finger with a hammer someday and say 'shoot' and who knows what might happen."

"Hey, that's cute, Mr. Socarides. Very cute. I'll remember your advice. For now, though, I'd still like to talk. This time you pick the spot."

I thought for a few moments. "Sure. I know just the place."

I gave him directions and hung up. Geetch, my little ant, had done a good job navigating the shell and come out on the other side. And the Hermes gambit had once again proven its worth.

CHAPTER 25

——

Guglielmo Marconi was looking cross-eyed at me, real unhappy to be where a sea gull could drop a load on his bronze pate. A couple of gulls already had. Marconi and I hobnobbed about a hundred feet from the easterly ramparts of the continent where the outer shore of Cape Cod drops steeply to the beach and the Atlantic Ocean.

Back in 1903 Marconi came here in the flesh to send the first transatlantic wireless message winging across the ocean from four high steel towers perched on the cliff. The note he relayed from Theodore Roosevelt to King Edward VII started off, "Taking advantage of the wonderful triumph of scientific research and ingenuity" . . . bleh, bleh, bleh, snore. The message wasn't exciting as messages go and neither was the king's reply. But it was history. So the National Park Service stuck a bust of Marconi on a granite pedestal just above the ruins of the old wireless station in South Wellfleet.

It was a good place to meet Mr. Jones. It was public. There was sometimes a park ranger about. And the ocean view from the bluffs was splendid. A steady procession of tourists came and went along the narrow blacktop walkway that led to the parking lot. The shutters of their motor-driven cameras made a constant *kerchunkwhizz,* capturing the scene on film again and again.

Arriving ahead of schedule, I leaned on a split-rail fence near Marconi and kept a lookout for Mr. Jones, zeroing in on faces like the lens in a Hitchcock movie. Still, I hardly noticed the short, pudgy man until he broke from the parade of sightseers and sat at a nearby bench. He had a goatee, curly balding black hair cut short, thick horn-rim glasses, and a cherubic butter-wouldn't-melt-in-his-mouth smile on his moist lips. He wore wrinkled chinos and a white long-sleeve shirt with the sleeves rolled up. There was a clear plastic pen holder with a couple of ballpoint pens and a calculator sticking out of his pocket. He looked at the stylized sculpture of Marconi, then he looked at me.

"That's quite a face. Lots of character, intelligence, and determination."

"I dunno," I replied. "Looks like Mussolini."

"Well," he said. "I'll bet you're Mr. Socarides."

I nodded slightly.

"My name is Jones." He came over and stuck out his hand.

I didn't take it. "What can I do for you, Mr., ah, Jones?"

"Hey, man, I don't blame you for being a little irritated. My two guys were way off base. I've given them hell."

"That's okay. Good help is terribly difficult to find these days. But I'd suggest you send them back to the worm farm you got them from."

Jones chuckled. "Worm farm. Hey, that's cute. Very cute. You ever think of doing standup stuff at one of the comedy clubs around Boston?"

"No." I said, "Let's go for a walk."

We strolled down the short incline to the concrete foundation of one of the old wireless towers. It used to be further inland, but erosion chews off around three feet of cliff a year, and the remains of the foundation lie at the edge of the bluff. I stopped next to a snow fence that borders the cliff. Ribbons of surf advanced on the beach far below, their roar a distant whisper.

Jones stepped out of the way of a skinny tourist with a camera. I guess he didn't want his face gracing the photo album of some family from Iowa. We continued along the path and paused, off by ourselves, next to the big-timbered sand anchors and rusty chains that once held the wireless tower guy wires.

"All right, Mr. Jones," I said. "What can I do for you?"

"Okay, man," Jones said. "I'll come right to the point. A few days ago someone calls and says you're asking questions about Arthur Scannell. I get a little curious, so at first I just have the boys sort of check you out."

"They tripped all over themselves tailing me. Go on."

"So they did a lousy job, but they find out it's no big deal. So I'm all set to forget about it, when I hear about you again. Someone tells me the word is around that you're going public with some info about July thirteenth. That is a big deal."

"Gee," I said. "July thirteenth. That's too late for Independence Day and too early for Bastille Day. I give up. What *did* happen on that date?"

He shook his head. "Hey, look, I don't want to come on strong. It's just not my style. But I think you've got a pretty good idea of what I'm getting at. Maybe you don't know the whole story. But maybe you know enough to rock the boat. So just forget it, man. Believe me. It would be much, much better for your health."

"Thanks for the advice. I'll be sure to tie an aspidistra bag around my neck. Suppose I agree to keep my mouth shut. What can you do for me in return?"

"I can keep you alive."

"Talk like that just makes me stubborn, Mr. Jones. You might catch me some night in bed with my teddy bear. But killing is always messy. Unless you do it yourself, you've got to deal with other people. Then one day the cops nail one of your Boy Scouts for kicking an old lady and he turns you in on a plea bargain. It would be far easier to hear me out. You could always change your mind."

Jones took off his glasses and wiped them on his shirt. His eyes were small. Replacing the glasses and carefully adjusting them, he let out a long, deep breath.

"You're right. You got me pegged. I'm no tough guy. Would it surprise you to learn that I'm a college grad? MIT, in fact. Electrical engineering."

"Not at all, Mr. Jones. Lots of guys have degrees tacked onto their cell walls over the picture of their mother."

"C'mon. I'm not bragging. I just want you to know we're coming at this from the same place, but different directions. So let's talk. What are you looking for? Maybe I can oblige."

I led the way up a wooden boardwalk to the observation platform. When we were at the top, I said, "Kip Scannell had some papers that belong to my client. Kip's dead. The papers are missing. My client wants them back. I want to know if

Kip's extracurricular activities had any bearing on my case. That's all."

"That's easy. I don't know about any papers." He chuckled. "Arthur was pretty careless with other people's property, I guess."

"I don't get you."

"Man, I'm only telling you this so you'll understand that you're in way over your head. I'm in the business end. Profit-and-loss sheets. Bottom lines. But still a lot more fun than computers. Arthur was in transport. He took delivery of goods from sea to land. He was pretty good at it, until July thirteenth. The shipment he was in charge of went astray."

"Is that why he was murdered?"

Jones's mouth dropped open.

"Whoa, boy. That's the first I heard of anything like *that*. I read it was an accident. Sure, a lot of people might *like* to murder Kip if he were still alive. He was the person last responsible for the goods. Losing a shipment is one thing. A risk of doing business. But no one likes to take a hosing. Sets a bad example. What makes you think he was hit?"

"Just a wild guess, Mr. Jones."

"That doesn't make sense. The money guys would want to recover the goods first. They might knock someone off later as an example, or maybe not. As you say, it gets messy. It's bad enough the shipment is missing. You got to move stuff quickly and quietly. Once there's a delay, a shipment becomes too hot to handle. Word gets onto the street. Every drug enforcement cop in the region soon knows about it, and they all want a promotion. So I'll repeat my suggestion. Forget this one. Tell your client you're up against a wall. I've heard that you're an insider but that you've got a conscience. Just asking questions could make some people nervous."

"Please stop. My knees are shaking."

"Okay. I don't scare you. My boys don't scare you. So what? There are some heavy dudes in this, and they scare *me*. On the other hand, if you do hear something about the missing package, you could make a good day's pay."

I did a slow 360-degree spin as if I were taking in the view from the observation platform. There was the flash of a green and red Hawaiian shirt on the dunes near the sign that says EROSION CONTROL AREA—PLEASE KEEP OFF.

We walked back down the boardwalk and to the parking

lot. A pair of Harley-Davidson motorcycles with raked forks and high handlebars were parked side by side. One of them had a decal of a white cobra on its gas tank.

I stopped and looked at Jones, thinking about how badly I wanted to jam my fist down his throat.

"Look, Mr. Jones," I said. "I really wouldn't want you to get the wrong impression about me. You think I'm like those trained apes you sent to my house. All you have to do is flip me a banana and you'll own me. You are right about one thing. I've got you pegged. You're a dilettante. You're someone who doesn't like to get his hands dirty and has a pedicure three times a week. You consider yourself just a friendly young guy who gets a big thrill outsmarting the cops. I'd toss you over that cliff but there's a fine for throwing garbage on the beach. Tell you what," I added, "I'll keep you out of it as best I can."

Jones frowned, an ugly grimace. "Sorry, Mr. Socarides," he said coldly, "but I can't take any chances." He held his right hand high above his head.

Two figures on the dunes started running toward the parking lot. They were moving fast and would cut me off before I got to my truck.

There was a tall park ranger in a Smoky the Bear hat standing near the entrance to the white cedar swamp walk. He wore a gun and might even know how to use it. I stepped over to him and said, "Pardon me. I don't mean to be a tattletale, but perhaps those gentlemen on the dunes don't know they're not supposed to walk on the beach grass because of the erosion problem."

The ranger looked off to where I pointed.

"You did right, sir. There are signs all over the place. Those guys are going to end up in court." Setting his jaw, the ranger strode to the edge of the grass and motioned Skinhead and Fungus over. He had pulled a pad and pencil from his hip pocket. I got into my truck and started the engine. Jones stood there smiling.

The smile didn't last long. Gosh, I can't believe what a sloppy driver I can be. The truck's heavy-duty rear bumper smashed into the motorcycles. Both Harley Hogs crashed to the ground. I kept going in reverse.

Sproing. Snap, crackle, and pop. Just like the breakfast cereal.

My wheels bumped over the bikes, mashing metal, plastic, and glass. I stopped, not wanting to puncture my new tires, threw the truck into low, bumped off the miniature junk heap I had created, and took off down the road without stopping to bid a fond adieu. Rude, maybe. And mean. But cute. Very cute.

CHAPTER 26

The call from Geetch came around nine o'clock that night. He sounded frantic. "Soc," he cried. "I'm in big trouble. You gotta help me."

I had been scrubbing engine grease off my hands when the phone rang. Sam had come by the boat house after my enlightening meeting with Mr. Jones. With his hauler working, naturally his engine went bust and he could use help fixing it. Sam is hard to refuse. Detecting is a nice hobby, but Sam's fishing boat keeps the wolf from my door. Besides, he's a heck of a nice guy.

We spent most of the day and early evening before we got the engine going. From the fish pier I went directly to the Hole, chugged down a couple of beers, and caught up on current affairs, broken marriages, new babies, and obituaries. It was refreshing to hear about the trials and tribulations of normal people with normal problems. Now this. Fooey.

"Hey, slow down," I said. "What kind of trouble?"

"Somebody's after me."

"What the hell are you talking about, Geetch? Who'd be after you?"

"I don't know, Soc. I don't . . . But you gotta—"

"Okay, okay. Take it easy, Geetch. You want me to come by your boat or meet you at the Hole?"

"Come by my cottage. I'm not moving."

"All right, I'll be there in half an hour. That be soon enough?"

"Yeah, yeah, Soc. But no later or . . ." He hung up.

Geetch tended to be excitable, but his plea reverberated with a raw fear. I decided to head over immediately. My hand was on the front doorknob when the phone rang. I went back and answered the call. A voice came on identifying itself as belonging to the overseas operator.

"I have a person-to-person call from London for a Mr. A. Socarides."

London. I didn't know anyone in London. Maybe the queen was calling. Or Princess Di.

"Go ahead," I said.

A clipped English accent that sounded like Winston Churchill doing Basil Rathbone cut in.

"How do you do, Mr. Socarides. This is Anthony Smythe-Covington of the Strand Investigation Service. Norma Sheldon, the young lady at Beacon Research in Boston, asked me to call you concerning some historical information which I believe has a bearing on a case you are working on. I'll be sending a packet along, but she thought you would appreciate hearing from me immediately."

Norma didn't miss a trick. "I do appreciate your calling, it must be quite late over there."

"Wee hours of the morning, but not to worry, lad. Mrs. Sheldon asked me to keep trying until I got you. She said you were keenly interested in a particular dairy."

"That's right. I've read the journal kept by Lieutenant Thomas Powers up to the shipwreck he was in. I wondered if there were additional entries."

"Precisely. I went directly to the horse's mouth, so to speak. I talked to a descendant of Lieutenant Powers. He kindly allowed me to examine the diary which was in his possession. The diary contains a few entries after the wreck of the *Gabriella*, but nothing about the lieutenant's naval career. He began keeping a daily journal when he moved to the country, but he had his fill of the sea, I assume. The entries are mostly about his flower gardens."

That tallied with what Eileen said.

"There's nothing in the diary about the money that was on the ship?"

"Correct. The diary was something of a red herring in that respect."

"Well, thanks, Mr. Smythe-Covington, I really appreciate—"

"But I *do* have the letter I read to Mrs. Sheldon. She said you'd be most interested in its contents. It's something I picked up when I went to see the Powers family about the diary. I was shown this document, which I copied and can read to you. It will only take a moment."

Remembering Geetch, I looked at my watch. "Okay, it's your dime," I said.

"Fine," he said. "This is a letter written by Lieutenant Powers to his mother." He cleared his throat. " *'My Dearest Madame. I am now going to give you an account of my last cruise in the* Gabriella. *But first I must enquire as to the welfare of my dear sister Emily whose illness I have only just become aware of—'* "

I cut in. "Mr. Smythe-Covington, I'd love to know how Emily made out with the vapors, but I'm in something of a hurry. Could you leave out the nonessentials and get to the part about the cargo. That's what I'm really interested in. The money."

"No problem. Actually I believe Emily was pining for some army officer whom she eventually married and had seven children by, but that's another story of course." Mumble, mumble. "Ah, here 'tis. The ship had gone aground, mizzen mast fell, wiped out some of the crew, that sort of thing. My word, they did have rather a dicey time of it. Lieutenant Powers says: *'The captain ordered me to make ready to launch his gig. But first to take a crew of strong men and load six large chests of important cargo from his cabin lazaret into the boat. Whilst we were complying with his orders, the captain proceeded to burn important documents and charts.'* "

That tallied too.

The voice droned on from three thousand miles and more than two centuries away.

" *'The gig loaded, it was put over the side on its davits and we awaited the captain. As we sat in the gig a mighty wave knocked the craft into the sea. We attempted to row to shore but were upset in the breakers, and all men in the gig perished, except myself, for which I thank God and my dear late father who had the wisdom to instruct me as a child in the exercise of swimming. Shortly after the gig upset, the ship rolled over on its side and the captain, too, was drowned.'* "

"What happened to the chests that were in the gig?"

"Coming to that. Well, to make a long story short, the lucky chap makes it to shore and is picked up the next morning by another British boat which had seen the *Gabriella* go down."

"That would be the *Nautilus*," I said.

"Correct. I had a friend who served in a ship by the same name during the big war. Destroyer, I believe. Or was it a minesweeper—"

"I'd truly like to hear about your friend sometime," I said. "But we were talking about the chests."

"Just getting to that, old chap. Hmm. This really is fascinating stuff, you know."

"I'd be grateful if you shared it with me."

He said, "Of course. Powers goes on, '*The wind having abated, the sloop* Nautilus *sent in a boat to where I directed. At low tide on this coast, the sea recedes several hundred feet, so that the point where the gig overturned was not far from land. On board the* Nautilus *was a Negro of great strength who had experience swimming down to Spanish ships in the Caribbean. We were able to find the chests, which were in shallow water, and he affixed lines to them. By the use of pulleys and rope we were able to save all the chests. Also a substantial quantity of gold. The* Nautilus *took aboard the handful of other survivors and dispersed the local populace, who had begun to swarm onto the shore like vultures on a corpse, with a few shot from its cannon.'* "

"Does he say what happened to the chests after they retrieved them?"

"Getting to that. He says, '*After a swift voyage with fair winds we arrived in London where I had the pleasure of returning payroll for His Majesty's Army in America, and gold, to the crown. And certain property belonging to others, among them Sir Charles Harcourt, late quartermaster in charge of naval prisoners for Philadelphia. Sir Charles expressed his gratitude in many ways.'* "

And what better way to express his gratitude than to ease Powers through the court-martial.

"Was there anything else?" I asked.

"Just one more sentence, probably not important. '*Sir Charles has invited me to visit his estate in Surrey, where I have met his lovely daughter Sarah.'* "

"And nature took its course," I said softly.

"What say?"

"Nothing, Mr. Smythe-Covington. From that letter would

you conclude that a good part of the cargo aboard the *Gabriella* may have been retrieved?"

"It would seem so, old chap. Probably all been spent too. Even though the pound was worth a great deal more before socialized medicine and labor unions. I've always voted conservative myself—"

"Well, thank you very much, sir. It must have been quite a job to dig out that letter."

"Ordinarily it would have been a task. But Lieutenant Powers's descendant unearthed the piece several months ago for one of your countrywomen who was doing some research on his ancestor. So he knew precisely what I was searching for."

"Someone else was interested in this? Did he remember the person's name?"

"I asked him that, but he couldn't recall. Chap's in his eighties now, and a bit on the senile side, but he still has an eye for the ladies. All he could remember was the fact that she had the loveliest red hair he had ever seen. A real blue-eyed Celt, that one, he said, with . . . well, you know what I mean."

"I think I do," I said. "Thanks again, sir. You've been a great help."

"My pleasure. Stop by and see me if you're ever on this side of the pond."

I hung up. The words from across the Atlantic echoed like a shout in the chambers of my mind.

A real blue-eyed Celt, that one.

Damn. Geetch. I had almost forgotten him. I hurried out to my truck.

Geetch's tiny cottage was in a scrub-pine forest at the end of a dirt road. I took two wrong turns before I found it. Geetch's pickup truck was in the yard, but the house was dark. It seemed unlikely that in his jittery state he'd gone to bed. It had only been a few minutes since I'd talked to him.

The night was oddly quiet; even the crickets were taking a coffee break from their mindless chirping. Maybe it was the Vietnam jitters again. Or the cop's memory of fetid slum hallways and the fear of death lurking in the shadows. I reached under the seat and pulled out the five-battery flashlight from my police days. The heavy flash made a good substitute nightstick.

I walked light-footed to the door and tried the knob. The door was unlocked. I pushed it open and reached around to the right, hoping I wouldn't find somebody's hand on the switch ahead of me. I clicked the switch and looked around. *Migod!*

The living room looked as if a herd of cattle had ridden through it. Cushions from the sofa and chairs were ripped open and tossed on the floor. Tables were overturned. Even the back of the television set was pried off and thrown to the other side of the room. Every cupboard door in the kitchen area was open. Pots and pans were scattered all over the floor. Geetch had never been a great housekeeper, even though he kept his boat as shiny and neat as if he had bought it at Tiffany's. But this mess wouldn't be cured by a few sweeps of the vacuum cleaner.

I walked over and picked up the telephone. The cord dangled from where it had been yanked off the wall. There were only two other rooms, a small bathroom and a bedroom. I checked the bathroom. Empty. The bedroom door was shut. A closed door can be a problem if someone behind it wants to go somewhere in a hurry and you're in the way. I went up to the door, stood off to one side, and knocked softly.

"Geetch?" I said.

No reply.

"Geetch," I repeated. Louder. "You in there?"

Still no answer.

I took a deep breath and opened the door. Peering around the corner of the doorway, I probed the bedroom with the flashlight. The spot came to rest on Geetch's pale face. He stared into the powerful beam without blinking.

"Goddamn," I muttered.

I stepped into the room and hit the light switch.

"Hello, Geetch," I said quietly.

I don't know why I bothered with a greeting, because Geetch was in no shape to answer. His was lying on his bed, his head propped up on a pillow. His hands were crossed on his chest as if he'd been laid out at Dolan's Funeral Home in Dorchester. The room even smelled faintly of flowers.

There wasn't a mark on him. No bullet holes, no punctures from a sharp implement, no blood. I walked over and touched the carotid artery in his neck with the tips of my fingers. He was still warm but there was no pulse. I had checked out enough auto accidents on the Southeast Expressway to hazard a reasonably accurate guess as to cause of death. Geetch's neck was broken.

CHAPTER 27

The murder of Geetch must have been the biggest thing to hit town since high tide. His doll-size cottage was bursting with burly men in police and rescue-squad uniforms. You could see them through the windows, milling around and trampling evidence. Geetch never had that much company when he was alive.

After my one-sided conversation with Geetch's corpse, I drove to a nearby service station where I called the police, told them he was dead, hung around for a few minutes to let things happen, then headed back to the cottage. The pulsating lights of three cruisers and a rescue-squad truck illuminated the front of the house in red and blue flashes.

A clean-cut patrolman saw me get out of the truck. He stepped smartly over. He was a new cop. He could have sliced potatoes with the creases in his freshly ironed trousers. His uniform wasn't shiny the way it would get eventually from sliding in and out of the cruiser a few thousand times. He stuck his left hand out to block me. His other hand snapped to his pistol holster for emphasis. No fooling with this guy. He was ready to draw his heater if I gave him any lip.

"Sorry, sir. You can't proceed any further. This is the scene of a crime."

Small-town cops can be a pain in the butt. "I know it's the scene of a crime. I'm the one who called it in."

The news confused him. Probably trying to decide whether to drill me or handcuff me to a tree, then drill me. I was obviously a case for deadly force. Fortune smiled. Chief Snow came out of the cottage and saw me talking to his officer. He gave a friendly wave and walked over. The chief is a tall thin man who smokes $2.99-a-dozen generic cigars made from tobacco substitute. He never gets excited about anything. He doesn't carry a gun, which amazes his younger officers, who would tote a Stinger antiaircraft missile if they were allowed to. He shook hands and grinned.

"Evenin', Soc. You got a police radio now so you can help the boys out on calls?"

"Hi, Chief. Not exactly. I was the one who found Geetch and called in from Seymour's gas station."

"My," he said. "Isn't that interesting? Why don't we just set in my car away from all this commotion. You can tell me about it while the boys are pokin' around."

We got into his unmarked car and the chief lit a cigar that belched smoke like the smokestack of a garbage incinerator. I cranked the window down and stuck my nose out like a cocker spaniel. The chief took a puff and savored the cigar as if it were a Havana.

"Damn shame about Geetch. Nice little fella. Never hurt anyone. Kept that boat of his shinier than my wedding silver. Guess he never did use it much for fishing. Well, now, hear you been havin' a busy week, Soc. First your gun was stolen, now this. How'd you come to be here? You just stop by to talk about fishing? Or Geetch a client of yours?"

I gave him just enough to think about. The excited summons from Geetch, the discovery of the body, the call to the police department. Nothing about the perfume scent in Geetch's bedroom. Nothing about the sweet smell of jasmine.

The cigar went out. The chief gnawed thoughtfully on the soggy end. I prayed that he had run out of matches.

"First murder case in this town since when I was a rookie," he reminisced. "Guy blew his neighbor's head off for fooling around with his wife. Fella was watching television. Milton Berle, I think. Still on when we got there. Always liked that show. Lord, what a bloody mess. Not the show, I mean. The house. Brains all over the rug and wallpaper. I guess you seen worse up in Boston. This one's much neater. Looks like a broken neck. I'll take that over a pistol anytime." He relit his cigar. "How you figure it?"

"I'd guess somebody was looking for something. Maybe Geetch wouldn't tell where it was. Or maybe they didn't want any witnesses. I can't figure why Geetch was laid out that way, though. Even down to his cap placed near the foot of the bed. Strange. It's the kind of thing you might see in a ritual slaying, but this doesn't have any of the other signposts to suggest that kind of deal."

"Uh-huh," the chief said. "I noticed that cap too. Never saw the little fella without it. What do you figure they were lookin' for?"

It was hard to know whether the chief was probing or honestly interested in my opinion. He kept his Yankee shrewdness and college education well disguised beneath his country-cop routine. The best course was to lay it out, within limits. He'd know if I were bending the truth.

"Doubt it was money," I said. "Never knew Geetch to have more than twenty bucks on him at a time, and that was only when I loaned it to him." I looked at the chief. "You got any ideas?"

"Nope. I kinda like to collect all the information in my head and let things harden up a bit like when my wife makes strawberry Jell-O."

"My favorite flavor is mint," I said.

He glanced at me to see if I was pulling his leg and, when he saw I wasn't, said, "Yeah, I like that second best. Some people put it on the side dish with a hunk of lamb. Never could figure why they did that. Lamb and green Jell-O. Hmmm. Doesn't seem like a marriage made in heaven. You goin' to be around if we need more information?"

"No problem, Chief. Sam's boat's out of the water for a few days. I'll be around. I won't be flying off to Las Vegas for a while."

Chief Snow said, "Heard you lost quite a wad out there."

"Blackjack isn't my game. By the way, you might want to have your boys check Geetch's boat. Same person who redecorated his house might have stopped there." I got out of the car. "Sometimes I like to let things gel too. If anything occurs to me, I'll give you a call."

The chief got out and leaned his lanky frame across the car roof. "I know you will. Good suggestion about the boat. Once a flatfoot, always a flatfoot. Already sent a car over there. Now, if you'll excuse me, I've got to get back inside and keep the boys from tearin' things up before the county identification fellas arrive." He ambled back into the house as if he were going on a social call. He was relighting his cigar.

I drove to a spot that overlooks the ocean and breathed the cool salty air coming in off the deep water. Polaris, the north star, twinkled brightly in the black sky. Odd. I could look straight up and see for millions of miles. Back on earth, visibility was zero.

The words kept repeating in my mind.

A real blue-eyed Celt, that one.

I slammed my palm against the steering wheel. What the hell was going on? Eileen. It couldn't have been anyone else. She knew about the Power's letter. She knew the *Gabriella*'s treasure had been retrieved centuries ago. Yet she never let on. She never told Mike that it didn't matter if he found the *Gabriella* or not, that he was chasing a pipe dream either way. Another instance of her not wanting to break her brother's heart? The last time something hit me in the gut like that was when the big Georgia cracker sucker-punched me in a Saigon bar after I told him only fags wear berets even if they are green. I pinched my chin like Rodin's *Thinker*. I needed a strong drink.

When I got to the Hole, I ordered a shot of ouzo and guzzled the liquorishy firewater down as if it were cream soda. Maybe Geetch might still be alive if I had put Mr. Smythe-Covington on hold. I tried not to think of it, but Joshua, who was on duty behind the bar, said, "Hey, wasn't that something about Geetch. Just heard from one of the guys on the rescue squad who picked it up on his radio. What happened? You know anything?"

"Looks like somebody wanted Geetch dead," I said.

"You mean, naw, I can't believe that. He was such a harmless little guy. Who'd want to hurt him?" He sighed. "I guess the Lord moves in mysterious ways. That's real funny, first Kip, then Geetch, all within a couple of weeks, and them being buddies too."

I was only half listening, so it took a minute for my brain to digest what the ear had heard. I clunked my drink down. "Run that by me again, Joshua. What you said about Geetch and Kip being friends."

He poured another shot of ouzo and put it on the bar. "Here, this one's on me. Yeah, don't blame you for being surprised. It wasn't the kind of thing you'd expect, Kip being such a hotshot and Geetch, well, you knew Geetch. One of the Lord's children, the kind He protects." He shrugged his big shoulders and started washing some beer mugs. "Except when He decides to call them home. That's just His way."

"How long has this friendship been going on?"

"I don't know exactly. But a few weeks ago I saw them drinking together. I remember hoping Kip wasn't stringing Geetch along just so he could play a joke on him, but they really seemed to hit it off. They were just chatting away over a couple of beers. Glad to see it. Like I was telling the big guy yesterday, Geetch would do anything if you were nice to him. Well, you know that. He liked you, liked you a lot—"

I sipped my drink and nodded absentmindedly.

"—so maybe you're the one who would know what I should do with this."

Joshua wiped his wet hands on a towel and reached behind him. "Geetch gave it to me for safekeeping. I'm not sure what to do with it now." He took a cardboard tube off a shelf under the hard-liquor case. I had seen the tube sitting there before, but assumed it was a bar calendar and never gave it a second thought.

I stared fish-eyed at the cardboard tube, which had been cleverly disguised as a cardboard tube. Aha, Poe's Monsieur Dupin was saying in his snotty Inspector Clouseau accent. You simply *assumed* the Purloined Letter was concealed, when in reality it was literally right under your stupid Greek nose all along. Voilà! I reached over and took the tube from him as if it held plastique explosives. I didn't have to look inside. "Don't worry. I'll see this gets to the rightful owner. Trust me."

Halfway to the door a light bulb went off over my head the way it does in the comics. I turned and walked back to the bar. "Hey, Joshua, you said something a minute ago? About talking to the big guy?"

Joshua finished drawing a couple of drafts and came over. "Yeah, Barrett, the treasure hunter. He stopped by last night for a beer. Nice guy. Don't see him in here too often. Anyhow, we started chatting about Kip, and the talk led to Geetch. You know how it is."

I turned to go. "Yeah. Thanks, Joshua," I said. But I was lying. I didn't really know how it is.

CHAPTER 28

I drove as if my pickup truck were a Ferrari at Le Mans. The GMC complained bitterly, screeching on the curves, coughing on the hills, and rattling her bolts on the boat-house road. I mumbled a guilty promise to bring her in for a wash and tune-up, ran into the boat house, and set the cardboard tube on the kitchen table. With a quick swipe of my razor-sharp buck knife, I lopped off one end, pulled the papers out of the tube, and unrolled them, pinning the corners with four Boston Celtics glasses.

Lying on top were a half-dozen underwater photos. I picked up the first one and studied it. The photo showed a group of cylindrical and spherical lumps lying dark against the pale sandy sea bottom. Someone with a red grease pencil had labeled the cylinders as cannon and marked the roundish objects as ballast or cannonballs. All were incrusted with a rough, blackish covering that had become a condominium for hundreds of barnacles and grassy clumps of marine growth.

In another picture the incrustation had been partly chipped off one cylinder and the camera had gone in close to reveal a mark inscribed on the bare metal. It was a broad arrow design. This crummy old piece of sea junk had once been the proud property of the British admiralty.

Clipped to the photos were textbook pages containing black-and-white line drawings of ten different British cannon and details on their weight, length, caliber, and shot size. They ranged in size from a nifty little yard-long number named a Robinet that fired half-pound shot, to a ten-foot monster that hurled bowling balls. A direct hit between the eyes by either weapon had the potential to ruin your day. A couple of cannon pictures were circled in red. They matched the specifications on another paper designated "*Gabriella* Gun List."

There was more. A dated list of coins, Spanish and English, and descriptions of pieces of wood and unidentified metal, a drawing that showed the location of an anchor, cannon, and ballast, and a shore current diagram similar to the one Eileen had shown me.

The papers included a biography of the *Gabriella*. She was built in 1775 by Randal and Brent at their Cuckold's Point boatyard on the Thames River. The contract specified every detail of construction. For instance, her timber and plank had to be "Growth of England," and she had to have three coats of paint. In the years between her fitting and demise, the *Gabriella* had distinguished herself in battle, capturing merchant ships, destroying American privateers, and damaging a couple of vessels. She had taken a pounding from bad weather on one of her last patrols, though, and maybe that's why she was leaking before she went down.

There were some fairly detailed drawings of the *Gabriella* based on sketches and plans from the British National Maritime Museum collection at Greenwich. She was a pretty ship. Sleek lines, three masts, all square-rigged, and a full-length figurehead surmounting the graceful rounded bow. A side note explained that the British admiralty later abolished the full figurehead on smaller vessels, replacing it with a scroll head, but relented after an outcry and approved the use of a bust. Sailors had to have something to remind them of what they were fighting for, after all.

Some of the sketches showed the location of artifacts on the bottom. Their placement roughly approximated a ship's outline. Most of the archaeological documentation bore the signature or initials of Eileen Barrett. I scratched my head. Eileen had made a fairly solid case for the *Gabriella*. There was nothing in the packet about another ship. I couldn't figure it.

The next items in the pile were eighteenth- and nineteenth-century maps and an up-to-date National Ocean Service chart of Cape Cod. Penciled on the newer chart was a cluster of circles designating an ocean area off Provincetown. Attached were a dozen or so smudgy-lined linear graphs similar to the sub-bottom profiles Barrett showed me on our first encounter. There were a couple of pages describing landmarks that could be used to verify a position.

I picked up the last sheet of paper. Eureka! I was looking at a chart marked with the codelike groups of numbers and letters that signified Loran bearings. Someone had marked the chart with an "X." This was the critical document, the ribbon that would neatly tie up the hodgepodge of information into a pretty package.

Considering the energy I had expended, I should have been bouncing excitedly off the walls. The best I could muster was a profound *hmmph*. In fact, I felt rather dumb. While I had been performing a prefrontal lobotomy on myself with generous infusions of alcohol, Barrett's stuff was literally almost within arm's reach.

I sat at the table and sifted through the pile again. A half hour later I got up and walked onto the deck. Another clear night. I leaned back in a chair and picked out the constellations. Hydra, the water serpent, slithered across the southern horizon. Hercules knelt almost directly overhead, his club poised high. The nine-headed sea monster had given Hercules a rough time. He'd whack off one head and two would grow back.

Finding Barrett's packet was equally frustrating. Answer one question, two more surfaced. Barrett's material told me where the *Gabriella* lay. It did not say who murdered Kip and Geetch. Or why Eileen Barrett kept the truth about the *Gabriella*'s illusory treasure from her brother. And what the scent worn by Laura Nichols was doing in the same bedroom as Geetch's warm and very dead body.

The papers *did* tell me one thing, though.

Cherchez la femme. Look for the woman.

She had been there all the time. The *Gabriella*. Whenever I opened a door, she was on the other side, probably laughing at my blind stupidity. Quite a lady. More than two centuries old, a moldering mirror image of her old lovely self, she still drove men crazy with her charms. For hundreds of years she had been a sea-guarded mystery. No one even knew where she slept. Now mortals had brazenly interrupted her slumber. And the *Gabriella* was reaching out from her five-fathom grave, beckoning to her unwanted suitors in a deadly flirtation. I leaned back and examined the wooden lady who graced the bow in the sketches of the *Gabriella*. She was a leggy blonde. Her wooden body would have been taken by the sea long ago, but with *Gabriella*, you could never tell. She had displayed an amazing resiliency so far, and maybe she was still on the ocean's bottom, arms ready to throw around you.

Barrett's papers would not unlock her secrets, but they could show me where to find the key.

I went back into the house and switched on the NOAA radio weather report. Barrett was right about the storm. It was working its way up the coast, preceded by unusually calm weather. The forecaster droned out a prediction for a fair and almost windless morning, breezing up in the afternoon. I sat at the kitchen table and drummed my fingers lightly on the papers, thinking about the advice I gave that newspaper reporter.

There's only one way to get at the facts. Go down there and take a look.

Okay, the material belonged to Barrett. He had to have it for the board meeting in two days. But he never said I couldn't borrow the stuff for a few hours. This case had been more than I bargained for and I was entitled to resolve the doubts nagging at me. Rationalization completed, I scooped the papers off the table before I changed my mind and ran duplicates off on a copying machine a client had given me in lieu of payment. The originals I stashed on a closet shelf.

I laid out my diving gear and called Larry. He promised a couple of filled air tanks would be waiting in the shed behind his shop. I set the alarm, went to bed, and drifted off to fitful sleep. Visions of flashing police cruiser lights and broken little men with white caps danced in my head.

The alarm buzzed almost instantly. I sat up and blinked at the clock. Couldn't be 6:30 A.M. so soon. But it was. From my bedroom window I could see the night sky turning morning gray over the barrier beach. I took a wake-up shower, gulped down two cups of coffee, then dressed, packed a lunch, loaded the diving equipment, charts, and a couple of extra gas cans into the truck and drove to Larry's. The air tanks were in the shed. Next to them was a large canvas bag. A note dangled from the handles.

Hi, Soc. Thought you might like to have a helper along. Your pal, Larry.

Fifteen minutes later I turned into a small gravel parking lot that adjoined a boat ramp and short floating pier with room for a half-dozen boats. The shore was deserted except for two shellfishermen who scratched for clams in the shallows and a young couple holding hands. Gulls wheeled hungrily over the sun-sparkled waters. The yellow morning light had a creamy softness to it.

My pride and joy was tied up at the pier. The twenty-two-foot Privateer had a fiberglass ocean hull and two outboard motors, a seventy-five-horsepower for traveling, and a ten-horsepower for trolling or searching. When I'm not working with Sam or making princely sums detecting, I use the skiff to fish for cod and flounder, or harvest bay scallops in the golden days of the fall. I had taken some grief from fellow fishermen because of the two eyes I painted on the bow, the way boats were decorated in old Greece. But I told my pier group they helped me find fish.

I loaded my gear into the boat, started the motor, cast off the mooring line, and headed into a cove, following a winding course between acres of grassy marsh and low bluffs crowned by big expensive houses. There wasn't much boat traffic in the channel. A couple of fishermen commuting to work, some picnickers headed for the outer beach. The air was still and heavy the way it gets when a storm is brewing. The water was flatter than my bank account.

The cove's entrance, a quarter-mile-wide cut in the barrier beach, was guarded by a line of toothy breakers. Even in summer the inlet is a treacherous passage, so I exercised special care threading the path between two sandy points. The boat bumped its way over the washboard wavelets into the Atlantic. I gave her the throttle. The Privateer skimmed along the blue satin ocean surface. Two hours later, about a half mile from shore, I was off Peaked Hills, looking at the rolling dunes of the Province Lands and the tall granite spike of the Pilgrim Monument.

Slowing to a crawl, I compared the digital readings displayed on my Loran set to Barrett's figures and the bearings printed on my navigational chart.

I cruised in crazy patterns until the readings matched Barrett's numbers. For good measure I checked my position in relationship to a water tower and church spire. This was as close as I was going to get. I decided not to throw a red and white floating flag over the side. The flag would warn other boats a diver was below, but I didn't want to attract undue attention, so I simply dropped anchor and pulled Larry's "helper" out of its bag.

The sea scooter's bright red high-impact plastic casing gleamed in the morning sunlight. This model was a Tekna DV 3X about two feet long and a foot across. At the back end of the streamlined housing was a propeller and two black handgrip controls. Up front was a powerful headlight. Set into the top of the propeller guard were a depth gauge and compass.

Larry's foresight would save me a lot of work. The scooter's battery-operated motor could pull a diver along up to two miles an hour. Range on a single charge was about three miles. It was like carrying an extra air tank. You can cut your air consumption as much as fifty percent if you don't have to kick with your fins.

I pulled on my wet suit and tank and tucked two small spherical pop-up buoys under my belt. Then I slipped over the side, manhandling the fifty-pound scooter into the water, and tucked the cruise seat, actually a bar attached by a strap to the propeller housing, between my legs. I pointed the scooter down along the anchor line and squeezed the trigger on the right hand control.

The six-hundred-rpm motor started with a high-powered whine and the scooter headed for the bottom with me stretched out behind. A few exhilarating seconds later and I was circling the anchor as playfully as a dolphin. It was like flying in a dream. I was in a universe where the standard rules of gravity do not apply. Gliding, hovering, and soaring in a graceful slow-motion ballet through an eerie transluscent atmosphere of greenish blue, like some great cyclops-eyed bird skimming over a strange planet. A plume of bubbles trailed in my wake.

After a few moments I cut the motor and looked around, trying to get my bearings. The depth gauge told me the water was thirty-one feet deep. The shimmering surface light was filtered to a brownish haze by thousands of mung-weed motes. Beyond fifteen feet visibility faded.

The anchor would be the center point of my search pattern. I rode the scooter due north for one minute. Then I turned around and headed due south for two minutes, passing the anchor at the halfway mark. I followed the same procedure with the east–west axis and came back to the anchor.

With a search area quartered, I began to make one-minute runs out from the center point on the in-between directions, zigzagging back to the anchor. It was a primitive way to conduct a survey, but it would give me relatively thorough bottom coverage over a large circular area.

I found some undersized lobsters. A few curious fish checked me out and darted away when I reached out to tickle their whiskers. But the ocean bottom was bare. I released the pop-up buoy at the anchor to give me a reference point, surfaced, and moved my boat about a hundred feet to the east. Loran is remarkably accurate, but it's a big ocean.

I made three more surveys, checked my air tank, and tried a fourth sweep. Negative. This was frustrating. If only I had a magnetometer. Even a hand-held metal detector might help. I pondered my next step. That's when I noticed a vague shadowy patch near the perimeter of my search zone.

I rode the scooter over to the dark puddle and squeezed the trigger in the left hand control. The headlight beam cut through the veil of mung weed, outlining the edge of an irregular conical depression. I went in closer. The crater was about thirty feet across and maybe two yards deep. I moved the light down. A sandy ridge about six inches high protruded from the bottom of the crater, running for several feet. Interesting. Nature rarely draws a straight line.

I checked my pressure gauge in the instrument panel hanging from a hose off my vest. About fifteen minutes left. Then I swam into the center of the crater and swept the light around in a circle. The beam picked out other cylindrical forms, each from six to eight feet long, lying on the slope of the conical hole.

Resting the scooter on the bottom, I brushed the sand off the concrete-hard crust of one cylinder. Somebody had used a hammer and chisel to chip off several hand-size chunks, exposing black metal. Iron, I guessed. I ran my hand over a bare section and with my finger traced three lines engraving in a broad-headed arrow design.

There were seven cylinders in all. Were these the big guns from the *Gabriella*? I wanted to investigate further, but my air supply was uncomfortably low. I needed a fresh tank. I released the second pop-up buoy to mark my position. Then I made a final sweep around the crater's perimeter, coming to a skidding stop.

Hello. An eighth cylinder.

It was off by itself at the outer range of visibility. I moved closer. My hand touched the surface. Smooth metal, steely in color. Nothing like the ancient hand-forged hunks I had just looked at. The cylinder was about eight feet long and a foot in diameter, rounded at both ends like a double-ended torpedo. No markings of any kind. There was something, though.

A tight seam circumscribed the cylinder about a foot from one end. Next to the seam were fittings made for an open-end wrench. Welded onto the metal, one at each end, were two large eyebolts.

About six feet away was another, identical cylinder. I swam over and put the scooter down. Standing on the sea bottom to give me purchase, I gripped an eyebolt and heaved with all the power in my legs and back. The thing didn't even quiver.

I had about ten minutes' supply left. Time to head up. I grabbed the scooter, pointed it toward the surface, and squeezed the trigger.

Three things happened in rapid succession.

First, a shadow passed overhead and there was the loud thrumming of an engine.

Then a volcano erupted under me.

And finally, someone turned the lights out.

The sea bottom exploded in a whirling, sandy vortex. I spun in a gut-wrenching cartwheel. My stomach jumped up to my Adam's apple. The sea scooter twisted out of my hands and sailed off into oblivion. The world became a muddy blur of green and brown. I couldn't tell what was up or what was down.

The metal instrument panel hanging off the air tank whipped crazily at the end of its hose and smashed into my face mask. The lens became a spiderweb of hairline cracks. It could have been worse. It could have crushed my skull.

I was being tossed around in a huge undersea blender with old spinach leaves and coffee grounds, and slammed down hard with a gritty shock that knocked the regulator from my mouth. I grabbed onto my mask so as not to lose it and blindly flailed with my right arm, trying to retrieve the mouthpiece. It snaked wildly at the end of its slippery rubber hose, out of reach of my clawing hand. Precious air bubbled away.

It is not true that your whole life flashes before your eyes at moments like this. There simply isn't time. Only parts of it, like the night long ago, when I was still young enough to hold my father's hand, and we walked by a photography studio whose owner, an old Greek man, had died a few days before. My father looked at the darkened windows and said, "Jimmy the photographer is dead. Now all the Greeks are afraid."

"Afraid of what?" I said innocently.

"They're afraid they're going to die too."

Pop is like a lot of Greeks of his generation. Quick-minded, opinionated, and philosophical, viewing life with black humor. I didn't really understand until years later that he was saying we only think of death in personal terms when something reminds us of our frail mortality. Something like tumbling around on the ocean bottom.

The violence stopped.

I rolled my body and reached over my right shoulder, sliding my hand along the regulator hose until I found the mouthpiece. I jammed it into my mouth and bit down hard, cleared the mouthpiece of water, and gulped in air. There was the muted roar of an engine, the sea bottom went kazowee again, and I did another lousy imitation of a Flying Wallenda.

This was getting monotonous. True, I wasn't floating belly-up—not yet, anyway—but my minutes had dwindled down to a precious few. I could make an emergency ascent and play dodge 'em on the surface, assuming I could find up. Or I could try swimming away from the surface buoy which seemed to be attracting all the deadly attention. When my air ran out, I would simply improvise. Not a great plan, but it was a plan.

To the east was three thousand miles of open ocean between me and Portugal. Swimming parallel to the beach in either direction would still leave me offshore and vulnerable. So I would head for land. First, I had to figure which way was up. I took a deep breath to increase buoyancy. My body rose slightly. I exhaled and felt the direction of the bubbles with my hand. Orienting myself in a more-or-less up-down posture, I looked at the barely visible face of my wrist compass. Then, with a flurry of fin strokes, I headed south-westerly toward the good ol' U.S. of A. Half a minute later I broke into slightly clearer water. I swam down and dragged my hand along the bottom to give me some reference as I tried to go in a straight line.

From behind and above came the growl of an engine.

I concentrated on the downward thrusts of my legs. One-two, one-two. I picked up the pace. Onetwothreefour. Onetwothreefour. My aching thigh and calf muscles screamed pain messages to my brain. My feet tendons were taut as bowstrings.

Rumrumrumrum.

The engine's roar grew ominously louder. I pumped my legs harder, harder. My kicks had lost their rhythmical cadence. The long, ground-covering power strokes had degenerated into a series of jerky energy-draining flutters. I must have looked ridiculously like one of those little toads you catch in your headlights, desperately hopping across a busy highway on a rainy night. One. More. Hop. And. I'll. Be. *Squish.*

The engine sound thundered in my ears. I tried zigzagging. The boat followed my trail of bubbles like a bloodhound homing in on a hot scent. I thrashed the water erratically, waiting for the blast that would send tons of ocean crashing down on my head.

But for a change, I got lucky.

A reddish smudge loomed in the murk just ahead. I stared in astonishment through the spiderweb cracks on my face mask. It couldn't be! A few kicks and I was hugging the sea scooter's plastic casing.

Doxa to Theos! Thank God. My old Greek school lessons coming back. I examined the scooter. It looked okay, but the motor could have been damaged. One way to find out. I grabbed a handgrip and squeezed the trigger. The obnoxious whine was like a Mozart symphony to my ears.

The sound was drowned out by the roar of the boat passing overhead. I braced myself and waited to be pounded onto the muck again, but it didn't happen. Giant invisible fingers plucked me off the bottom instead. The spinning propellers had gone into reverse thrust. Someone badly wanted to make pâté out of me. The same water column that flattened me a minute earlier was sucking me up toward the surface, into the whirling prop blades.

I squeezed the scooter's trigger and let it tow me away

from ground zero, cruising for several minutes, letting my breath out slowly to conserve air and reduce the bull's-eye ripples my exhalations etched on the surface. I had just a few minutes of air left. I couldn't outrun my pursuer, but if I got closer to shore the boat might not follow me into shallow water where it would go aground. In realistic terms, my choice would be made for me. I would run out of air or the scooter would conk out. Then I would either surface or start learning to breathe like a fish.

I stopped and listened, like a U-boat crew waiting out a depth-charge attack. The engine sound was fainter.

I headed southwest again, the scooter slowing perceptibly as its batteries ran down. My pressure gauge said the air tank was on empty. As if I couldn't have guessed it. My rib cage seemed to have shrunk three sizes. A smothering weakness afflicted every muscle in my body. And I was suffocating. When you run out of air, the flow continues, but it becomes increasingly more difficult to pull life-giving air out of your tank. I practically swallowed the regulator trying to suck the last cubic inches into my oxygen-impoverished lungs. Then the scooter died.

Time to go up.

I released the scooter and yanked the quick-release buckle on my weight belt as I kicked off the bottom. The belt dropped off. Newly buoyant, I rose toward the beckoning silvery surface. The residual air in my tank expanded slightly with the change in pressure, giving me one last belabored breath. The seconds crept by. I was on a skyscraper elevator that paused for passengers at every floor. The moments seemed to stretch into long, agonizing hours.

My head broke the surface. I spat out my mouthpiece and gasped in sweet burning lungfuls of air. Then I blew into the BC's manual inflation tube, puffing up the vest to keep me afloat, and swiveled in the water, expecting to see a keel bearing down on the tempting target offered by my bobbing head.

There were a few boats in the distance, nothing near me, but a wind had picked up, ruffling the surface, and I couldn't see much detail from sea level. My skiff was nowhere in sight. Sunk, scuttled, or towed, I guessed.

I eyeballed the distance to shore. About an eighth of a mile. Not a tough swim under ordinary circumstances. But I was dizzy from the battering I had taken and worn out by the struggle to escape the killing blasts. I rested for five or ten minutes, inhaling deeply until my breathing slowed. Then I struck out for shore, breast-stroking slowly and resting every few minutes. Each movement of my leaden arms and legs was torture.

Just outside the surf zone where the waves gathered energy for their assault on the beach, I stopped to evaluate my situation. I was still a hundred yards from land, but the breaking waves indicated a sandbar and shallow water closer to me. I moved in, letting the surge pull me toward shore, working the energy from the rollers. I was being carried in at an angle by the longshore current, but that didn't bother me. Any help was welcome.

The rumble and hiss of breaking waves echoed in my ears. I unsnapped my vest and pulled off my tank and let it drop. My cracked face mask followed. I caught the breaking crest of a slow-moving sea and body-surfed forward. I did it again, playing the rollers, gaining a few precious yards each time. A couple of tanned surfers schooned by on either side and waved.

My fins touched bottom. I pushed into foamy waist-deep water. Only a few more feet. I was on my knees at the edge of the steeply inclined beach. The slope was only about five feet, but it looked like Mount Kilimanjaro. I pulled off my fins, then stood and flung my upper body onto the shore, clawing out handfuls of wet sand.

The sea wasn't through yet. A powerful undertow from the back-rushing waves sucked greedily at my feet. Hundreds of loose, gravel-sized stones, hurled by the last-gasp waves breaking against the beach, pummeled my ankles and left black and blue marks that would last for days.

Choking with exhaustion, I crawled on all fours up the crumbly incline, like a slimy amphibian escaping the primordial ooze, and lay with my face in a pile of foul-smelling seaweed, spitting out half the Atlantic Ocean.

A few minutes later I sat up. I was pulling off my hood when one of the surfers, a gangly kid in wildly flowered bathing trunks, dragged his board over and squatted next to me.

"Hey, dude. You okay?"

I nodded weakly.

His concerned face cleared. "Man, where'd you swim in from? England?"

I slapped the hood down on the beach and looked at him blearily. "Pip, pip, old chap."

"Radical, dude," he said.

I wiped the stinging seawater from my eyes. The other surfer was still skimming the low wave tops on his light plastic board. On another day I would have enjoyed watching him work the incoming rollers. But I was scanning the water beyond the surf line, fearfully contemplating the great blue-green ocean where I had nearly joined the *Gabriella* in her watery tomb.

CHAPTER 29

The back of the Jeep Wrangler wasn't made for anyone taller than a fire hydrant. I elbowed aside a couple of dripping surfboards and adjusted my butt more comfortably on the soggy wet suits, cupping my hands over my ears. The stereo was cranked up as high as the moon, Jeep zipping along Route 6 in a happy blitz of decibels. Real romantic stuff. Some heavy-metal riff about death and destruction. It fit my mood.

My newfound surfer buddy and his girlfriend had offered me a ride to my truck. He conceded that losing my boat was almost as radical as swimming from England, and I had to admit he had a point. It was dark when the Jeep jerked to a stop at the parking lot where I'd left the GMC that morning. They pried me from the back and I found the spare ignition keys I keep in a magnetic case under the truck. I assumed the Privateer had gone to the ocean bottom with the other keys and my lunch. I hoped the fish were enjoying my bologna sandwiches.

The young man shook my hand, and his girlfriend gave me a sisterly peck on the cheek. Somehow that made me feel ancient. Then they piled off in the direction of a surfers' bar in search of new and greater challenges to their eardrums.

I stripped off my wet suit to my bathing trunks, wrapped a Mexican blanket I keep in the truck over my shoulders, Navajo style, and drove home hunched over the steering wheel, truck heater on full blast. Back in the boat house, I popped a Bud and called Larry to say I had an accident and lost his sea scooter. He told me not to sweat it, his insurance premiums were up to date.

After I showered, changed into dry clothes, and ate a

peanut butter and grape jelly sandwich on Wonder Bread, I felt better, but I was still in a foul temper. I was probably being overly sensitive, just because somebody deep-sixed several thousand bucks' worth of boat and motor I was still paying loans on and tried to kill me for no apparent reason. I paced from one end of the boat house to the other, which wasn't very far, slamming my fist into the palm of my hand. I wanted to punch somebody in the nose. Real bad. But who?

Taking a wild guess, I ventured that I'd been blasted underwater by prop-wash diverters. It would be nice to think my quick wits saved me, but I knew better. Without tie-down anchors, the boat would have fishtailed all over the ocean when it used its mailboxes. Finding the sea scooter was sheer luck on my part.

I took the cardboard tube holding Barrett's papers out of the closet and put it in the truck. I was thankful that I'd had the sense to make copies and left the originals safely at home. I don't remember anything about the trip to Provincetown except that I got there fast. Thoughts churned in my mind. I wanted to see Lucas, but the *El Toro* wasn't in the harbor. I asked a few people working on the dock where Lucas was and finally found a fisherman who had seen his boat go out the night before.

Barrett's boat was tied up at its usual space. Lights glowed in the cabin. I got the cardboard tube out of the truck and I was walking toward the *Shamrock* when I tripped over a thought. I sat near a piling for a few minutes and ran my eye over Barrett's boat, from the stern to the bow and back to the stern again. Then I went back to the truck and put the tube under the seat.

My dive bag was still in the truck. I pulled out my fins, an old but serviceable spare mask, and a ten inch, three-cell Seatec waterproof flashlight. I tested the batteries. The beam was strong. Then I carried the gear onto the beach and ducked into the cool dank shadows under the pier. I stripped to my underwear, put the fins on, and slipped into the water up to my knees. It was chilly without a wet suit, but not unpleasant. If I only stayed in a few minutes I wouldn't turn blue. I kept going.

Oily mounds of seaweed and plastic debris floated near shore. I pushed them aside and breaststroked slowly into the harbor, staying close to the boats moored along the pier, using them to shield me. I didn't want anyone asking why I was swimming around in my underwear playing navy frogman.

As I passed under the stern of a cabin cruiser someone on the aft deck coughed. I froze. Maybe I had been spotted. Steps edged closer. I took a deep breath and readied for a quick surface dive. The footsteps stopped. A cigarette butt sailed through the air in an orange arc and landed with a *phht* about a foot from my head. The coughing started again, drowning out any ripples I might make. Guy really should give up smoking.

I pushed on. A few strokes short of the *Shamrock* I stopped and treaded water. The boat loomed over me like a skyscraper and I couldn't see on deck, but all was quiet. I hyperventilated, taking several deep breaths to build up my lung capacity, then ducked below the hull from the port side. When I thought I was safely out of view, I flipped on the light, running the beam along the slimy underside of the hull, which looked enormous from this angle. I came out on the starboard side, moved a few feet closer to the stern, caught a breath, and dove again.

I was on my third underwater crisscross when I found what I was looking for.

I made two more dives just to make sure, then swam back to the beach. Once under the pier, I stripped off my underwear, dried myself with an old sweatshirt, then dressed. I took my gear back to the truck. I smelled slightly of harbor oil but didn't look any worse than your average wharf rat after I combed my hair in the side mirror. I retrieved the tube from the truck and strolled over to Barrett's boat. For the second time that night I stopped short of my goal.

The wharf lights glinted off a sleek shape parked near where the *Shamrock* was tied up. I took a closer look. Nice car. Black Porsche 911. I went over and sat next to a piling where I had a clear view of the car and boat.

Twenty minutes later, the *Shamrock*'s pilothouse door opened and two figures were silhouetted against the interior illumination. One was a giant bearded man. Barrett. The other was a woman, a svelte woman with her hair in a ponytail. I could feel the heat of their clinch from where I stood. She broke off the embrace, murmured something, then left the boat, climbed into the sports car, and drove off. Nothing surprises me. But this surprised me.

I took the charts back to the truck again. I needed a beer. Maybe two.

An hour later I climbed aboard the *Shamrock* and yelled down the hatchway. Barrett came onto the deck. He didn't smile right away when he saw me, and when he did, it seemed forced, as if he had other things on his mind.

"I guess I'm not the only one who drops in out of the blue," he said. "Come below and have some coffee. I'm just brewing up a pot."

"Maybe you'd like some reading material to go with it," I said, handing over the cardboard tube.

Barrett glanced at me, a question in his eyes, then he reached out and took the tube from my hand. We went into the pilothouse. He stripped off the masking tape I had resealed it with, pulled out the roll of papers, and spread them onto his chart table. A moment later he looked up and grinned.

"Dammit, Soc! It's all here. Every single bit. The photos, the Loran, the charts. You're a genius. Where'd the hell you find this stuff?"

"In a very unlikely spot, I must admit. I'll tell you in time. Look, I'm not trying to be cute about this; I'll explain the whole thing when I give you my written report, along with my bill."

Barrett clamped me on the shoulder. It didn't hurt for more than a minute. His mood had changed to one of ebullience. "Ask and you shall receive," he declared.

"I guess you'll be making a *Gabriella* run now that you have this stuff."

"Yeah," he said, scratching his beard. "Tomorrow, if I can, but I've got to iron out some engine problems. The state board meets tomorrow. I'll get the info they want to Eileen. She can deal with them and get the permit straightened out. I'm anxious as hell to get moving before that storm hits and reburies the whole damn site. I'll let you know, just in case you're interested in tagging along."

"Lucas could still raise hell and screw up your permit," I said.

Barrett looked up quickly and said, "Lucas won't be a problem."

"I'd like to be there when you relocate the wreck. Call me."

"I'll be sure to do that. Damn, Soc, I don't know how to thank you."

"No problem," I said. I got up, and we went onto the deck. I stepped onto the rail and paused. I don't know what I was waiting for. Barrett and I stood in the damp evening coolness, saying nothing. Barrett was smiling and he had his papers clenched tightly in his big hand as if they were a bird that would fly away. Finally I saluted with my forefinger and climbed onto the dock.

There was little traffic on Route 6. I drove past the silent dunes that curved darkly against the star-speckled sky like the contours of a reclining nude. I kicked the truck along at a respectable speed, but the drive home seemed very, very long indeed.

The phone rang shortly after I got back to the boat house. It was Laura Nichols. Laura said her husband was going to make his move within the next day or two. She said he would be going by boat. She said he would be carrying a lot of cash and needed protection. She said she would call me tomorrow with the details. I said okay, okay, okay, okay, and okay and hung up. Then I went out on the deck and listened to the dark waters of the incoming tide gurgle against the shore.

CHAPTER 30

Barrett called just before sunrise the next day. He had worked all night, fixed his engine, hoped to catch the morning tide, and couldn't wait for me. Sorry. Maybe the next time. He had put the packet containing the information for the state archaeological board on the late bus to Boston. Eileen would meet the bus and plead his case to the board. She'd make a hell of a better impression than he would anyway, he said. I wished him luck and hung up. It was nice of Barrett to call. I didn't expect him to.

I lay back on my pillow and stared at the wall, watching it grow paler as Homer's rosy-fingered dawn reached through the windows. Pictures flashed there, like slides from a projector. Images of dead divers trussed up like haddock, of old cannon and sea mung, of pretty blue eyes that lied.

The reflected sunlight became blinding. I got out of bed, made coffee, and called Chief Farrell. Then I phoned the wharfinger, the town official who watches over the pier in Provincetown. Yes, he said, looked like the *Shamrock* was getting ready to go out. No, there wasn't a black sports car parked on the wharf. Come to think of it, he'd seen a car like that on the other pier, where the marina is. Damn right he noticed the driver. Who wouldn't? I asked if he'd seen her before. Couple of times this summer, he recalled. She'd been talking to that diver. The blond guy who drowned. I thanked him, hung up and tapped the kitchen table for a minute, then dialed another number.

A cool male voice answered. "Nichols residence."

"I'd like to speak to Mr. Nichols, please."

"I'll see if he can come to the telephone. May I say who's calling?"

"Yes, tell him it's Tom Johnson. And if he doesn't remember my name, say I'm the man he met at the Harbour Club, the condo builder from Maine who owns that Chatham property."

Nichols's affable voice came on the phone a minute later. "Well, Mr. Johnson, nice to hear from you. Did your deal on the land sale fall through?"

"Sorry to disappoint you, Mr. Nichols. There never was any land deal. And my name isn't Johnson. It's Socarides and I'm a private investigator." No sense beating around the bush.

"I'm afraid I don't understand, Mr. Johnson or Socarides or whoever you are. What's your game?" The polished veneer had peeled off as if I'd held a blowtorch to it.

"No game, Mr. Nichols. I was hired by your wife to keep an eye on you. Can we talk about it?"

"My wife? Laura? I don't believe that. No, hold on. I have forty-five minutes free at ten this morning. Can you come to my house? I'll give you directions."

"No need to, Mr. Nichols. I'll find it. Just let the man at the gate know I'm coming."

I rang off and tried to picture Nichols at the other end. Was he phoning a battery of lawyers, or cops? I doubted it. I arrived at the gatehouse a few minutes before ten. The gateman had my name and passed me through.

The entrance to the Nichols driveway was flanked by massive fieldstone pillars. The drive was nearly a mile long, with glimpses of water and sailboats through tall evergreens, lovingly tended rosebushes, and blue explosions of hydrangea.

On Cape Cod it's considered tacky to display wealth ostentatiously. Not like Newport, where the rich call their places summer cottages but build them to look like Buckingham Palace. The Cape Cod wealthy try to hide their affluence behind a tasteful covering of silver-gray shingles and white trim. The masquerade doesn't quite do the job. The houses are simply too big to belong to anyone who works by the hour. The billiard-table lawns are the color of money and the sleek cars in the garage are not the kind you buy with a hundred dollars down. The architect had tried to "quaint" the Nichols house by putting a nonfunctional windmill at one end. It only made the mansion more imposing.

I parked in front of a portico and hoped my truck wouldn't

be removed by the hired help and taken to the dump with the household trash. A silver-haired man in a black suit opened the front door with the gracefulness of a ballet dancer while I still had my finger on the bell. I recognized his frosty voice from my call. He ushered me into a darkly paneled circular reception room. It had a crystal chandelier that could have come from Versailles and a parquet floor like the basketball court at Boston Garden.

"Mr. Nichols is waiting for you in the sunroom," the butler said in a reverential whisper, indicating a door to my right. I stepped in. The door closed behind me with a quiet click.

The room was hospital white. Light streamed in through the curving bank of French doors that opened onto a brick patio and bounced off the walls and ceiling with an intensity that hurt the eyes. Someone had decorated the room with large-leafed tropical plants that looked like they would eat you if they got a chance. The furniture was bleached wicker with sky blue cushions. A breeze smelling of manicured flower gardens and newly cut grass wafted through the doors and tossed the pale gauzy curtains. Nichols was expecting me.

He sat at a mahogany desk only slightly darker than his tan, his back to the patio. He was going over some papers but pushed them aside and got to his feet when I came in. He was wearing white slacks and a cotton V-neck sweater that was coordinated with the room's seat cushions. He smiled, shook my hand, and said with a straight face how glad he was to see me.

"Mr. Socarides, am I pronouncing it correctly?"

"Close enough. Everybody has trouble at first. By the time you learn to say it right we'll be old friends."

He raised a skeptical eyebrow. "Let's go onto the patio. It's a beautiful morning." He led the way to a white metal table and two chairs under a striped umbrella. The patio extended out from the house like the prow of a battleship. The house sat in turn on a promontory that jutted into a large bay. A stairway led down a cliffside and I'd bet there was a private dock and a cabin cruiser at the end of it.

The butler brought us a silver tray holding a bone white porcelain coffeepot and two cups with handles too small for my fingers. He poured the coffee, but neither Nichols nor I touched it.

"You know," Nichols mused, "it really is a shame you don't have that Chatham property. I'd be most interested in it. Well then. Let's get right to the point, shall we? You say my wife hired you to follow me. I find that hard to believe."

"Truth is stranger than fiction, Mr. Nichols. I don't usually discuss an investigation with anyone other than the person who hired me, but technically, since you're paying the bill, you contracted for my services, whether you know it or not." I laid out what Laura had said about his former connections to the Mob, his fear it would murder him as a potential government witness.

His face flushed. "That's ridiculous. I've never had anything to do with organized crime."

"I know that, Mr. Nichols. I also know you're on the hit list of a much bigger organization. It's called the federal government. Frankly, I might prefer the Mob to the feds if I were in your place."

"What exactly do you want, Mr. Socarides? Money? Are you trying to blackmail me?"

"No, I don't want money. I want information. I think your wife was trying to set us both up and I want to know if I'm right."

He said nothing. I went on.

"Let's look at the facts. Your wife could have hired a slick detective agency that used unmarked cars with two-way radios and listening devices that can hear you think. Instead, she hires me to keep an eye on you. My cases tend more to finding missing lobster pots or spouses that have run off to Boston for a weekend tryst with a lifeguard. Real low-end stuff. Hell, I'm not even in the Yellow Pages."

"If you were so suspicious, why did you take the case?"

"Simple. I needed the money. And your wife can be very persuasive, as you know. I went along against my instincts, thinking I was smart enough to handle anything tossed at me. It's called hubris. Greek word. Means excessive pride that makes you arrogant and, in my case, stupid."

"I still don't believe Laura hired you. But assuming she did, why you?"

"Once I learned the Mob-connection story was a phony, I asked myself the same question. If she didn't really need my detecting abilities, what *did* she want me for? I'm a loner, a dropout and cop-out and something of a lush. She might have talked to people who said I'm an unstable character. I quit a responsible job in Boston to grub for a living by the shore. I'm a Vietnam vet, and we all know 'Nam vets are screwballs with agent-orange hangovers and post-traumatic stress syndrome. Ticking psychological bombs. I was the perfect candidate."

Nichols furrowed his brow. "Perfect? The perfect candidate for what?"

I took a sip of lukewarm coffee and leaned across the table. "To be your murderer," I said.

Nichols's face went pale under the tan. His cup clinked down on the saucer and coffee sloshed onto his white pants. He reached under his sweater and pulled out a gun and pointed it at me. Served me right. I had forgotten about the bull's-eye on my chest that everybody could see but me. The .22 Ruger target pistol Nichols held wouldn't make any more noise than a loud hiccup if he squeezed the trigger.

"You can put that away, Mr. Nichols." I took another sip. "I don't murder for money or love. Just relax and we'll talk about it."

"Let us, indeed, talk about it." Beads of sweat glistened on his forehead, but his voice was calm. The pistol stayed where it was.

"As I was saying, your wife hired me, sought me out in fact, and I'm not easy to find. But she knew exactly what she wanted. Someone considered eccentric and reclusive, someone who knew how to use guns and might even have one. Someone who might do anything for a buck. You're in trouble, Mr. Nichols, and not because of me. The feds want you for laundering drug money and for a few other trifles. That's no secret to you, I'm sure. You've probably got a whole law firm lined up that will work like demons to keep you out of jail."

Nichols didn't flinch. He said only, "Go on, Mr. Socarides."

"Your wife is a poor girl become rich. She knows that when Uncle Sam moves in, you'll be paying a platoon of lawyers at two bucks a minute. The feds will freeze your assets and grab everything not nailed down. Even if you win, you're likely to be left with a financial house of cards that could tumble at the slightest breath. But worse, from your wife's point of view, you could implicate her. You could plea-bargain for immunity and say she's really the brains behind the operation, which she may be. Spouses have turned on one another when the stakes have been much lower than twenty years in a federal prison. Even with time off for good behavior, that's a life sentence at your age. For a beautiful young woman like your wife, it's more like a death warrant."

"That's absurd and insulting. My wife and I love each other."

"Not the way I read it. Remember, she didn't tell you she . hired me. Maybe she didn't want to worry you, but I'd hazard a guess that the missus knew your heart wouldn't break if she had to work for a nickel a shirt in a prison laundry. Wives usually sense what their husbands are thinking. The way you look at her, or something you mumble in your sleep, or giving her expensive presents with no apparent reason. Hell hath no fury and so on. . . . But the bottom line for Mrs. Nichols was clear. You were more valuable to her dead than alive."

"Mr. Socarides, this is fascinating melodrama. Assuming it is true, what were my wife's plans? You can understand my interest, of course?"

"Of course. I think she wanted me in the picture for a couple of reasons. First, simply to watch you so she'd know what you were up to. I joined the parade, not knowing that a gaggle of state and federal troops were part of it. They've probably logged my license plate onto their computer, but even if they haven't, somebody, maybe even Mrs. Nichols, would have remembered seeing my truck around if anything happened to you. Next would have been to have something happen to you and to frame me."

"How would she go about doing that?"

"I have a rough idea. My gun got stolen and I think your wife had something to do with it. Then last night she called. She told me you were going to take a lot of money out of your sock or wherever you keep cash in this big old house, get into a boat, and ride it somewhere. You'd have a body-guard, though. Me. Surprised?"

"Granted that I am," Nichols said, "what was her pur-pose in telling you?"

"The feds are watching your house from the road, but they're not too imaginative sometimes, and notoriously cheap, so they wouldn't patrol the water. Even so, I'd guess you've something that could outrun them, and your chauffeur is a pretty handy guy on a boat, I hear, which is probably one of the reasons you hired him. You'd go off to the Bahamas or someplace where you could negotiate with the government guys from a safe distance. You haven't been charged yet, but you seem like a cautious fellow and probably wanted a fallback position."

"You still haven't explained why she called you."

"Your wife said she wanted me to protect you. If past performance is an indication, she wants just the opposite. I'd wager that in the morning some boaters would find your body, maybe with a few empty money bags and some hundred-dollar bills lying around. You'd be shot with my gun, which would be found in the nearby bushes. That would pin the murder on me. Your wife paid me in cash, so she could deny she'd ever hired me. Or I'd simply be made to disappear. I don't know if she had the plan going from the start or if it occurred to her after she hired me to shadow you. Pretty crude, but it could work. Your wife would have the dough, get rid of a possible prosecution witness, and the feds would be left trying to untangle your finances, something that could take years."

"And my wife would do this all by herself, I suppose," Nichols said.

"Naw," I said. "By the way, where's your chauffeur today?"

"Laura gave him the day off. She drove herself to Boston early this morning to do some shopping at Bonwit's. Why do you ask?"

"You should screen your help more carefully, Mr. Nichols. Your chauffeur's got a court record longer than a novel by Tolstoy. Edward is not the kind of guy I'd trust a $70,000 automobile with, to say nothing of a wife. You asked me what I wanted. Simple. I've had to put this little scenario together from bits and pieces, and it may have more holes in it than a fishing net. I wanted to run it by you to see how it played. What do you think, Mr. Nichols? Think I'm pretty close, give or take a few details?"

Nichols stared at me for several seconds. He looked amused but not really happy. Obviously reassured by my trustworthy face, he lowered the gun and rested it on the table. His fingers remained on the grip. He turned his head and gazed out over the bay, silent as the waters.

"Thanks for being so cooperative," I said. "How's this one? Was there anything between your wife and Kip Scannell?"

"Why should I tell you anything, Mr. Socarides?"

"Fair question. Let's see if I can answer it. I could say confession is good for the soul, but I'm not sure I believe it myself. Kip was murdered. He knew your wife, which links him to you. Kip was in the drug trade. He laundered some of the money himself, but he needed help getting rid of a lot of it. If the cops are right in saying you're in the laundry business, you put some of his cash on the spin-dry cycle. It's possible he and your wife were having an affair. As a jealous husband, you'd be a prime suspect. So it might be in your best interests to help me find his murderer. Unless, of course, you are the killer, but I don't think so."

Nichols took his time replying.

"Very well," he said finally. "Kip and Laura were lovers. Laura and I had long passed the love, honor, and cherish stage. Perhaps we never had it. We were strictly business partners. She may have derived some pleasure from her affair with Kip, but knowing Laura as I do, I believe it was strictly one of the costs of doing business. It gave her some leverage over Kip, access to his innermost thoughts. Pillow talk and all that. And you're right about Kip. I'm not his murderer. I don't know who is."

"What was your wife's relationship with Barrett?"

"Who is Barrett?"

"He owns the boat Kip worked on."

"That's a new one." Nichols shrugged. "Nothing, as far as I know. I don't really know anything about him. Our dealings were with Kip." He caught the look in my eye and smiled sardonically. "Oh, no. Don't tell me. Laura's wrapped Mr. Barrett around her finger."

"What do you know about a big dope drop on July thirteenth?"

"Nothing, really. Laura would have been more privy to that information. I knew there was going to be a delivery of some sort this summer. But I was only interested in how cash can be converted into real estate and other legitimate enterprises."

"Who do you think might have killed Kip?"

Nichols laughed, bitterly. "Could have been anyone. Kip was not well liked."

I rose to go. "Thanks for the coffee. Don't bother, I can find my way."

Nichols ignored me. He had turned back to look out over the water, his thoughts elsewhere.

I stepped off the patio, feeling the lawn like a shag rug under my sandals, and walked around the house to the driveway. I was glad to see my truck still there.

Nichols would be turning over possibilities, calculating odds, weighing options, revising his escape schedule to fit the turn of events, making his move, getting away.

Not if I could help it.

As soon as I found a pay phone, the feds would get an anonymous tip alerting them to the possibility Nichols might take a boat ride. I looked around at the mansion and the vast lawns rolling down to the low cliffs overlooking the bay. Impressive spread. Maybe the government would turn the place into something useful. Like a drug rehabilitation center.

CHAPTER 31

A summer storm was in the making, building up power like a runaway dynamo. The humid air was heavy and suffocating, charged with the impending threat of nature's violence. On a brooding evening like this, Eugene O'Neill would have written a play, inspired by the elemental forces pounding at the door of his Province Lands dune shack. But I saw no romance in my surroundings. The festering sky and leaden atmosphere evoked morbid stirrings in my soul. I watched and waited in the shadows of the marina pier, across from MacMillan Wharf, trying to imagine what it must be like to drown, and thinking about restless corpses rotting on the ocean bottom.

The heavens glowed, and the brief incandescent light cast the rough granite of the Provincetown monument and the dun cliffs of Truro in stark relief against the sooty sky. A few seconds later came a rumble, like distant artillery pounding an infantry position. The storm was advancing across Cape Cod Bay behind a phalanx of angry black clouds, rolling toward Provincetown, moving fast.

Another flash followed. I counted chimpanzees, a chimp for each mile, calculating the storm's distance like a child trying to calm his nervous fears.

One chimpanzee, two chimpanzee, three chimpan ... *caruump!* Three miles.

A wettish williwaw rolled in from the bay and slapped sailboat halyards against their aluminum masts in a brief chang-chang chorus. Then the wind died and the sleeping harbor was deathly still again, but only for a moment.

From out near the red beacon on the breakwater came the throaty gargle of a boat exhaust. A gray daub blossomed in the darkness and hardened into the cone of a spotlight that probed the gloom. The boat moved cautiously toward an isolated, unlit docking area near the big vacant shed at the end of the wharf. Then the engine cut and the hull thudded softly against the dock fenders. I moved closer, slipping from one pool of darkness to another.

Footsteps padded cautiously up a ramp to the parking lot. A figure crossed to the small office where the night watchman napped, emerged moments later, and got into a pickup truck. The truck backed up to the edge of the dock without turning on its headlights. The driver got out and disappeared down the ramp. Moments later a boom winch motor growled.

I descended the ramp, flashlight in hand, and crept stealthily along a long catwalk, stopping a few yards from the spectral outline of the boat. A hint of perfume came my way.

Jasmine.

There was something else. A ghostly whitish patch floated about ten feet in the air, midway between the boat's cranking boom and the dock. I switched on my flashlight. The finger of light picked out the dirty brown fabric of a canvas tarp, slung over the load swinging from a cable.

The winch motor whined to a sudden halt. I swept the beam toward the boat. The bull's-eye fell on the pale faces of Laura Nichols and Edward, her chauffeur.

"Hi, folks," I said, real friendlylike. "Can I give you a hand?"

Barrett had been operating the winch. He stepped forward, his features grotesque in the angled illumination. He raised his hand in an unenthusiastic gesture of greeting, then let it drop.

"Hello, Soc. You should have let me know you were stopping by. I would have put the coffee on."

"No problem, Mike. I don't drink coffee this late. Caffeine keeps me awake. Say, looks like you were right about the storm. Some real nasty stuff shaping up."

Barrett glanced around and sniffed the air. "Yeah, I could smell it coming. Weather's been thickening all day. Sky had a real bloody look to it at sunrise."

"You know what the old-timers say: Red sky at morning, sailor take warning."

The conversation had an air of unreality to it. I decided to bring it back to earth. I pointed the flashlight up again, reached out, and whipped aside a corner of the tarp like a magician in the vanishing-lady trick. The canvas fell to the catwalk.

The metal cylinders were slung side by side in a nylon cradle, their shiny surfaces shimmering in the light of the electrical fireworks display over Race Point. Thunder rolled across the harbor. A two-chimpanzee count.

I waited until the last resonating echo had faded. "Those are damn funny-looking cannon, Mike."

No one spoke, so I continued my hilarious monologue. No sense quitting when you've got them rolling in the aisles.

"Hey, wait a minute. Maybe they're not cannon," I said. "Maybe they're torpedoes. This is one for the books. Congratulations, Mike. You'll have the archaeologists in a tizzy, just the way you wanted. I'll bet they had no idea you could get hardware like that back in the 1700's."

Still no reply. I kept on.

"Hell, Mike, you won't believe this, but I saw a couple of things like that on a dive yesterday, before somebody tried to blast me out of the ocean."

I flicked the light back to the boat, playing it from face to face.

"For God sakes," Laura said harshly. "He doesn't carry a gun."

Her chauffeur reached into his windbreaker and pulled out a .38 Smith & Wesson that resembled the gun stolen from my truck the night I tried to crawl into Laura's shorts. Eddy pointed my pistol at me and said, "What do we do with him?"

"We don't have any choice," she said.

"Sure you do," I said cheerfully. "We could all go over to the police station and dictate a statement. Let's make a party of it. I'd spring for the cotton candy."

Laura laughed as if she had just heard some droll chitchat at a lawn party. "Mr. Socarides, I'm really going to miss you. You have no idea how sorry I am we were interrupted that evening on my boat."

She wasn't the only one. Even with a gun pointed at me, even with Laura talking as if I were a horse with a broken leg who would have to be put out of its misery, I still marveled at what a lovely creature she was. When God created woman, in her case, He had outdone Himself. The denim of her designer jeans was tight against the curve of her hips and her long legs. Her perfect mouth was partly open in a perfect smile that showed her perfect white teeth.

"Yeah, I'm sorry too," I said. I meant it. "But don't forget the new tires you bought me, Mrs. Nichols. That was swell of you. It almost makes up for the damage to my skull."

"I do apologize for your truck. Edward was only supposed to put you to sleep for a few minutes to help remove any doubts you may have had about my case. And to take your gun. Sometimes he gets carried away." She glanced at Barrett. "I'm sorry, Michael. I should have explained, but you had so much on your mind."

"I might forgive Eddy if you answer one question," I said. "Did you plan right from the start to set me up?"

Laura brushed a long blond tress back from her face in that careless and graceful and incredibly sensuous move I had seen her use before. Drops of moisture glittered like jewels in her hair.

She said, "It was Michael's idea to hire you. He was convinced you'd be able to move in Kip's world far more effectively than any outside detective agency. When he told me about your background, I decided you might be helpful in solving my own rather daunting problems."

Barrett cut in. "Where did you find my site papers?"

He was talking to me, but his eyes were on Laura.

"I hate to be the one to tell you this, Mike. The papers were behind the bar at the Hole. Geetch put them there for safekeeping. They were just a few yards away when we had our first conversation. I guess we underestimated Geetch. Kip was a shrewder judge of character. He saw that Geetch had a strong sense of honor. That he'd die before he'd betray a trust. Is that why you had to kill him, Mike? You did kill him, didn't you? Kip too."

"How did you know?" Barrett sounded sick.

"I wasn't certain until now. After I learned about Kip's drug connection, the compass needle just started swinging in your direction. But there were signals from the start. You left too many loose ends. His weight belt was far too heavy for a normal dive, and he never went for his sheath knives. But what really gnawed at me was the fact Kip went diving without his hood. What happened to it?"

Barrett said, "Kip was coming to, so I put his mask on without the hood."

Laura made an impatient sound. We ignored her. For now, it was just Barrett and me.

"As simple as that," I said. "It must have been tough, stuffing an unconscious man into a dry suit, pulling the fins onto his feet, buckling the air tank on."

"Tough, but not impossible."

"Not half as tough as dumping him over the side. You must have wanted him dead real bad, Mike." I was taunting him, but I didn't care.

"There wasn't any other way."

"There were other ways, Mike. Lots of them."

A gust that was more rain than wind whirled around us. Barrett pawed the drops off his anguished features. "It was an impossible situation, Soc. He was planning to take delivery and go into business for himself. It would have meant the end of the *Gabriella* project."

"I guess that's what fooled me, the fact that you had to find the *Gabriella* at all costs. I couldn't figure out why you'd sabotage your own project by murdering your diver and losing the site data."

"Losing the data wasn't in the plan."

"I didn't think so, Mike. Still, I might not have made a connection if I hadn't learned that the *Gabriella*'s treasure was probably long gone. That made me wonder what all the fuss was about. If there were no pot of gold at the end of the rainbow, why were you so intent on trying to relocate her? Conclusion? There must be something else you were after."

Barrett took a step forward. "What the hell are you talking about?"

"There's no treasure on that ship. It was salvaged the day after the *Gabriella* went down. Ask Eileen if you don't believe me."

A jagged bolt of lightning split the sky. Barrett's words were blotted out by the clap of thunder in its wake, but his mouth and brow were carved in a classic mask of fury, like the king in a Sophoclean tragedy who learns the dark truth about his past.

"That's right," I yelled over the ebbing rumble. "No lousy treasure! Maybe you never even hit the *Gabriella*."

"Goddammit, I found those coins! I found those cannon!"

"I'll say it again. Ask your sister."

"If Eileen knew, why didn't she tell me?"

"I don't know, Mike. I don't understand about Geetch, either. You still haven't told me why you killed him."

Barrett hesitated. His thoughts must have been in turmoil. His sister had betrayed him. Laura had carved out her own agenda and hadn't told him. Even if he had found the *Gabriella*, his beloved ship was an empty shell. He had killed for nothing. There was a hush, as if the storm were gathering itself for a major assault. Ordinary sounds, like the hollow slap of waves against the *Shamrock*, were magnified to sledge-hammer blows. The atmosphere was thick with danger.

He spoke, finally, unemotionally. "The bartender at the Hole told me Geetch and Kip had been spending a lot of time together. I knew Kip. He never would have said two words to Geetch if it didn't benefit him. I went to see Geetch on his boat. He denied he had the papers, but I could tell he was lying. I went to his cottage that night. He still wouldn't come through. I got angry. I tried to scare him. I picked him up and shook him. . . . He died so easily. I put him on his bed. Maybe I hoped he would wake up in the morning."

I remembered how Barrett had easily lifted the 150-pound artillery shell that day on his boat. Geetch would have snapped like a fragile feather in his massive hands.

"He didn't wake up," I said just loud enough to be heard. "He never will, Mike."

Laura had run out of patience. "That's quite enough, Mr. Socarides." Her wet hair had fallen in lank straggles into her face and her eye makeup was running.

"Just one more question. Did you lend a hand, Laura? Or did your perfume get in Geetch's room by itself?"

"Well." Laura said, surprise in her voice. "I was getting tired of that scent anyhow. Yes, you're right. I was waiting outside. I heard the altercation, but by the time I got in the cottage it was too late. Michael doesn't know his own strength." She shrugged. "It's quite possible Geetch would have had to be disposed of in any event." Matter-of-fact, like taking a load of old clothes to the Salvation Army bin. I marveled. God, what a beautiful cold-blooded bitch she was.

Barrett interrupted. "I didn't know that was you diving yesterday, Soc. I saw the boat. I thought maybe it was just some poacher after the *Gabriella*. I couldn't let that happen."

"No problem, Mike. Hell, what's another dead diver? By the way, what's the stuff in the cylinders worth? Half a million?"

It was Eddy's turn to get into the act. "Way off, cowboy," he said. Keeping the gun aimed at my chest, he climbed off the *Shamrock* onto the catwalk and faced me. "Get on board."

"No boat ride tonight, Eddy. I've got other plans."

"I just canceled them." He pressed the gun to my forehead and took the flash out of my hand.

"I wouldn't advise it, Eddy. I've got you surrounded."

He thought I was kidding. He curled his lip the way Edward G. Robinson used to do when he got the drop on Jimmy Cagney. It was time for John Wayne to arrive with the cavalry.

A bullhorn voice boomed: "Drop that gun, dirtbag, and freeze!"

Eddy whirled. Farrell was standing there, out of uniform, his badge pinned to the front of the blue shirt barely buttoned over his stomach. He had a Cheshire cat grin on his face. Not exactly John Wayne, but the .357 Magnum in his hand looked like something out of the OK Corral.

"Hi, Soc," he said eagerly. "Heard everything. Looks like we can wrap this one up." He took a couple of quick steps forward.

Eddy was a quick thinker. He flashed the light in Farrell's eyes, momentarily blinding him. The chief's shoe caught on a metal dock cleat. He pitched forward onto his hands and knees. The gun leaped from his hand and skittered across the catwalk like a hockey puck. So much for the cavalry.

Farrell pushed himself up. Eddy raised the pistol in his hand and pointed it at me again. He kicked Farrell's gun out of reach and handed the flashlight to Laura, who kept it trained on us.

"Shit," Farrell said. "Sorry about this, Soc."

"So am I, Chief. But it was a great entrance. What do you do for an encore?"

"I'm afraid there's not going to be an encore," Laura said. "You and your friend will have to come with us, Mr. Socarides. I regret it turned out this way."

"Yeah," I said. "Me too. This will really mess up your

plans. You'll have to figure another way to set up your husband."

"What are you talking about?"

"I had a nice little chat with Charles earlier today. Just before I called the feds and told them he was planning to take a boat trip. I would guess that right now he's in an interrogation room with a couple of DEA guys who are playing good-cop bad-cop with him. He's probably told them everything about you except your shoe size."

"You've become immediately dispensable," Laura said.

She sounded as if she meant it. I tried to change the subject. "What do you think about all this?" I appealed to Barrett. "You think that a dead ship is worth a couple more killings?"

"No." Barrett's voice was hollow, as if he were talking in a cave. "This has gone far enough, Laura."

"Michael," she said soothingly. "Everything will be fine. But we can't turn back now. We have to follow through to the end. Events have been taken out of our hands."

A light pattering rain began to fall.

"I'm taking them back into our hands," Barrett said.

"Don't you understand?" Angry now. "You have no say in this." She produced a .25-caliber automatic and held it where he could see its shiny nickel-plated barrel.

"You're the one who doesn't understand, darling." He stepped toward her.

Laura swung to face him.

The storm had resumed its advance while we talked. It was almost on top of us. Lightning danced everywhere you looked in the sky.

Raising her voice to be heard over the near-constant rumble of thunder, Laura said, "For the last time, Michael. I'm not going to throw my whole life away because you're tormented by a guilty conscience." It was a warning, as subtle as the hiss of a cobra, but Barrett did not hear it, or chose to ignore the lethal message.

He took another step and reached out for her gun.

"You fool," Laura said. She cracked off two shots, the gunshots sounding like snaps in the muffling noise of the storm. The bullets tore into his big frame. Barrett hesitated as if he'd been stung by a couple of bees, then lurched forward, his eyes ablaze, hand extended, grabbing for Laura's slim arm.

Laura backed away. She moved awkwardly, without her usual litheness. Her sleeve caught for an instant on a boat fitting and she had to jerk it free. I think she was terrified. People don't usually keep walking when you've pumped two slugs into their body. She racked off another shot. This one did it. Barrett stopped, grabbed at his chest, then crumpled over the side of the boat and onto the catwalk.

Laura was a cool one. She could have regained her composure, powdered her nose, and taken us all out if she'd had the chance to think about it. But she was distracted by an agonized voice screaming "Michael!" from the bulkhead above us. Eileen.

Eddy had been standing a few feet from me, watching the scene play out on the boat. His head swung up and around. I chopped at his shooting arm. He yelled with pain. My .38 clattered onto the catwalk.

Holding his arm with one hand, Eddy lunged toward the pistol. I went after him, ready to slam his face into the deck.

There was a loud click overhead.

My scalp prickled from the static electricity.

Then came a deafening crash, and more lightning and more earthshaking clamor. The smell of ozone was so strong I could taste it. The storm was all around us now, slashing the sky white in a dozen places, unleashing a molecule-jarring barrage, challenging the darkness with a stroboscopic intensity.

The catwalk, the boat, all the players in the opening-night performance of *Drama on the Docks,* were bathed in brilliant light. Laura stood there, frozen in time, like Antigone defiant. Her sweater was disheveled and ripped. But her mouth was set in a tight line of determination. She pointed her pistol at me. I stopped. Our eyes met.

"Eddy," she barked. "Get us out of here."

He picked up my .38, scrambled onto the boat, and untied the mooring lines, then he staggered into the pilothouse. Seconds later the engine roared. The boat moved slowly away from the dock, the cylinders swung wildly from the boom. Laura was in the stern near the prop-wash diverters, still pointing her pistol. When they were safely out of reach she turned, and with a parting, insouciant wave that may have been meant for me, joined Eddy in the pilothouse.

The clouds had opened like a busted water pipe, sending down torrents of heavy raindrops that were whipped to bullet velocity by wild gusts of wind. Eileen was with her brother now, cradling his head in her arms, trying to shield him. Farrell was on his hands and knees nearby, searching for his gun.

I raced along the catwalk. A few slips away from the *Shamrock* was a fourteen-foot wooden-hulled Novi with a big outboard. I was in luck. The boat's owner had left the gas tank. I would have preferred a PT boat, but this would have to do. I scrambled in, started the motor after a couple of pulls, cast off, and pointed the bow into the whitecapped harbor waters.

It dawned on me that I had absolutely no idea what I was doing. Once beyond the protection of the breakwater, I'd be lucky to stay afloat. And even if I caught the *Shamrock,* what the hell would I do, write them a ticket for a moving violation? Laura and Eddy were armed and weren't likely to respond to a citizen's arrest. I would have to improvise.

Farrell saved me the trouble.

I was starting to round the end of the pier when I discovered why the owner of the outboard had been so casual about leaving his boat. The motor sputtered, coughed, and died. I was out of gas. The *Shamrock* was a good hundred yards away. I watched in frustration as the boat picked up speed, passed the jetty, and paused momentarily, maneuvering for a dash into open water.

There was movement near the end of the pier. Farrell, loping along, then standing, motionless as a statue, was caught for just an instant in the electrical light. He had retrieved his pistol and clutched the cannon in both hands, regulation firing position, aimed at the *Shamrock*.

I remembered the wooden box in the blue storage locker.

"Farrell, no!"

My shouted warning was swallowed by the racket of the storm.

Farrell cranked out three shots. I could see the crimson muzzle bursts. Paused. Then fired three more times. The fifth or sixth round found a mark.

Christ!

The *Shamrock* simply disappeared. In its place was an enormous fiery swirling ball of yellow and red. There was a tremendous roar louder than any thunder. I stood up in reflex. Blistering heat seared my face. I threw my arm out in front of my eyes. The boat pitched violently. I clawed the air for one fruitless moment before I lost my balance and tumbled into the harbor. I went under twice and came up thrashing. I kicked off my sandals and half floated, half swam as best I could in the choppy water, until I heard shouts of "there he is," and strong hands were reaching down.

CHAPTER 32

It was two days later when Farrell called and woke me from something that resembled sleep but really wasn't. His voice sounded as if it were coming through a megaphone. "Sorry to get you outta bed. The EMTs do a good job putting you back together at the police station the other night?"

"I'll survive. I didn't really need eyebrows."

"That's good. I've got something you'd be interested in. Feel fit enough to make a quick dive?"

"Yeah, I guess so. Is it important?"

"Could be. See you at our town dock in forty-five minutes. We'll get some air tanks and diving gear at the fire department."

"Aye, aye, skipper," I mumbled.

I took a shower and made coffee, then went out on the deck. As often happens in New England, the weatherman had been fooled. The big storm Barrett and everyone else expected took a right-hand turn north of Cape Hatteras, only brushing us with a line of thunderstorms. The air was cool and the humidity low. It was the quintessentially perfect Cape Cod summer morning, but I couldn't appreciate the pristine beauty of the bay. Not today. I felt as empty inside as a gutted codfish. Kip. Geetch. Barrett. Laura. Eddy. All dead. And for what? I was feeling sorry for myself too. I had moved here to escape the troubles of the outside world, and they had followed me, snapping at my heels like a pack of mangy curs. After the appropriate dose of fresh air and self-pity I went back into the house.

Farrell and the harbormaster were readying the patrol boat when I arrived.

"Fisherman called in early this morning on Channel 16,"

Farrell explained as we cast off from the pier and moved into the channel. "The only diver in the fire department quit a couple of months ago and there's no money in the town budget to certify a new one until next year. I coulda brought someone in from the next town, but I had the feeling this might have something to do with us, you and me. Flatfoot's instinct. Holy Mother of God. Looks like everything is landing in my backyard. Well, it's sure a helluva lot more interesting than rousting college kids for sleeping on the beach."

The boat entered the harbor and picked up speed, heading into Cape Cod Bay. Twenty minutes later we came to a halt about a mile offshore, inside the curve of the Cape. The wind was light and the water surface unruffled.

"There it is," said the harbormaster, pointing.

A mast and radar antenna protruded from the water. He eased the boat closer, cut the motor, and dropped anchor. I got into the scuba gear Farrell had thoughtfully brought along and jumped overboard, following the mast down to the bow deck. I swam into the pilothouse and explored the galley and bunk room. There was a lot of junk floating around, but no sign of anyone, dead or alive.

Coming from below, I moved off the deck and kicked my way toward the gravelly bottom. The water was about twenty-five feet deep and clear. The boat lay with its black hull at a slight angle. From this perspective the vessel looked like a dead whale. I noted the registration numbers on the bow before circling the boat, gliding a few inches above foot-tall vegetation until I was back where I started.

I ran my eye over the wooden hull, stopping at a shadow on the bow, just below the waterline. Splotch of marine growth, maybe, or patchwork. I moved in closer.

The dark spot was actually a hole about two feet across. I touched the jagged wooden edges, peering into the black interior, thinking. Then I returned to the stern for another look at the boat's name and the two stovepipes mounted aft. I had seen all there was to see. I looked up to locate the patrol boat, hit the inflate button on my buoyancy compensator, and began a slow ascent. Less than half a minute later my head popped into the open air.

Farrell helped me aboard. "Well?" he demanded when I pulled off my mask.

"It's the *El Toro*. Lucas's boat."

"I had the feeling it might be. Didn't think much about it when you said yesterday no one had seen Lucas. Then I heard he didn't show for his big hearing in Boston, so I asked around. He told some people he was going out into the bay for a couple of hours to check his dive equipment so it'd be all ready when he got his permit. I figured something was up. When I got the call about this sunk boat, I put two and two together."

"There's a hole at the bow big enough to crawl into," I said. "She would have gone down in a few minutes. Crew might have had time to go overboard, but they left in a hurry because their survival suits were still on board, not doing a hell of a lot of good."

"Maybe it hit a rock."

"Yeah," I said, thinking of the unobstructed sea bottom. "Maybe."

A Coast Guard forty-four-footer approached as we moved off. The harbormaster relayed my findings over the radio and we headed back to port. I got out of my dive suit and leaned on a gunwale looking back at the frothy wake behind the patrol boat, inhaling the clean morning air. Spray dashed cool in my face. It felt good.

Farrell came over after a while and leaned beside me. "Sorry about messing things up the other night. Jeez, I still can't figure it. I couldn't hit the side of a barn door when I used to practice on the pistol range. I feel bad about those two people. No one deserves to be blown to smithereens."

"It's not your fault, Chief. You couldn't have known about the explosives on board. We're all lucky that the breakwater broke some of the force of the blast."

"I guess you're right. I was just trying to poke a few holes in their boat so maybe they'd get a leak that'd slow 'em down. I never expected anything like that." He clapped me on the shoulder. "This'll look terrific on my record. The selectmen won't dare touch me with a major drug bust under my belt. Nice of you to give me the collar, especially with the way I almost got us killed, but I'll have to share the credit with the P'town cops. They were pretty peeved at me messing around in their town. Can't say I blame them. Mostly they were embarrassed dope was coming in right under their noses." His chuckle was positively evil. "Hell, one time they actually sent a police detail over to stand guard duty for Barrett. Supposedly unloading gold."

"It's not entirely their fault," I said. "It was a hell of a cover. The whole police force would be out if a strange boat came in with cargo that wasn't fish. But after Barrett brought in a few things and started talking to the press, people got used to him. He'd check in with the dockmaster who'd just see stuff covered with a tarp if he bothered to come out of his office. If anyone asked, Barrett could say he had to keep his artifacts wrapped up so the metal wouldn't deteriorate."

"Yeah," Farrell said. "Barrett had lost a lot of blood, but he was still conscious when I rode the ambulance to the hospital. He said Scannell got the idea in Florida. Smugglers down there would fly up from Colombia and drop a load of cocaine at sea in metal canisters. Stuff had beacons that would send out a signal. Dope would float just below the surface, spotters would come in and pick it up. Brought in thousands of pounds that way."

"You'd need a major support system to back up something like that," I said.

The patrol boat overtook a fishing dragger from town. Farrell waved at the crew as we went by. "Right. So Scannell simplified the deal. There's a lot of ocean traffic off here. Mother ship would detour in and make a night drop at the *Gabriella* site."

"Then Barrett and Scannell would make the pickup," I said. "Anyone seeing the boat out there figured they were diving on the old ship."

"You got it. They used air bags and the winch to lift the containers. Hooked the cylinders to those fittings you saw on either side of the keel the night you dove under the *Shamrock*."

"Santos said the *Shamrock* handled funny sometimes."

"Santos didn't know anything about it," Farrell said, "and neither did Barrett's sister. The runs were timed so they wouldn't be on board, but maybe the stuff couldn't be offloaded one time and Santos felt the difference. The boat was rigged with quick-release bolts so the dope could be dropped in a hurry and picked up later if the Coast Guard got nosy."

"Did Barrett say how much they were bringing in?"

"Uh-huh. They tried a few dry runs just to see if it worked. Then they picked up a few deliveries of grass worth in the six figures. This last drop was a biggie. Couple hundred kilos of coke. More than four hundred pounds. Price has gone down in the last few years, but it was worth millions retail."

The patrol boat was running parallel to the shore. Rectangles of color, beach blankets, were starting to dot the sand. I tried to picture a mere million dollars and gave up.

"A load that size would make a few people rich, and a few crack customers dead," I said.

"Right about that too. Anyway, the mother ship had other drops to make, but it got busted off Maine. The crew tossed the info on the Cape package overboard so the Coast Guard wouldn't find it. That left Scannell holding the stakes. Who knows how long the deal would have worked if he hadn't decided to cut Barrett out, grab this last package, and skip town. He got greedy, I guess."

"It wouldn't be the first time greed was a fatal mistake."

"Yeah, and his second big mistake was talking about his plans to the Nichols woman," Farrell said. "She didn't trust Kip. Thought he was planning to skidaddle on her with the profits from this load. She wanted the money, bad, 'cause of the feds closing in on her husband, so she went to work on Barrett."

"Whose idea was it to do away with Kip?"

"Dunno, Soc. Laura helped set him up for the hit. She arranged to meet Scannell at that P'town bar. Barrett had been stalking Scannell for days, figured to get him alone at a spot he and Laura had cooked up. He was watching when Scannell got up to take a leak out on the beach, and bushwhacked him there. It was just luck."

"Not entirely. He must have been thinking about how to do it because he'd swiped the net off the Santos boat," I said.

"So that's where he got the damned thing. God, that was a hell of a way to go, being trussed up like a sardine and tossed overboard. What would make a guy do that to someone?"

We were rounding the first outer harbor buoy. The patrol boat cut speed as it approached the breakwater and the outgoing traffic in the channel. I didn't reply right away, and when I did, I said, "Nothing that makes sense. Barrett say anything else?"

"He rambled a lot. Kinda crazy stuff."

"That doesn't surprise me. He was pretty shot up."

"Naw. It wasn't like that, Soc. You ever hear of someone named Dinsmore?"

I squinted at Farrell, surprised he knew the name. "Yes," I said. "Captain Morton Dinsmore. He was skipper of the *Gabriella*. Went down with the ship."

"No kidding. Barrett was talking like he . . . Naw, jeez, it's too weird."

"I'd like to hear what he said, Chief."

"Okay. I could have this wrong, but Barrett talked like it wasn't him that killed Scannell. It was this Dinsmore guy. Something about defending the crown's property against moon cussers. Thought I'd heard everything."

Only half joking, I said, "Maybe there were ghosts on the *Gabriella*."

"Hey, don't talk like that. My mother was from the old sod. She had a bunch of ghost stories that'd make your hair stand on end. Brrr. Still gives me the creeps."

The patrol boat sidled up to the pier. I jumped off and cleated the mooring lines. Farrell handed the gear over, then we walked up the ramp to the parking lot. I got into my truck and leaned on the steering wheel, watching the flock of gulls diving in the wake of the fishing boat we had passed on the way in. Farrell peered in through the window.

"You want to take on the bad guys again, give old Fumblefoot Farrell a call. Next time I'll try to stay vertical."

I turned and smiled. "Diversionary tactics. Confuses the enemy. Old marine trick. Code name SNAFU. Gets 'em every time."

"Diversionary tactics. I like that. Hah. One more thing," Farrell said. "Barrett's sister told me she wanted to talk to you. She'll be at the little fried-clam joint out at the end of the MacMillan Wharf around noon if you're in the neighborhood. She seems like a nice gal who could use somebody to talk to."

I nodded. "I'll be there."

"Good. I kinda said you would."

CHAPTER 33

The clam shack was filling with the noisy lunch crowd when I arrived a few minutes before noon. I grabbed a coffee and a window table and kept a lookout for Eileen. The restaurant sits on pilings at the end of MacMillan Wharf next to the fishing-boat anchorage and has a good view of the harbor and town.

Eileen was walking along the wharf toward me. She appeared small and frail. I rapped on the window as she went by. She came into the restaurant and over to my table. She looked tired. I asked if she wanted something to eat, but she surveyed the crowded restaurant and said she'd rather get some fresh air.

We found a quiet corner of the wharf where we could sit. She glanced around at the fishing boats, the circling gulls, and the camera-toting tourists. "Things seem so much different in the daytime, don't they?"

"Eileen, I'm very sorry about Mike. I really liked him."

She searched my face with puzzled eyes as if she were trying to find something she had lost.

"I don't understand," she said. "What sort of a person are you? After what he did to those people. After what he nearly did to you. Michael could have gotten you killed."

"But he didn't, Eileen."

"That's still no excuse for what he did to Kip and Geetch. And what he did to himself. How could Michael do those things? I'm his sister. I've known him since he was a child. He'd get in fights, everybody in our neighborhood did. But he never gave any indication of being capable of such focused and terrible violence. How could that happen?"

I was watching an old fishing schooner outfitted for charter taking out a load of happy day-trippers. The boat was under full sail. Pretty. I looked away from the boat and into Eileen's sad blue eyes.

"I've been trying to figure Mike out and doing a lousy job of it," I said. "He just seemed to be two entirely different persons. His rational side looked on like a horrified spectator, shocked by the enormity of what he was doing, but unable or unwilling to prevent it. I've seen guys like him who put their humanity on hold. Officers so intent on victory they'd order troops into a mine field. Cops who think you clean up a neighborhood by wiping out the two-legged rats; tough if a few innocent people get in the way. Their obsession makes their emotions go dead."

"And I helped feed that obsession." Tears welled in her eyes. "I lied to Mike. I lied to you. I *knew* the *Gabriella* didn't have a treasure. If I told Michael, he might . . ." She turned away. A shudder went through her body, but she didn't make a sound.

I put my arm around her shoulders. Her hair was scented with perfume. "Mike wouldn't have believed you. Real or not, the dead man's gold was a means to an end. Salvaging the *Gabriella* was a way to show the world. Every time he talked about her he seemed in a different world. When Kip threatened Mike's dream, a veil dropped over his eyes. He was on a self-destruct course, Eileen. If it hadn't been the *Gabriella*, it would have been something else. There was nothing you or anyone could do about it."

She shook her head. "I just don't know. Maybe someday I'll understand, but now . . ."

"Don't try to understand. Just give it time."

Eileen looked at her watch. She stood up and we faced each other. "Thanks for reminding me," she said. "I have to go. I'm awfully sorry. The police want to talk some more although I'm not sure what else I can tell them."

"Then what will you do?"

"Go back to Cambridge and try to finish school." She stared out into the harbor. "Maybe I can get a job in New Mexico or Arizona, far from this. I hate the ocean, I think; I really have to get away from it. Don't you sometimes find yourself hating it?"

I picked a clamshell shard off the pier and absentmindedly fingered its sun-bleached surface, thinking about what Jacques

Cousteau said about his almost sexual need to dominate the sea the way a man tries to possess the woman he loves. It was a love affair that produced moments of ecstasy, moments of pain, and sometimes, when he sensed he was being trapped by his emotions, moments of resentment.

"No," I said. "The sea is why I'm here, close to where I can see, hear, and smell it. The ocean's the one constant in my life, the one thing I can trust to be what it really is. Sure, I hate it sometimes when it doesn't do what I want it to, and love it when it does. But mostly I respect it." Tossing the shard into the water, I said, "I try to remember that the sea barely tolerates us, and it can swallow me just as easily as that clamshell."

We walked to Eileen's car in the town parking lot.

"There's one thing I don't understand," I said. "Why did you tell me Mike hadn't found the *Gabriella* when you knew he had?"

"I hoped it would discourage you from looking for Michael's site data."

"What about the pewter plate you showed me?"

"Michael had taken it off a wreck in Florida. It was a clumsy ploy on my part."

Eileen analyzing her performance again, weighing it against past efforts, vowing to do better next time. Maybe I was wrong about Eileen. Maybe I'd been exercising male hubris, mistakenly thinking a woman's heart beat under Eileen's breast, that behind her cool intellectual exterior smoldered a fire that only needed a little stoking by me. I wondered if we ever really communicated. Was it me, imagining that we had touched each other, if only for an instant, on some subtle emotional level?

I could understand Laura Nichols, who, in her own calculating, black-widowish way, had acted out of raw emotion. But Eileen's motivations were far less clear because they were based not so much in passion, but in a sort of perverse logic, where truth is expendable.

She stopped by her car. "I was delayed in Boston yesterday and tried calling you to say I couldn't make our dinner date. How absolutely ironic. The reason I came by the boat last night was to tell Michael the good news about his permit. The state board upheld it." She unlocked the truck and reached in. "Here," she said. "This is probably evidence.

The police may ask for it. You'll know better than I what to do."

I took the cardboard tube. "Are you sure?" I said.

Eileen nodded unequivocally. "If you're ever in Cambridge . . ."

Her face crumpled. Then she hugged me, got into her car, and drove off. I noticed she hadn't given me her address. Nobody likes bad memories knocking on their door. Which was just as well, because I had no plans to call.

As I watched the car disappear in traffic I thought about my dive that morning on the *El Toro*. I thought about the dark burn marks around the hole I'd seen and the way the wood was splintered. Not in, the way it would be if the boat had hit a rock, but out, as if it had been blown from the inside. Had obsession claimed another victim? I'd leave that to others. Lucas's body might float up on the beach someday and tell the story, but I wouldn't bet on it. The sea has a way of hiding dark secrets, and in this case, maybe that was just as well too.

Sam was as ecstatic as his Yankee reserve would allow. It had been a super day. Our fish hold was stuffed with cod that would fetch a hefty price on the market. The boat engine and hauler had performed like champs on their trial run. And we were heading home.

While Sam set the boat on course, I finished coiling line in a plastic tub and took a Stop and Shop supermarket paper bag out of my duffel bag. I leaned over the stern and held the open bag over the churning wake. Shreds of paper poured out like confetti at a parade and whirled into the foam. When the bag was empty, I bunched it into a ball and threw it over, watching as it bobbed for a few seconds on the surface before being sucked under. The material Eileen had given me the day before was committed to the sea. It belonged there.

I stepped up next to Sam in the wheelhouse. "Ever wish you could hit Megabucks so you could quit fishing or maybe cut back?" he said. "God, my back hurts."

"Many an honest heart hath the false lure of gold seduced to walk in ways of shame."

"Hey," Sam said. "That's real pretty. You make that up?"

"No. It was a guy named Sophocles."

"Friend of yours?"

"I guess you could say so."

Kojak was waiting for me in the front yard when I got home that night. He rubbed up against my leg and purred noisily. Ordinarily I would have welcomed a friendly greeting after a hard day, but Kojak, I knew, has a neurotic fear of the outdoors, especially when it is dark. A moth will terrify him and an encounter with a field mouse spawns a week of nightmares. So if he was out, someone had thrown him out. Which could mean only one thing. Uninvited company.

The past week or so had not been a stellar time. Within the space of a few days I had been knocked out, had my boat sunk and my truck busted. I had nearly drowned, looked down the barrels of more guns than you'd see at an Al Capone alumni party, and lost two clients before I had the chance to send them bills.

Now somebody had invaded my castle.

I walked around to the side of the boat house, where I almost tripped over a black van. I stood in the dark. Should I quietly get back in my truck and make a run for the nearest telephone? I mulled that thought for a moment. Naw. People who throw my cat out where it can be molested by wild animals need to be taught a lesson.

I went into my shed and came out with a thick piece of lumber about four feet long. I had been saving it for some forgotten and ill-conceived construction project, but at the moment it suited my purposes just fine. I walked behind the van and hefted the hunk of lumber like a baseball bat.

Smash! The rear taillight disintegrated in a shower of red plastic.

I walked to the front. I was humming "Whistle While You Work." I demolished a headlight. Then I climbed onto the van's roof and started on the windshield. I stopped to admire the pretty free-form web pattern I'd created in the safety glass. The front door creaked open and slammed shut.

I jumped off the van and ran around to the back door. It was unlocked, as usual. I went to the hall closet where I'd placed the ASP automatic I had taken away from Skinhead on his first visit. Damn. It was gone. Except for the hunk of wood, I was unarmed. Great.

Wait a minute. I did have another gun in the house. I ran into the bedroom and reached under the bed. I came out with a mouthful of dustballs and an old flintlock rifle. A client who couldn't pay me for finding his stolen outboard motor had given me the old cannon in lieu of payment. I planned to mount the shooting iron and hang it over my fireplace, but that was something else I had never gotten around to it. Good thing.

I dashed out the back door onto the deck, stopping in the kitchen to give a light switch a flick of the finger.

Then I climbed the ladder from the deck onto the roof and crept over the asphalt shingles. Near the edge I looked down. The floods bathed the yard in light. My old friends Skinhead and Fungus stood next to their van and they weren't happy. I could understand why. The damage was extensive. Imagine what I could have done in the daytime. Skinhead was circling the van, swearing. Fungus stood with his hands on his hips, glancing nervously around.

I stuck my head over the roof like a gargoyle. "Yoo-hoo, boys, I'm up here."

They both looked up at the same time, blinking against the lights, and reached under their jackets.

"Hold it right there unless you want a load of twelve-gauge buckshot right between the eyes." I slid the musket barrel over the edge of the roof and pointed it at them. "I can get both of you with one yank of the trigger. And don't bother moving apart to make it tougher for me. I've got more than one shell. Now what can I do for you?"

Their hands came out of their jackets. Skinhead shook his fist at me. "You bastard. You wrecked our bikes and got us fired."

"Yeah," chimed in Fungus. "And we had to pay a fifty-dollar fine to that lousy park ranger for walking on the grass."

It was tough, but I resisted the urge to weep. "You boys are breaking my heart. You can always collect unemployment until there's a couple of vacancies in a haunted house. Fun's over. I'm beat and my trigger finger is starting to twitch, so get in your van and move out before I turn you into salt-and-pepper shakers. Go. Bye-bye."

It was sort of a dumb move when I thought about it later. If they had called my bluff, Sam would have had to dump an urnful of my ashes at sea.

Skinhead said, "Who's going to pay for my van?" He sounded tearful.

I can't stand crybabies. "That's what you get when you park in a seedy neighborhood. Now roust! Get your asses out of here!" I jerked the musket for emphasis.

They gave me a dirty look and got into the van. They had a little trouble getting out of the yard, what with the windshield and the lights, but they managed to grope their way down the dirt road and out of sight.

I heaved a big sigh of relief and went downstairs, where I picked up the phone and called the police department. I put a dishcloth over the telephone to disguise my voice the way I'd seen William Powell do it in *The Thin Man*.

When the dispatcher answered, I said, "This is a concerned citizen. There's a black van going through town with its headlight and taillight out. The guys inside are carrying guns. Thought you might be interested." Just so there wouldn't be any mistake, before I hung up, I gave the cops the van's license number. I wondered if Skinhead and Fungus were as dumb as they looked. Massachusetts has a mandatory year-long jail sentence for carrying an unregistered and unlicensed gun. Faced with that kind of incentive, and the fact of their precipitate dismissal, the boys might offer up Mr. Jones as a morsel on a plea-bargaining plate. One could only hope.

I went to the front door and called Kojak. He came in, bristling with indignation at being left out in the dark with the beasties. I assuaged him with a whole can of 9-Lives. I took a Bud and the box of baklava Mrs. Pappas had given me into the living room. I was looking forward to a little peace and quiet. The telephone rang.

"Aristotle," my mother said. "Sunday we are having roast lamb for dinner. Your favorite."

The offer was tempting, but I was worn out. "Gee, Ma, I don't know if I can come. I've been working awfully hard lately—"

"I know, Aristotle. But I'm making it just for you. Your sister is coming too."

"Really? Okay, Ma, I'll be there." I couldn't turn down a reunion. Our family was rarely all in the same place at the same time.

"Good. I knew you would say that. There's one more thing. We've invited Father Demetrios."

I wasn't surprised to hear the family priest was coming. He was a kindly old guy with a white beard, moist eyes, and a healthy appetite. "That's nice, Ma. How is Father Demetrios?"

"Good. And not so good. His health is fine but he is very upset. Someone took the icon of St. Basil from the church and the police can't find it."

"Ma . . ."

"So I told Father Demetrios how my son Aristotle found the money so quick for Mr. and Mrs. Pappas."

Oh hell. I suddenly felt incredibly weary. I sat down in my overstuffed chair and whispered, "I'll do my best, Ma."

"I know you will, Aristotle," she said. "You've always been a good boy."

If you enjoyed the first Aristotle "Soc" Socarides mystery, you'll enjoy his next adventure.

NEPTUNE'S EYE.

Here's an exciting preview of Paul Kemprecos'
next suspenseful novel, NEPTUNE'S EYE.

PROLOGUE

1945

The sound of doom was remarkably prosaic.

It came as a muffled metallic crash, like a firecracker
going off in a distant rubbish barrel. In the control room at
midship, the commander looked away from the depth gauge
he'd been studying and cocked his head to listen. He frowned
in puzzlement. This was like nothing he had heard in years at
sea.

Another crash reverberated through the pressure hull, louder
this time. Then another. The bearded helmsman and the
equally bewhiskered hydroplane operator turned to the commander and watched his lined and weary face intently, waiting for instructions. There was panic in their eyes. The
commander reached for the microphone hanging from an
overhead cable and barked the order.

Close all watertight compartments.

The whole procedure, from the first explosion to the
commander's directions, had taken about ten seconds. It
might just as well have been ten years. Even as crewmen
from one end of the boat to the other leaped to follow
orders, a deafening blast rocked the pressure hull.

The deck lurched violently. The commander was thrown
off balance. He wrapped his arms around a vertical conduit
pipe attached to the arched bulkhead and kept his foot-

ing. The crewmen grabbed onto the controls in front of them to keep from being thrown out of their seats. The boat shuddered and listed toward the stern. The diesels died. Forward motion came to a halt. Water must have entered the engines.

They were sinking.

The commander called for battery power to drive the boat.

The control room went dark. Water in the electric motors.

The auxiliary power system came on and the control room was illuminated in a dim red glow. The commander glanced around at the hellish scene. Incredible. A minute ago they had been peacefully cruising at snorkel depth, recharging their main batteries. All was calm. All was secure. All was routine. All organized. Now this. Within seconds. Pandemonium.

He responded coolly. He had a reputation for a methodical go-by-the-book attitude that bordered on the phlegmatic. It was the reason he had been picked for this important mission. He ordered the crew to dump ballast. Compressed air hissed into the main ballast tanks.

The boat continued to sink stern-first.

They blew all the tanks. The added air should have been more than enough to restore buoyancy.

But the boat plunged further.

The nose-up angle of descent became sharper. The emergency lights went out. Anguished shouts in the darkness. Thuds and crashes. Bodies and objects smashed into the steel bulkheads.

The commander slid down the pipe and sat on the floor. Crouching in the dark, strangely detached from the bedlam around him, he knew it was over. He wondered briefly about the steel box in his quarters, if its contents were worth the end of his fine new boat and its young crew.

Water was pouring in from the stern, surging from compartment to compartment, lapping around his feet. The commander felt a strange serenity he had not known since the madness began.

Die decently, the higher-ups had said. What a laugh. As if men could be ordered to go with dignity when they were gagging under tons of seawater. He twisted his mouth in scorn. Moments later, when death finally found him, his mouth was still frozen in a rictus of contempt.

CHAPTER 1

The telephone call that launched me into the search for Leslie Walther came on a delicious Cape Cod morning in late spring. Sunlight bathed Pleasant Bay in a soft buttery glow and the sea-cool air was sweeter than strawberry wine. From time to time the breeze freshened and a perfume of salt spray, rose, sedge and beach-plum blossoms wafted onto the deck of my boathouse where I lounged, half-comatose, with Kojak the Maine coon cat stretched out beside me. The boathouse I call home has deteriorated since it was part of a large estate whose owners kept it in good repair. The roof leaks in a rainy southwest blow, and I have to crank the wood stove up to red-hot when the cold winter winds sweep down from Labrador. But the view of the misty barrier beach with the dark Atlantic beyond is a visual mantra, and I frequently sit outside, gaze off at the ocean rim, and pretend the world is flat.

I was trying to sell my flat-earth theory to Kojak, who wasn't buying it. He was pretending to listen while he stared cross-eyed at a muscular ant struggling under the weight of a large piece of tortilla chip. I was at the part about the world being balanced on the back of a gigantic turtle when the cordless phone on the driftwood coffee table rang. I snagged the phone, stuck it in my ear, and managed a drowsy hello.

"Mr. Aristotle Socarides?" a man's voice said.

"Speaking," I answered, keeping an eye on Kojak, who had hoisted his bulky body onto all fours for a stretch. I lip-synched: Hey buddy, don't go away. He yawned and licked one black paw.

"My name is Winston Prayerly," the man said in an English accent. "Would you be available this afternoon or early this evening? My employer, Mr. Frederick Walther, would like to discuss the possibility of retaining your services."

I sat up at attention. The prospect of a paying job stirred me from my lethargy. My last case was three months ago. A Wellfleet quahogger hired me to find the outboard motor stolen from his skiff. He suspected his estranged wife. She told me she took the motor but she bought the damn thing so the lazy bum couldn't use a busted motor as an excuse to stay home and loaf. She showed me the check to prove it. The quahogger refused to pay me because I hadn't delivered the goods, but the story had a happy ending, I'm pleased to say. The shellfisherman and his wife joined a Pentecostal church, renewed their wedding vows, and the last I heard they were taking a second honeymoon in Cancún.

I said: "I'll have to check my schedule, Mr. Prayerly. Could you tell me where Mr. Walther lives? That would have a bearing." Kojak sauntered toward the kitchen door. I tried to grab his scruffy tail, he bolted, and I fell out of the aluminum and plastic chaise longue.

"Not too far, Mr. Socarides. On Merrill's Island in Chatham."

I scrambled back into the chair. "In that case, I can fit you in after lunch, Mr. Prayerly. How about 1 P.M.?"

"Perfect. Let me give you directions."

Our destiny, Homer says in the *Odyssey*, lies on the knees of the gods. Or in my own less elegant metaphor, life is a crapshoot and somebody else is throwing the dice. Prayerly's call was a good example. My private detective work is incidental to my job as a commercial fisherman. I fit my investigations around the migratory patterns of groundfish, never forgetting that my success at catching cod, not crooks, is what pays my bar-bill tab. Ordinarily, it was the time of year when my fishing partner, Sam, and I would have been hooking cod from his line trawler. But Sam was in Florida with his wife Millie, enjoying a trip to Disney World and Epcot on a VFW raffle ticket I bought them. Sam had been reluctant to go. I don't think he's been off-Cape since Cal Coolidge was president. I told him the codfishing could wait and he agreed it was cheaper to take a vacation than to settle with Millie in divorce court.

I went into the boathouse and rummaged through the refrigerator for lunch goodies. The best I could do was two slices of fried bologna, rare, one egg over easy, and a stale Pepperidge Farm oatmeal raisin cookie for dessert. As I dined on the health-food special I thought about Winston Prayerly's accent. His speech had been brushed with a layer of culture, but his diction needed another coat of paint because the flaws showed through. If you listened carefully, you could hear him rough up a vowel or manhandle a consonant, like an East Boston tough trying to talk Back Bay Brahmin.

After lunch I shaved, showered, exchanged my jeans and gila-monster sweatshirt for a pair of tan Levi's corduroys, a button-down blue oxford cloth shirt, and a brown Harris tweed jacket I had picked up for $1.50 at the Catholic church thrift shop. I hadn't seen lapels that wide since my father wore them, and if the Al Capone look ever came back, I'd be right in style. I had haggled the thrift-shop ladies down from two dollars. They weren't happy about selling the jacket at a discount, but it had been a slow day.

The engine of my 1977 GMC pickup truck coughed asthmatically when I turned the key in the ignition and blue smoke billowed from the vibrating exhaust pipe, hanging free of its rusted brackets, that rattled against the frame like a machine gun. The truck is in the advanced stages of decrepitude and it's a toss-up which will go first, the body or the engine. I think both will die at the same time. The pickup started on the fourth try, a good sign. I offered thanks to the high god General Motors and the miracle mechanic at the Sunoco station who keeps the truck on life-support systems and then pointed it toward the half mile of sandy drive that leads to the main road.

Merrill's Island is a twenty-minute ride from my boathouse. Shortly before 1:00 P.M. I drove over the causeway that links the island to the mainland. The road is flanked by a shallow cove on one side and salt marsh laced by tidal creeks on the other. On Merrill's Island itself, the rough natural beauty bordering the access road gave way to lawns as smooth as golf greens, as verdantly close to Astroturf as chemical science could make of living grass. There were a half-dozen houses built on the shoulders of the island, an oblong hill about a mile long. They were great sprawling edifices as big as imperial mausoleums, owned by people who liked privacy and could afford to pay for it, hidden from the world and from each other by uninviting thickets of trees and sharp-thorned shrubs.

The Walther house was slightly smaller than a dirigible hangar. It sat at the southerly tip of the upland, surrounded like a game preserve by a high spiked stockade fence. The place was built in an English baronial style that was rare on the Cape. People who live on the Cape like their houses faced with white cedar that weathers to silver, and would put shingles on their mattresses if they weren't afraid of splinters. The house had Tudor timbers exposed in beige stucco and small windows with diamond-shaped panes except on the Atlantic Ocean side, where huge expanses of glass faced easterly onto a wide veranda. The view must have cost a thousand dollars a square foot, and it was probably worth every cent of it.

An olive-green Mercedes sedan with Maryland plates crouched in the circular gravel drive. I pulled in behind it, walked up onto the wide porch, and rang the bell. The thick darkwood door was opened a few seconds later by a man about my height, just over six feet. He had large meaty ears and balding black hair that could have been slicked back with two slices of buttered toast. His pale skin was as smooth as a salamander's and it looked even whiter because of the contrast with his clothes. He was dressed like a paid mourner. Black blazer, black turtleneck, black slacks, and black Chinese rubber-soled slippers. I was sorry I hadn't brought flowers and a message of condolence for the dearly departed, whoever it might be.

"Please come in, Mr. Socarides." It was the same softspoken voice with the English accent I had heard on the phone.

"Mr. Prayerly?" I said, stepping into a large circular lobby with high-beamed ceilings and a massive crystal chandelier.

He nodded. "Wait here, please." He went up a wide sweeping staircase. I strolled over to examine the exposed machinery of a tall grandfather clock. I was checking out the date on the face when Prayerly said, "Mr. Walther will see you now." He was standing a couple of yards behind me, looking as if he had caught me trying to stuff the grandfather clock in my hip pocket. A quiet one, Mr. Prayerly. He led the way up the stairs to a spacious landing and into a drafty oak-paneled room several times larger and a lot neater than my boathouse.

You could die happily in any one of the plump brown leather chairs or the sofa after checking your blue-chip stocks in *The Wall Street Journal*, giving a loud harumph and smoking a good Havana cigar. A log fire crackled in a walk-in medieval fireplace large enough to roast an elephant with an apple in its mouth. It was a room with a theme.

War. Old war, fought at spear's length. It reminded me of a set from one of the old Abbott and Costello haunted-house movies I used to see at the Saturday-morning kiddie show. Shiny suits of armor stared vacantly out from each corner. Shields and halberds and flintlocks and paintings of battle scenes with soldiers dressed up like fancy-ball ushers hung from the walls.

Near the fireplace was a billiard-size table. The green and brown baize top swarmed with hundreds of tin soldiers. Bending over the table was a slender man wearing a gray herringbone tweed jacket. It wasn't half as natty as mine. He turned and smiled, then walked smartly over to me, and giving a quiet click of his heels, he shook my hand. His bony grip was strong. He looked about sixty but was probably ten years older. His silver hair was cropped Prussian close to a long firm-jawed Nordic head. His thin lips were as bloodless as two strips of liver. His face was all hard planes and angles, not a soft or a curving line on it, like one of those ice sculptures they chisel for winter carnivals. If he stood near a stove long enough, he'd simply melt.

His cold blue eyes focused on a spot six inches behind my head. "A pleasure to meet you, Mr. Socarides. Please have a seat. These Cape Cod spring days still have a nip of winter in them, don't they. How about some brandy?" It was a cultivated voice, not much louder than a whisper, with no particular regional accent I could place. I was wondering why everybody in the place spoke in a whisper. Why I wanted to do the same.

The interview got off to a good start. Winston Prayerly poured us two snifters of Grand Marnier. "Thank you," Walther said, "that will be all." The valet disappeared, quickly and quietly. Walther lifted his brandy. "To your health." We sat in facing leather chairs, sipping the brandy in appreciative silence, the only sound the snapping of the fire. Walther put the glass down on a side table. "You're probably wondering how I happened to call you."

It had crossed my mind. People who live on Merrill's Island don't exactly ring my phone off the hook.

"Most of my cases are referrals," I said, which was true, because I don't advertise.

"Just so. You were recommended to me by Leonard Wilson. He said your methods were unconventional, but they worked."

Leonard Wilson was my old yachting buddy. Cape Cod has a lot of rich people like Wilson who are always looking for a free deckhand. Last summer an acquaintance asked me to crew in a sailboat race. The forty-nine foot sloop was owned by Leonard Wilson. We lost the race, but Wilson was grateful and bought drinks for us at the yacht club. Over gin and tonics Wilson told me he owned a large retail operation near Boston and that someone at his warehouse was stealing him blind. I offered my services as a private cop, went in undercover, studied the system, and recommended places where he could plug the leaks. Then I got lucky. The thief spotted my cop's flat feet and thought I needed a body to match. He tried to bury me under a pile of heavy boxes. That was his first mistake. Missing me was his second one. I get excited when people try to make me short and wide. I came up swinging and he spent a few days in the hospital nursing a broken jaw and three cracked ribs. With him out of the picture, things just sort of fell into place and the pilferage stopped.

Walther was saying, "I took the liberty of doing some further checking. I'm very careful about who I work with." A pile of manila folders sat on the table next to his brandy. He took the top folder and handed it to me. I opened it. Inside was a résumé I could have written myself. Born in Lowell, Massachusetts, studied the Greek and Roman classics at Boston University, dropped out to join the marines in Vietnam, did a stint with the Boston Police Department, now a fisherman and part-time private cop.

The most interesting item was an eight-by-ten color photograph. It showed a dark-haired guy with olive skin and a droopy mustache on the deck of Sam's boat pitchforking cod into the dockside conveyor bucket. The picture of me was taken by someone standing on the fish-pier observation platform.

"Frankly, I don't think it does you justice," Walther said. He was watching for a reaction, so I gave him one.

"It's not my best side, but I wouldn't mind a dozen copies to spread around the family at Christmas."

Walther smiled. He didn't know I was serious. "I'll see what I can do. Now, down to business." He opened the next manila folder on the table, took out another photo, and handed it to me.

"This is my daughter Leslie."

The picture was of a young woman in her late twenties. She had strawberry blond hair that was a color no amount of money could buy. She didn't resemble her father in the least. Even her blue eyes were different from his chill and distant ones. Hers sparkled with warm good humor. I memorized the soft features of her face without too much trouble and handed the photo back to Walther.

"She's lovely," I said, and I meant it.

"Yes." He studied the portrait dreamily as if he were seeing it for the first time. "Extremely so."

I waited.

Walther looked up. The dreamy look was gone, and in its place was the frozen stare. "Leslie has been missing for more than a month. I believe she is in the Cape Cod area. I would like you to find her. As a local, you'd be more effective than a team of city detectives getting lost on back roads."

"Have you gone to the police?"

"Yes, of course. But they don't have the facilities to launch a search. They can only put the information on file. Unless they suspect foul play."

"Is there any evidence of that?"

"No, not in the strictest sense of the term."

Walther was beating around the bush. "In what sense of the term, then?"

"Let me explain," Walther continued. "Leslie was a lab technician. She lived in Falmouth and worked for a man named Thomas Drake." He handed me another file. "This contains some background on Drake, as much as I have been able to cull from available sources. I believe this man had something to do with Leslie's disappearance."

"Why do you say that?"

Walther picked up the snifter. He swished the amber contents, studied their whirling patterns as if he were searching for auguries, then, without drinking from it, set the glass down. He ran a slender finger along one side of his pencil-line mustache, then the other, although every hair was exactly where it should be, and said, "She was involved with him, very much so." His voice had gained a carbon steel edge.

"Have the police talked to Drake?"

"Yes. But he told them Leslie simply didn't show up for

work one day, and that he hasn't seen her or heard from her since."

"Did she leave any indication of where she might be going? A note maybe?"

"No. Nothing. Her apartment was checked several times."

"How about a paper trail? Did she pay for a hotel or plane ticket with a credit card?"

He shook his head. "We've kept in touch with her bank. Leslie made a large withdrawal just before she disappeared, but she hasn't written any checks since then."

"Did she mention anything to friends? Or was she acting unusual?"

"No again, I'm afraid."

"Has she ever just taken off like this before? Perhaps when she was a teenager?"

"Leslie has never left without saying where she was going."

I looked at the photo again. A missing persons case always starts this way. A picture. A distraught relative. A story that may or may not hold the whole truth. Either you find them quickly or not at all. This case didn't seem too complicated. Rich daughter skeddadles. A few phone calls and interviews. I bet myself I could wrap it up in seventy-two hours, make some drachmas, and have a few days to play before Sam got back from Florida.

I said, "I would be glad to look into this for you, Mr. Walther."

"Thank you. It's been a strain, not knowing." I examined the frosty eyes and found it hard to believe anything could strain Walther.

He handed me the folder that held Leslie's picture. "This contains some background material on Leslie. I don't mean to tell you your business, but you might want to start with Drake. Perhaps you can be more persuasive than the police." He took an envelope from an inside jacket pocket. "This check should more than cover your services for the first week, I believe. We can go on from there."

I rose and said, "I'll call you within a couple of days, whether I have something or not, Mr. Walther."

Winston Prayerly appeared. Quietly.

Walther got up and shook my hand. "Fine," he said. "I'm ever so grateful. And Mr. Socarides . . ." He paused for emphasis. "I don't care what it costs or who you have to step on to find my daughter."

It wasn't the kind of comment that needed an answer and Walther wouldn't have liked the one I gave him. I picked a tin soldier off the battle table. The inch-high infantryman carried a shield and spear and wore a short pleated skirt.

Noting my interest, Walther said, "As you can see, I'm something of a military buff. This is the Battle of Chaeronea. Philip of Macedon crushing the Greeks with the phalanx." He bent over the table. "Several ranks of spearmen in close array, so if one fell, a fresh soldier took his place. It was perfected by Philip, father of Alexander the Great. Simple but effective. I have these tin soldiers custom-made, by the way. They're exact, down to the last detail."

Armchair generals turn me off even when I'm working for them. I felt the sharp point of the miniature spear with my thumb and put the soldier back on the table.

"Everything's real except for the shock, the bleeding, and the gangrene, Mr. Walther."

Walther chuckled. "Winston," he said without removing his gaze from the battle table, "please show Mr. Socarides to the door."

The interview was over. I was on the payroll. Dismissed.

Back in my truck, I tore open the envelope from Walther and looked at the check inside. It was drawn on a bank in Maryland. I wondered if Leonard Wilson had given Walther the wrong impression about my work. For a smart man, Walther hadn't the slightest idea of what he had just bought for his money. I'm not exactly a saint, but Walther didn't know me. I won't muscle anyone unless he tries to muscle me first, and even then I've got a lot of tolerance for stupidity, maybe more than I should have. I was tempted to tear up the check, tell him I was too busy, and go back and sit in the sun with Kojak until Sam got home. But I didn't. I folded the check and tucked it into my wallet. It would be unprofessional to refuse a case just because I didn't fall in love with the client. Besides, I was bored and broke. And there was always the chance Leslie Walther was in some trouble. Even if she weren't, I wanted to meet her in the flesh so I could see if her hair was really the color Titian liked to use in his paintings. It had been a long, long winter.

CHAPTER 2

The sun was starting to go down the sky as I drove off Merrill's Island. I debated heading to Falmouth immediately to chat with Tom Drake, but decided to cool the Walther job and get a fresh start early the next morning. It was just too nice an afternoon to waste in cross-Cape traffic. I live on the outer forearm of the Cape Cod peninsula, which hooks into the ocean like a big arm swinging in an uppercut toward the mainland south of Boston. Falmouth, where Drake had his lab, was near the shoulder. The population of the Cape has zoomed since the Kennedy family focused the attention of the world on their touch-football games and sailboat races at Hyannis Port, but most of the roads aren't any wider than they were back when they were handling horse carts. It's about an hour's drive to Falmouth with the last few miles on Route 28, the main drag in and out of town. Traffic would be bumper-to-bumper this time of day. I headed back to the boathouse and went into the kitchen for a can of Bud. Kojak was waiting by his empty dish, so I poured him some dry cat food. He despises the stuff and was giving me his pitiful how-could-you-feed-me-this-garbage look when the phone rang. It was my mother.

"*Tikanes*, Aristotle," she chirped. "How are you?"

I rolled my eyes toward the cobwebs on the ceiling and wondered if I could hang up and get away with the excuse of a bad connection. Ma was calling from Lowell, north of Boston, where the family lives and owns a highly profitable wholesale bakery operation called Parthenon Pizza. Don't get me wrong. I think my mother's a terrific lady. Intelligent, strong, compassionate. But she's run things for so long, she can't imagine her adult children coping with the world on their own. I've been a marine and a cop and I still have the physical and mental scars from both jobs. I've killed men and have almost been killed by them. But I'm expected to report in to my mother regularly with updates on my health and my professional progress. What there is of it. I hadn't phoned home in weeks. I braced myself for a scolding.

"*Kala*, Ma. I'm fine. How are you?"

"Fine, Aristotle. Everybody is good."

That was odd. No sermon. I took advantage of my good fortune and diverted the conversation from the well-being of the family to the health of the business. "How are the new Yuppie pizzas going?"

"Not Yuppie pizzas," she corrected. "*Gourmet* pizzas. Your brother George wants to call them the Olympus line so we can say food fit for the gods. I say okay to George so he doesn't get hurt. But we don't need fancy names. We put on the box All Natural. No chemicals. Light and lively. And we charge three times regular price. The artichoke, feta, and black olive pizza sells like . . ." She groped for the words. "How do you say it, Aristotle?"

"Like hotcakes?"

"*Neh*, yes, like hotcakes, Aristotle. Have you seen your sister Chloe?"

The leap from gourmet Olympic hotcakes to the whereabouts of my younger sister defied logic, but that was my mother. Chloe lives with my parents and helps out in the business. As the only daughter, she has to deal with the folks' ups and downs. She spends a lot of time away from home, and I can't say that I blame her. We talk occasionally, but probably not enough. She's a good kid and sometimes I wish I knew her better as a person. I hadn't seen her in months. The last I knew she was on a grand tour of Europe.

"Chloe sent me a postcard from France or Germany, Ma. But that was a while ago. Is she still traveling?"

"No, Aristotle, your sister is back. She came home last week."

"That's great. Hope she had a wonderful trip. How is she?"

Ma was silent for a few seconds. Then she said, "Good and not so good."

My mother is the original Cretan labyrinth. Her roots go back to the people who invented the maze. Crete is so mountainous it is virtually impossible to travel in a straight line from one village to another; you have to go up and down or around. She thinks in the same way. It was simple to communicate with her once you got the hang of it. She was trying to tell me something she didn't want to tell me. Or trying not to tell me something she wanted to tell me. Ma was obviously troubled by something, but I would have to dig with the patience of an archaeologist to find out what it was.

"What do you mean, Ma?"

She sighed. A mother's sigh. The kind that starts at the toes and travels up through heaving breasts before issuing from the mouth. In a single expulsion of air, it evoked the pain of childbirth, dozens of sleepless nights, thousands of meals prepared and laundry loads washed, and the unendurable burden of ungrateful children.

"Your sister is *very* angry at me."

This was going to be a more complicated than I expected. I knew how Schliemann must have felt when he started to excavate the mountain of earth that covered the ruined city of Troy.

"I don't understand, Ma," I said patiently. "Why would Chloe be angry at you?"

"For *nothing*, Aristotle."

"Nothing, Ma?"

"Yes. Only one thing. I told her she should get married."

"So. She probably should. She's old enough. Why did she get angry over that?"

Another pause. "I told her who she should marry. She didn't like that. But he's a very nice boy," she said quickly. "Nestor Evangelos, a friend of your brother. He owns *two* restaurants."

"Ma, you know Chloe doesn't like to be told anything."

"I know. She's like your aunt Demeter who married the Polish butcher in Chicago. Strong in the head. She leaves the house with a suitcase. Slams the door. She doesn't tell me or Papa where she goes."

Chloe inherited her stubbornness from my mother not Aunt Demeter, but I didn't say that. "I'm sure she's all right, Ma. Probably cooling her temper at a friend's house."

"Yes, I think so too. But, Aristotle, you and your sister were always very close. I want you to find Chloe. And talk to her."

I paced back and forth with the phone. It was my own fault for blowing off the Walther case until the next day. "Ma, I don't have any idea where to look."

"Aristotle, you are a detective, no?"

"Yes, Ma, I'm a detective, but—"

"This is for the *family*, Aristotle."

My frail defenses crumbled in the face of Ma's onslaught. She had trundled the ultimate weapon up to the front lines. The family. It was the final nail in the coffin of whatever argument I tried to muster. Too busy. Going on vacation.

Lying on my deathbed. There was always my obligation as the eldest son. I had broken away from the family to pursue my wayward ways, so my responsibility was a special one. This was implied, but never openly said. Whether my mother did it consciously or not, she knew how to strike the chord of guilt deep in my soul.

I caved in. Trying not to groan, I said, "Okay, Ma. I'll call some of her friends, check around. I'm sure everything's okay, so don't worry."

"*Kala*, Aristotle. Good boy. One more thing. When you find Chloe, tell her ..." She sighed again, impatient at herself for showing emotion.

"I know what to say, Ma."

"Yes, Aristotle. You tell Chloe that I love her. Bye-bye."

While I had the phone in my hand, I dialed the number of Beacon Research in Boston and gave my name. Norma came on the line a few seconds later.

"Soc!" she said. "How are you, my dear?"

"I'm fine, Norma. How's the information business?"

"Couldn't be better, love. This is a wonderful time to be a professional snoop."

I had worked with Norma when I was a Boston cop. A couple of white-collar felons were still makng license plates as guests of the state because of the information she dug up and I used in court. Her company, Beacon Research, was a child of the computer age. Some information about every one of us is stored in a computer database somewhere. Just count the pieces of junk mail you get or try to erase a bad credit rating if you don't believe me. Norma's electronic files could spit up the background on a prominent person with a few strokes of the keyboard. Nonentities and those who went to extremes to guard their privacy took a little longer. But nobody could hide forever. It was only a matter of knowing where to plug into the network. And that was Norma's specialty.

I said, "Are you telling me everybody wants to know everything about everybody else?"

"That's right, hon. Who do you want to know everything about?"

"A guy I just met. His name is Frederick Walther. All I know about him is that he's very rich, he has a house on Cape Cod and a car registered in Maryland." I gave her

Walther's address, the number of his car license plate as I remembered it, and the bank's name from the check he gave me. "While you're looking into it, could you poke around and see what you can turn up on a Winston Prayerly. He works for Walther. He could be English or maybe South African."

"No problem, sweetie pie. I've got to be in New York for a couple of days, but I'll get my staff on it. Call you when I get back."

"Fine, Norma. I'll talk to you later."

Kojak was sniffing at his bowl as if the food I poured him contained cyanide. I relented and opened a can of 9-Lives he knew I'd been rationing. I didn't want him complaining to the Society for the Prevention of Cruelty to Kitties. I finished my beer, popped another, and sat at the kitchen table thinking about the ironies that abound in my business. Walther hires me as an private investigator, and the first thing I do is investigate him. Maybe it was true as somebody once said that gentlemen don't read other gentlemen's mail. But I'm no gentleman. Nor, I sensed, was Walther, for all his money-green patina. And Prayerly's cultivated accent didn't mask the smell of thug. There was something else. Frederick Walther said he was careful who he worked with. He wasn't the only one who felt that way.

"[Lindsey] is in the first rank of mystery writers working today." -- *Houston Chronicle*

THE SUSPENSEFUL WORKS OF DAVID L. LINDSEY

IN THE LAKE OF THE MOON

The assault began innocently enough. Four envelopes delivered through the anonymity of the U.S. Mail, four mysterious photos, and then a picture that would draw Houston detective Stuart Haydon into a nightmare world of grisly death and dark obsession. For the fifth photograph was of Haydon himself...with a carefully drawn bullet exploding through the back of his head....

MERCY

Two weeks after the shocking and bizarre murder of a wealthy Houston woman detective Carmen Palma is faced with a second victim killed in an almost identical manner. After a third killing, Palma teams up with FBI special agent Sander Grant, an expert on serial murders. As Palma and Grant learn to work with each other, their investigation leads them to the dark underground of sadomasochism, and into the twisted mind of the killer.

Don't miss any of the heart-stopping thrillers by David L. Lindsey. Now on sale wherever Bantam Crime Line Books are sold.

AN231 -- 5/91